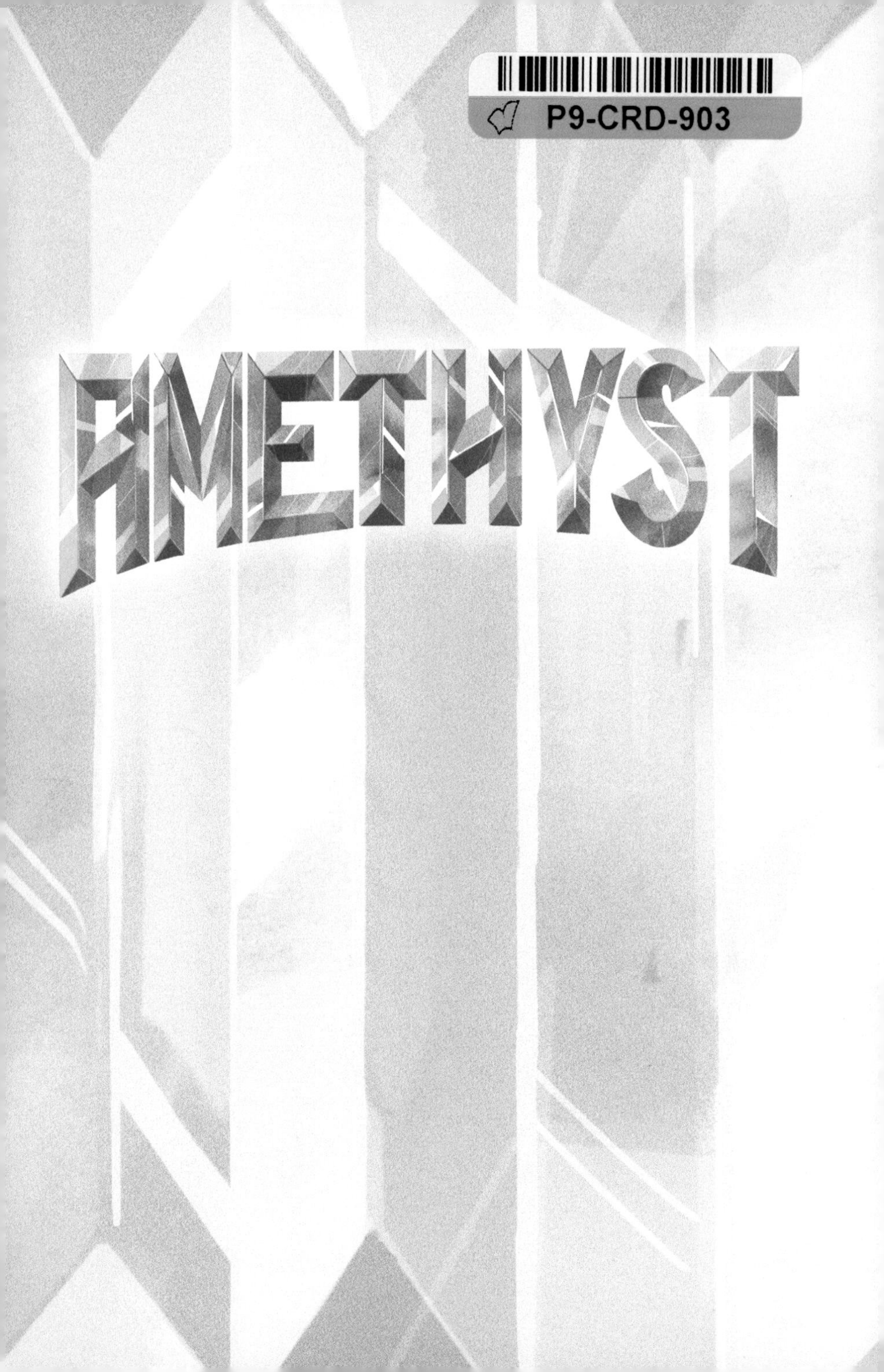
AMETHYST

WRITTEN BY
Shannon Hale & Dean Hale

DRAWN BY
Asiah Fulmore

LETTERS BY
Becca Carey

AMETHYST CREATED BY
Dan Mishkin, Gary Cohn, and Ernie Colón

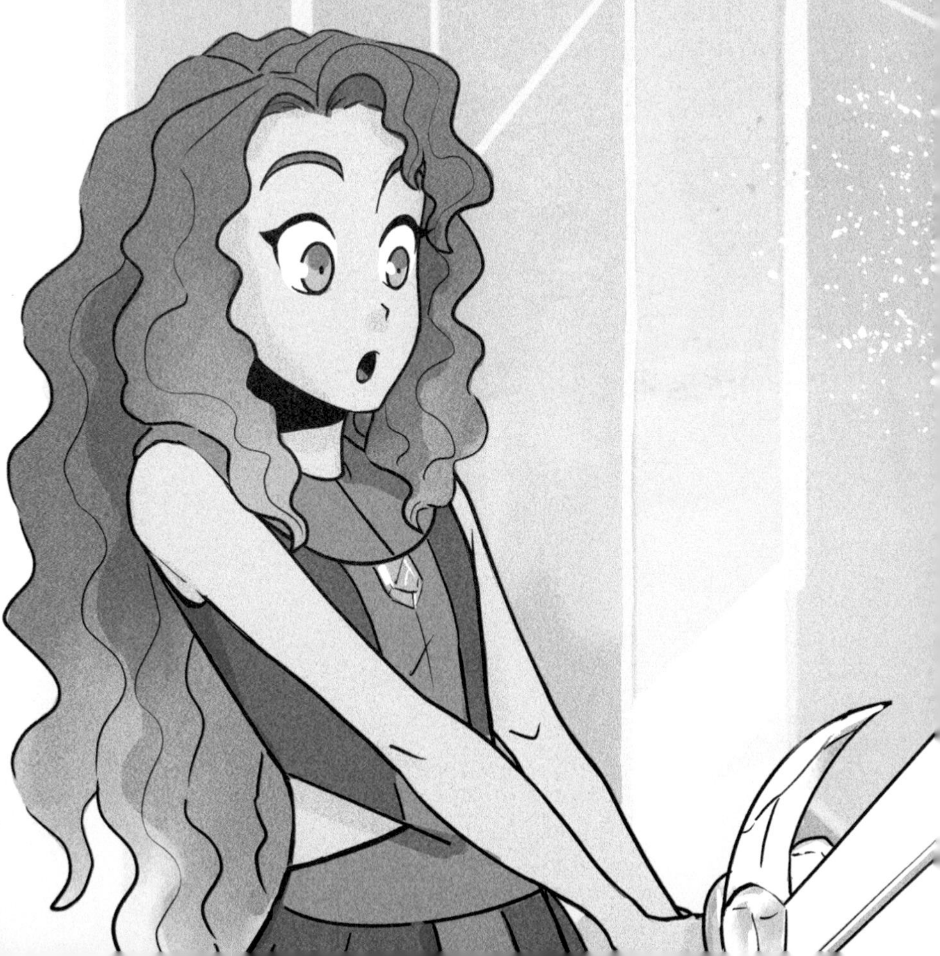

AMETHYST

princess of gemworld

KRISTY QUINN Senior Editor
COURTNEY JORDAN Assistant Editor
STEVE COOK Design Director – Books
AMIE BROCKWAY-METCALF Publication Design
DANIELLE DIGRADO Publication Production

MARIE JAVINS Editor-in-Chief, DC Comics

DANIEL CHERRY III Senior VP – General Manager
JIM LEE Publisher & Chief Creative Officer
DON FALLETTI VP – Manufacturing Operations & Workflow Management
LAWRENCE GANEM VP – Talent Services
ALISON GILL Senior VP – Manufacturing & Operations
NICK J. NAPOLITANO VP – Manufacturing Administration & Design
NANCY SPEARS VP – Revenue

AMETHYST: PRINCESS OF GEMWORLD

Published by DC Comics. Copyright ©
2021 DC Comics. All Rights Reserved.
All characters, their distinctive
likenesses, and related elements
featured in this publication are
trademarks of DC Comics. The stories,
characters, and incidents featured in
this publication are entirely fictional.
DC Comics does not read or accept
unsolicited submissions of ideas,
stories, or artwork.
DC – a WarnerMedia Company.

DC Comics, 2900 West Alameda Ave.,
Burbank, CA 91505

Printed by LSC Communications,
Crawfordsville, IN, USA. 10/1/21.

First Printing.
ISBN: 978-1-77950-122-6

Library of Congress Cataloging-in-Publication Data

Names: Hale, Shannon, writer. | Hale, Dean, 1972- writer. | Fulmore, Asiah,
   illustrator. | Carey, Becca, letterer.
Title: Amethyst, Princess of Gemworld / written by Shannon Hale & Dean Hale
   ; illustrated by Asiah Fulmore ; letters by Becca Carey.
Description: Burbank, CA : DC Comics, [2021] | Audience: Ages 8-12 |
   Audience: Grades 4-6 | Summary: Amaya, Princess of House Amethyst in
   Gemworld, is sent to mundane Earth to teach her that magic is a
   privilege, but after Amy has long settled into ordinary middle school
   life, a Prince of the Realm brings her home to restore her magical
   destiny.
Identifiers: LCCN 2021035968 | ISBN 9781779501226 (trade paperback)
Subjects: CYAC: Graphic novels. | Fantasy. | Princesses--Fiction. |
   Magic--Fiction. | LCGFT: Fantasy comics. | Graphic novels.
Classification: LCC PZ7.7.H35 Am 2021 | DDC 741.5/973--dc23
LC record available at https://lccn.loc.gov/2021035968

PEFC Certified

This product is from
sustainably managed
forests and controlled
sources

PEFC

PEFC/29-31-337   www.pefc.org

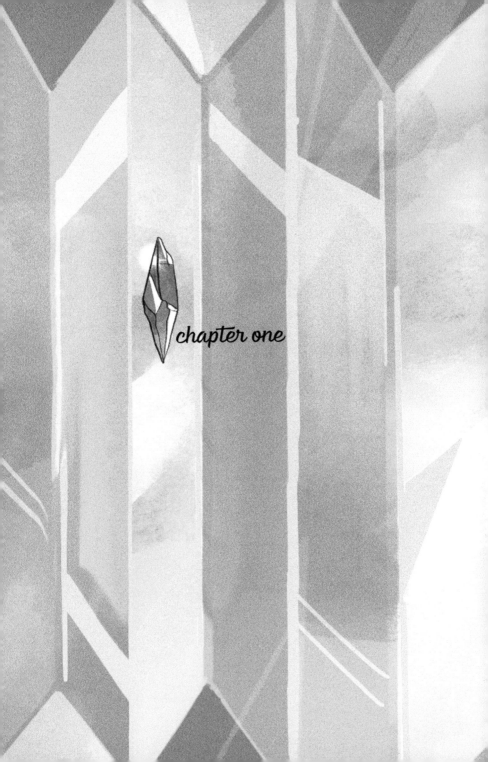

chapter one

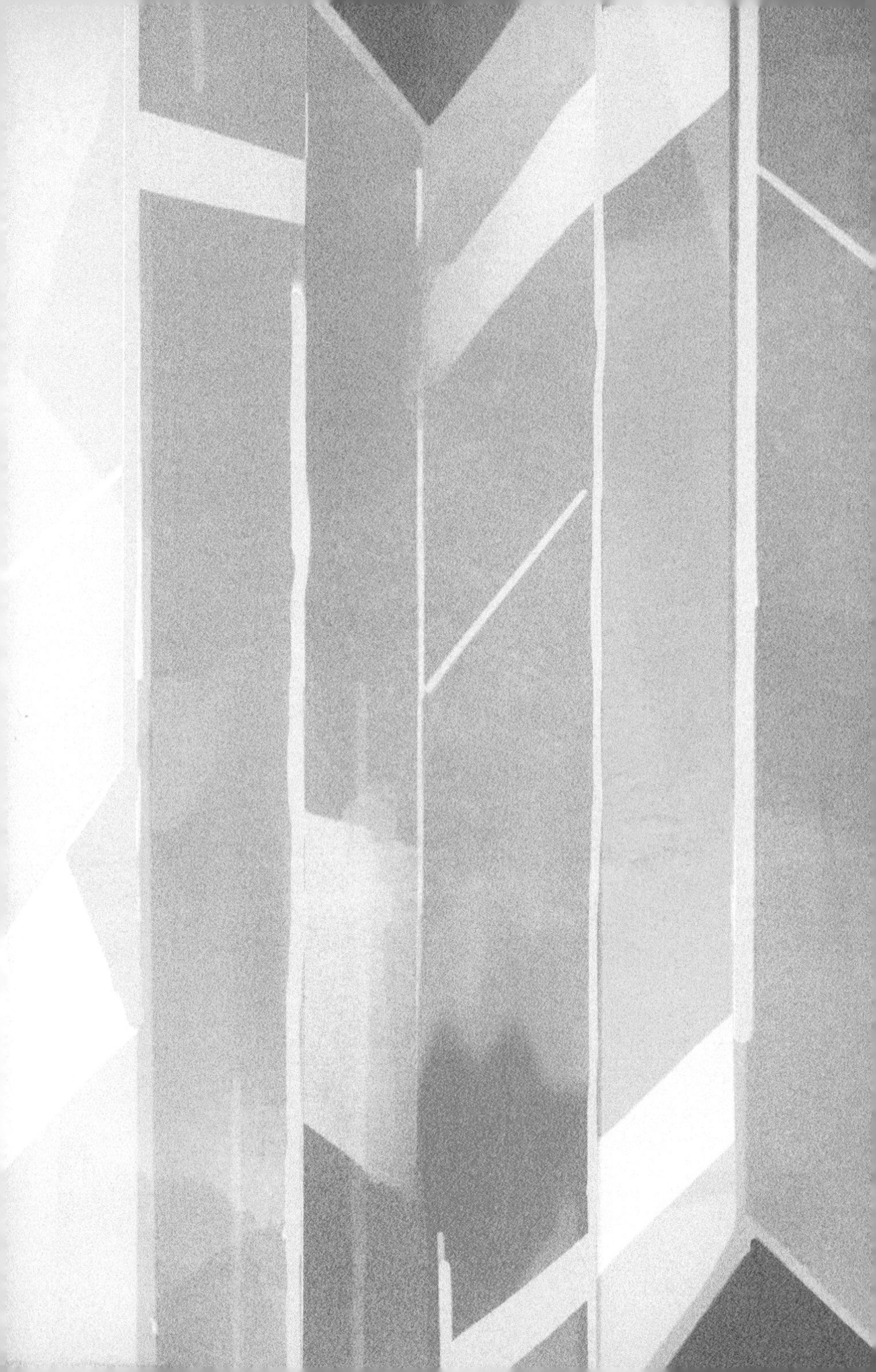

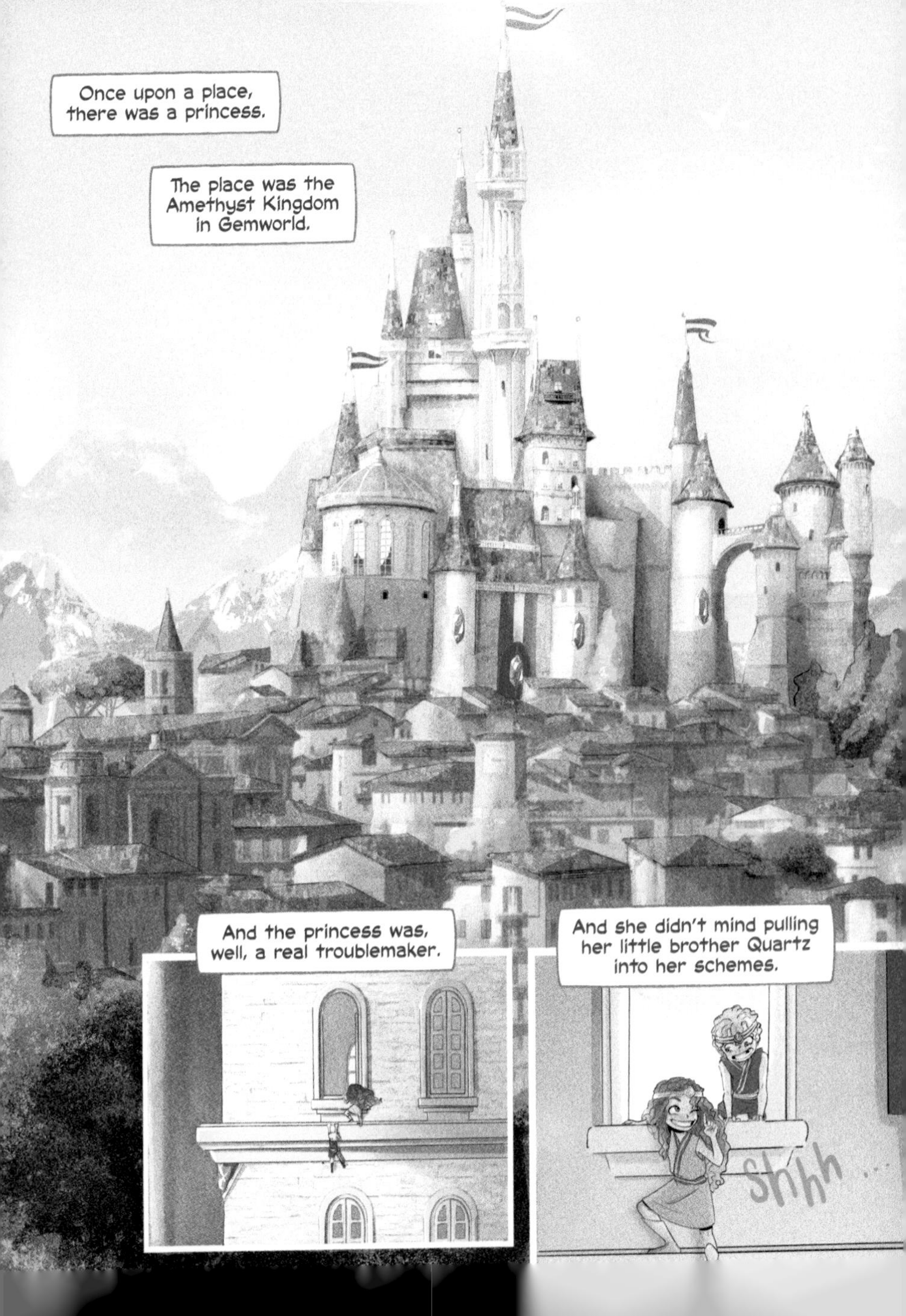
Once upon a place, there was a princess.
The place was the Amethyst Kingdom in Gemworld.
And the princess was, well, a real troublemaker.
And she didn't mind pulling her little brother Quartz into her schemes.
Shhh

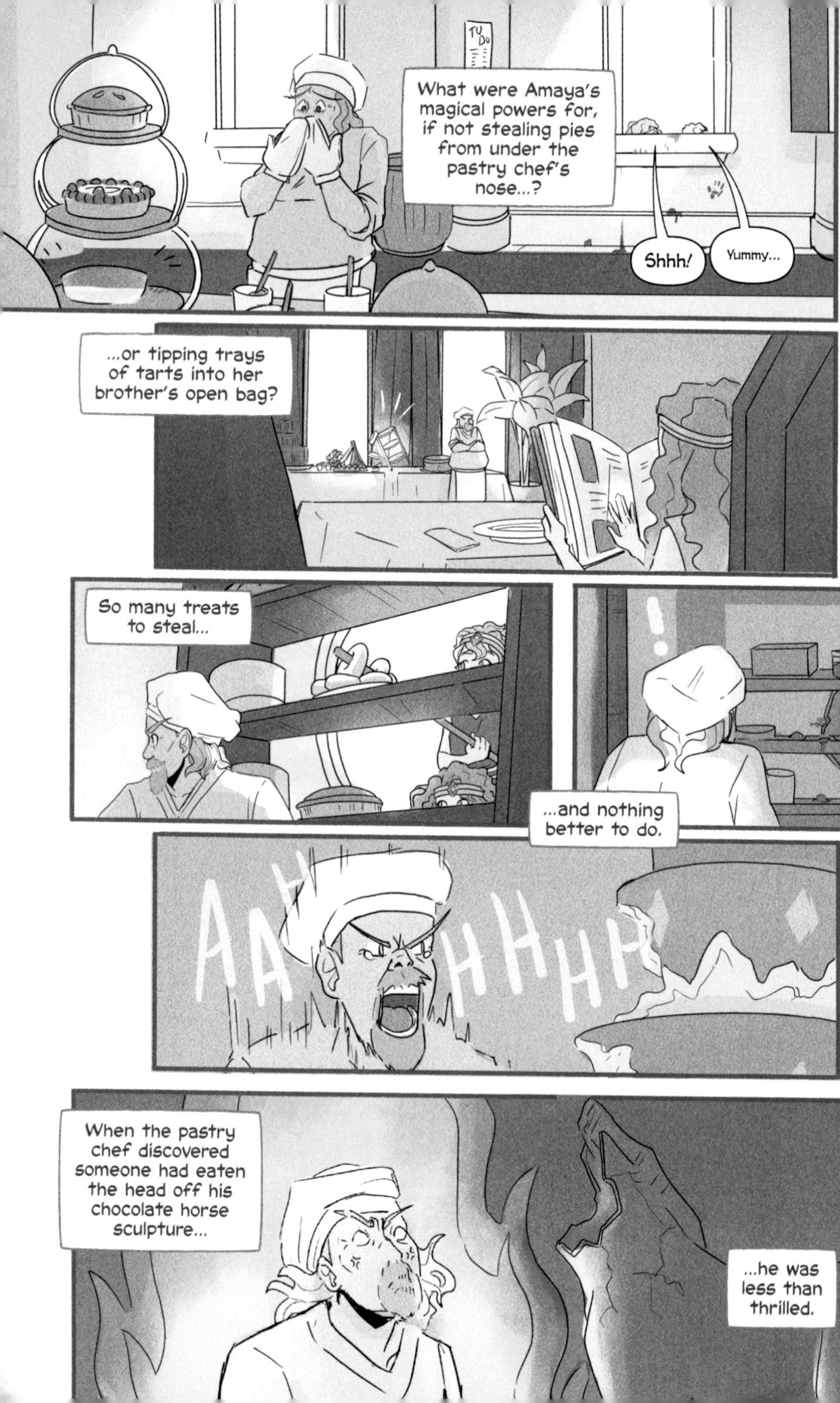
TO DO
What were Amaya's magical powers for, if not stealing pies from under the pastry chef's nose...?
Shhh!
Yummy...
...or tipping trays of tarts into her brother's open bag?
So many treats to steal...
!
...and nothing better to do.
AAHHHHHH
When the pastry chef discovered someone had eaten the head off his chocolate horse sculpture...
...he was less than thrilled.

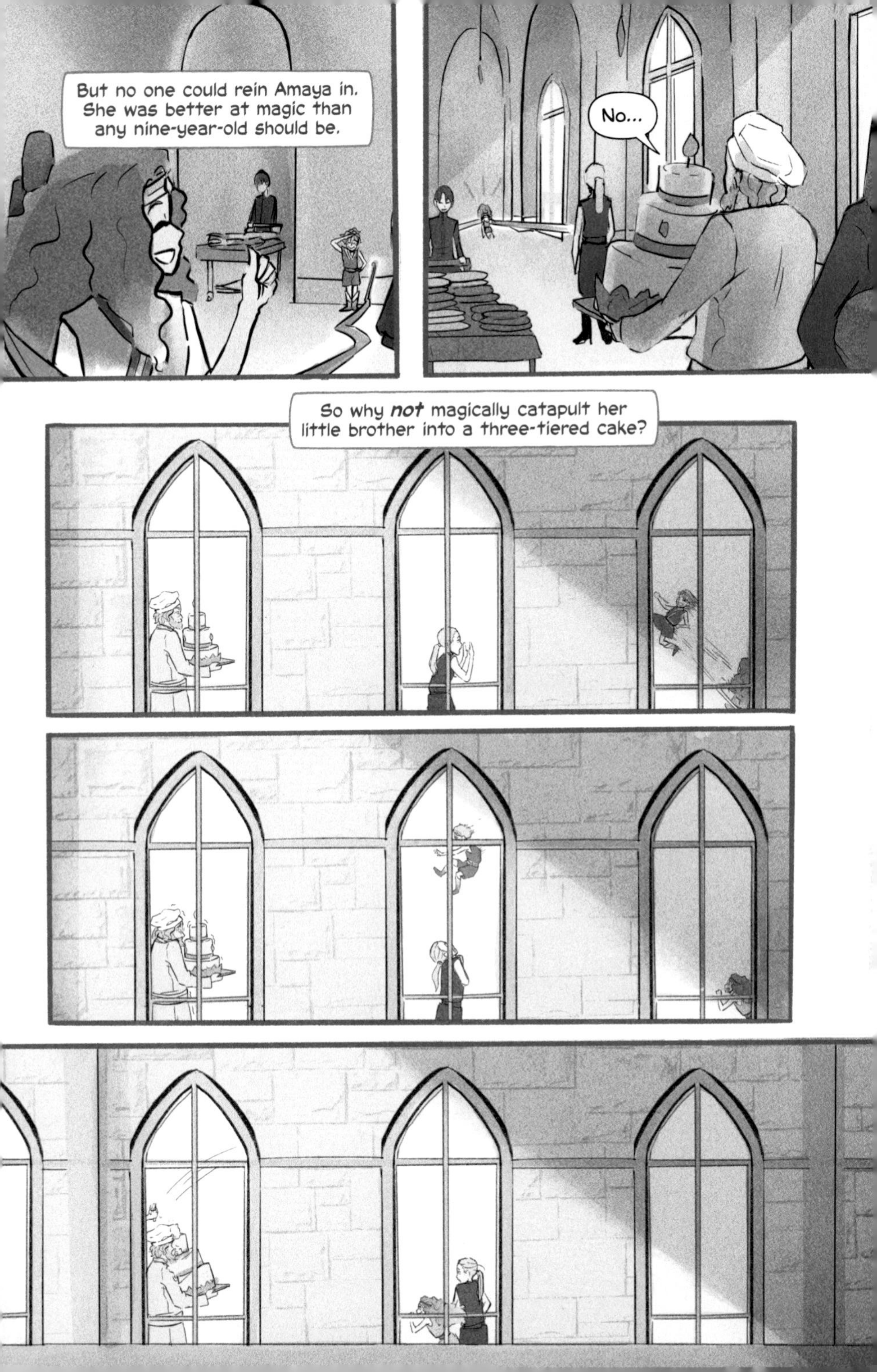
But no one could rein Amaya in. She was better at magic than any nine-year-old should be.
No...
So why *not* magically catapult her little brother into a three-tiered cake?

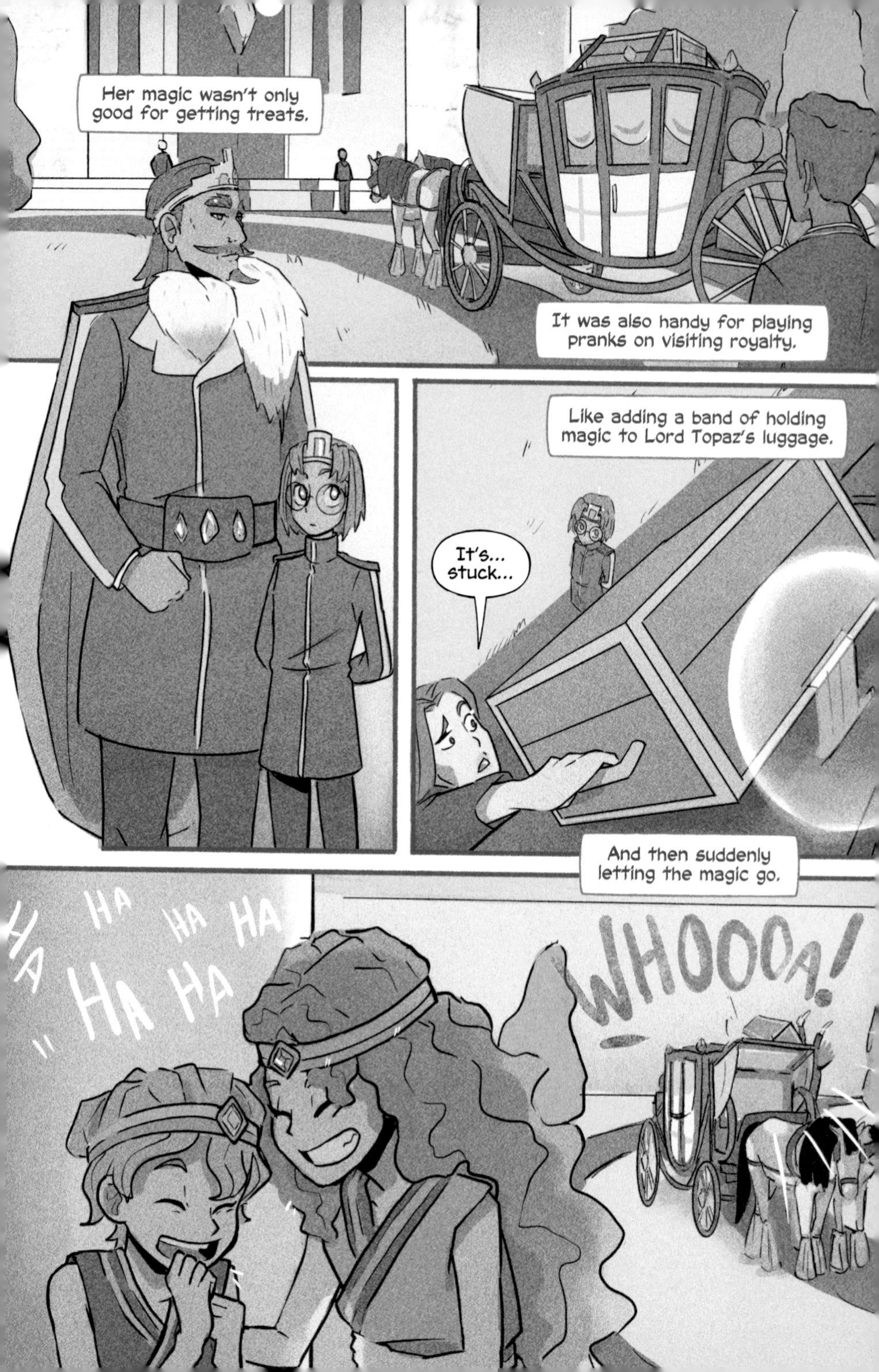
Her magic wasn't only good for getting treats.
It was also handy for playing pranks on visiting royalty.
Like adding a band of holding magic to Lord Topaz's luggage.
It's... stuck...
And then suddenly letting the magic go.
HA HA HA HA HA HA HA HA
WHOOOA!

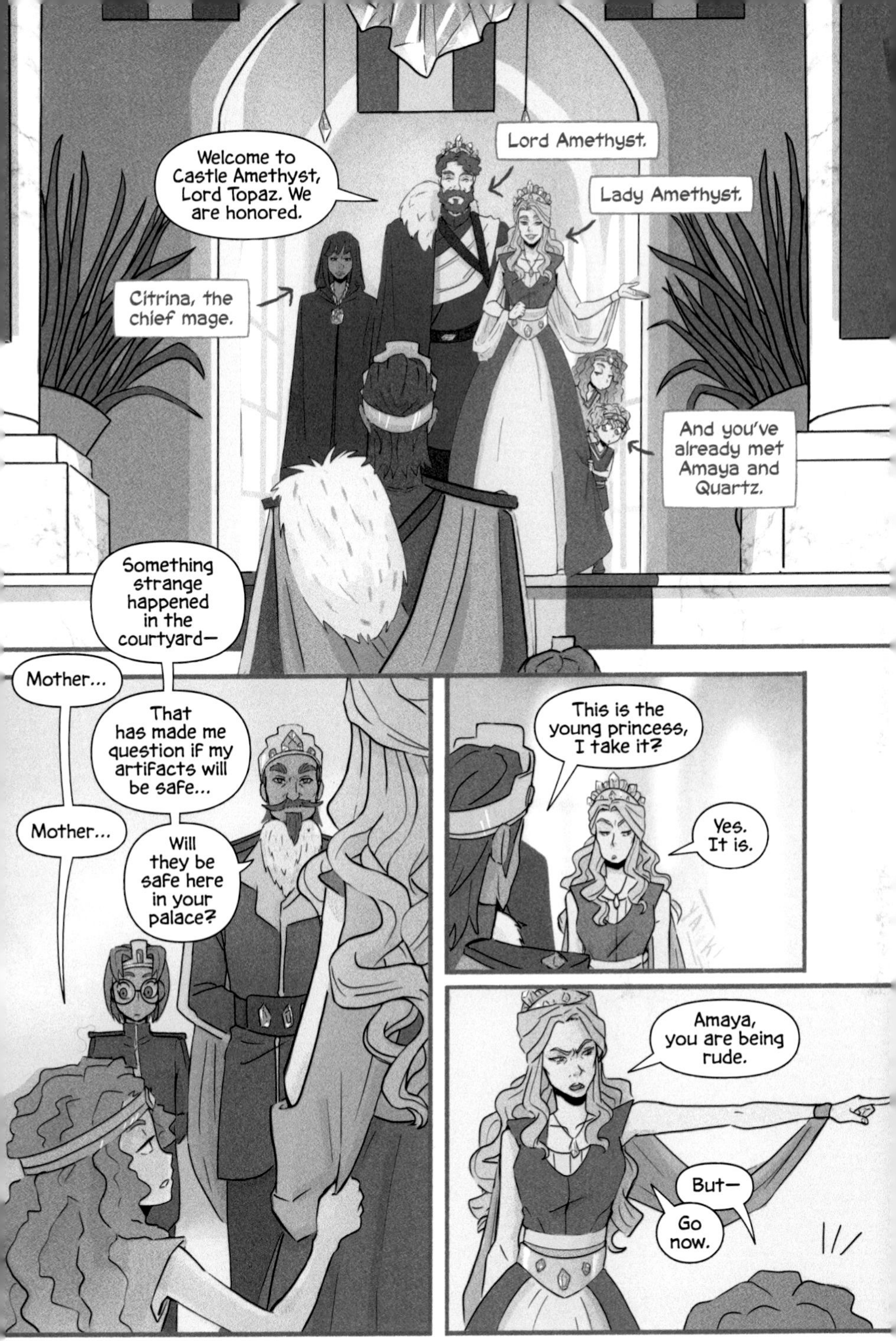

Welcome to Castle Amethyst, Lord Topaz. We are honored.
Lord Amethyst.
Lady Amethyst.
Citrina, the chief mage.
And you've already met Amaya and Quartz.
Something strange happened in the courtyard—
Mother...
That has made me question if my artifacts will be safe...
Mother...
Will they be safe here in your palace?
This is the young princess, I take it?
Yes. It is.
YANK
Amaya, you are being rude.
But—
Go now.

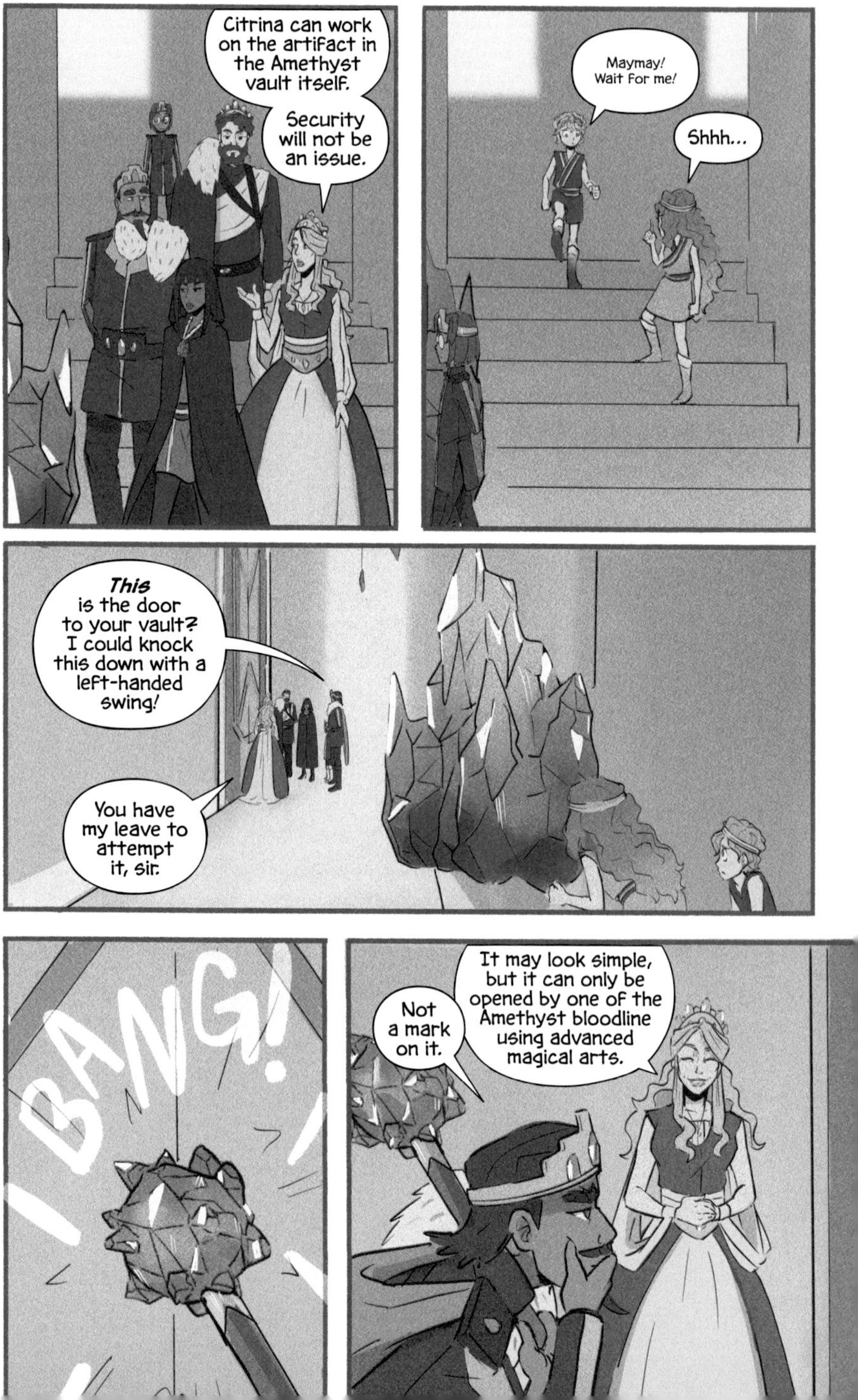
Citrina can work on the artifact in the Amethyst vault itself.
Security will not be an issue.
Maymay! Wait for me!
Shhh...
This is the door to your vault? I could knock this down with a left-handed swing!
You have my leave to attempt it, sir.
BANG!
Not a mark on it.
It may look simple, but it can only be opened by one of the Amethyst bloodline using advanced magical arts.

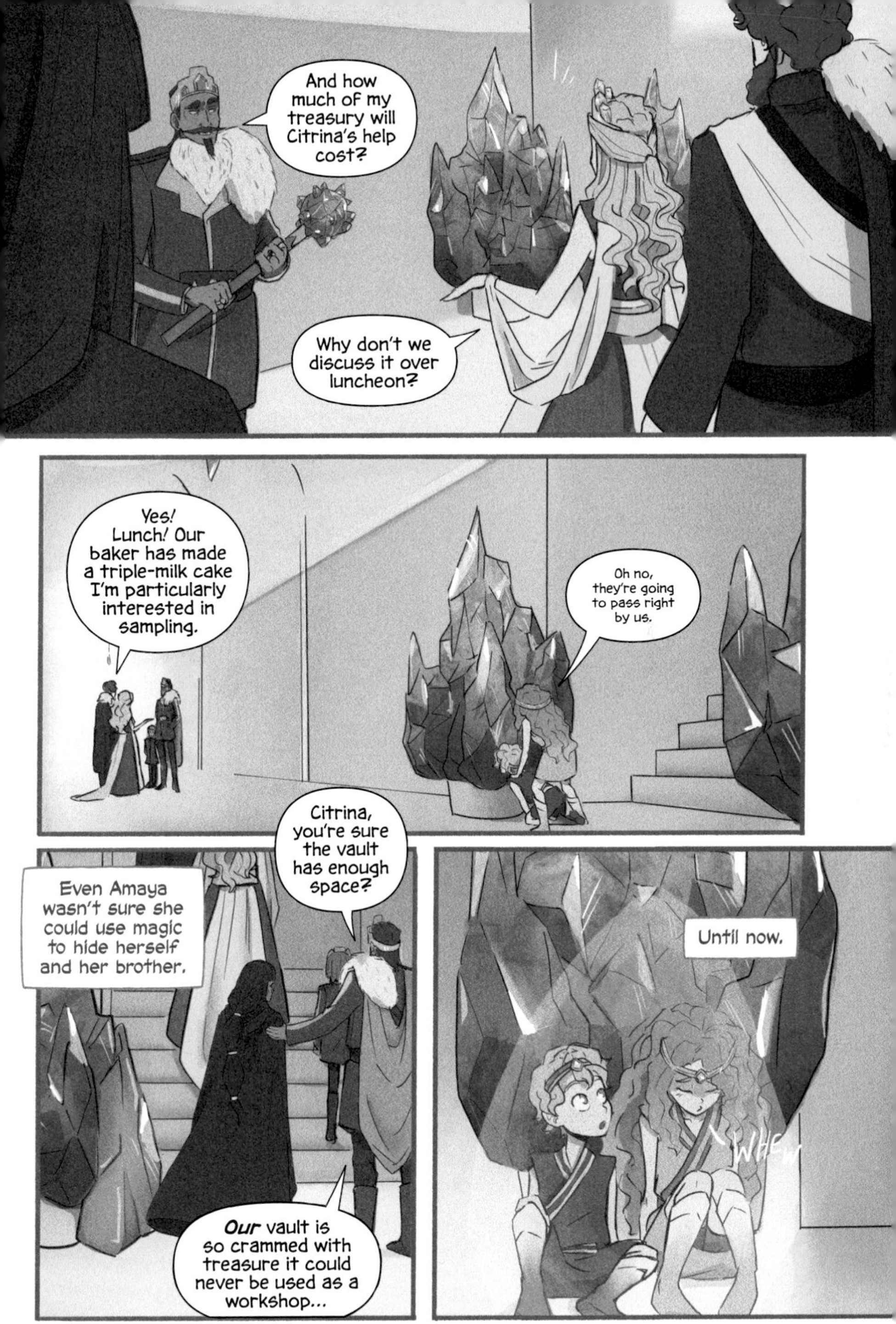
And how much of my treasury will Citrina's help cost?
Why don't we discuss it over luncheon?
Yes! Lunch! Our baker has made a triple-milk cake I'm particularly interested in sampling.
Oh no, they're going to pass right by us.
Citrina, you're sure the vault has enough space?
Even Amaya wasn't sure she could use magic to hide herself and her brother.
Our vault is so crammed with treasure it could never be used as a workshop...
Until now.
WHEW

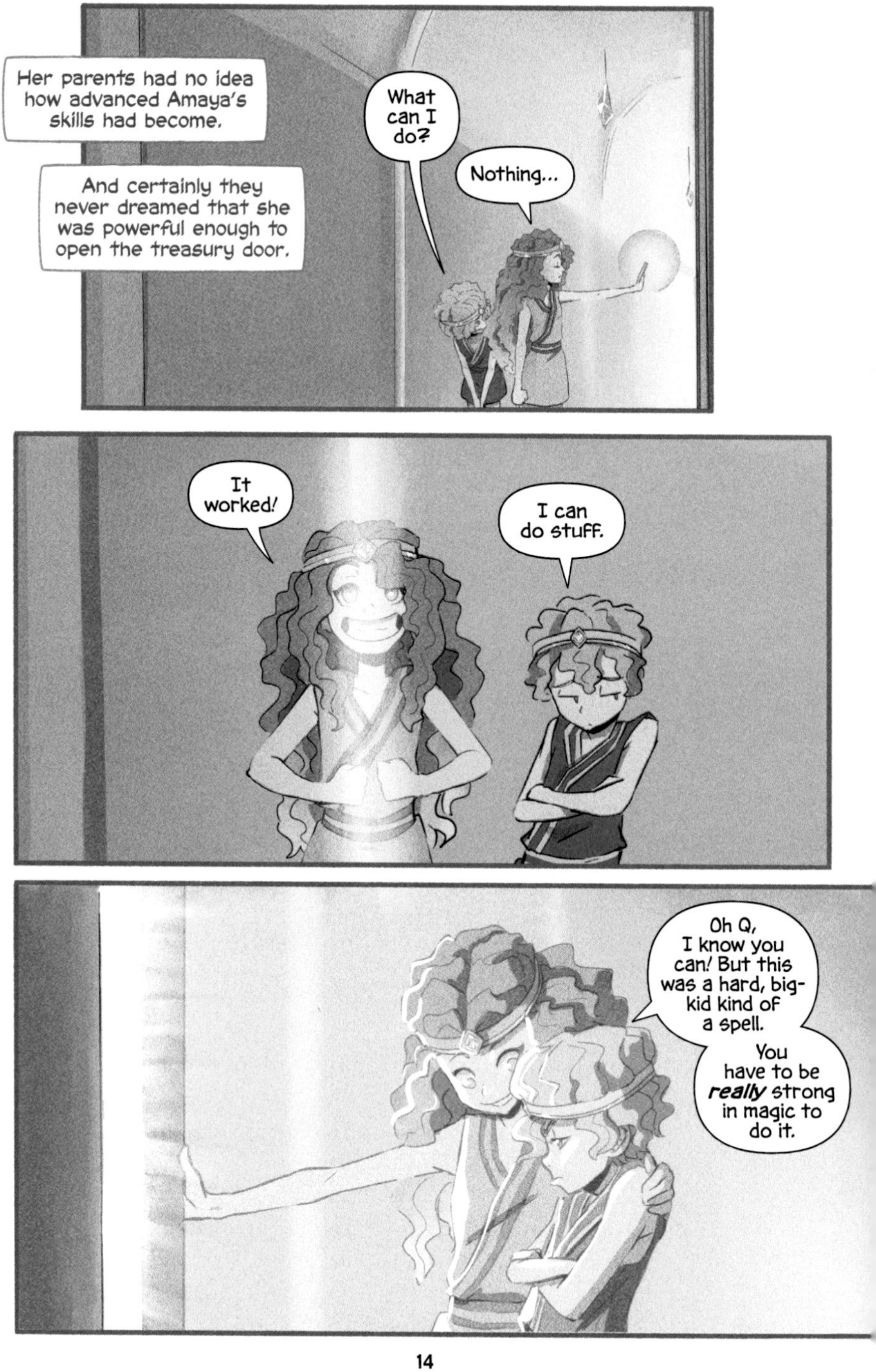
Her parents had no idea how advanced Amaya's skills had become.
And certainly they never dreamed that she was powerful enough to open the treasury door.
What can I do?
Nothing...
It worked!
I can do stuff.
Oh Q, I know you can! But this was a hard, big-kid kind of a spell.
You have to be *really* strong in magic to do it.

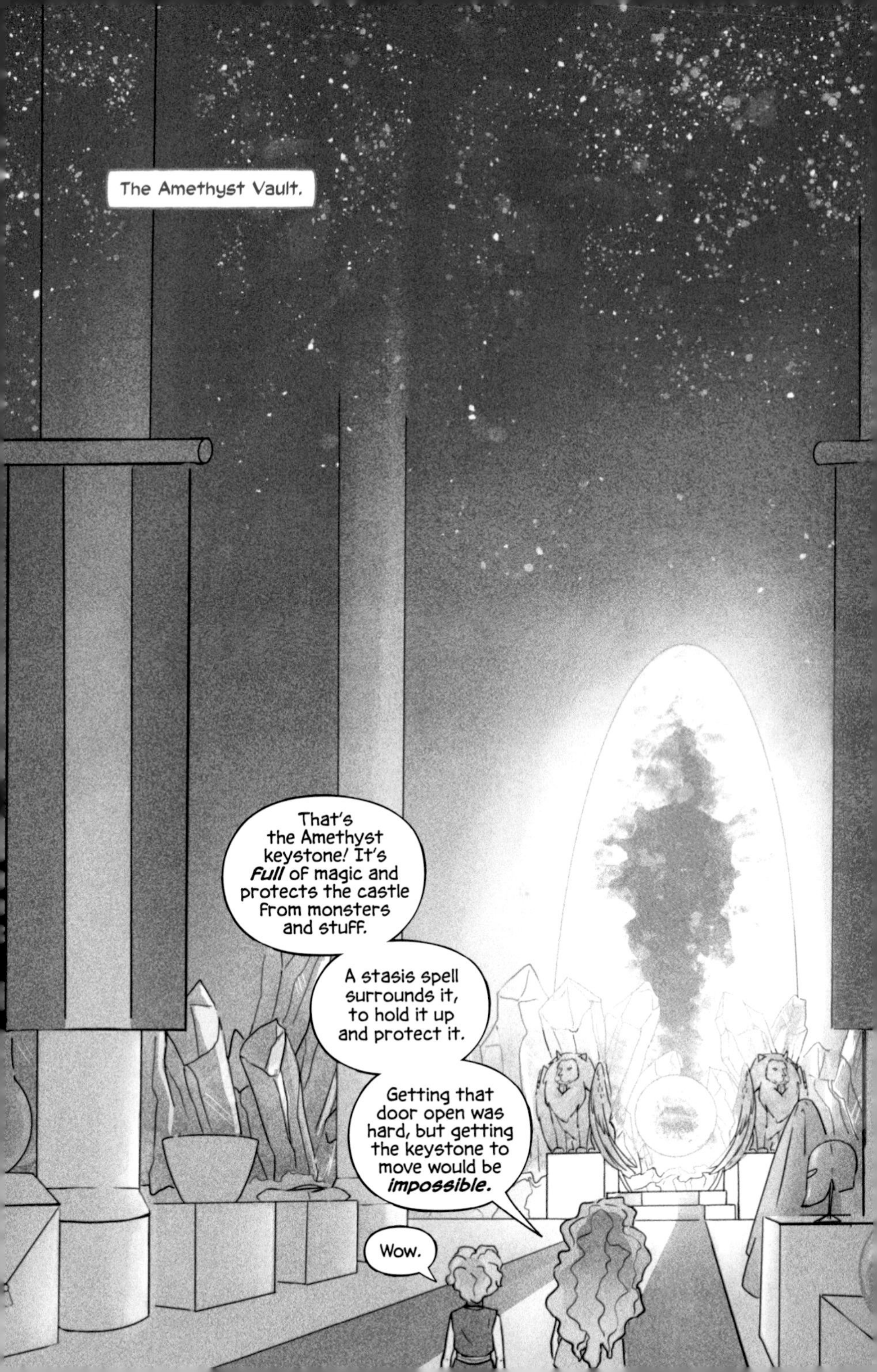
The Amethyst Vault.
That's the Amethyst keystone! It's *full* of magic and protects the castle from monsters and stuff.
A stasis spell surrounds it, to hold it up and protect it.
Getting that door open was hard, but getting the keystone to move would be ***impossible.***
Wow.

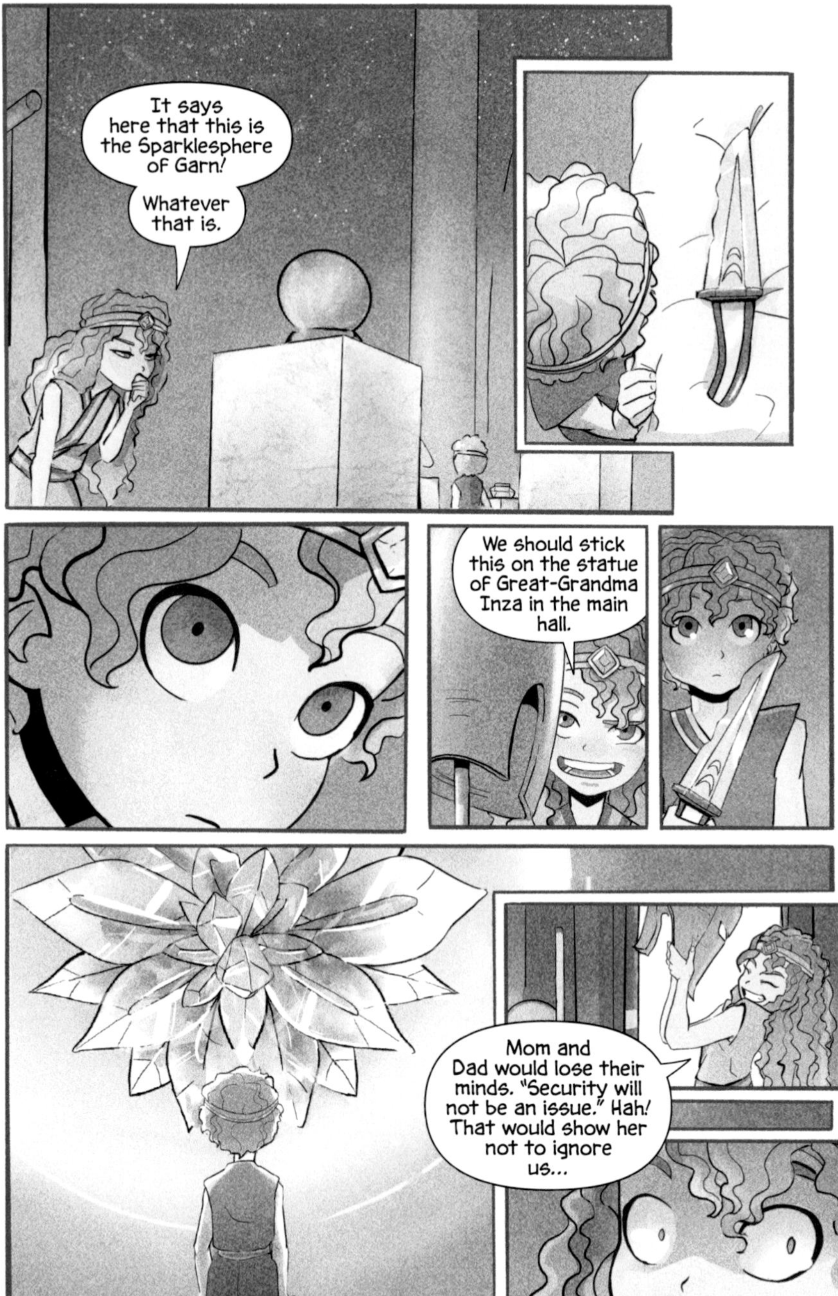

It says here that this is the Sparklesphere of Garn!
Whatever that is.
We should stick this on the statue of Great-Grandma Inza in the main hall.
Mom and Dad would lose their minds. "Security will not be an issue." Hah! That would show her not to ignore us...

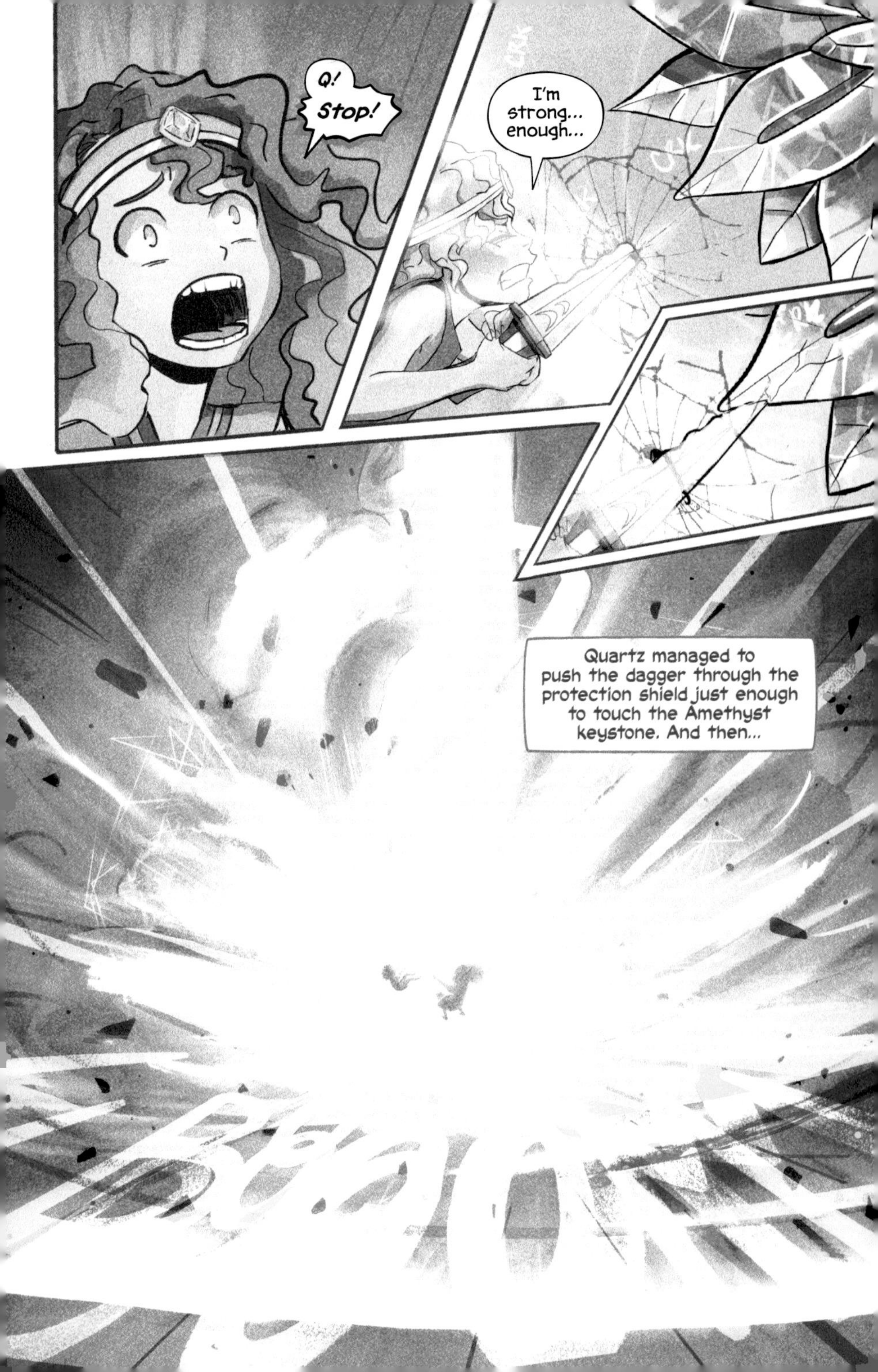
Q! Stop!
I'm strong... enough...
Quartz managed to push the dagger through the protection shield just enough to touch the Amethyst keystone. And then...

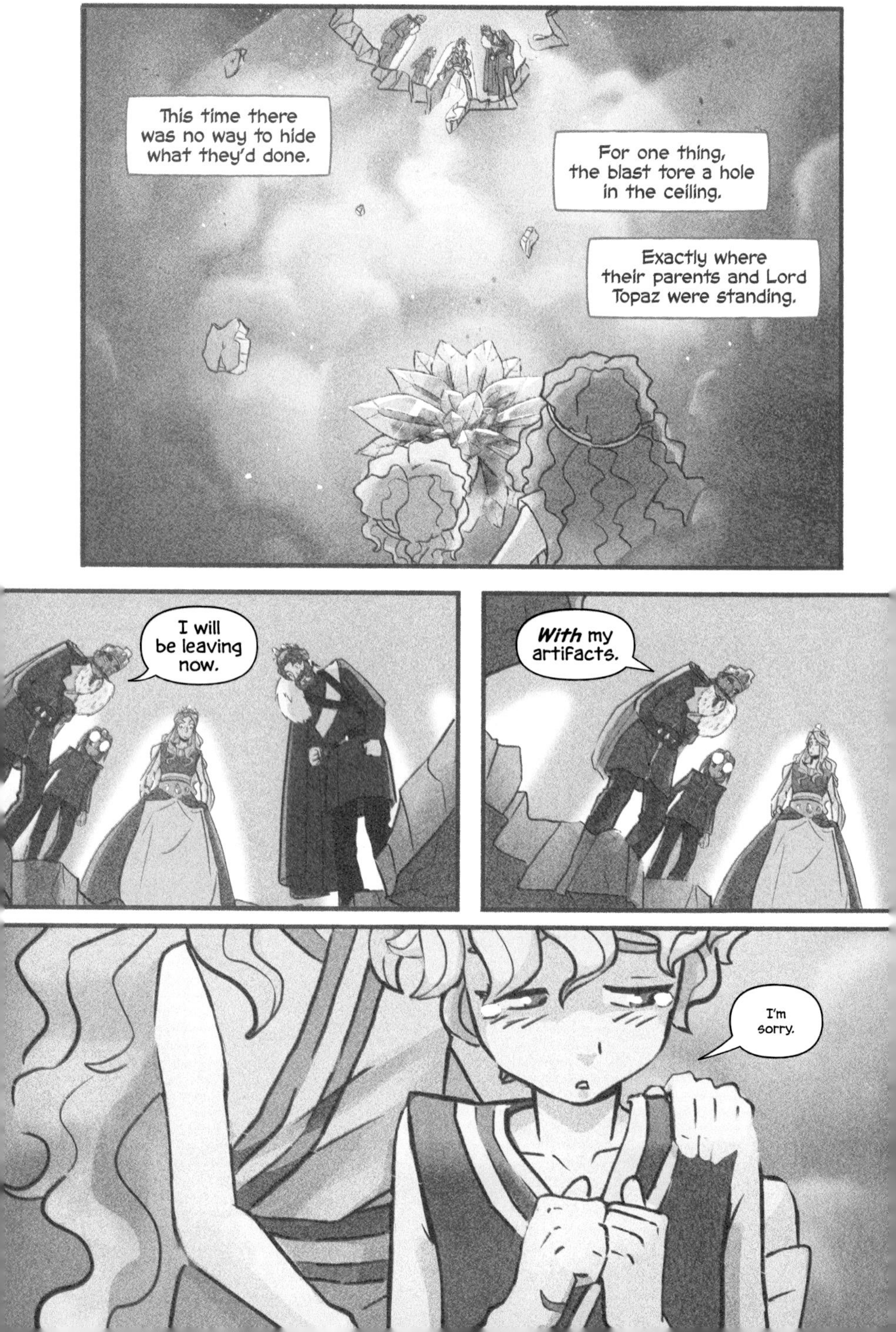
This time there was no way to hide what they'd done.
For one thing, the blast tore a hole in the ceiling.
Exactly where their parents and Lord Topaz were standing.
I will be leaving now.
With my artifacts.
I'm sorry.

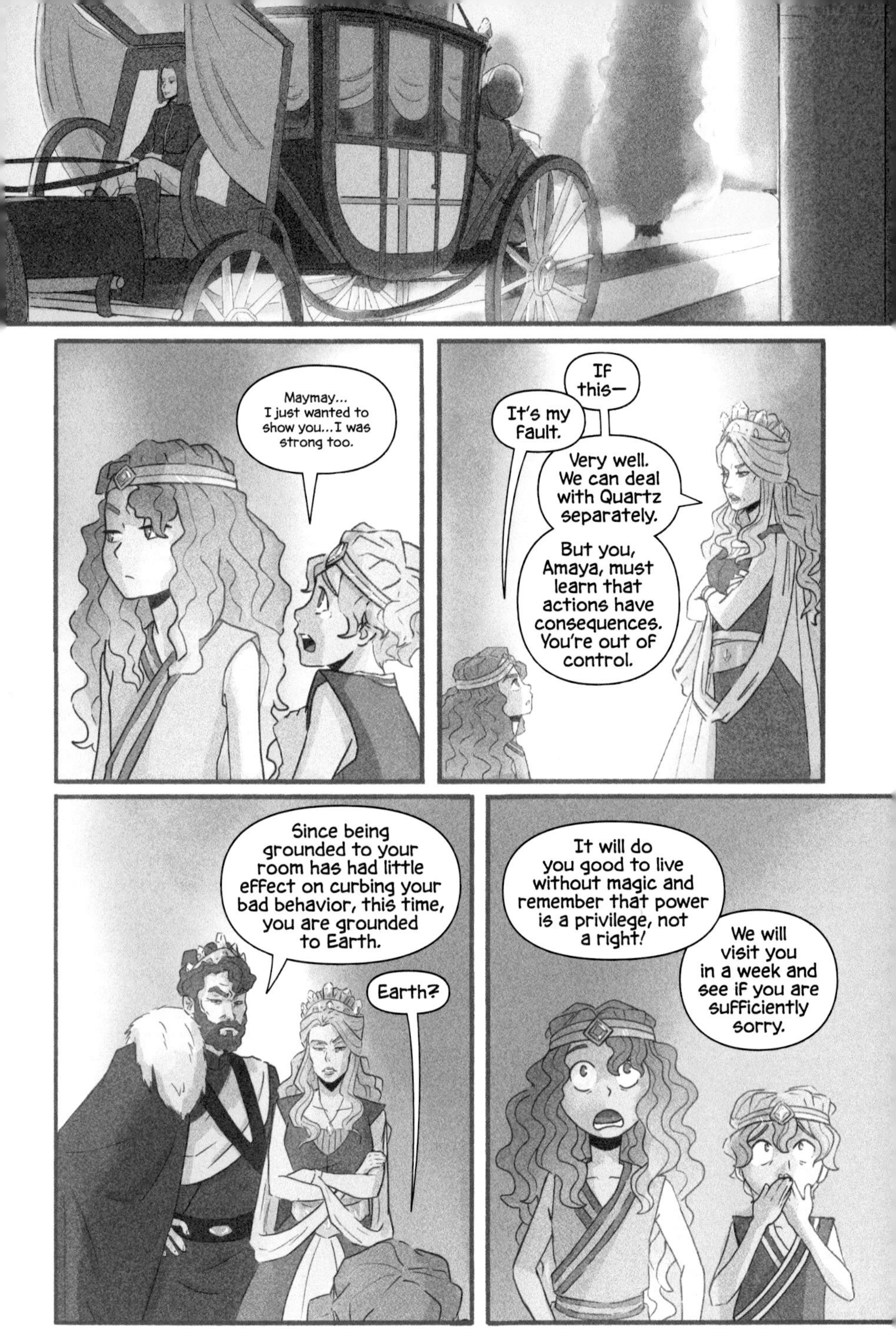
Maymay... I just wanted to show you...I was strong too.
If this—
It's my fault.
Very well. We can deal with Quartz separately.
But you, Amaya, must learn that actions have consequences. You're out of control.
Since being grounded to your room has had little effect on curbing your bad behavior, this time, you are grounded to Earth.
Earth?
It will do you good to live without magic and remember that power is a privilege, not a right!
We will visit you in a week and see if you are sufficiently sorry.

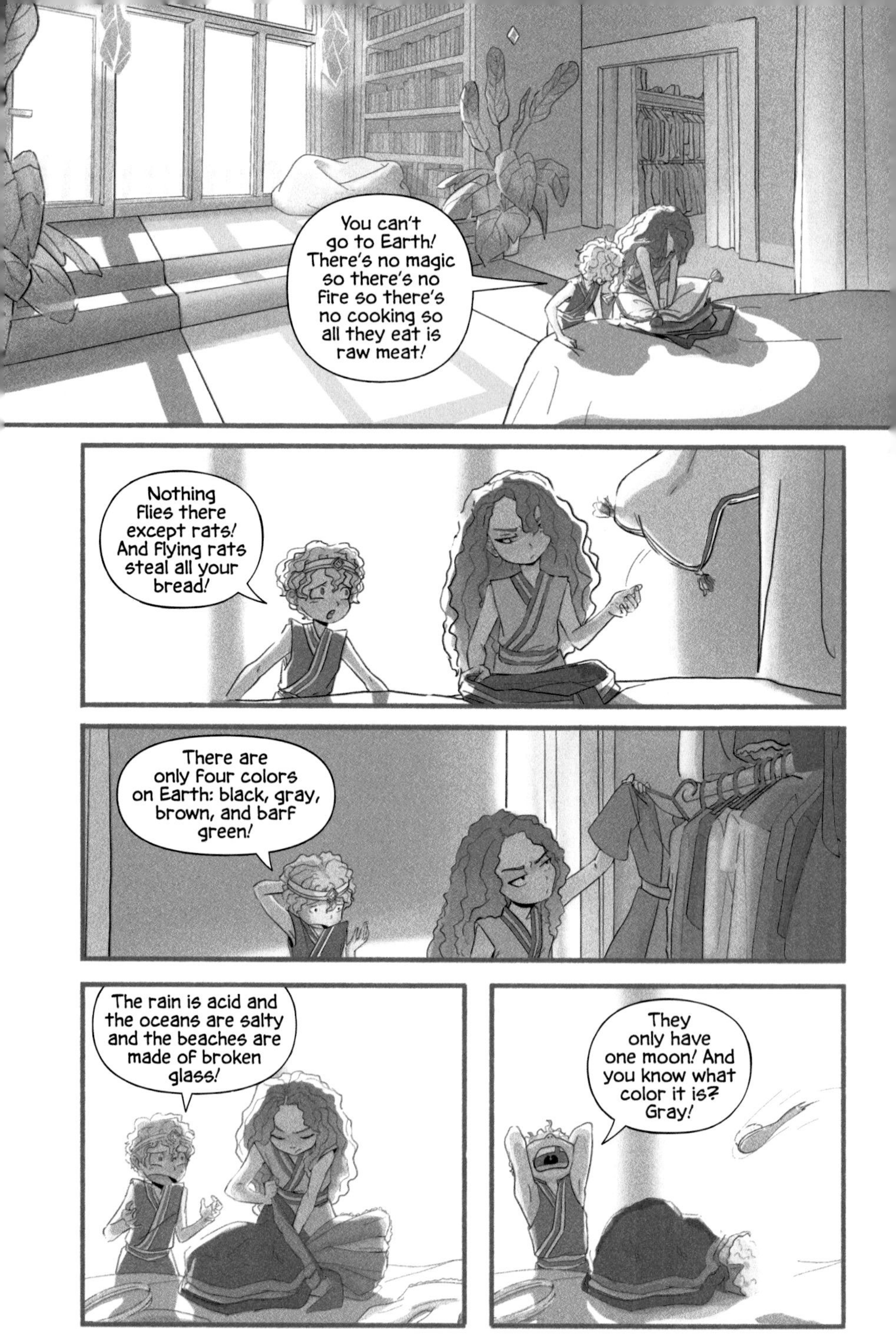
You can't go to Earth! There's no magic so there's no fire so there's no cooking so all they eat is raw meat!
Nothing flies there except rats! And flying rats steal all your bread!
There are only four colors on Earth: black, gray, brown, and barf green!
The rain is acid and the oceans are salty and the beaches are made of broken glass!
They only have one moon! And you know what color it is? Gray!

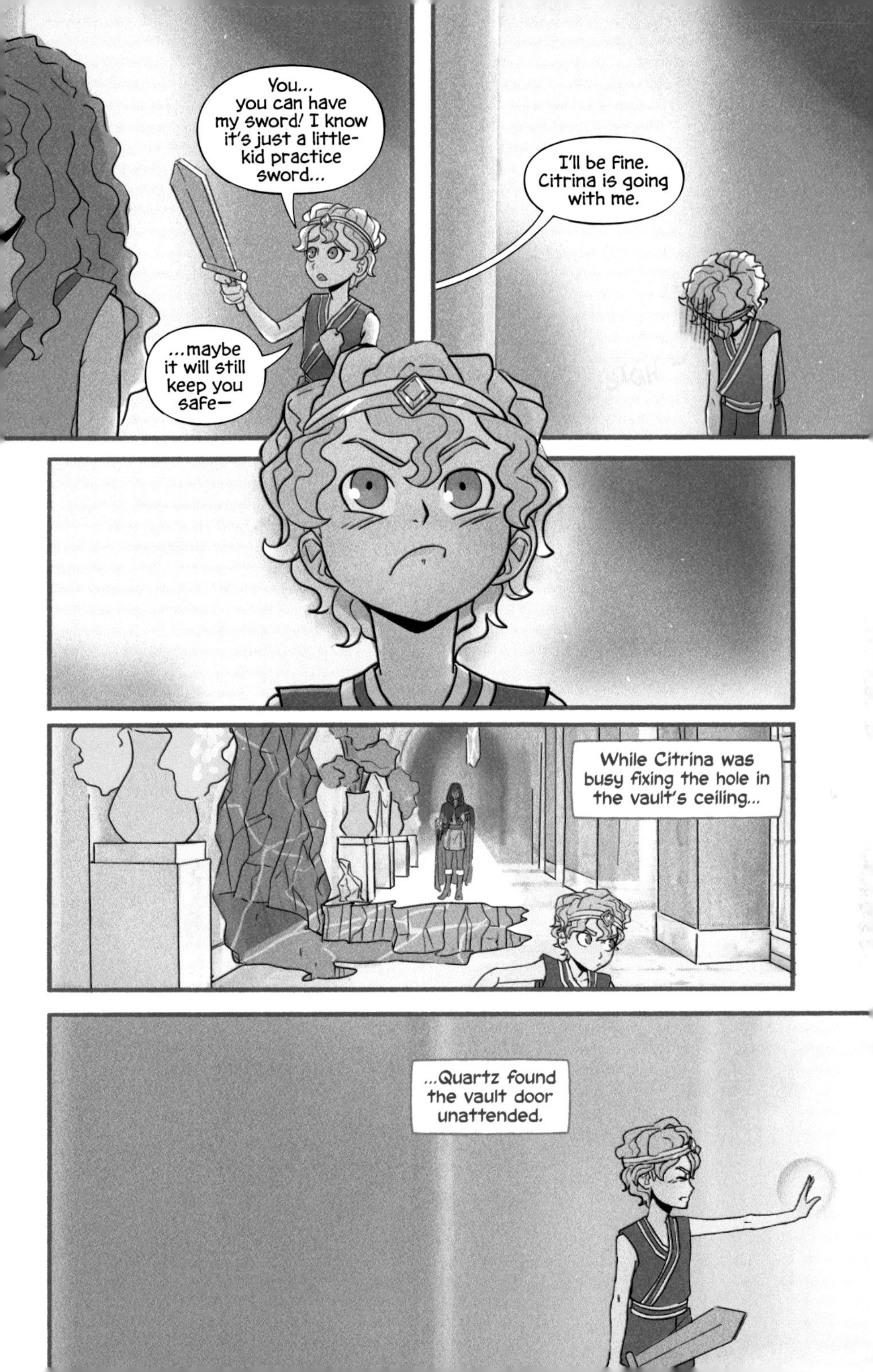
You... you can have my sword! I know it's just a little-kid practice sword...
...maybe it will still keep you safe—
I'll be fine. Citrina is going with me.
While Citrina was busy fixing the hole in the vault's ceiling...
...Quartz found the vault door unattended.

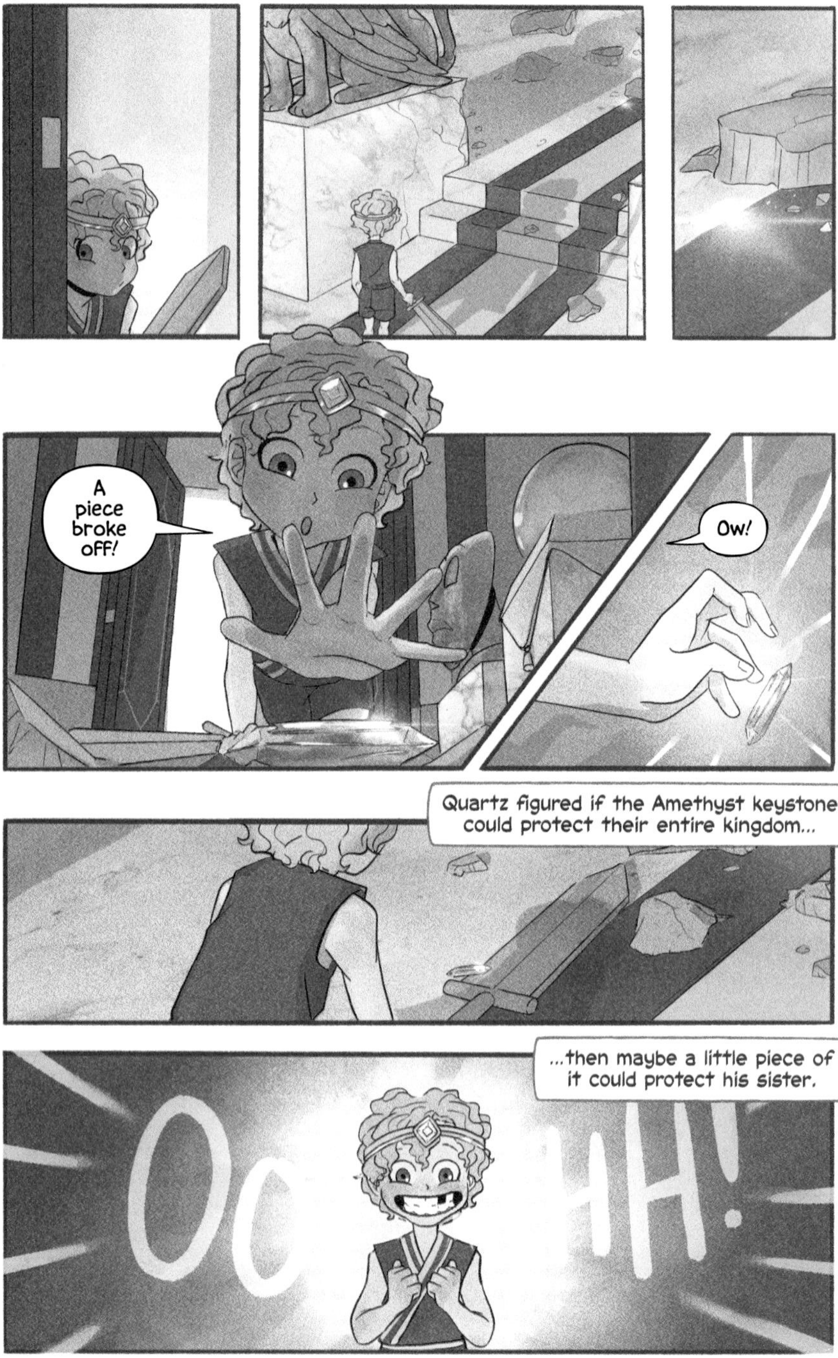
A piece broke off!
Ow!
Quartz figured if the Amethyst keystone could protect their entire kingdom...
...then maybe a little piece of it could protect his sister.

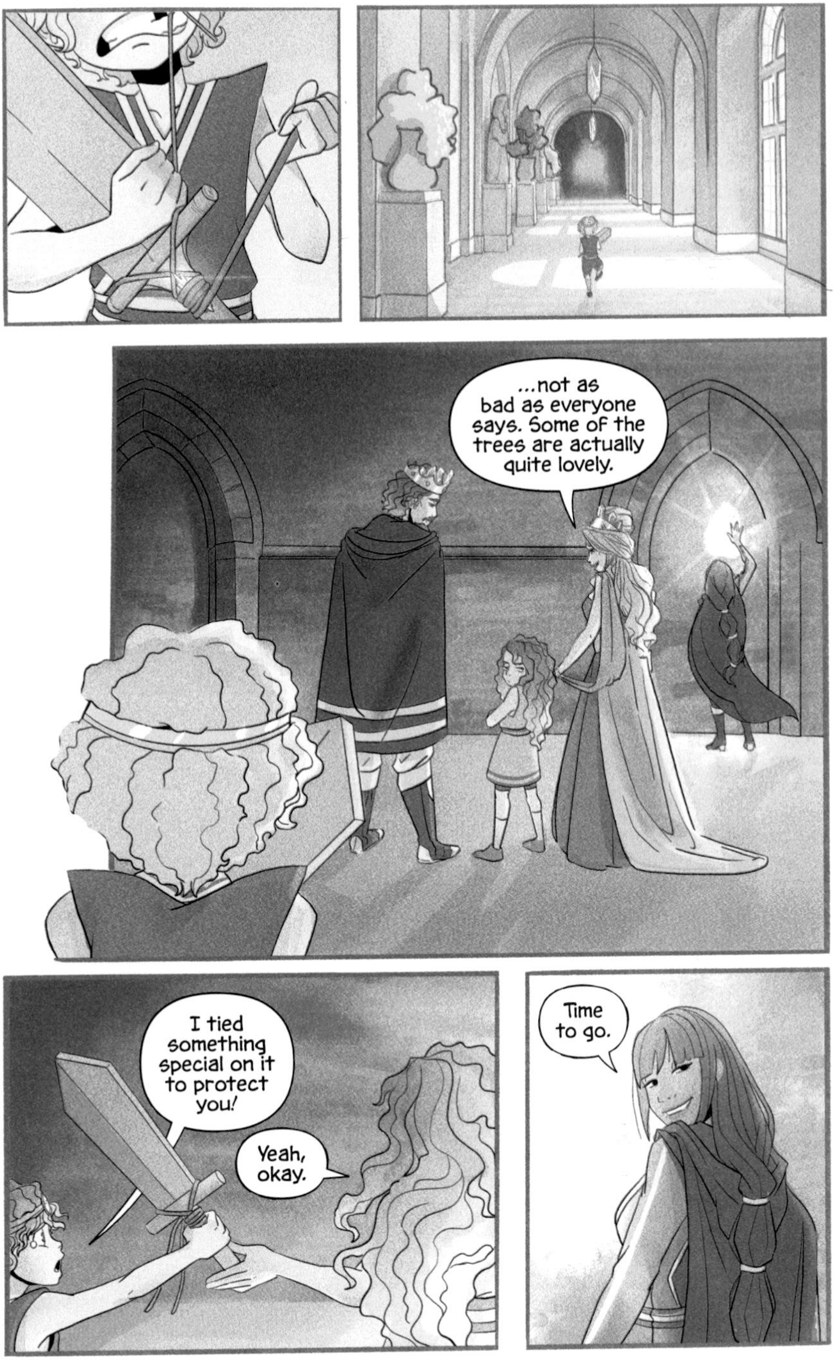
...not as bad as everyone says. Some of the trees are actually quite lovely.
I tied something special on it to protect you!
Yeah, okay.
Time to go.

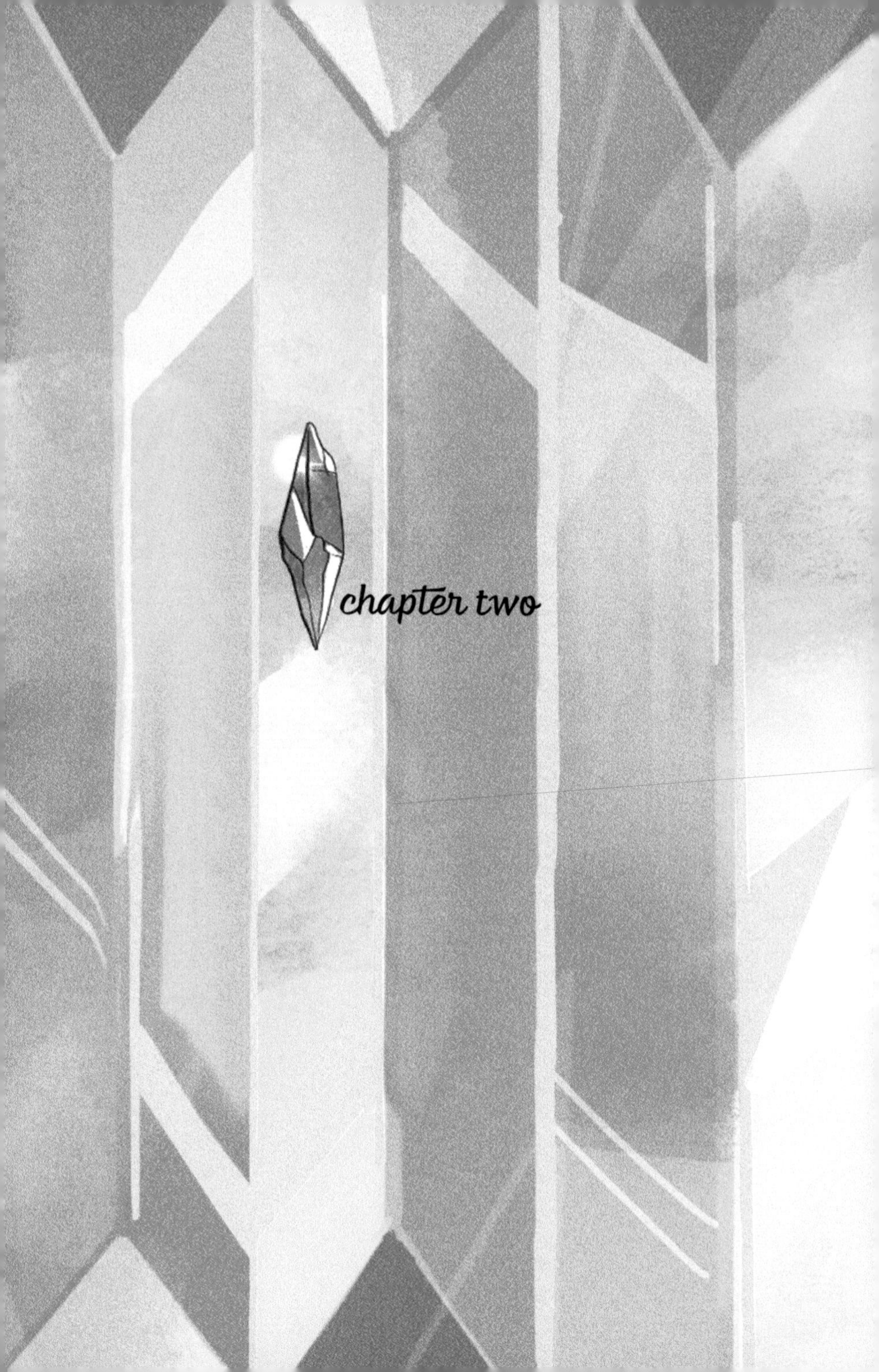

chapter two

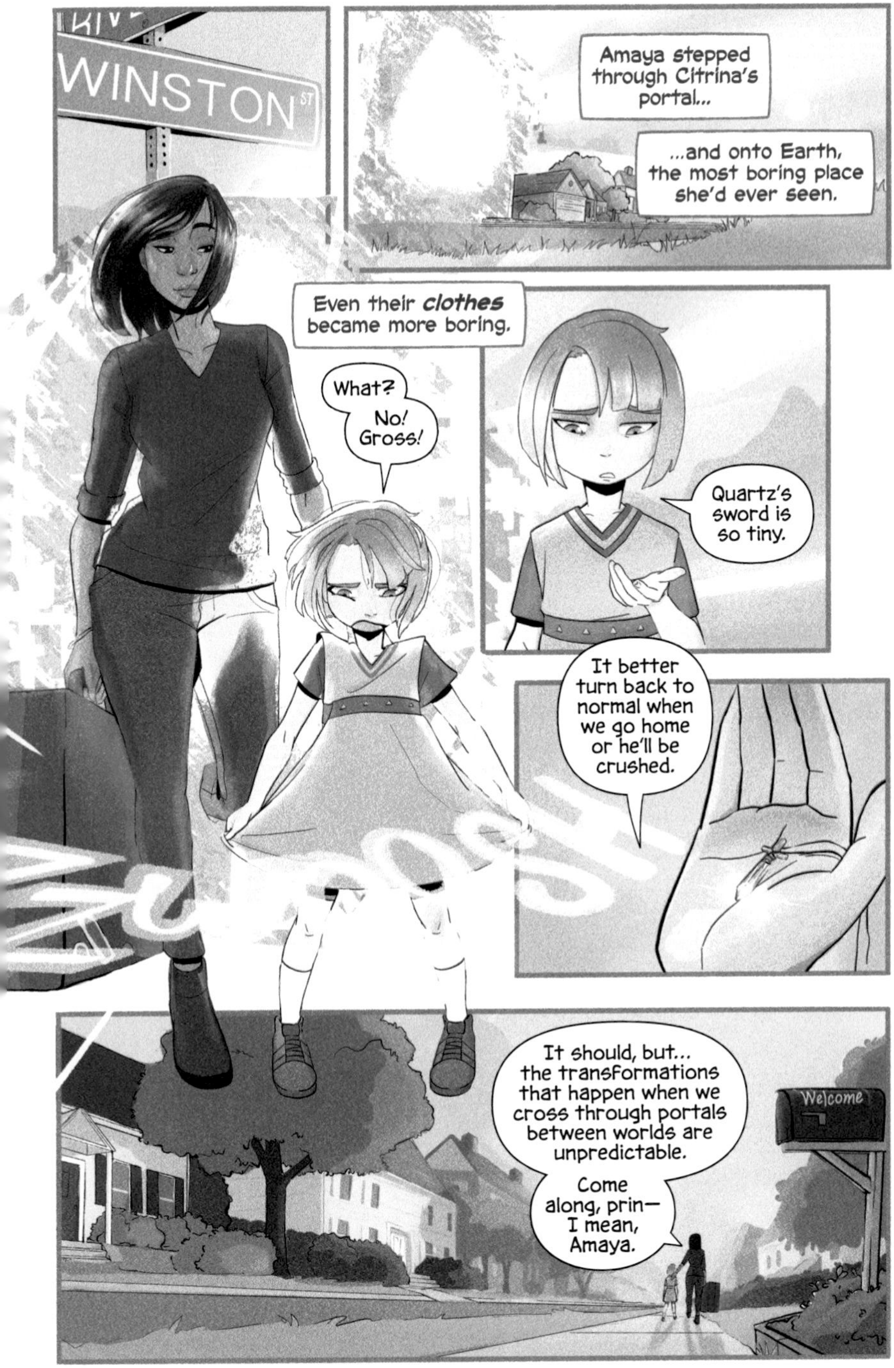
WINSTON ST
Amaya stepped through Citrina's portal...
...and onto Earth, the most boring place she'd ever seen.
Even their *clothes* became more boring.
What?
No! Gross!
Quartz's sword is so tiny.
It better turn back to normal when we go home or he'll be crushed.
It should, but... the transformations that happen when we cross through portals between worlds are unpredictable.
Come along, prin— I mean, Amaya.
Welcome

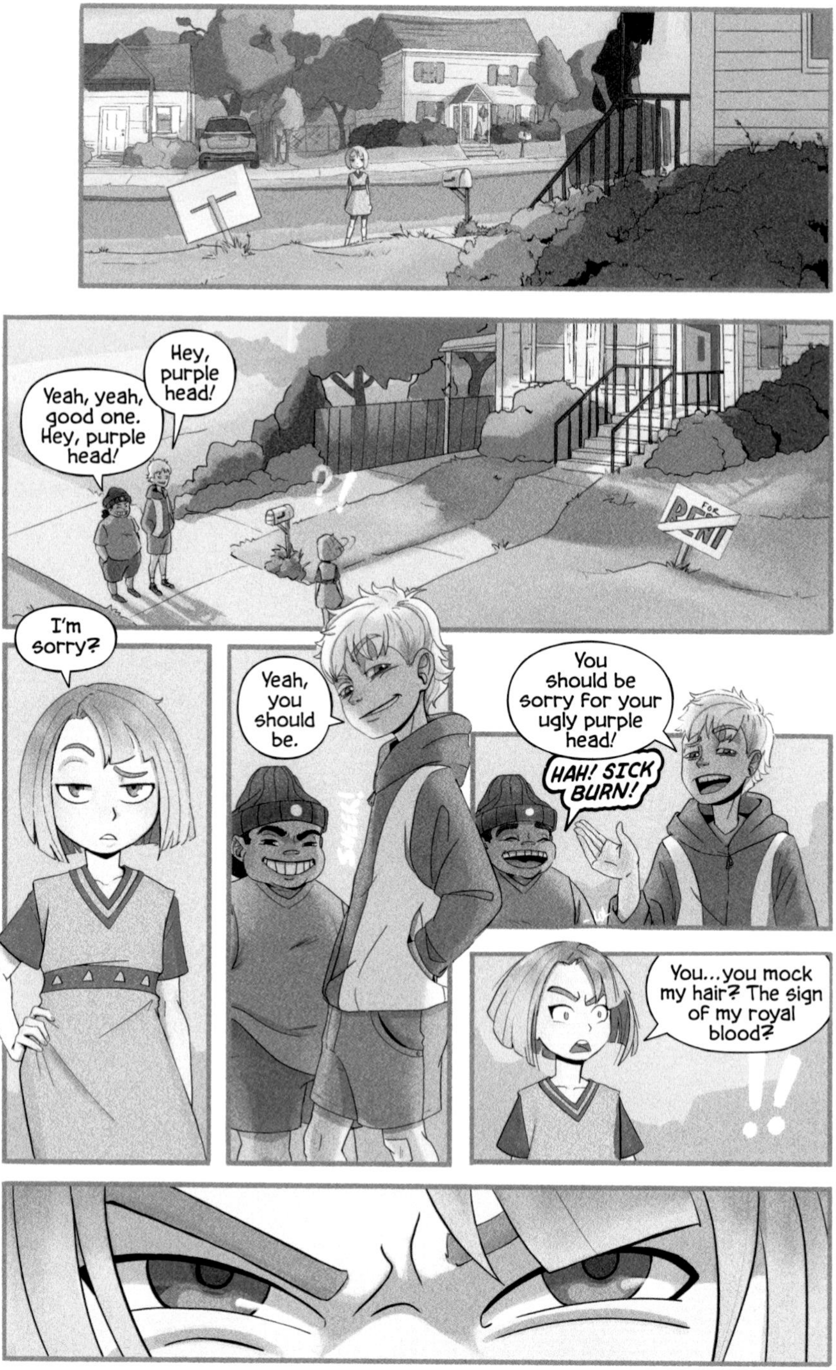
Hey, purple head!
Yeah, yeah, good one. Hey, purple head!
FOR RENT
I'm sorry?
Yeah, you should be.
You should be sorry for your ugly purple head!
HAH! SICK BURN!
You...you mock my hair? The sign of my royal blood?

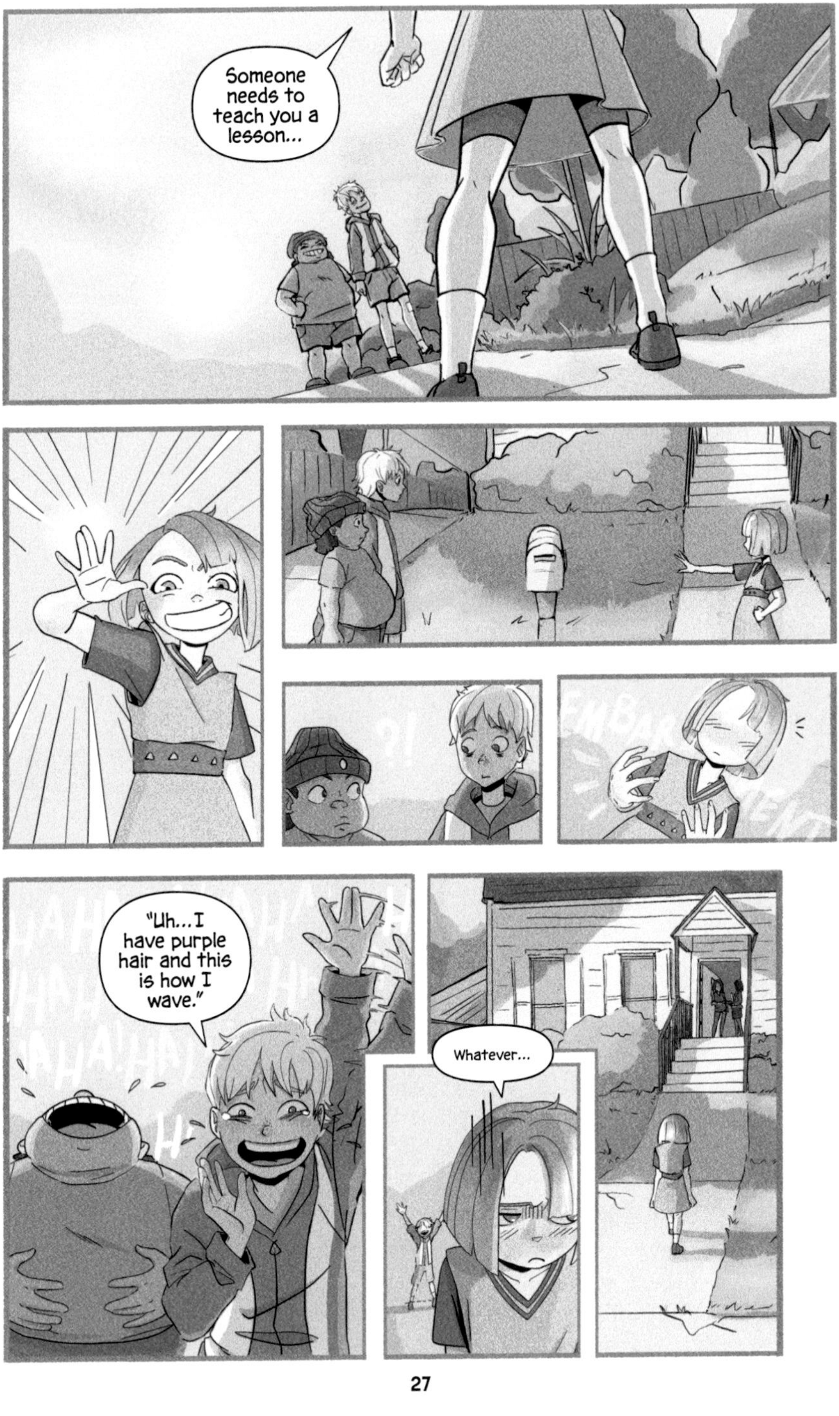
Someone needs to teach you a lesson...
?!
"Uh...I have purple hair and this is how I wave."
Whatever...

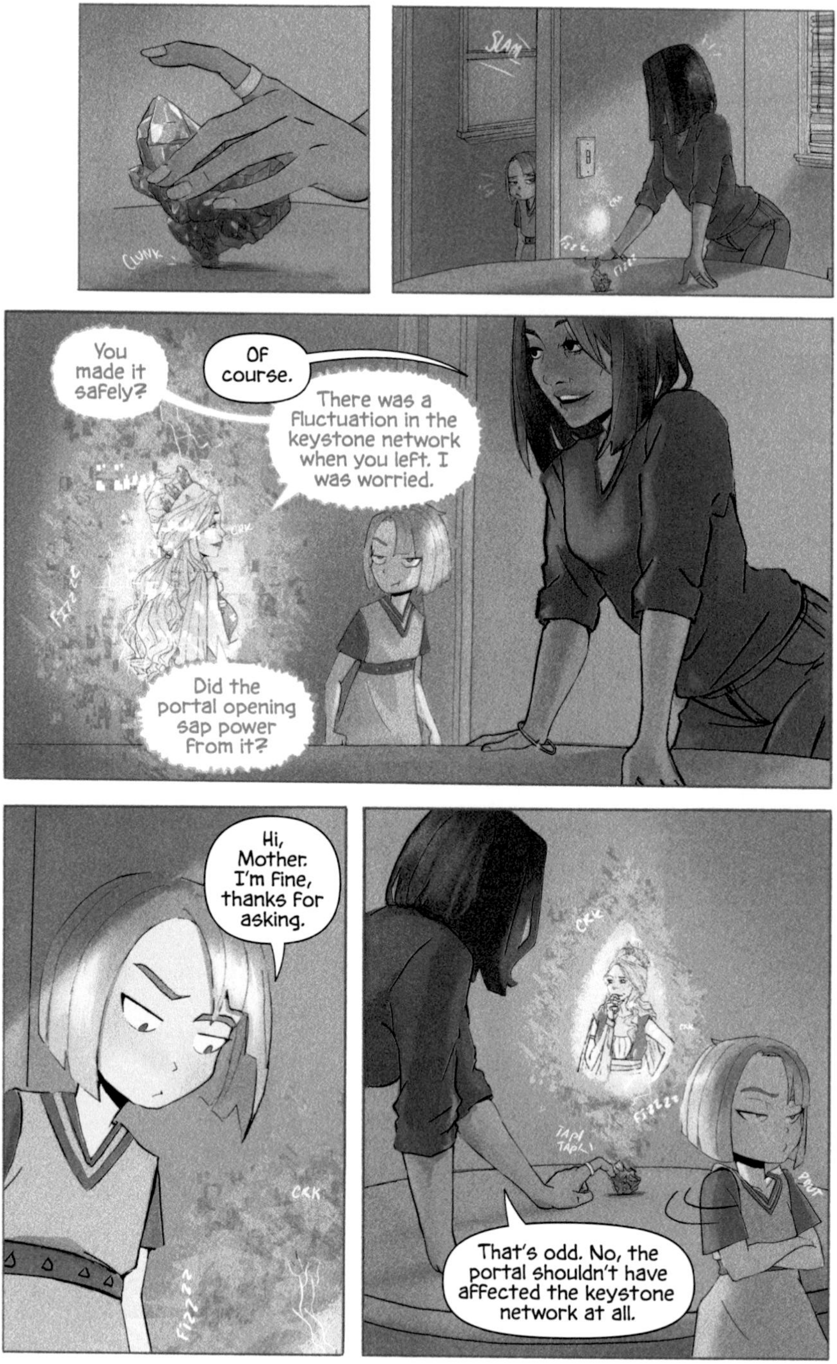
CLUNK
SLAM
You made it safely?
Of course.
There was a fluctuation in the keystone network when you left. I was worried.
Did the portal opening sap power from it?
Hi, Mother. I'm fine, thanks for asking.
CRK
That's odd. No, the portal shouldn't have affected the keystone network at all.
POUT

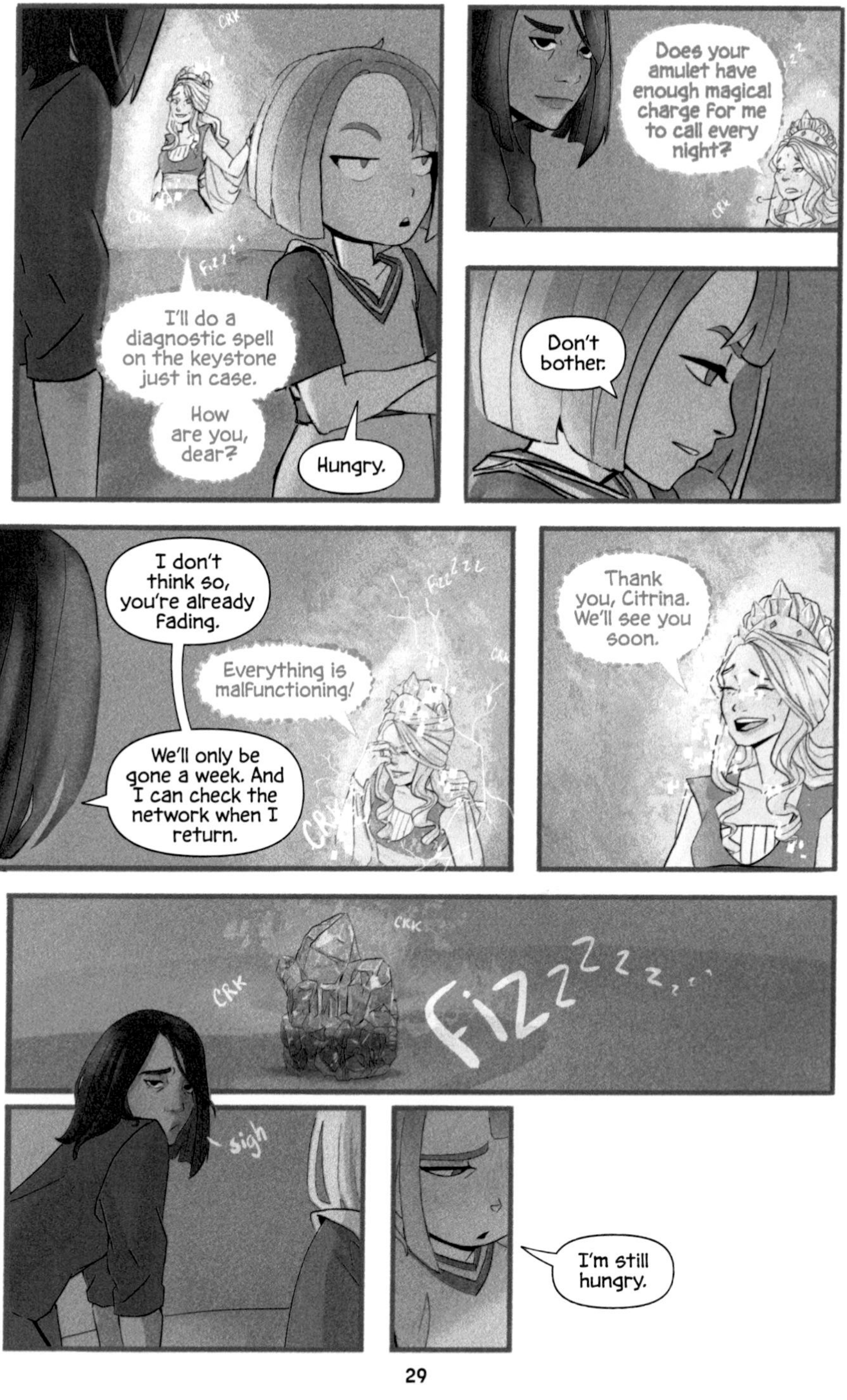
CRK
CRK
FIZZZZ
I'll do a diagnostic spell on the keystone just in case.
How are you, dear?
Hungry.
Does your amulet have enough magical charge for me to call every night?
CRK
Don't bother.
I don't think so, you're already fading.
FIZZZZ
Everything is malfunctioning!
CRK
We'll only be gone a week. And I can check the network when I return.
Thank you, Citrina. We'll see you soon.
CRK
CRK
FIZZZZZ...
sigh
I'm still hungry.

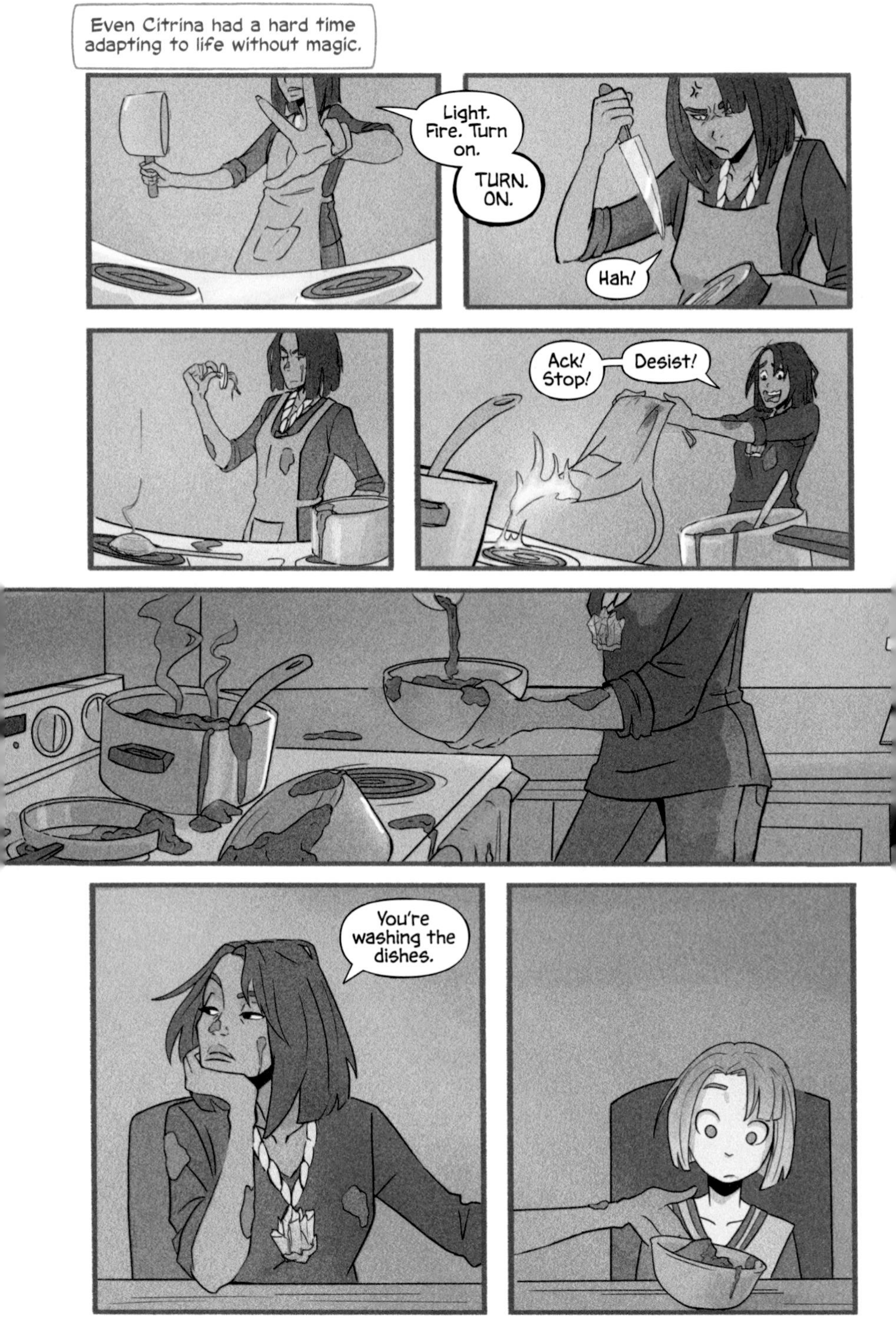
Even Citrina had a hard time adapting to life without magic.
Light. Fire. Turn on.
TURN. ON.
Hah!
Ack! Stop!
Desist!
You're washing the dishes.

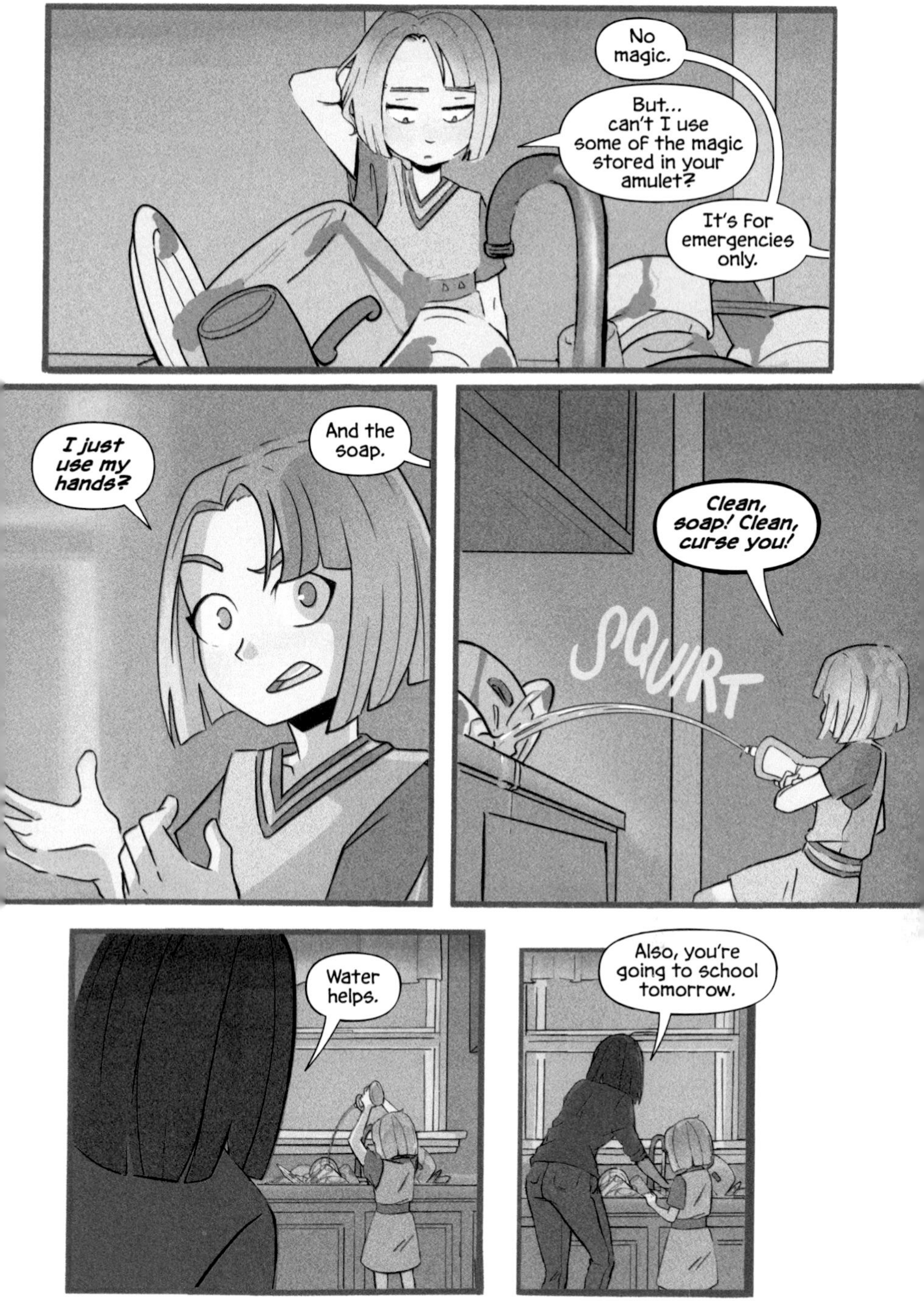
No magic.
But... can't I use some of the magic stored in your amulet?
It's for emergencies only.
I just use my hands?
And the soap.
Clean, soap! Clean, curse you!
SQUIRT
Water helps.
Also, you're going to school tomorrow.

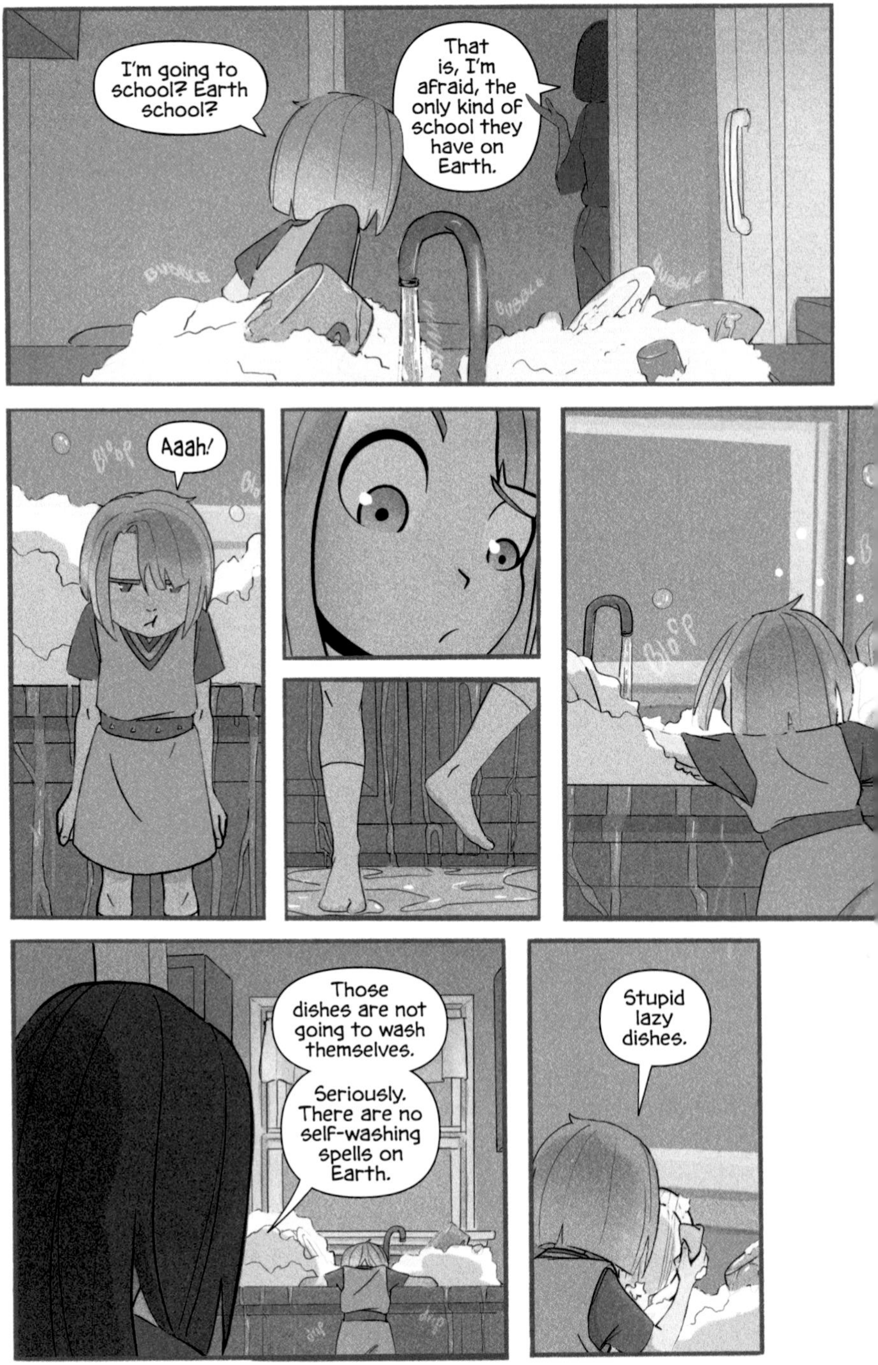
I'm going to school? Earth school?
That is, I'm afraid, the only kind of school they have on Earth.
Aaah!
Those dishes are not going to wash themselves.
Seriously. There are no self-washing spells on Earth.
Stupid lazy dishes.

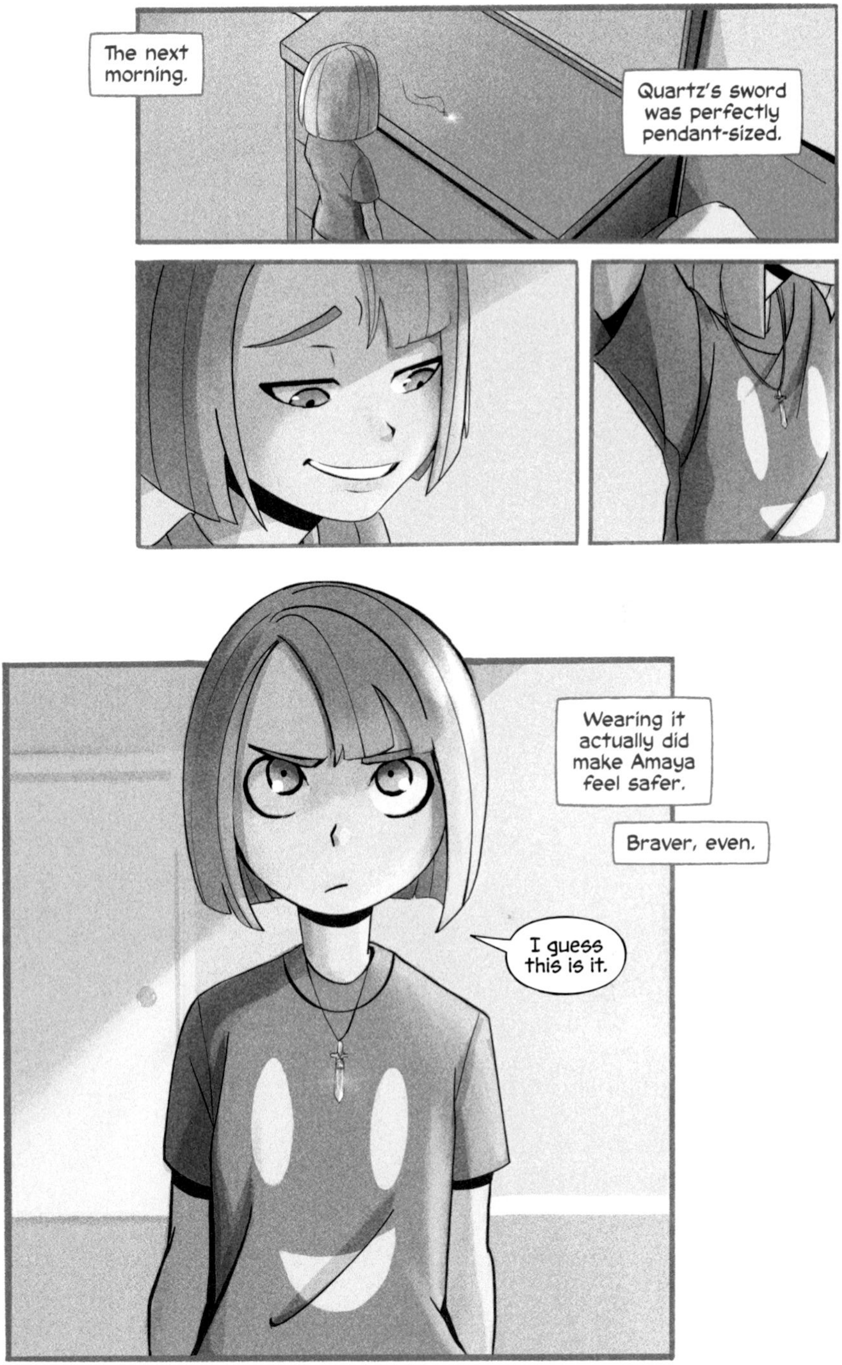
The next morning.
Quartz's sword was perfectly pendant-sized.
Wearing it actually did make Amaya feel safer.
Braver, even.
I guess this is it.

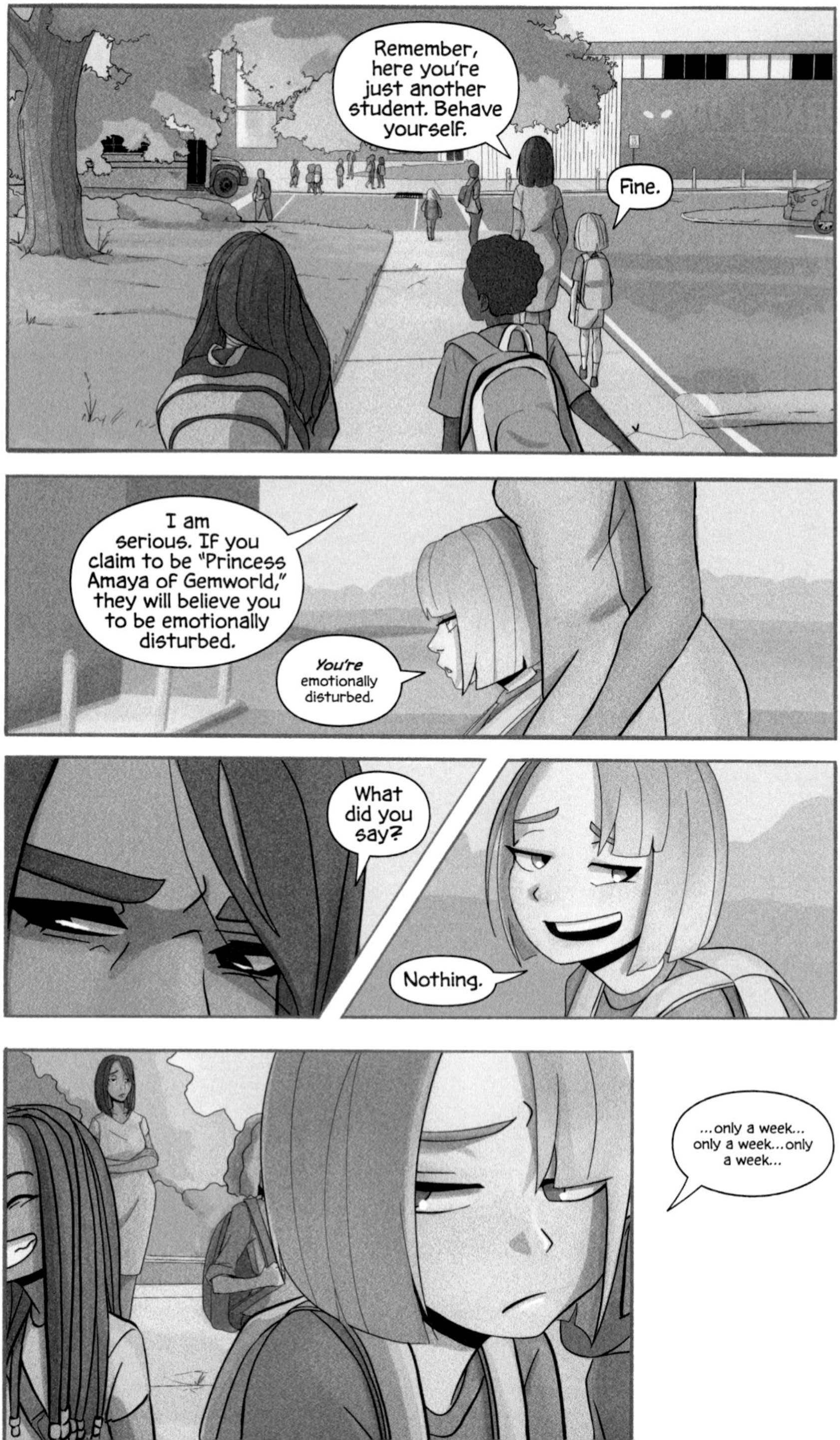
Remember, here you're just another student. Behave yourself.
Fine.
I am serious. If you claim to be "Princess Amaya of Gemworld," they will believe you to be emotionally disturbed.
You're emotionally disturbed.
What did you say?
Nothing.
...only a week... only a week...only a week...

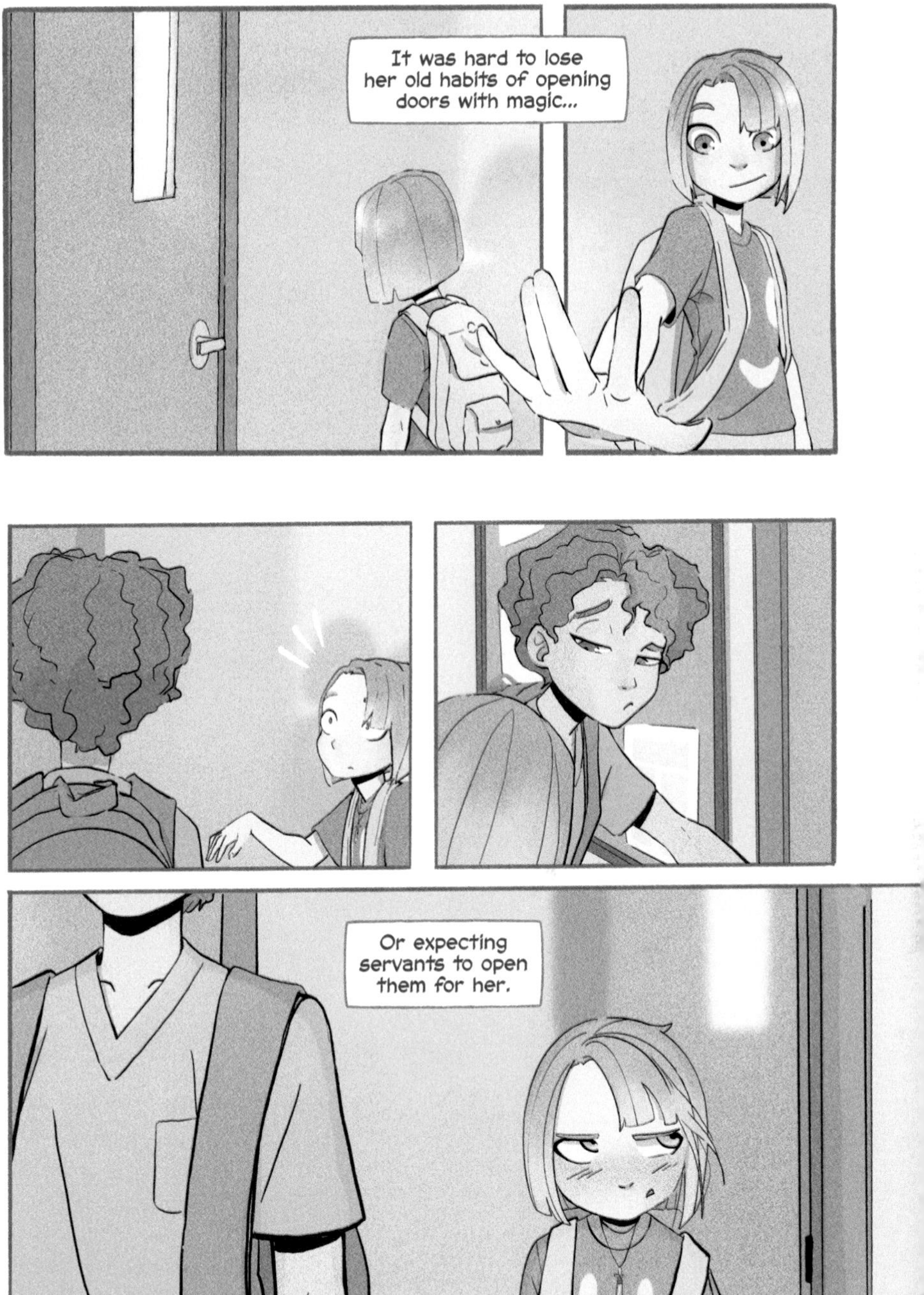
It was hard to lose her old habits of opening doors with magic...
Or expecting servants to open them for her.

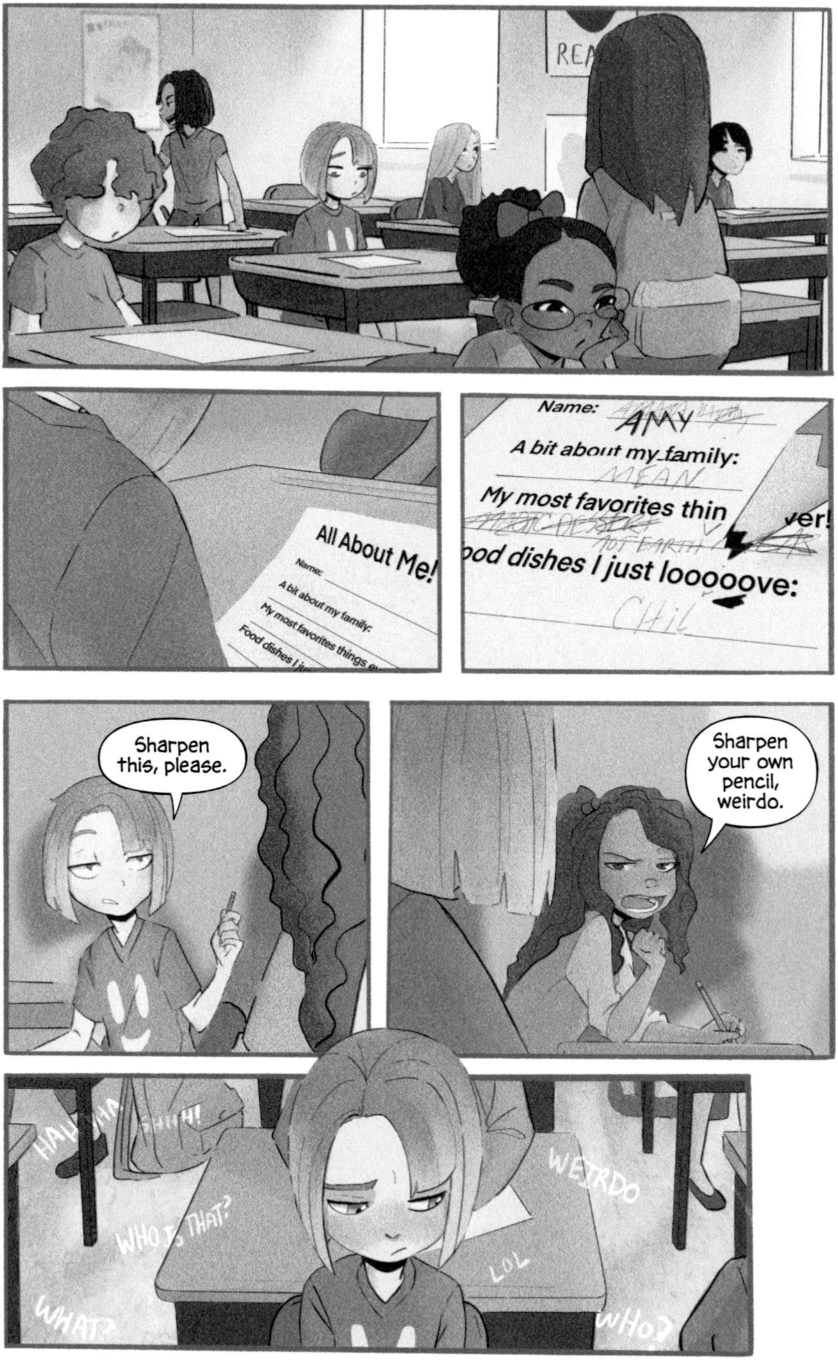
All About Me!
Name:
A bit about my family:
Name:
AMY
A bit about my family:
MEAN
Sharpen this, please.
Sharpen your own pencil, weirdo.
HA HA
SHHH!
WEIRDO
WHO IS THAT?
LOL
WHAT?
WHO?

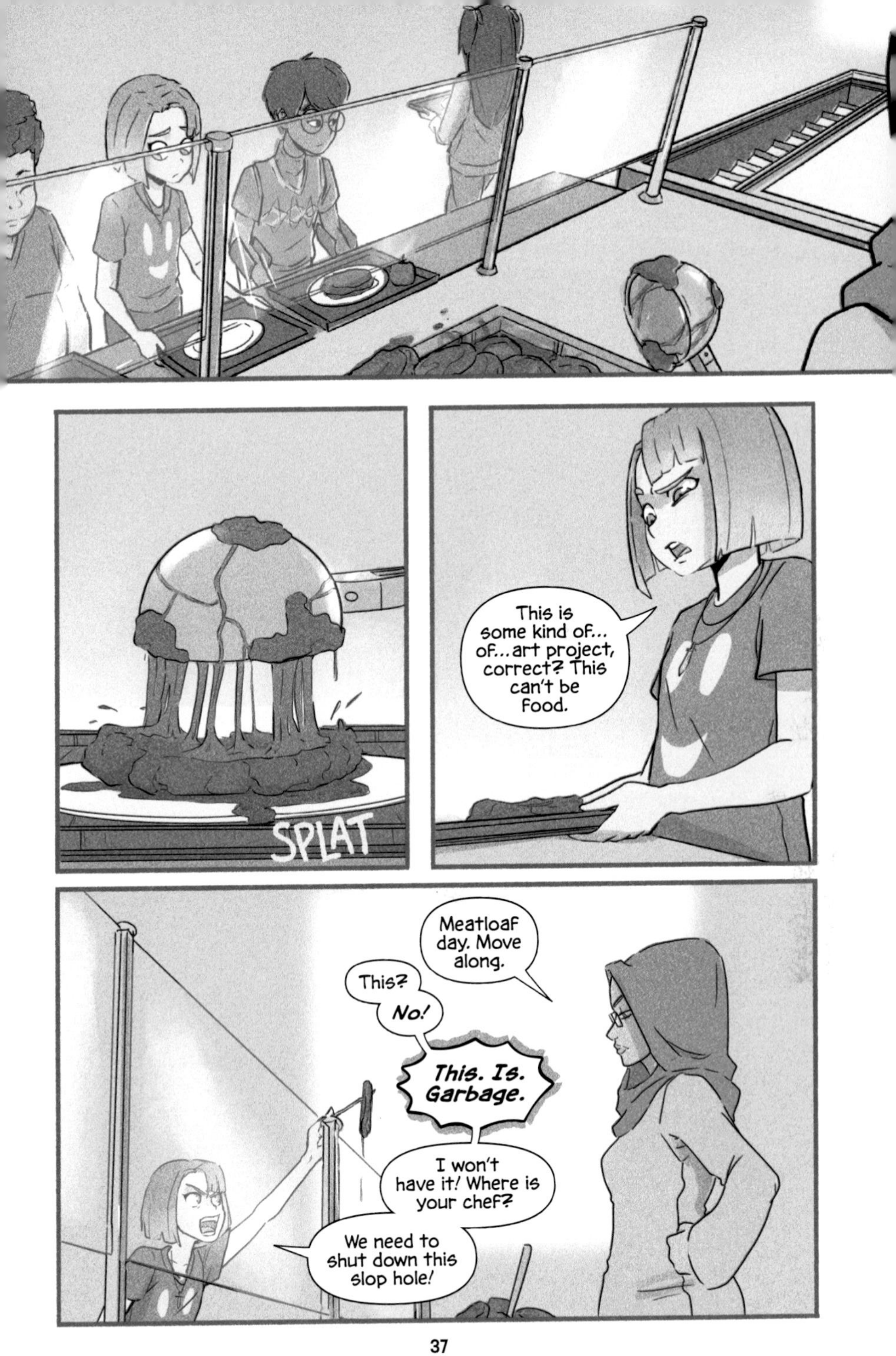
SPLAT
This is some kind of... of...art project, correct? This can't be food.
Meatloaf day. Move along.
This?
No!
This. Is. Garbage.
I won't have it! Where is your chef?
We need to shut down this slop hole!

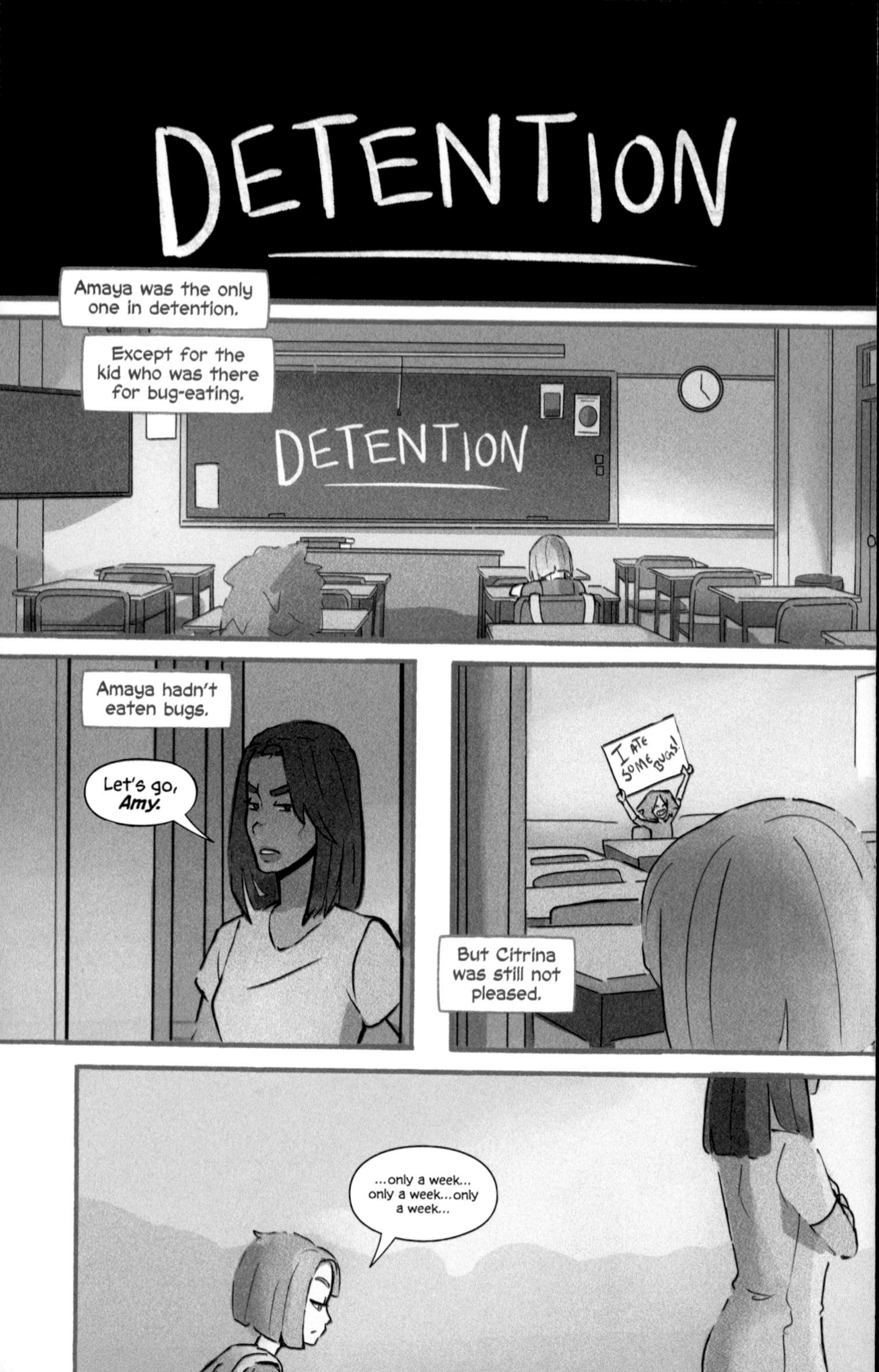
DETENTION
Amaya was the only one in detention.
Except for the kid who was there for bug-eating.
DETENTION
Amaya hadn't eaten bugs.
Let's go, *Amy.*
I ATE SOME BUGS!
But Citrina was still not pleased.
...only a week... only a week...only a week...

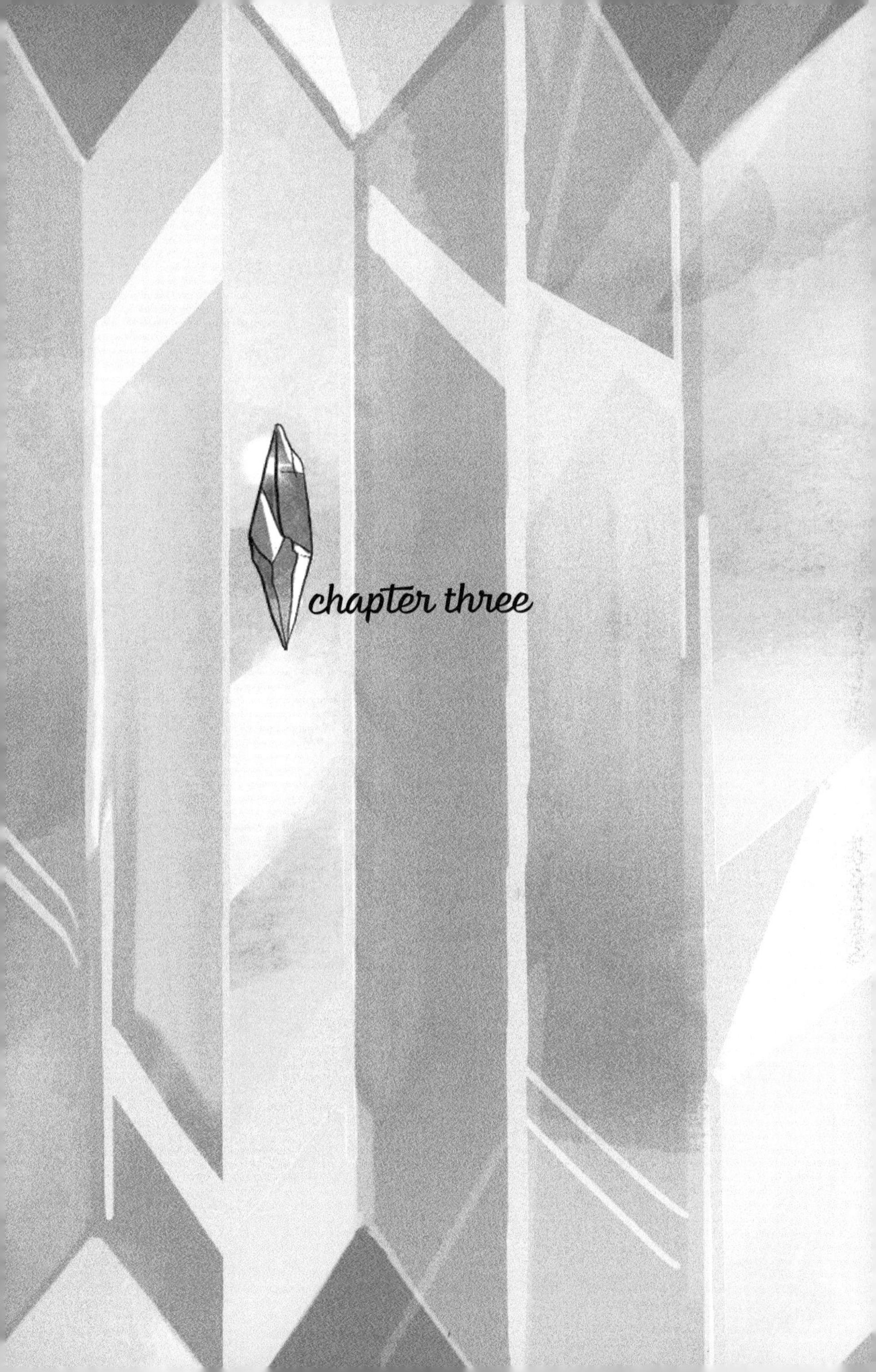

chapter three

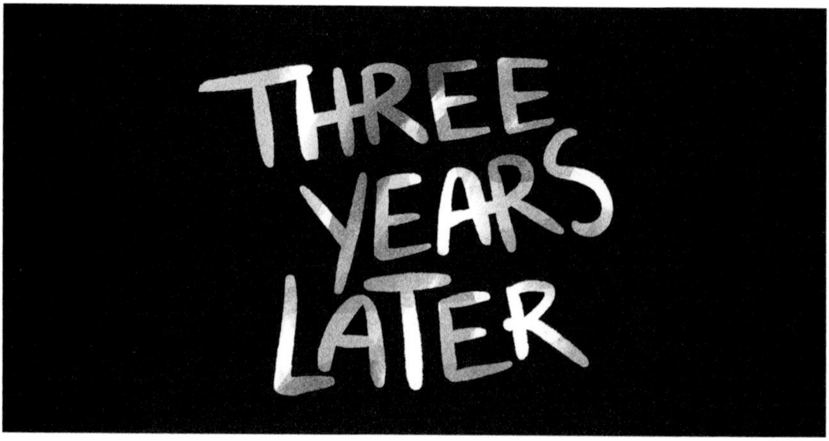
THREE YEARS LATER

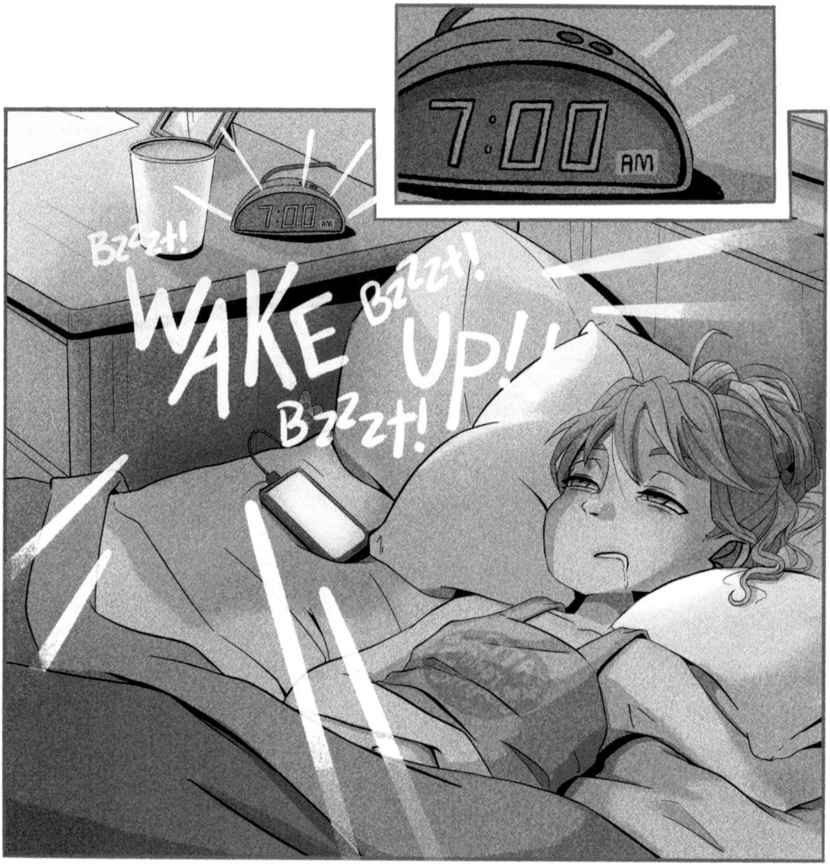
7:00 AM
Bzzzt!
WAKE
Bzzzt!
UP!!
Bzzzt!

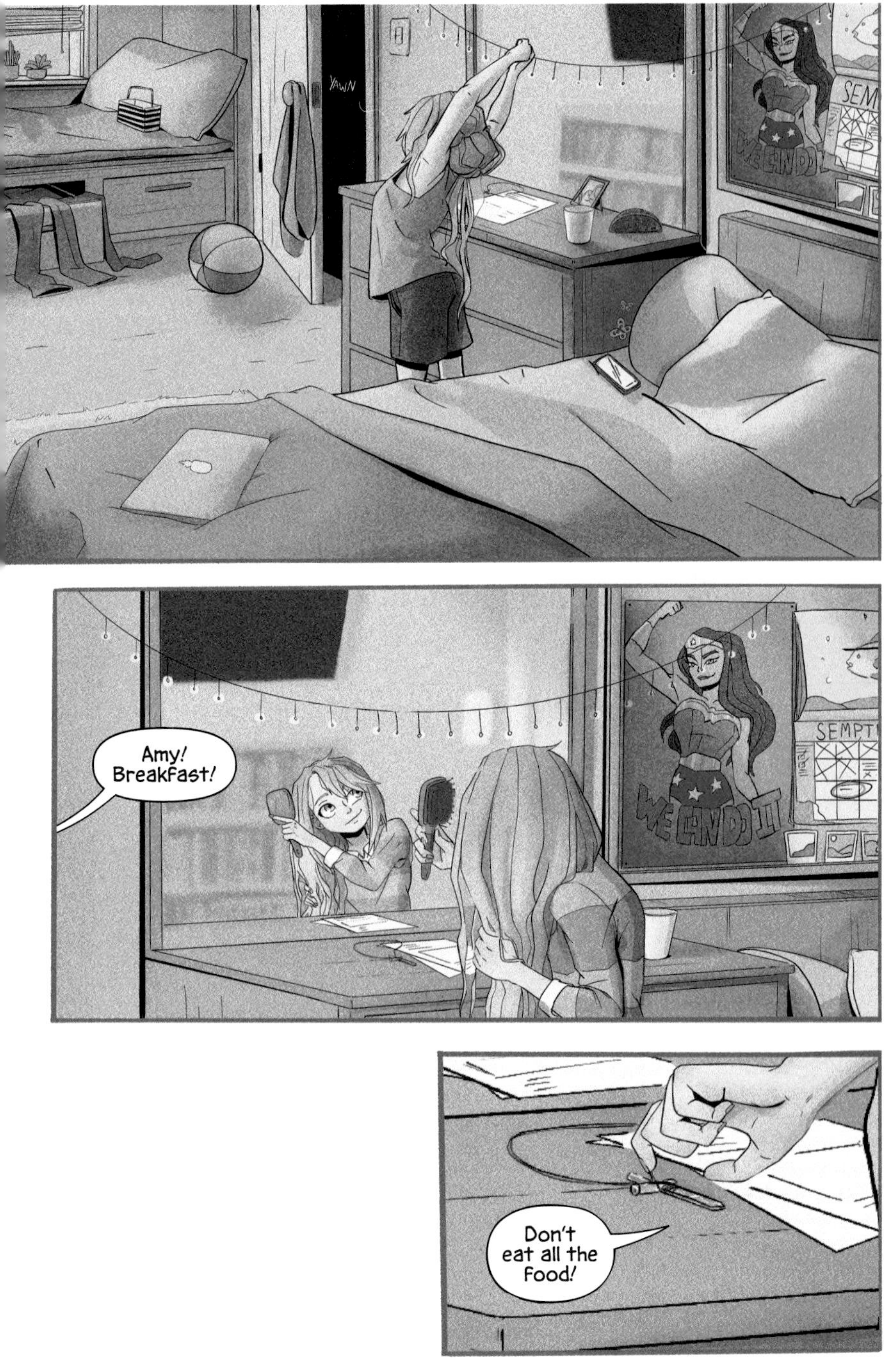
YAWN
WE CAN DO IT
Amy! Breakfast!
Don't eat all the food!

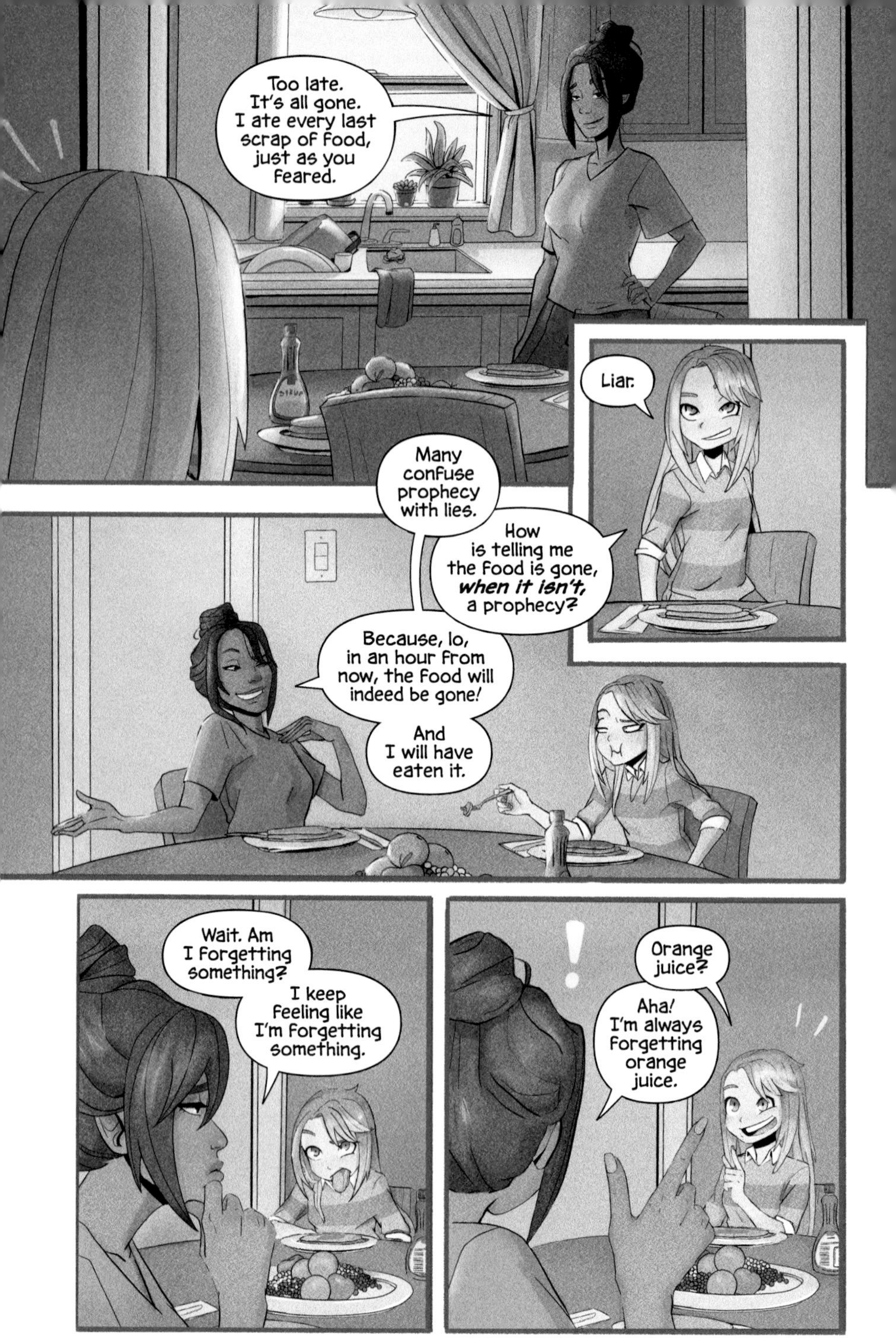
Too late. It's all gone. I ate every last scrap of food, just as you feared.
Liar.
Many confuse prophecy with lies.
How is telling me the food is gone, ***when it isn't,*** a prophecy?
Because, lo, in an hour from now, the food will indeed be gone!
And I will have eaten it.
Wait. Am I forgetting something?
I keep feeling like I'm forgetting something.
!
Orange juice?
Aha! I'm always forgetting orange juice.

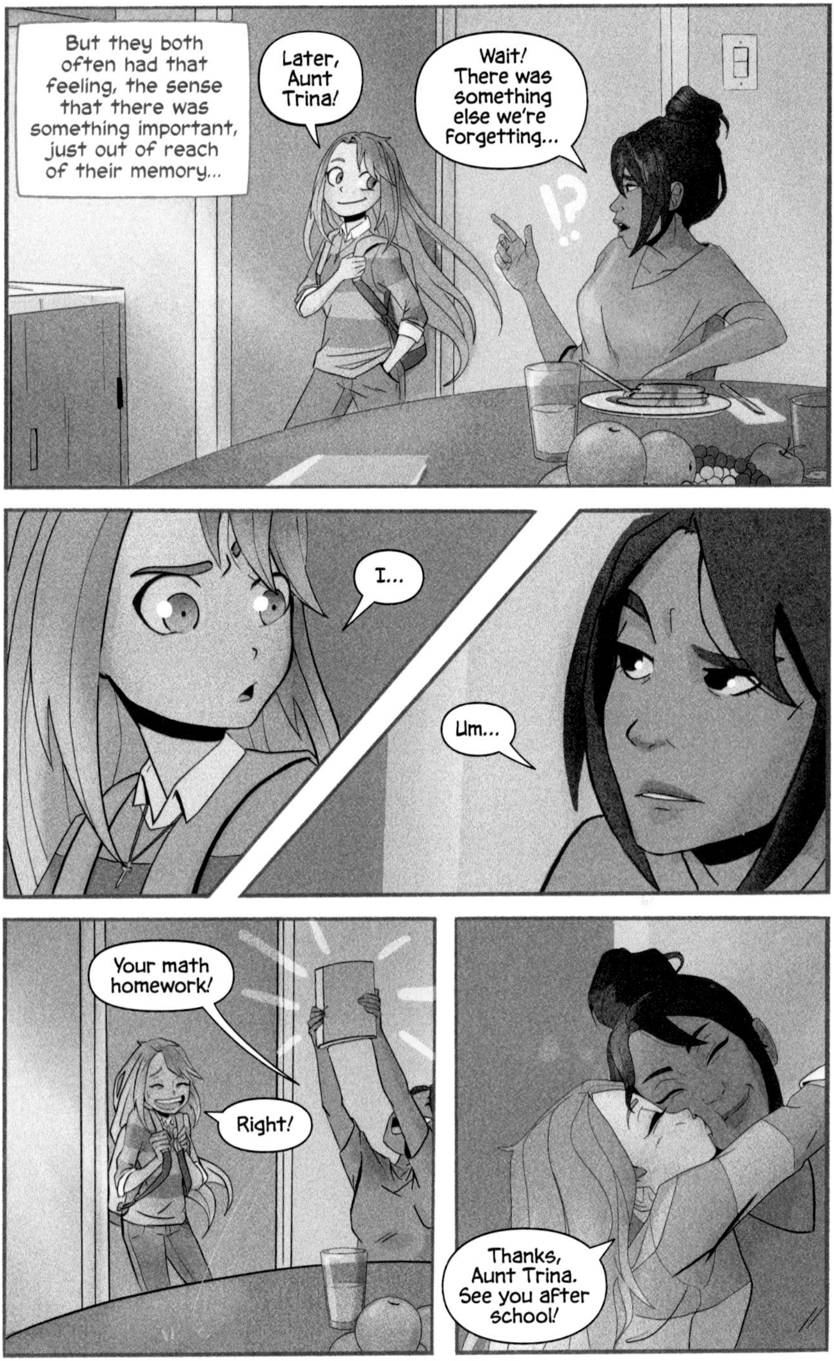
But they both often had that feeling, the sense that there was something important, just out of reach of their memory...
Later, Aunt Trina!
Wait! There was something else we're forgetting...
!?
I...
Um...
Your math homework!
Right!
Thanks, Aunt Trina. See you after school!

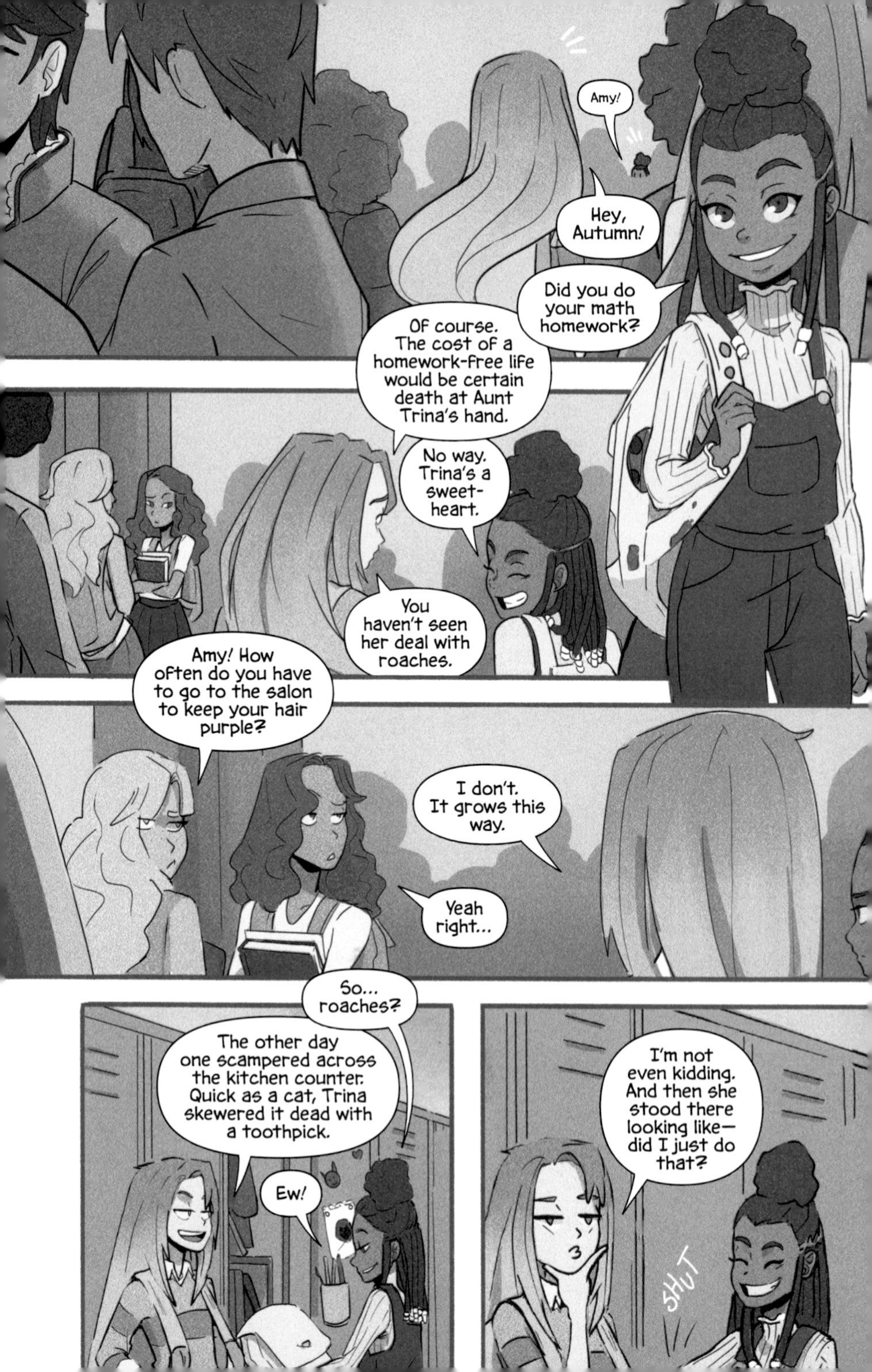
Amy!
Hey, Autumn!
Did you do your math homework?
Of course. The cost of a homework-free life would be certain death at Aunt Trina's hand.
No way. Trina's a sweet-heart.
You haven't seen her deal with roaches.
Amy! How often do you have to go to the salon to keep your hair purple?
I don't. It grows this way.
Yeah right...
So... roaches?
The other day one scampered across the kitchen counter. Quick as a cat, Trina skewered it dead with a toothpick.
Ew!
I'm not even kidding. And then she stood there looking like— did I just do that?
SHUT

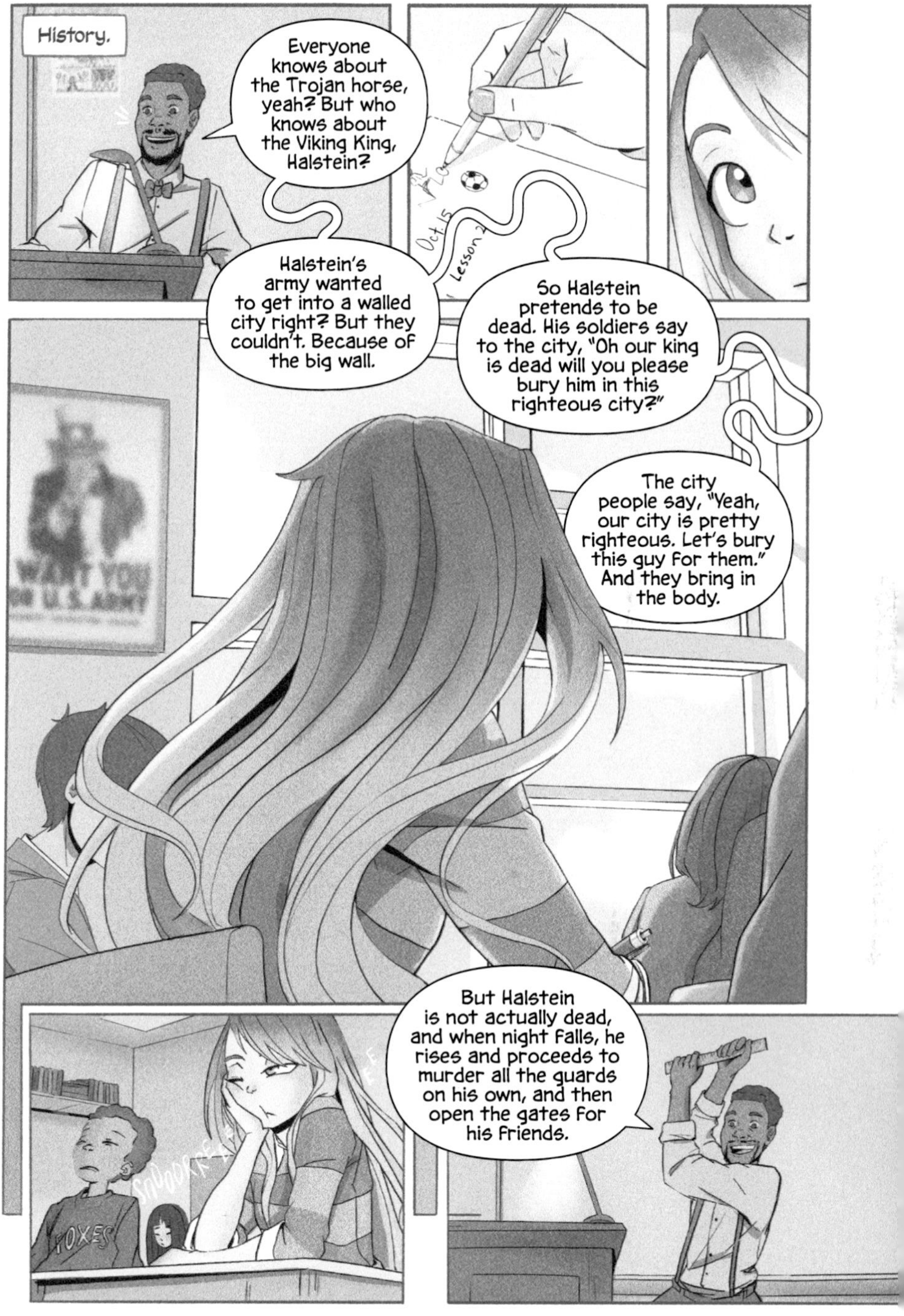
History.
Everyone knows about the Trojan horse, yeah? But who knows about the Viking King, Halstein?
Oct. 15
Lesson 2
Halstein's army wanted to get into a walled city right? But they couldn't. Because of the big wall.
So Halstein pretends to be dead. His soldiers say to the city, "Oh our king is dead will you please bury him in this righteous city?"
The city people say, "Yeah, our city is pretty righteous. Let's bury this guy for them." And they bring in the body.
FOXES
But Halstein is not actually dead, and when night falls, he rises and proceeds to murder all the guards on his own, and then open the gates for his friends.

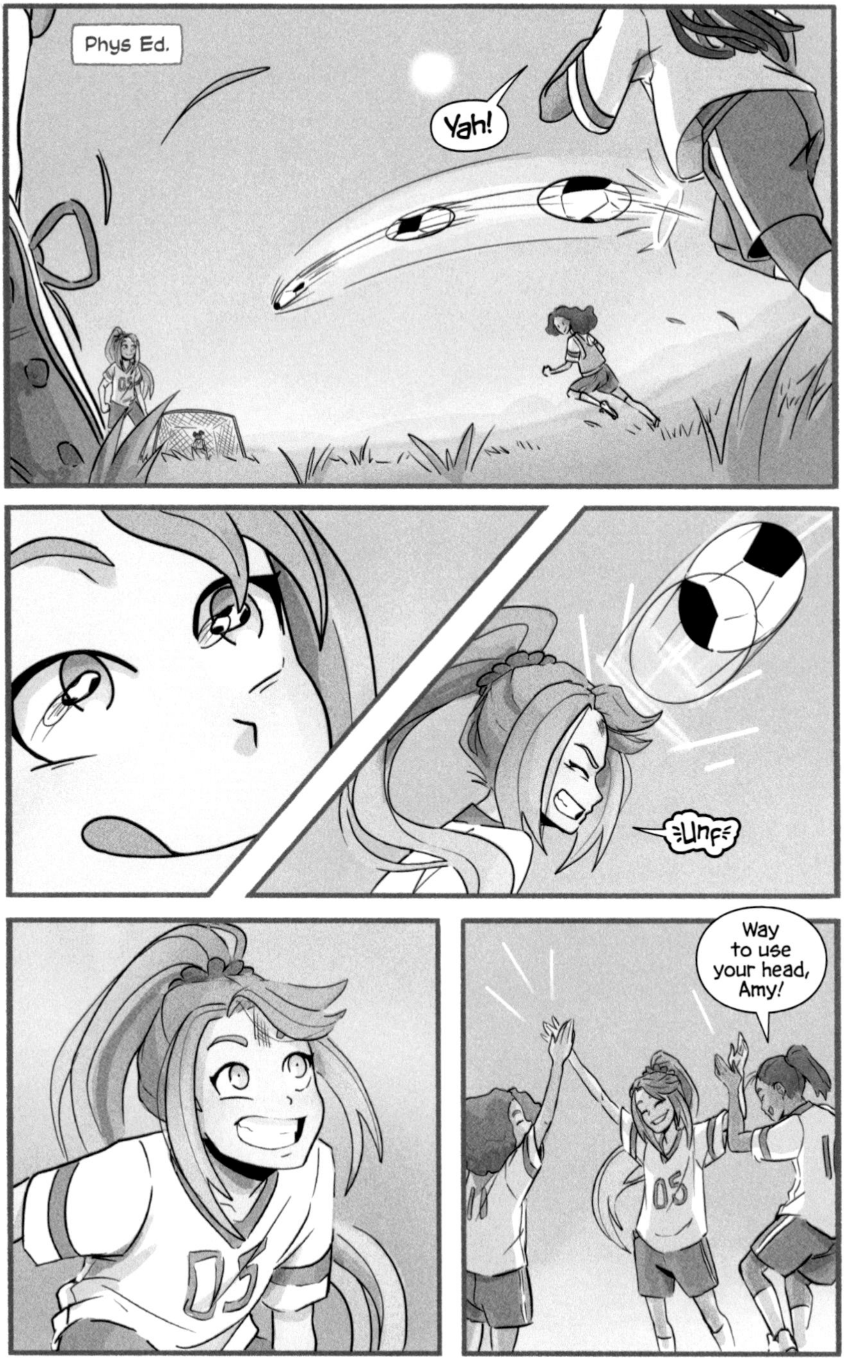
Phys Ed.
Yah!
Unf
Way to use your head, Amy!

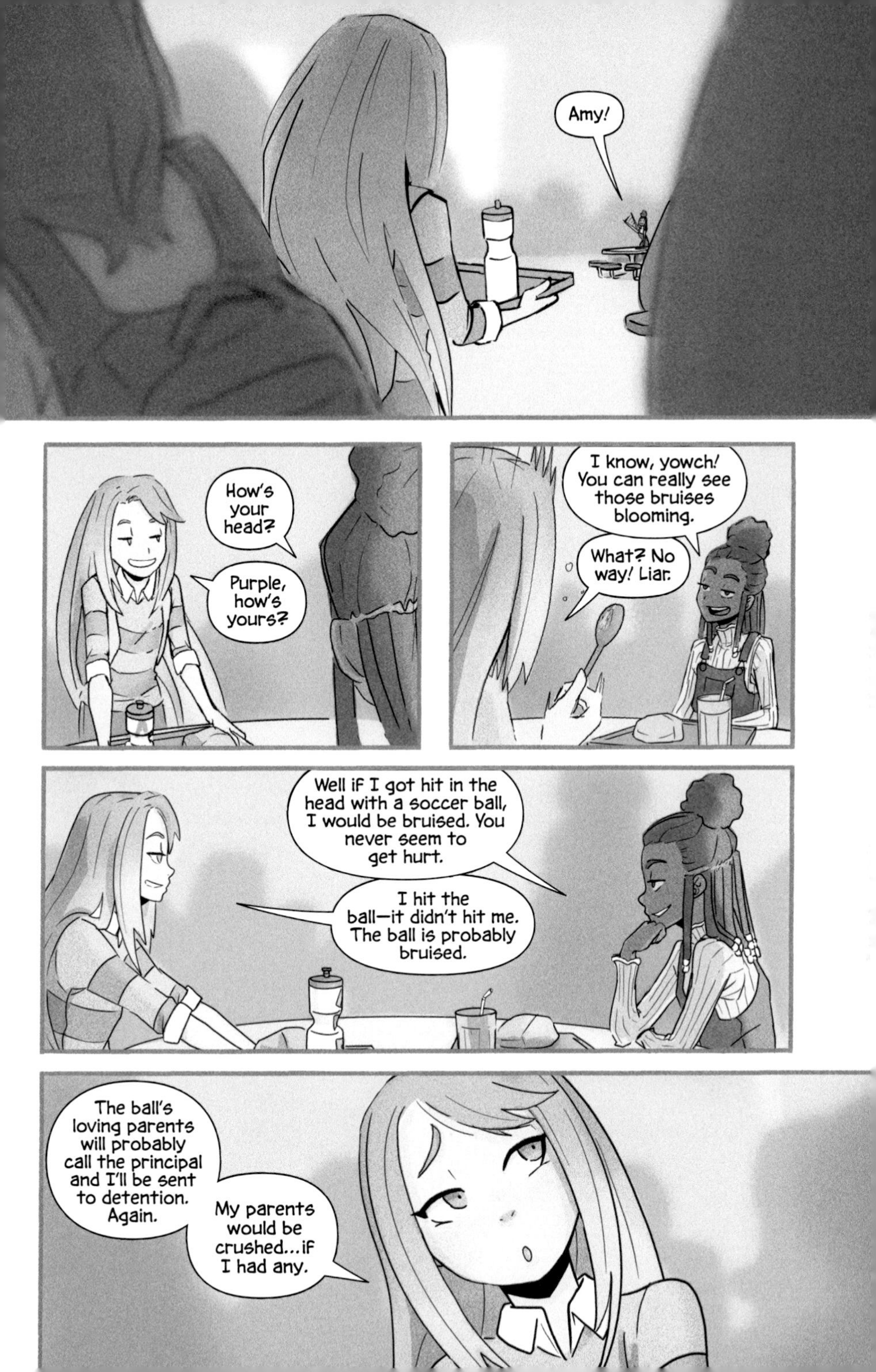
Amy!
How's your head?
Purple, how's yours?
I know, yowch! You can really see those bruises blooming.
What? No way! Liar.
Well if I got hit in the head with a soccer ball, I would be bruised. You never seem to get hurt.
I hit the ball—it didn't hit me. The ball is probably bruised.
The ball's loving parents will probably call the principal and I'll be sent to detention. Again.
My parents would be crushed...if I had any.

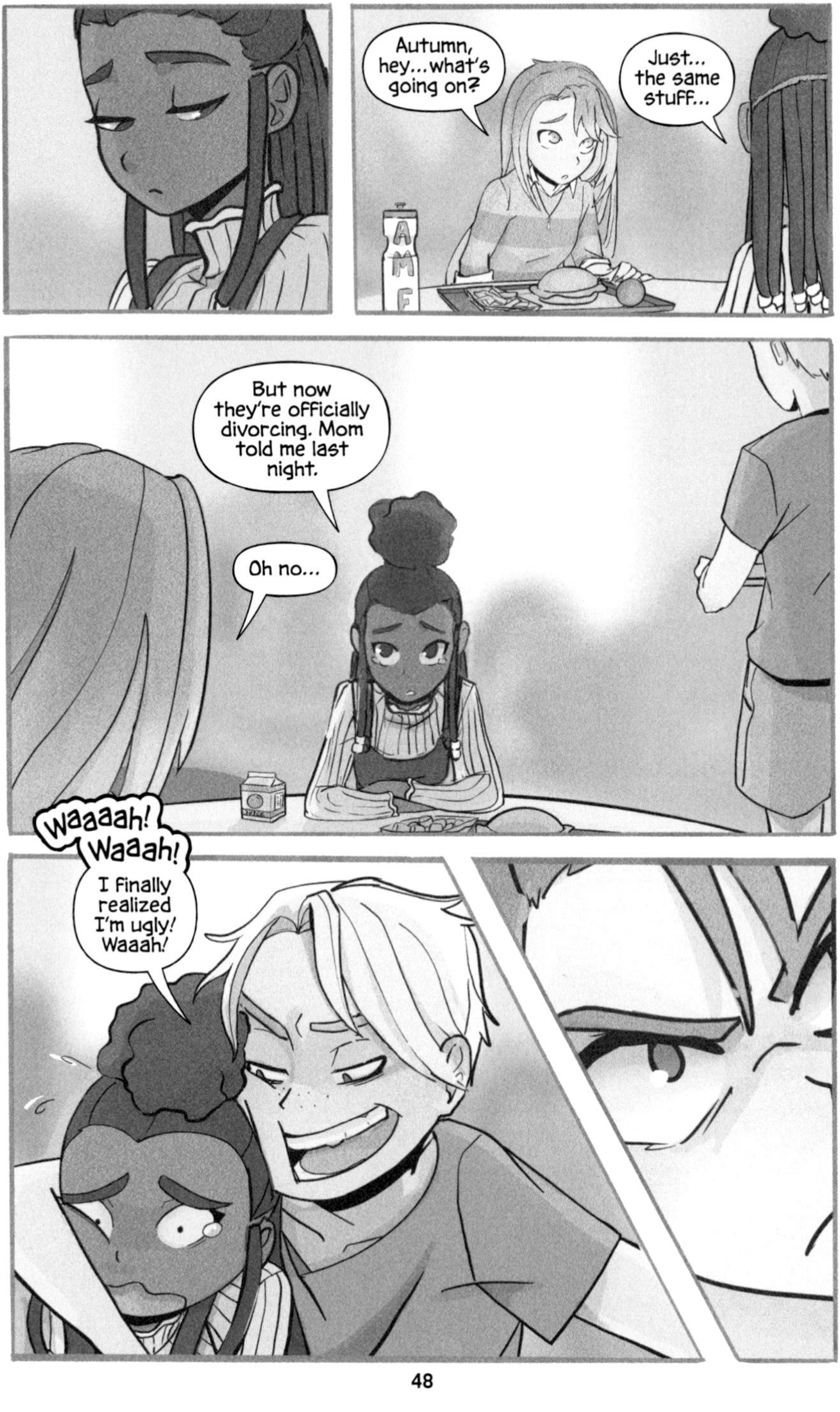

Autumn, hey...what's going on?
Just... the same stuff...
AMF
But now they're officially divorcing. Mom told me last night.
Oh no...
Waaaah! Waaah!
I finally realized I'm ugly! Waaah!

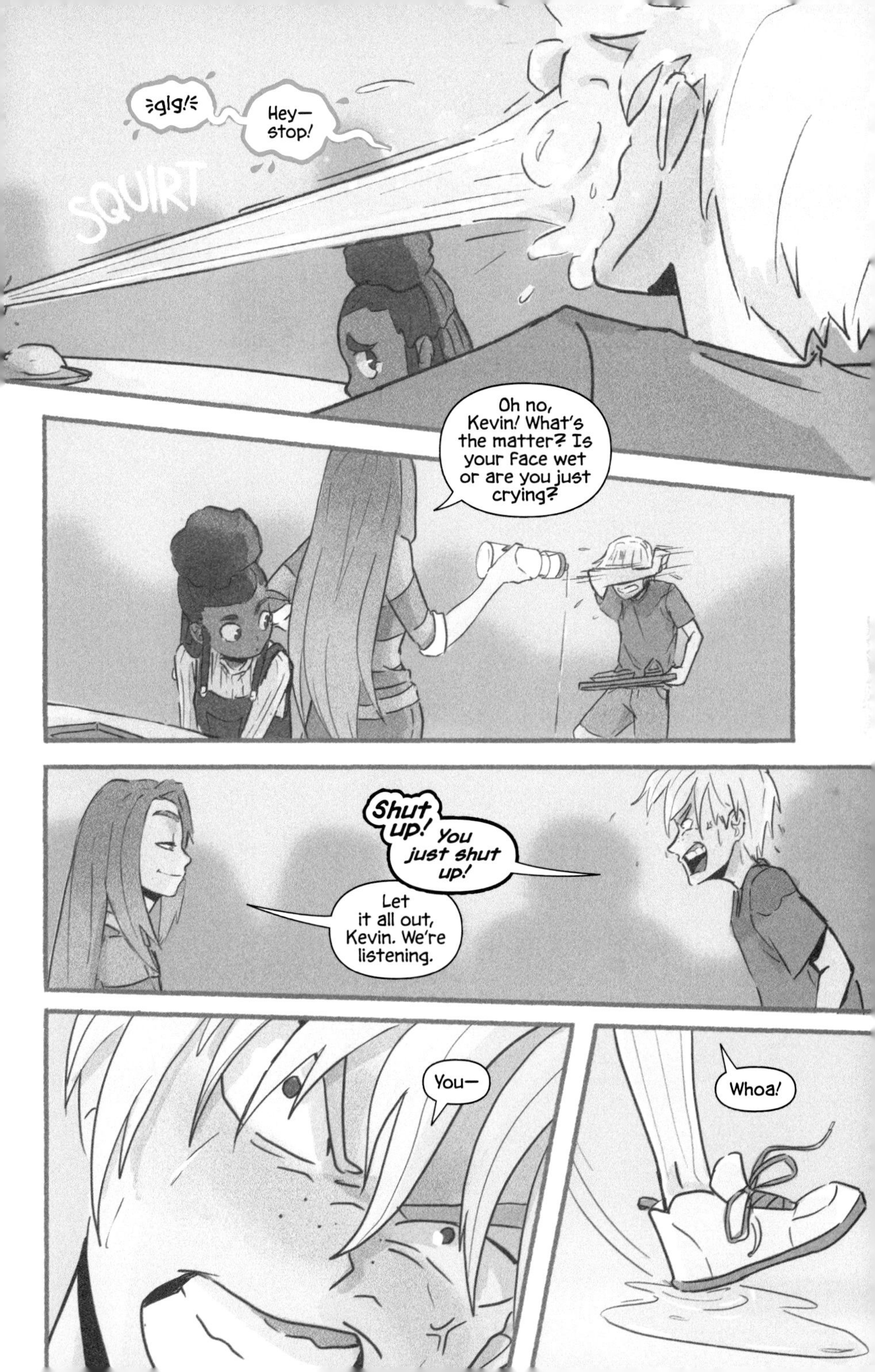

glg!
Hey—
stop!
SQUIRT
Oh no, Kevin! What's the matter? Is your face wet or are you just crying?
Shut up! You just shut up!
Let it all out, Kevin. We're listening.
You—
Whoa!

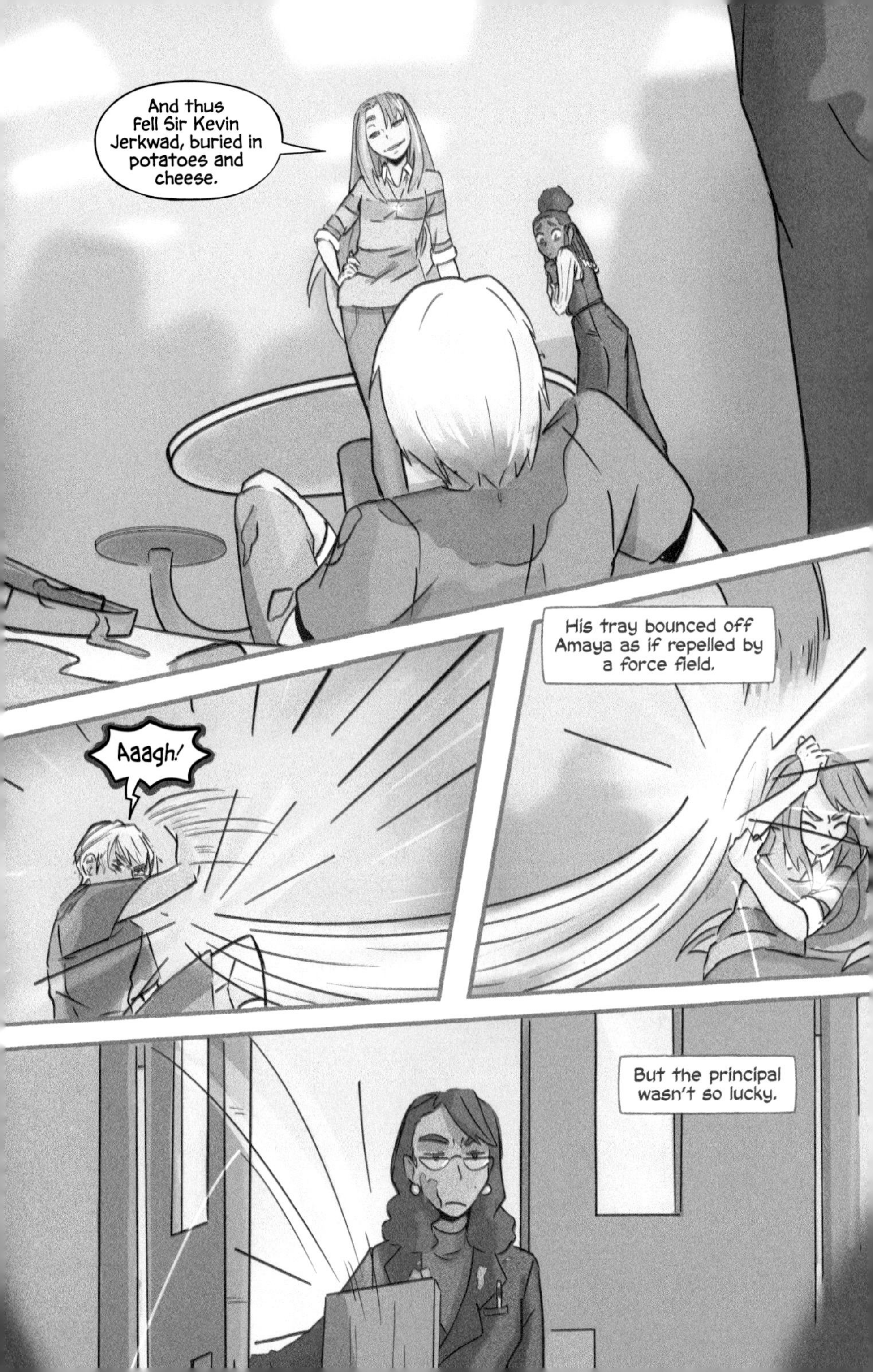
And thus fell Sir Kevin Jerkwad, buried in potatoes and cheese.
His tray bounced off Amaya as if repelled by a force field.
Aaagh!
But the principal wasn't so lucky.

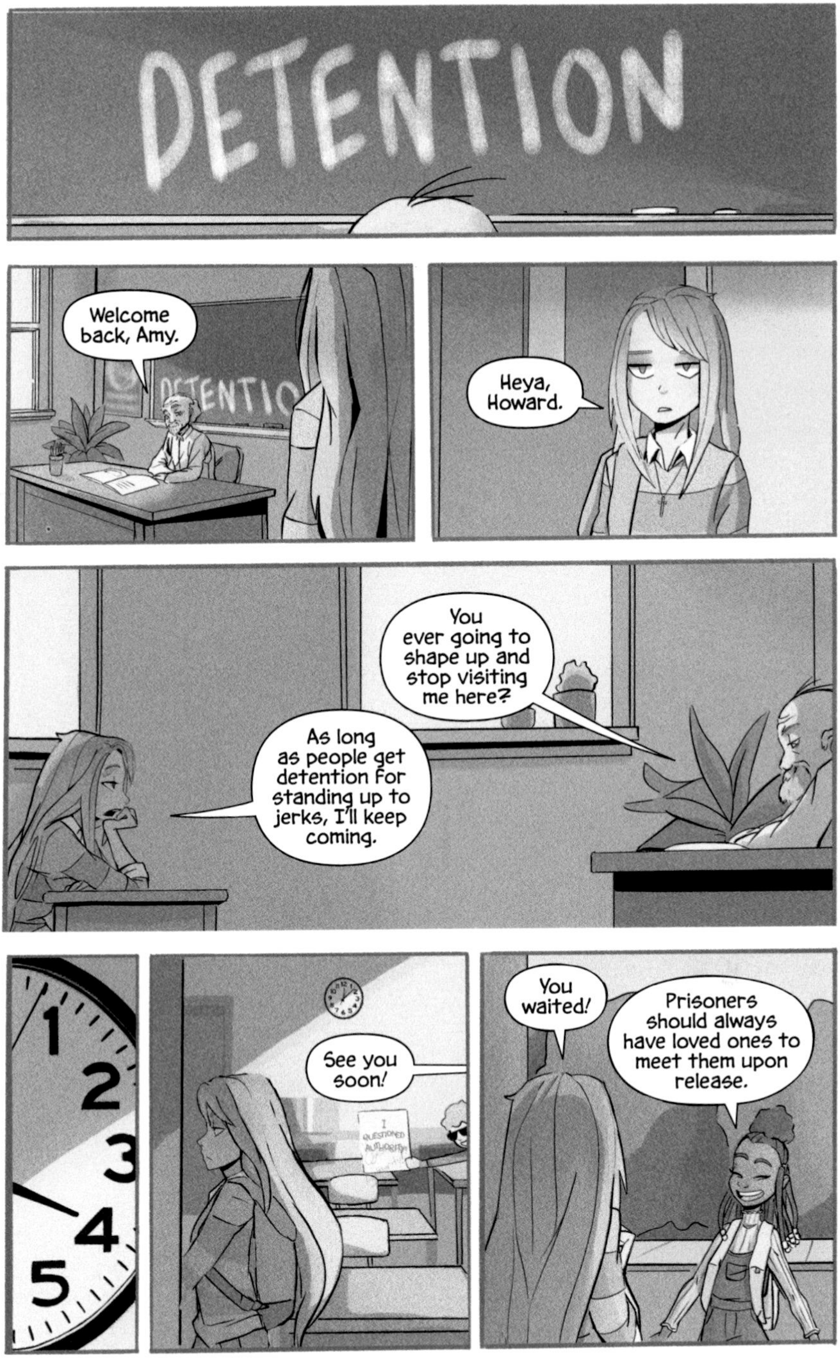
DETENTION
Welcome back, Amy.
Heya, Howard.
You ever going to shape up and stop visiting me here?
As long as people get detention for standing up to jerks, I'll keep coming.
See you soon!
I QUESTIONED AUTHORITY
You waited!
Prisoners should always have loved ones to meet them upon release.

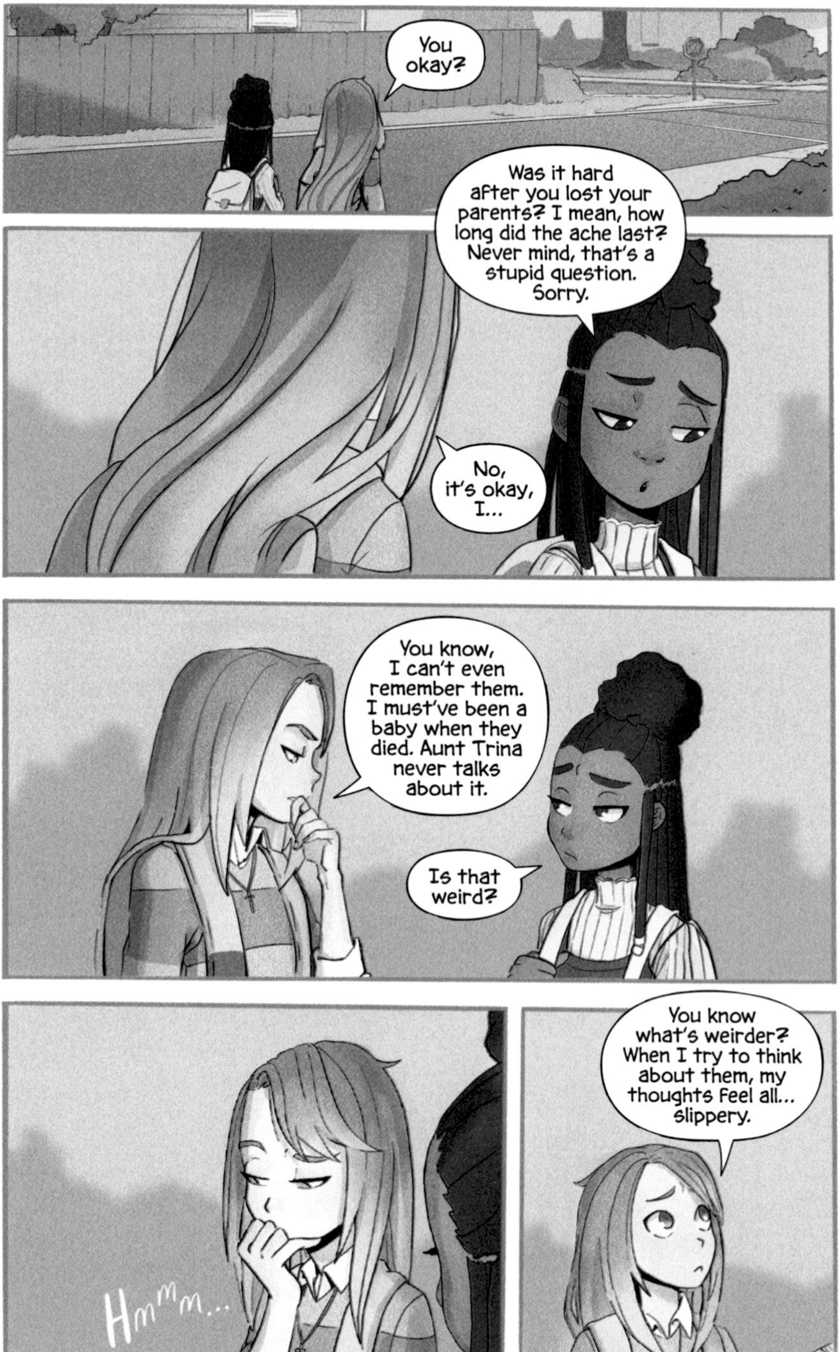
You okay?
Was it hard after you lost your parents? I mean, how long did the ache last? Never mind, that's a stupid question. Sorry.
No, it's okay, I...
You know, I can't even remember them. I must've been a baby when they died. Aunt Trina never talks about it.
Is that weird?
Hmmm...
You know what's weirder? When I try to think about them, my thoughts feel all... slippery.

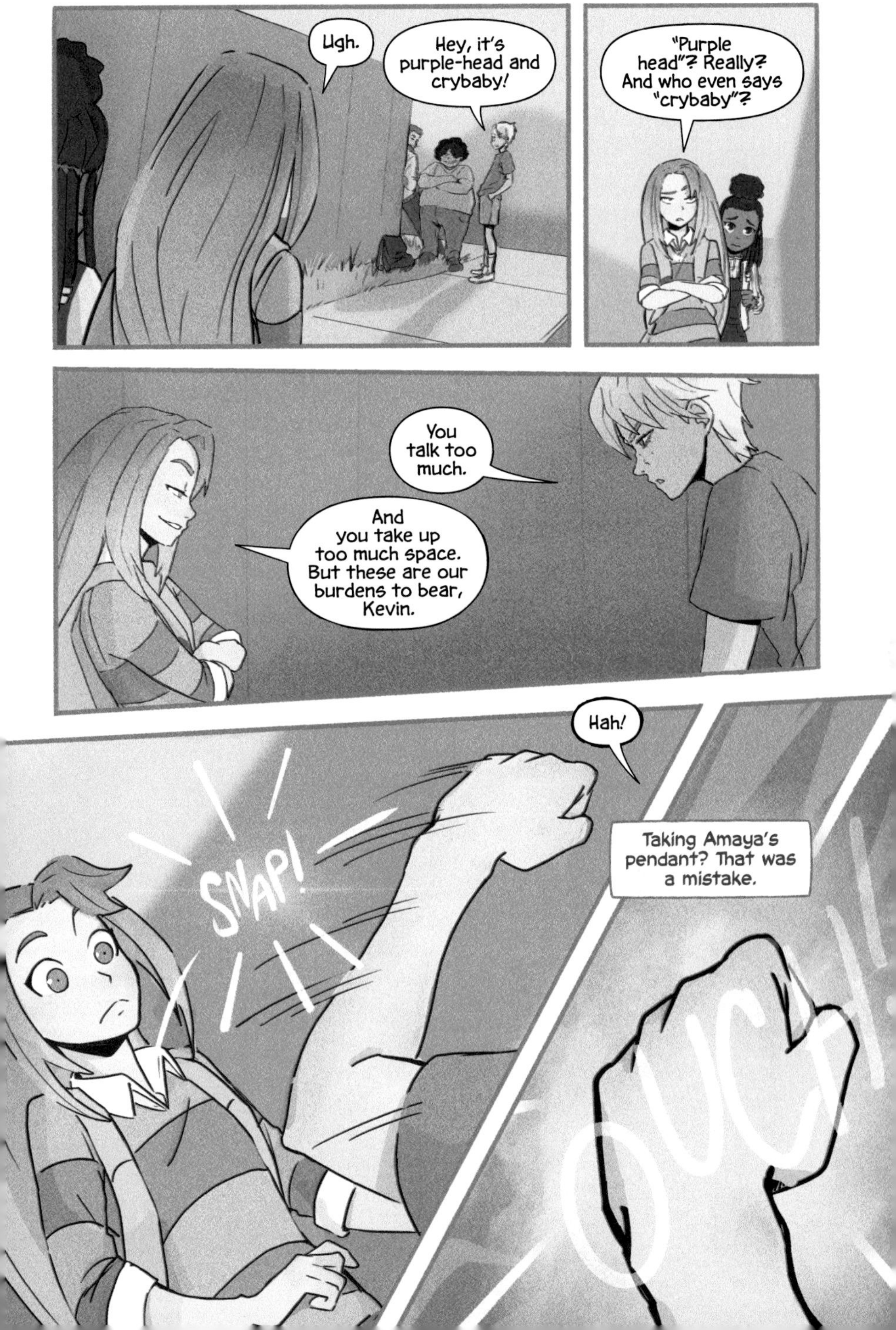
Ugh.
Hey, it's purple-head and crybaby!
"Purple head"? Really? And who even says "crybaby"?
You talk too much.
And you take up too much space. But these are our burdens to bear, Kevin.
Hah!
SNAP!
Taking Amaya's pendant? That was a mistake.

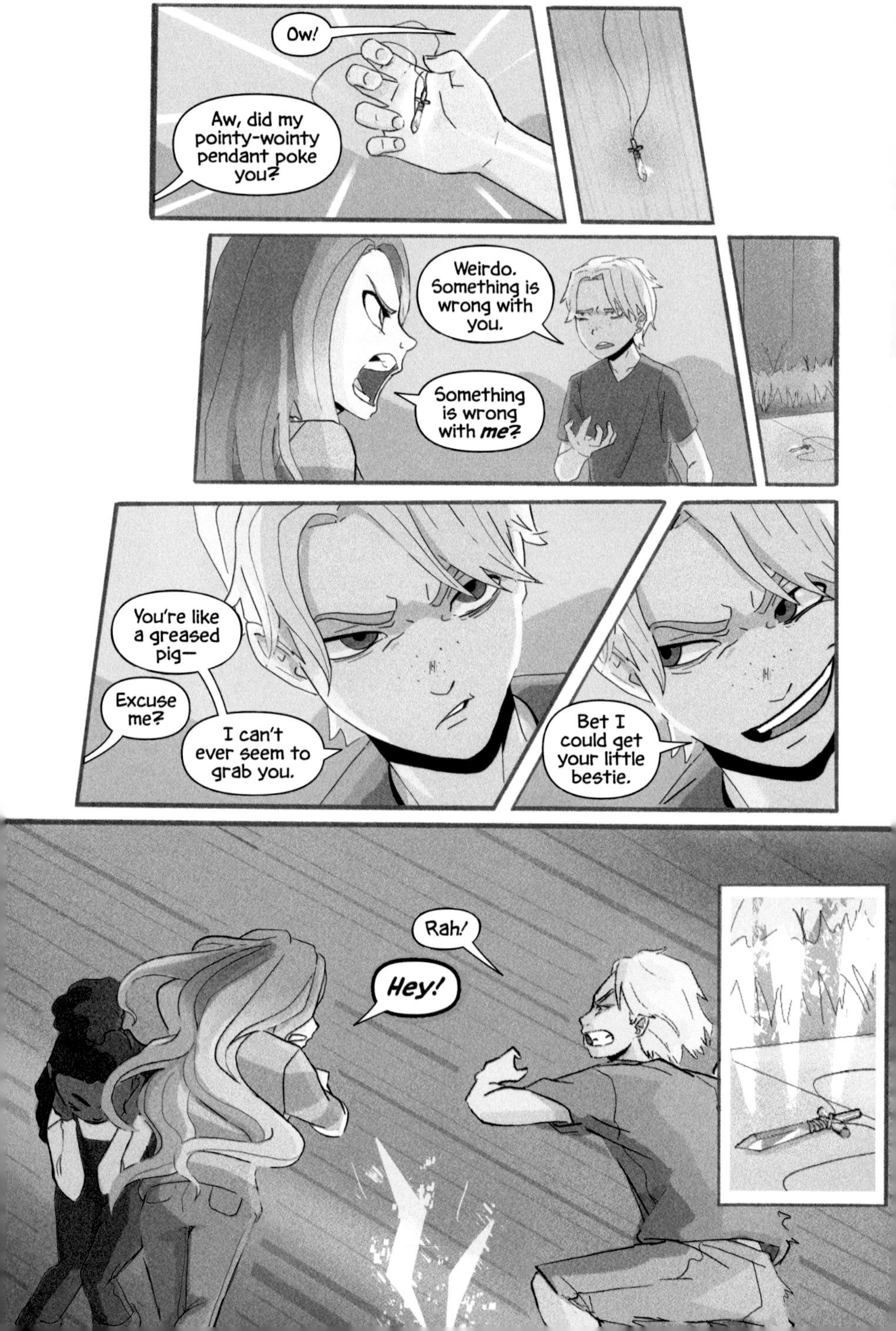
Ow!
Aw, did my pointy-wointy pendant poke you?
Weirdo. Something is wrong with you.
Something is wrong with *me*?
You're like a greased pig—
Excuse me?
I can't ever seem to grab you.
Bet I could get your little bestie.
Rah!
Hey!

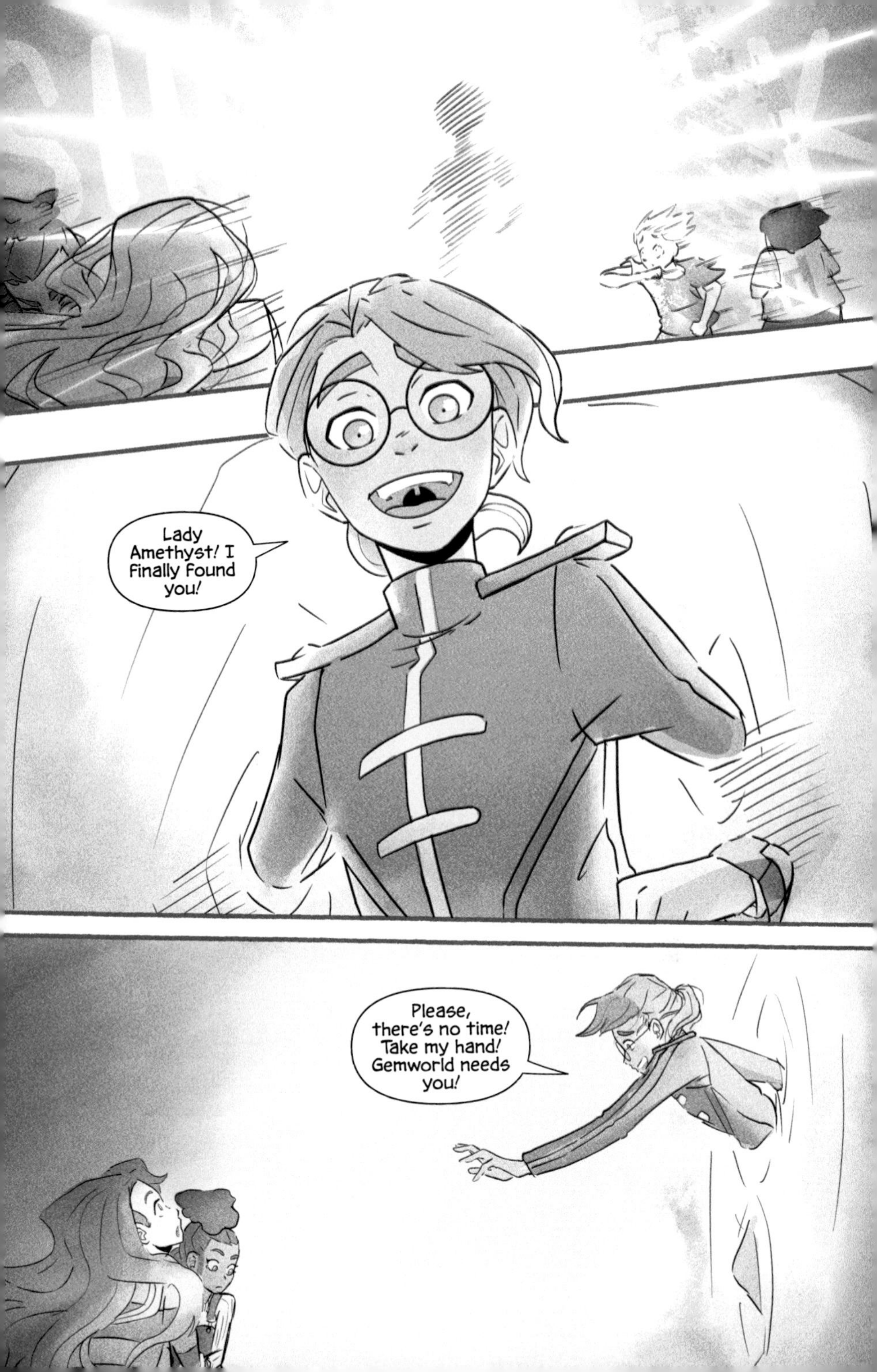
Lady Amethyst! I finally found you!
Please, there's no time! Take my hand! Gemworld needs you!

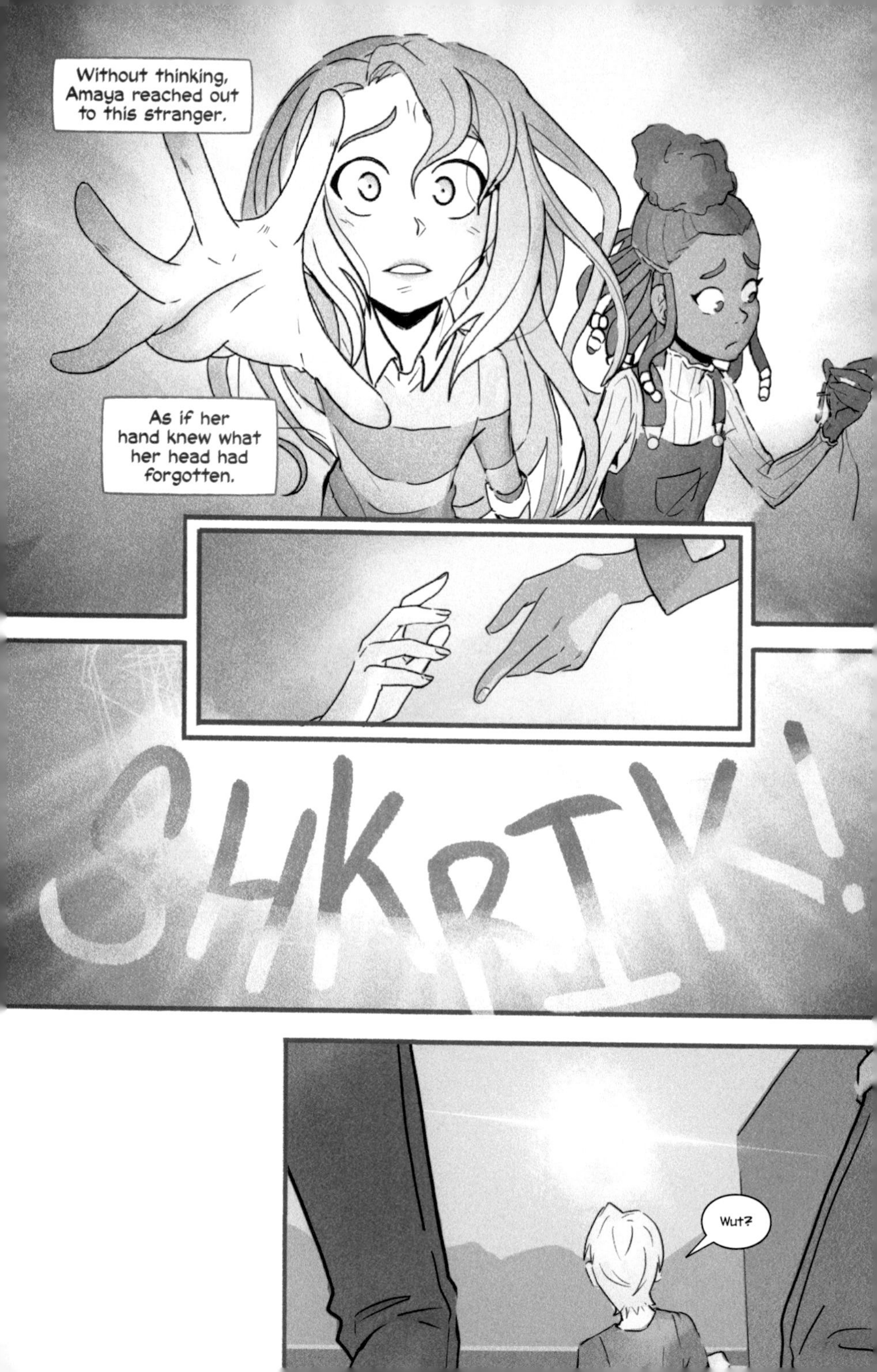
Without thinking, Amaya reached out to this stranger.
As if her hand knew what her head had forgotten.
SHRIK!
Wut?

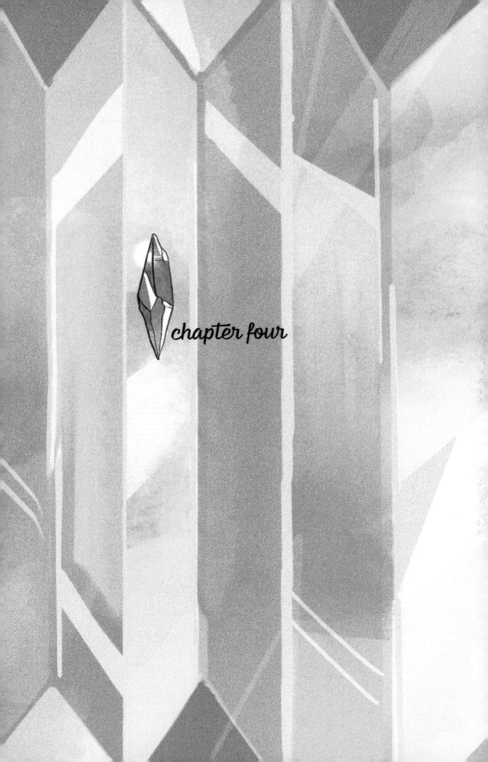

chapter four

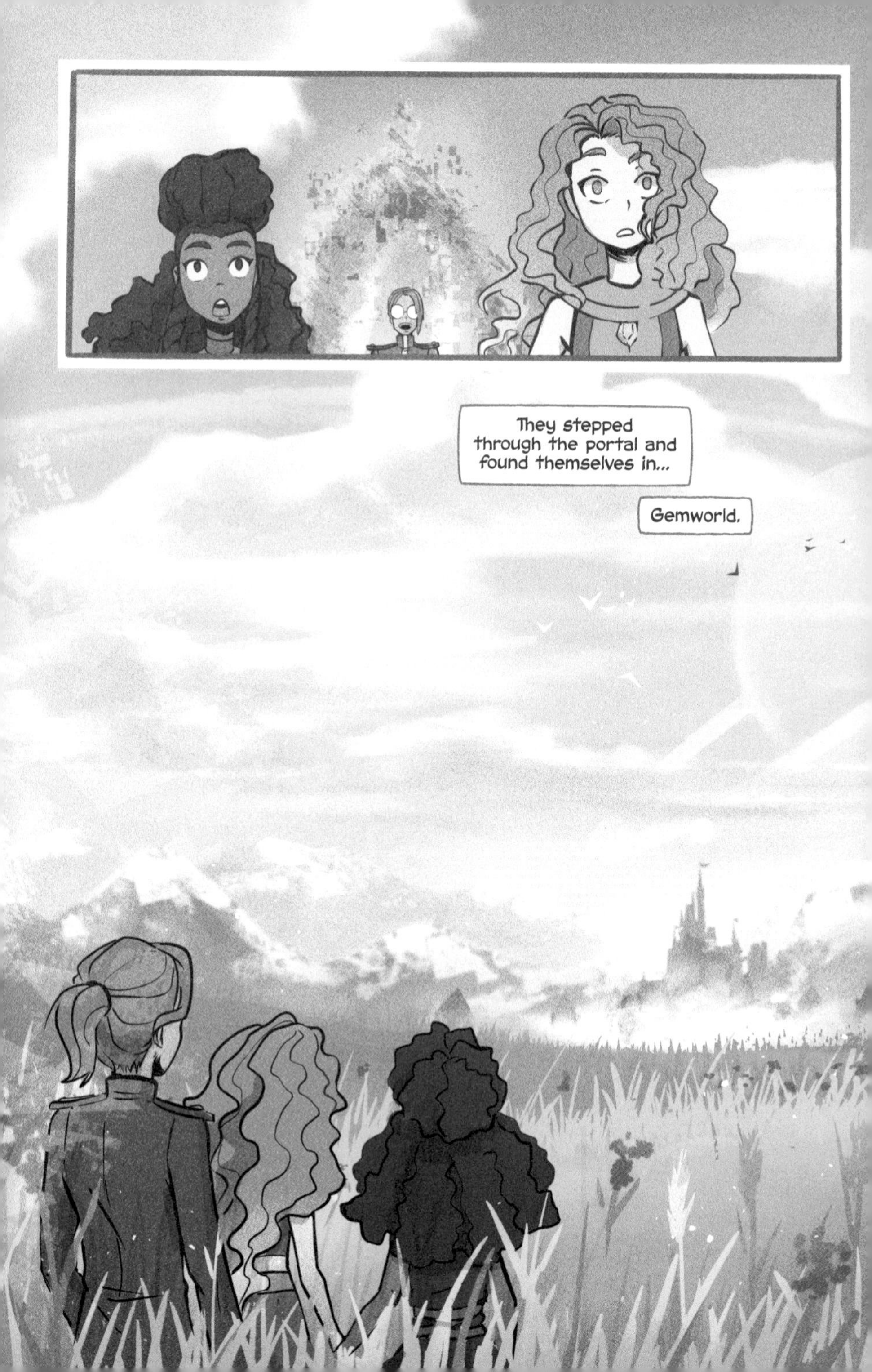
They stepped through the portal and found themselves in...
Gemworld.

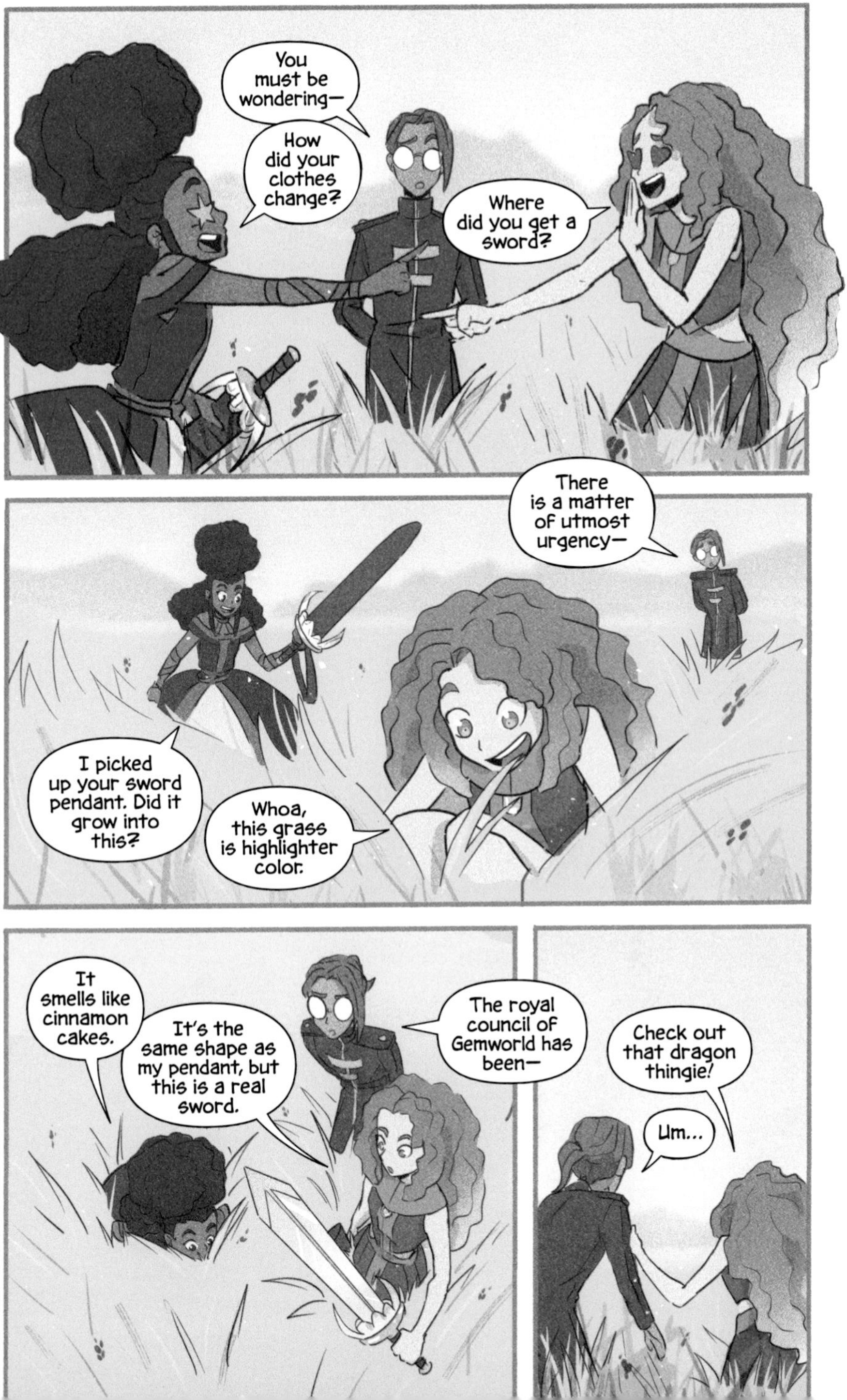
You must be wondering—
How did your clothes change?
Where did you get a sword?
There is a matter of utmost urgency—
I picked up your sword pendant. Did it grow into this?
Whoa, this grass is highlighter color.
It smells like cinnamon cakes.
It's the same shape as my pendant, but this is a real sword.
The royal council of Gemworld has been—
Check out that dragon thingie!
Um...

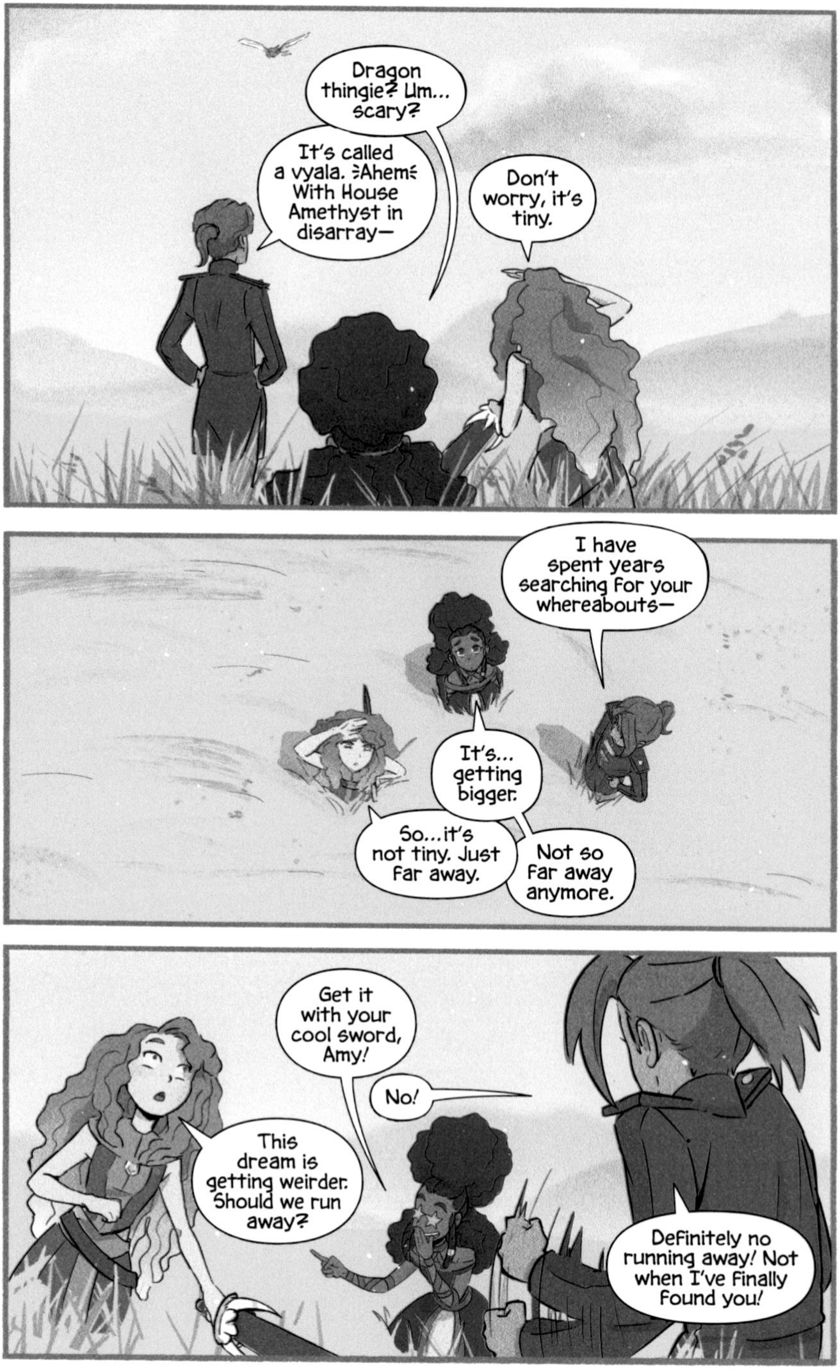
It's called a vyala. ≶Ahem≷ With House Amethyst in disarray—
Dragon thingie? Um... scary?
Don't worry, it's tiny.
I have spent years searching for your whereabouts—
It's... getting bigger.
So...it's not tiny. Just far away.
Not so far away anymore.
This dream is getting weirder. Should we run away?
Get it with your cool sword, Amy!
No!
Definitely no running away! Not when I've finally found you!

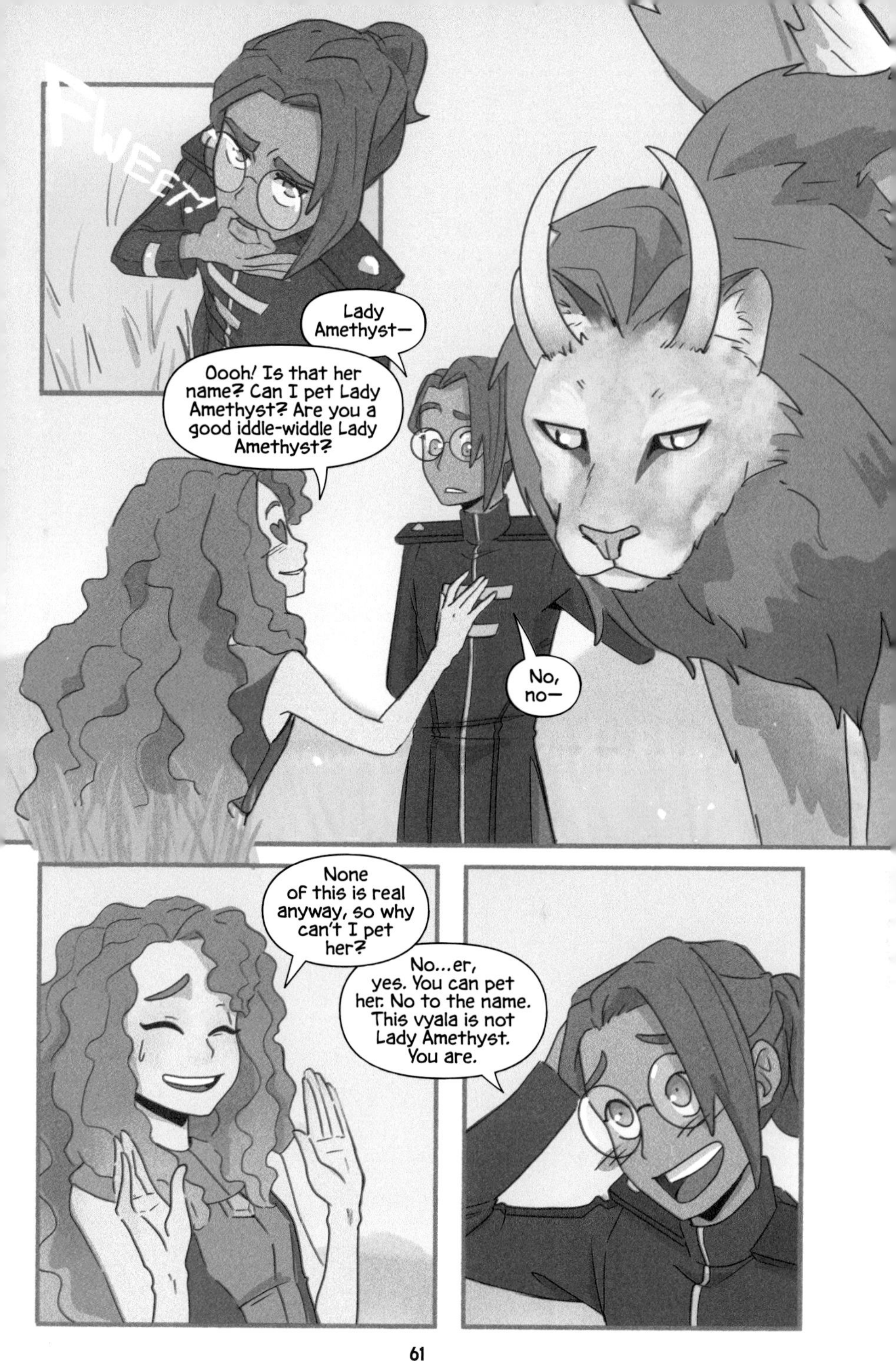

FWEET!
Lady Amethyst—
Oooh! Is that her name? Can I pet Lady Amethyst? Are you a good iddle-widdle Lady Amethyst?
No, no—
None of this is real anyway, so why can't I pet her?
No...er, yes. You can pet her. No to the name. This vyala is not Lady Amethyst. You are.

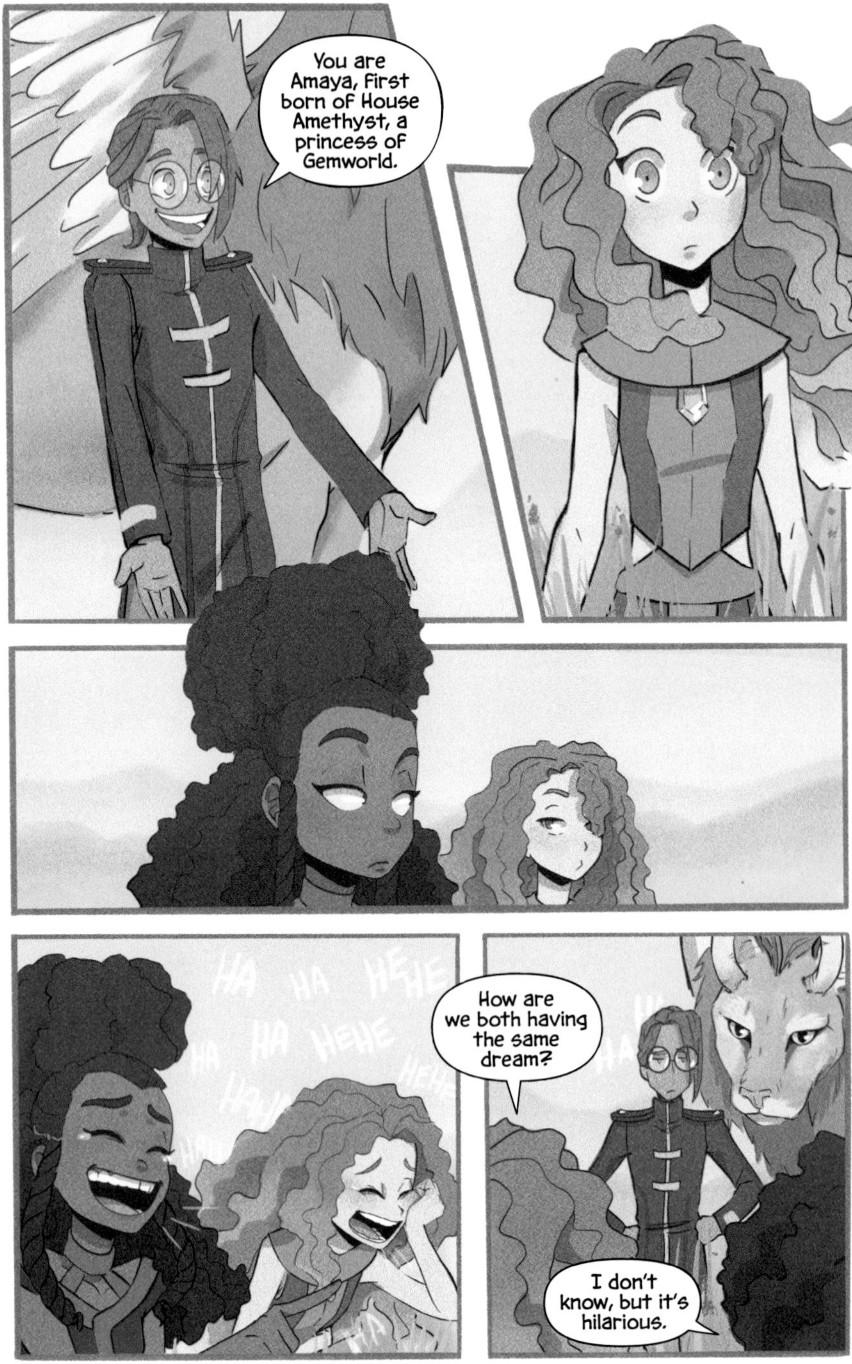
You are Amaya, first born of House Amethyst, a princess of Gemworld.
HA HA HEHE
HA HA HEHE
HEHE
How are we both having the same dream?
I don't know, but it's hilarious.

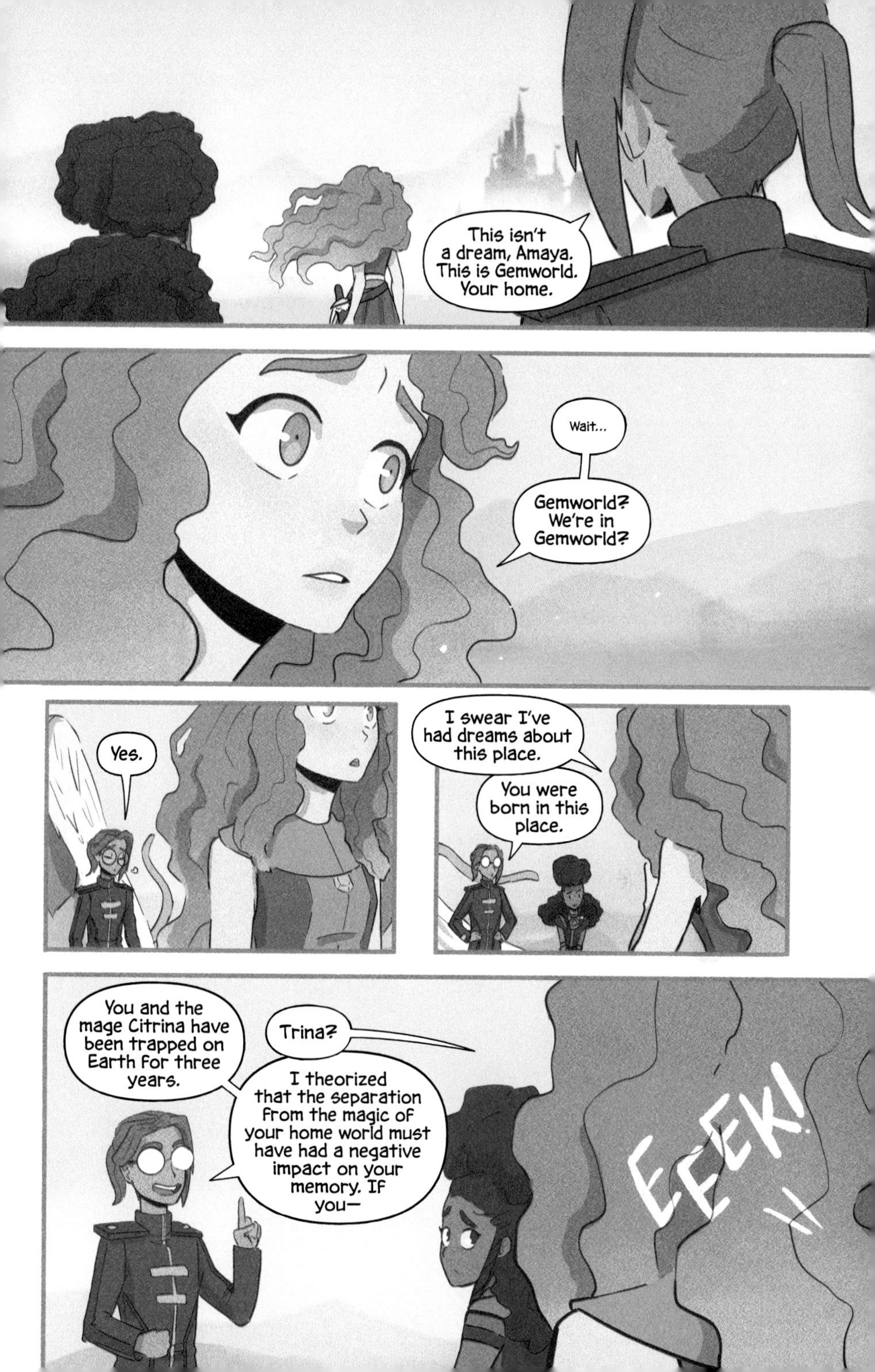

This isn't a dream, Amaya. This is Gemworld. Your home.
Wait...
Gemworld? We're in Gemworld?
Yes.
I swear I've had dreams about this place.
You were born in this place.
You and the mage Citrina have been trapped on Earth for three years.
Trina?
I theorized that the separation from the magic of your home world must have had a negative impact on your memory. If you—
EEEK!

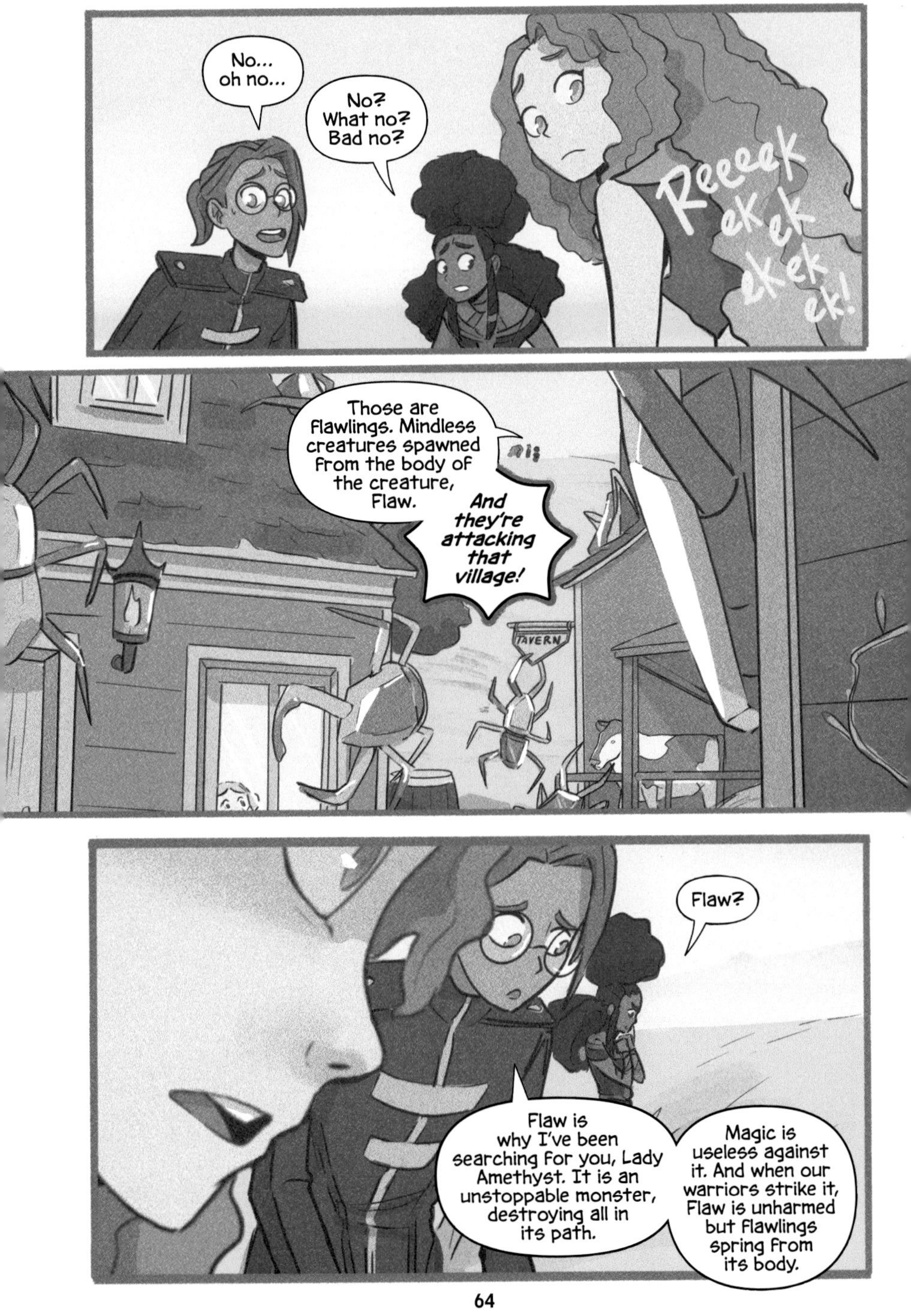

No... oh no...
No? What no? Bad no?
Reeeek ek ek ek ek ek!
Those are flawlings. Mindless creatures spawned from the body of the creature, Flaw.
And they're attacking that village!
TAVERN
Flaw?
Flaw is why I've been searching for you, Lady Amethyst. It is an unstoppable monster, destroying all in its path.
Magic is useless against it. And when our warriors strike it, Flaw is unharmed but Flawlings spring from its body.

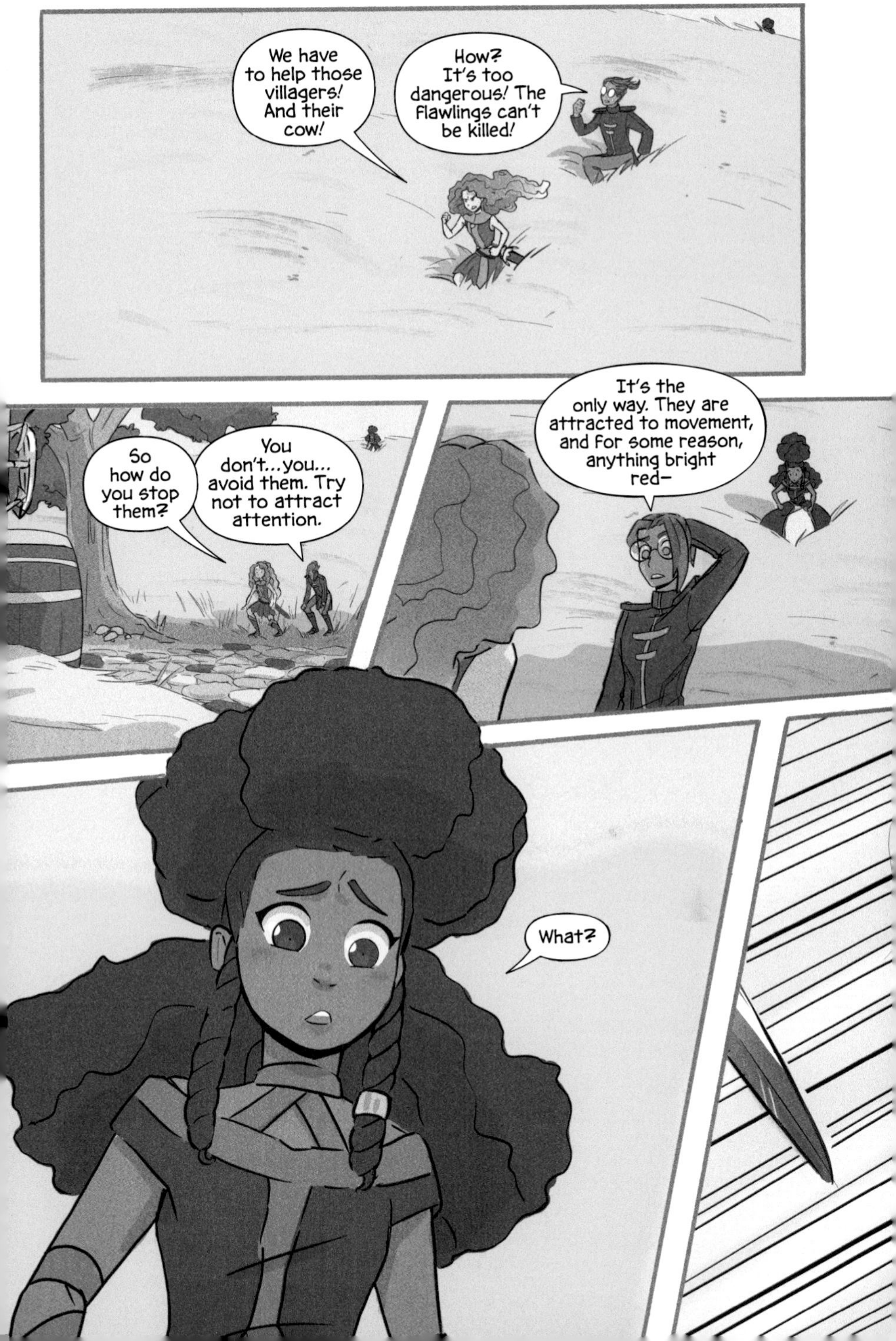
We have to help those villagers! And their cow!
How? It's too dangerous! The flawlings can't be killed!
So how do you stop them?
You don't...you... avoid them. Try not to attract attention.
It's the only way. They are attracted to movement, and for some reason, anything bright red–
What?

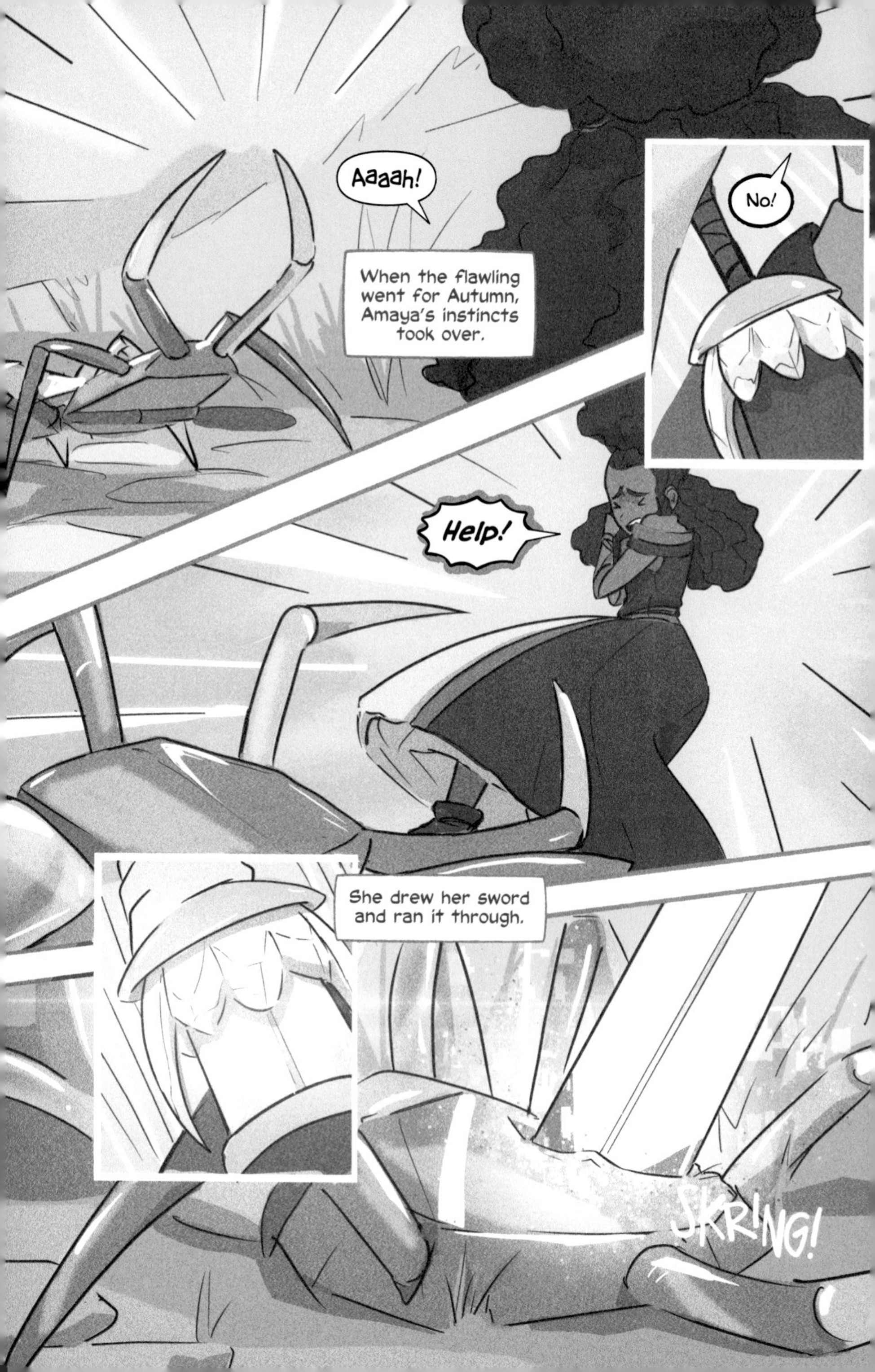
Aaaah!
When the flawling went for Autumn, Amaya's instincts took over.
No!
Help!
She drew her sword and ran it through.
SKRING!

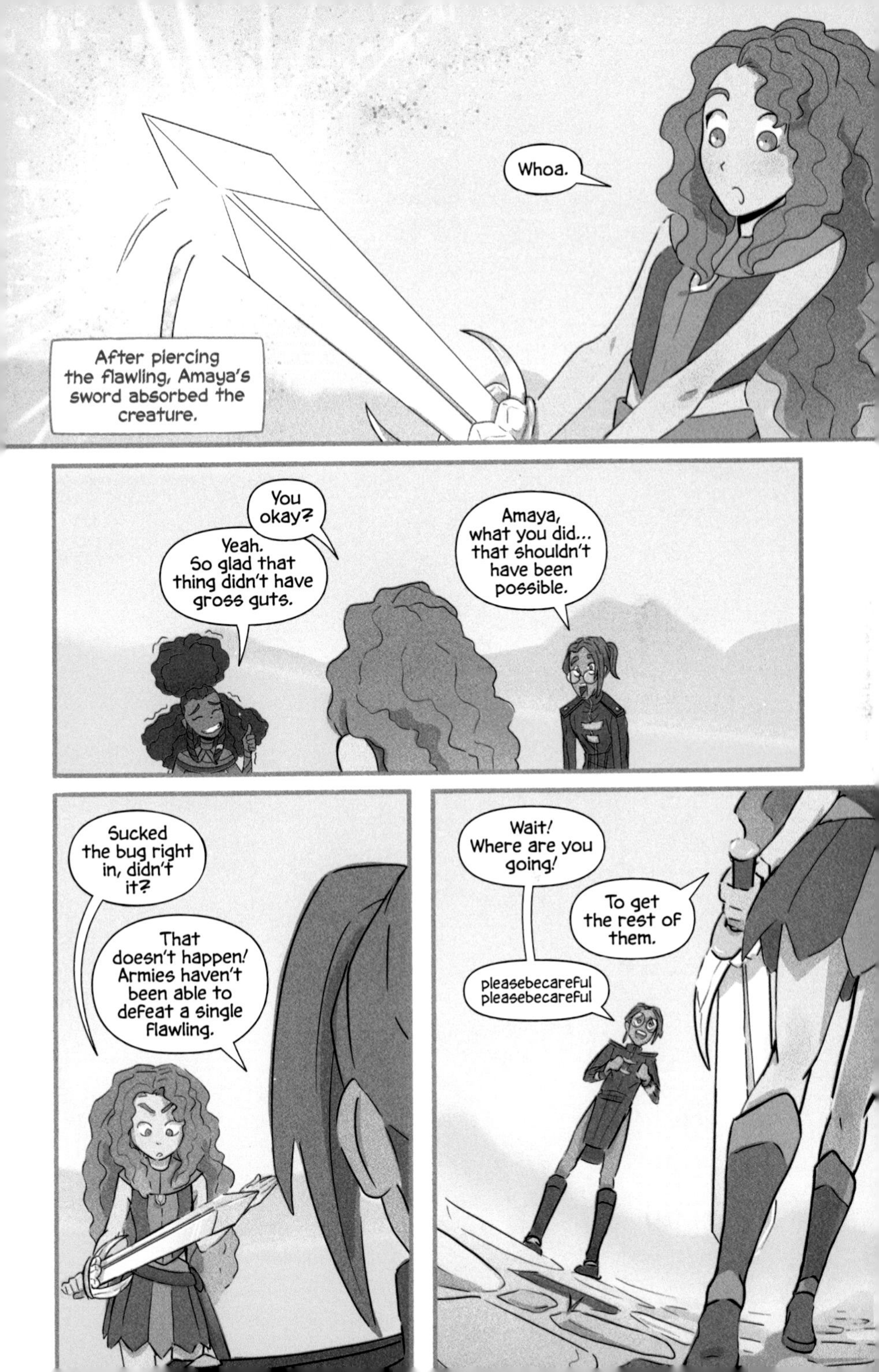
Whoa.
After piercing the flawling, Amaya's sword absorbed the creature.
You okay?
Yeah. So glad that thing didn't have gross guts.
Amaya, what you did... that shouldn't have been possible.
Sucked the bug right in, didn't it?
That doesn't happen! Armies haven't been able to defeat a single flawling.
Wait! Where are you going!
To get the rest of them.
pleasebecareful pleasebecareful

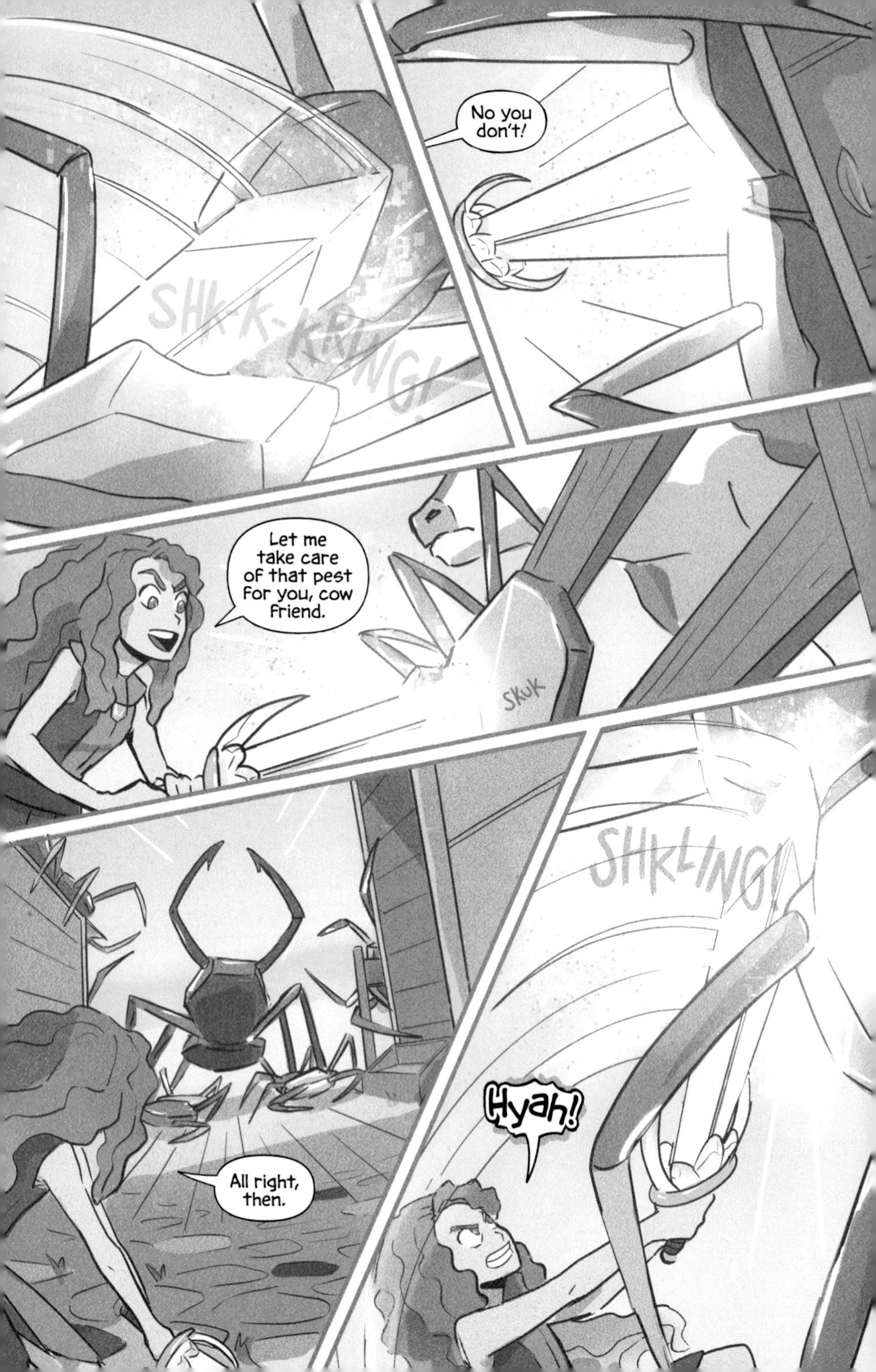
SHK-K-KRING!
No you don't!
Let me take care of that pest for you, cow friend.
SKUK
All right, then.
SHKLING!
Hyah!

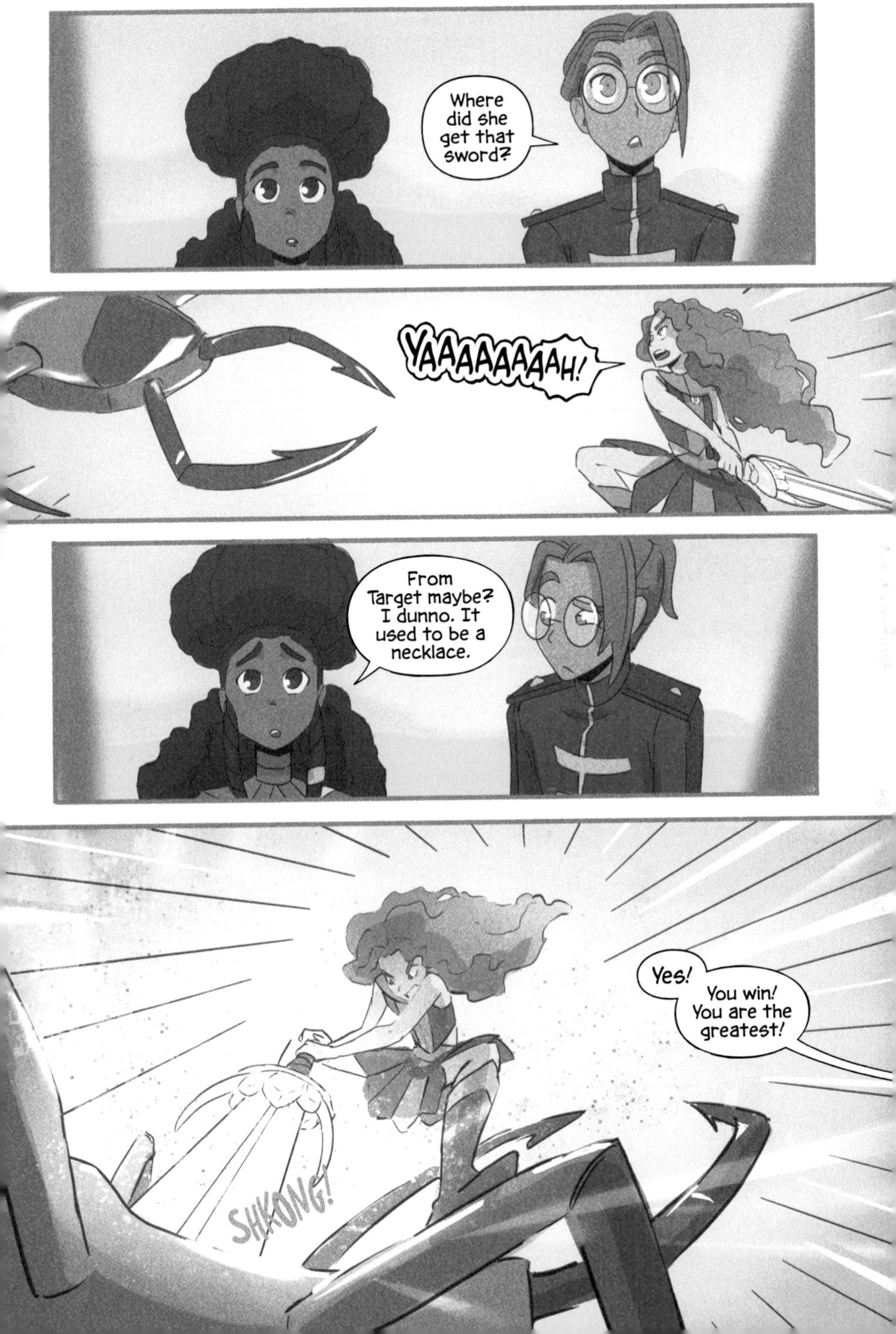
Where did she get that sword?
YAAAAAAAAH!
From Target maybe? I dunno. It used to be a necklace.
Yes!
You win! You are the greatest!
SHKONG!

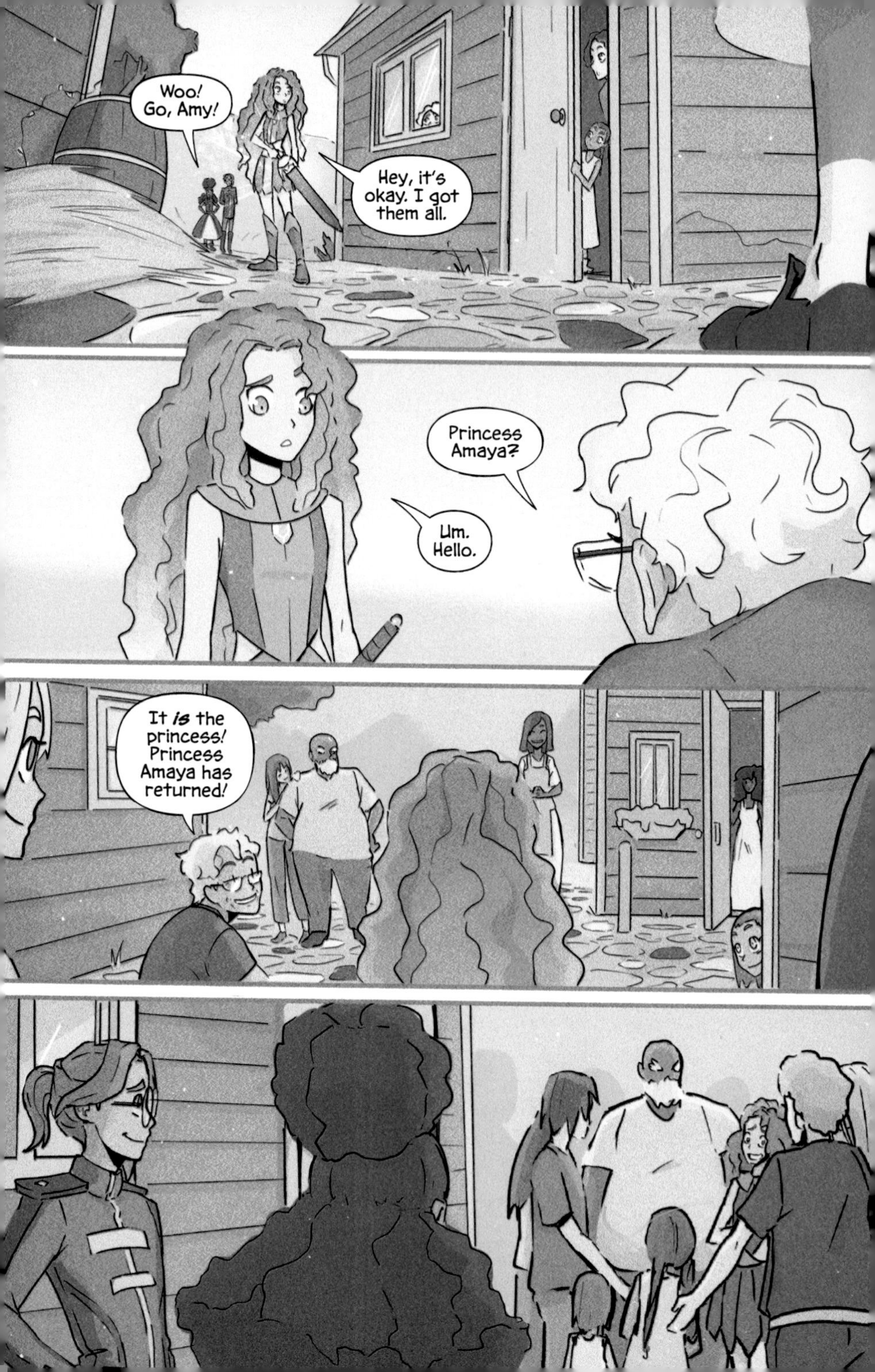
Woo! Go, Amy!
Hey, it's okay. I got them all.
Princess Amaya?
Um. Hello.
It *is* the princess! Princess Amaya has returned!

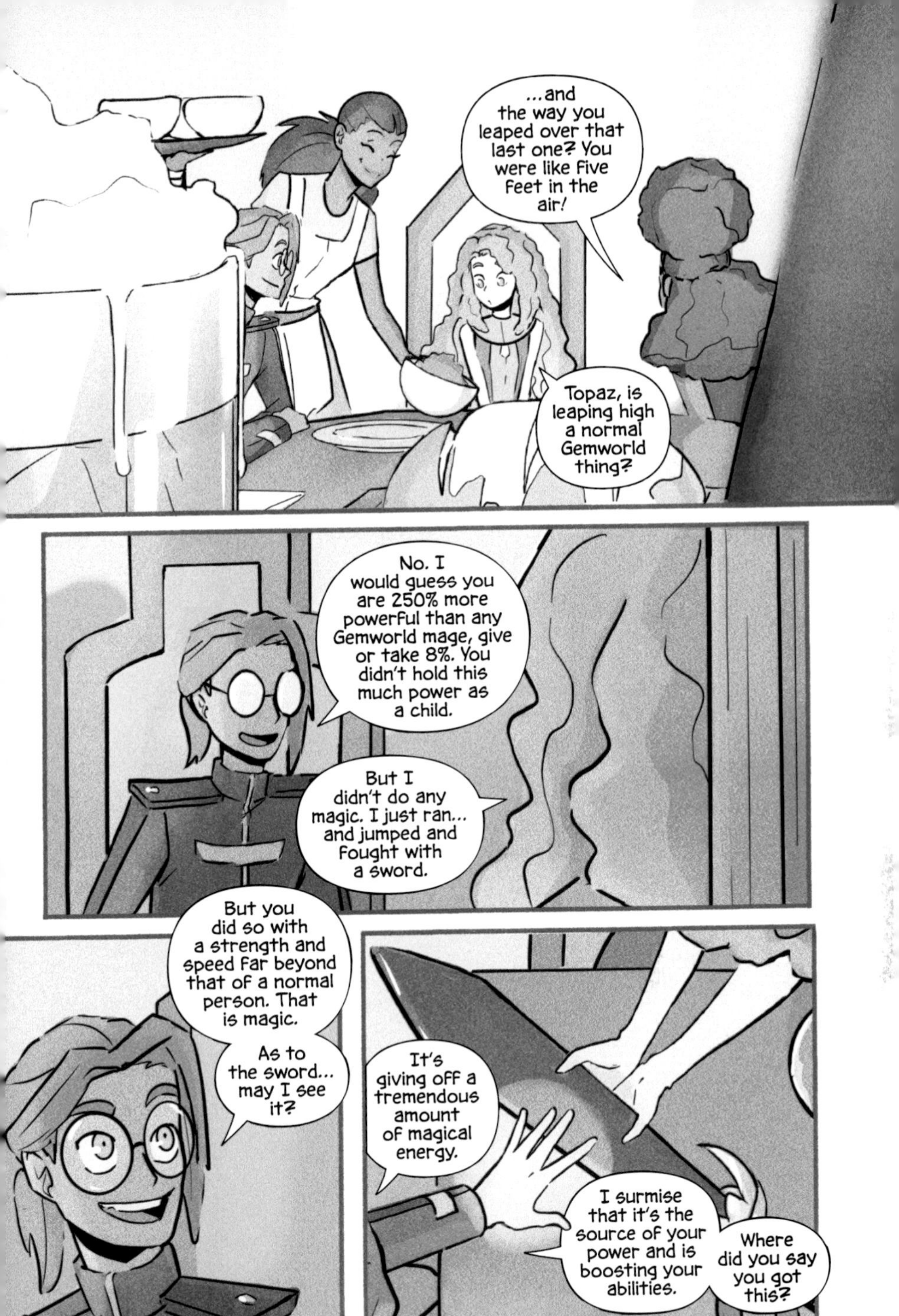
...and the way you leaped over that last one? You were like five feet in the air!
Topaz, is leaping high a normal Gemworld thing?
No. I would guess you are 250% more powerful than any Gemworld mage, give or take 8%. You didn't hold this much power as a child.
But I didn't do any magic. I just ran... and jumped and fought with a sword.
But you did so with a strength and speed far beyond that of a normal person. That is magic.
As to the sword... may I see it?
It's giving off a tremendous amount of magical energy.
I surmise that it's the source of your power and is boosting your abilities.
Where did you say you got this?

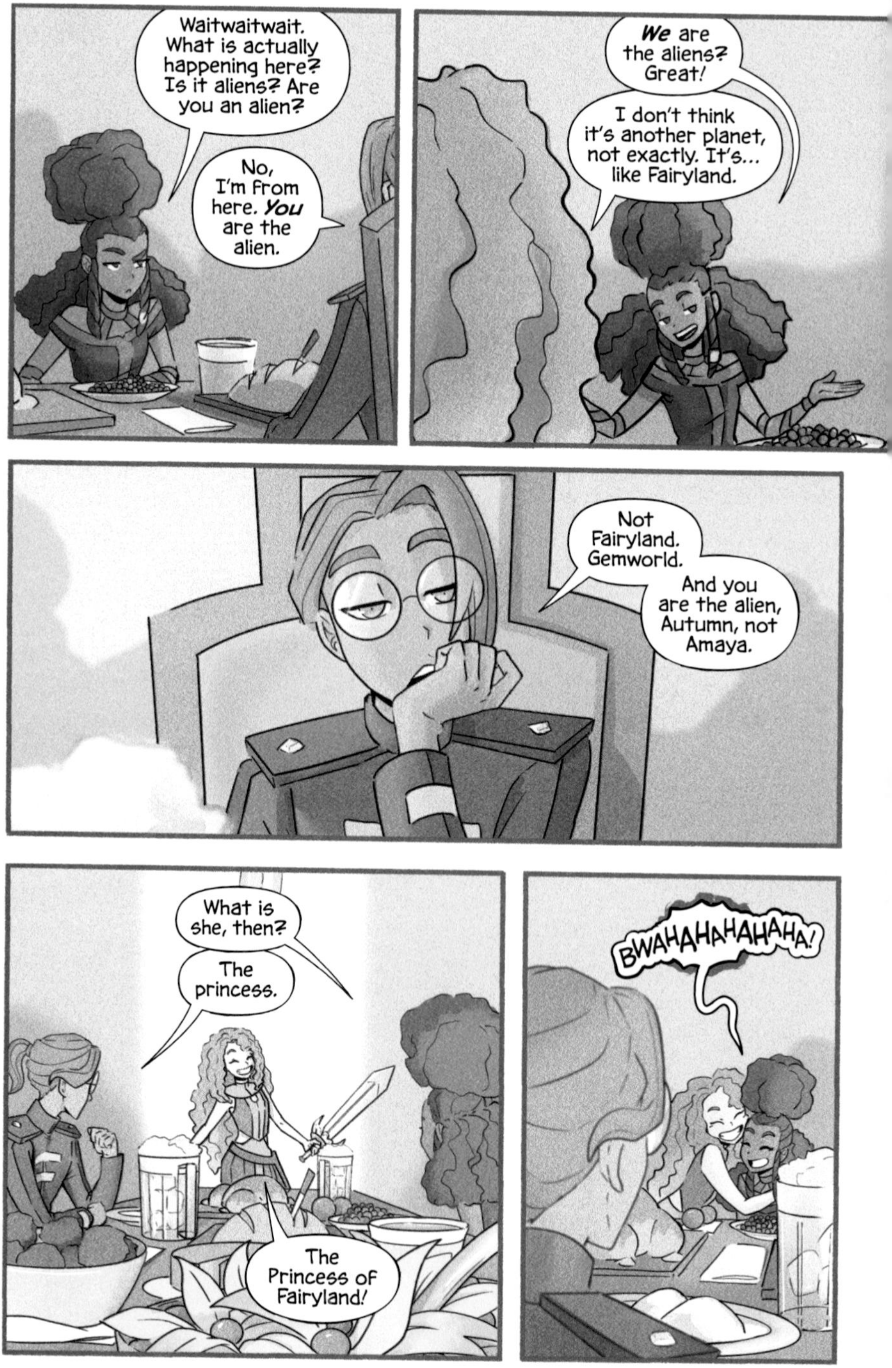
Waitwaitwait. What is actually happening here? Is it aliens? Are you an alien?
No, I'm from here. *You* are the alien.
We are the aliens? Great!
I don't think it's another planet, not exactly. It's... like Fairyland.
Not Fairyland. Gemworld.
And you are the alien, Autumn, not Amaya.
What is she, then?
The princess.
The Princess of Fairyland!
BWAHAHAHAHAHA!

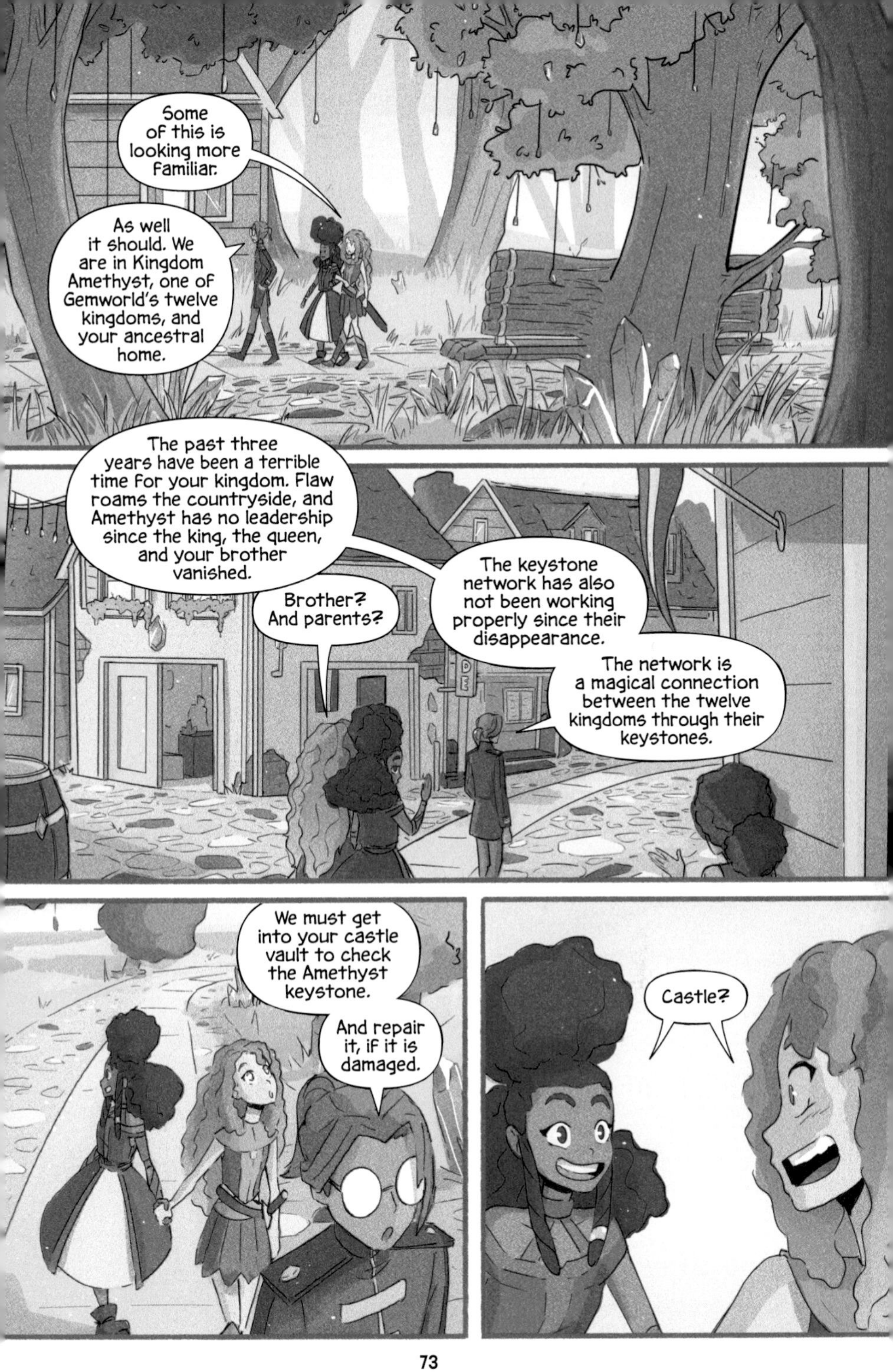
Some of this is looking more familiar.
As well it should. We are in Kingdom Amethyst, one of Gemworld's twelve kingdoms, and your ancestral home.
The past three years have been a terrible time for your kingdom. Flaw roams the countryside, and Amethyst has no leadership since the king, the queen, and your brother vanished.
Brother? And parents?
The keystone network has also not been working properly since their disappearance.
The network is a magical connection between the twelve kingdoms through their keystones.
We must get into your castle vault to check the Amethyst keystone.
And repair it, if it is damaged.
Castle?

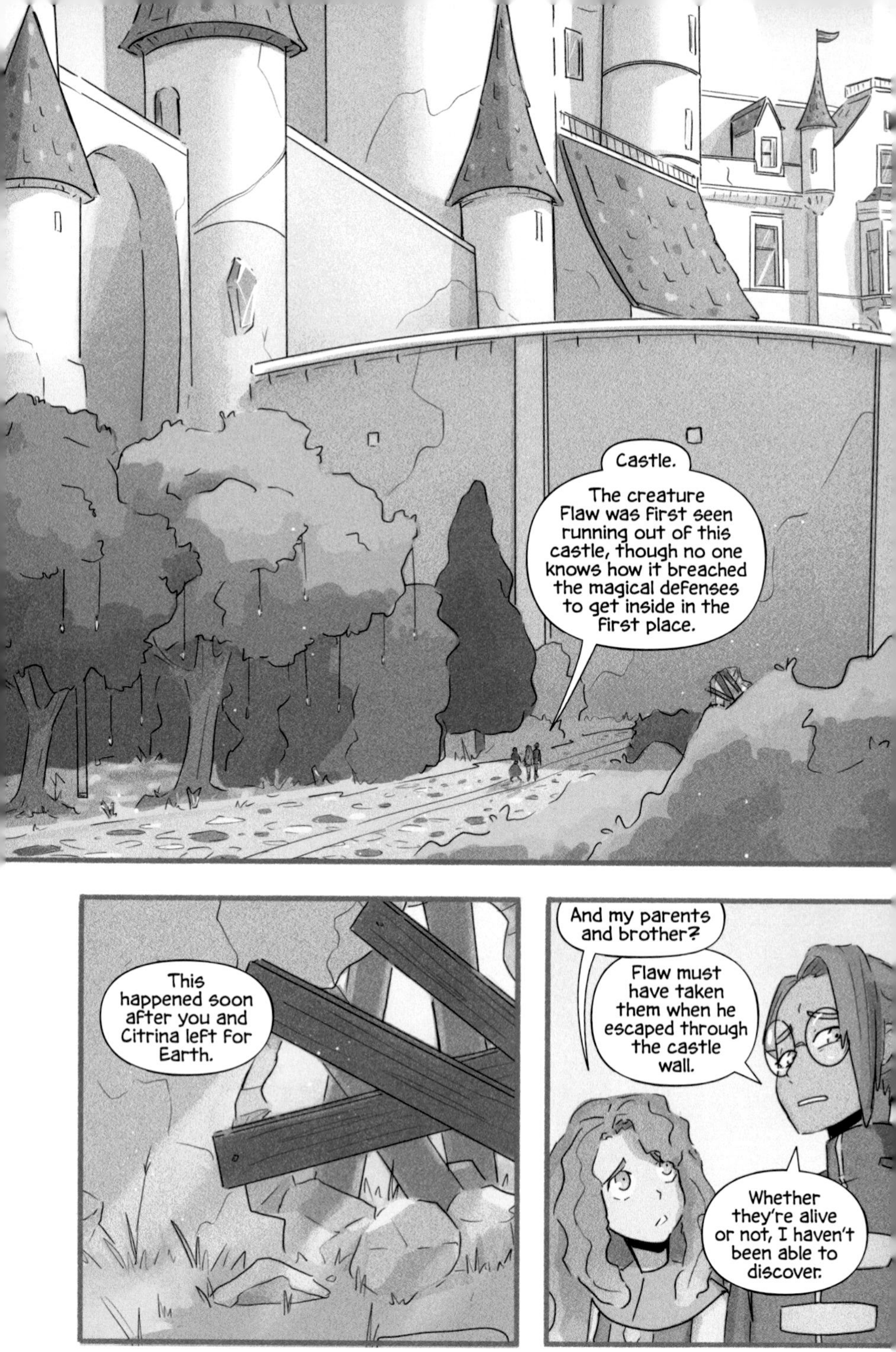

Castle.
The creature Flaw was first seen running out of this castle, though no one knows how it breached the magical defenses to get inside in the first place.
This happened soon after you and Citrina left for Earth.
And my parents and brother?
Flaw must have taken them when he escaped through the castle wall.
Whether they're alive or not, I haven't been able to discover.

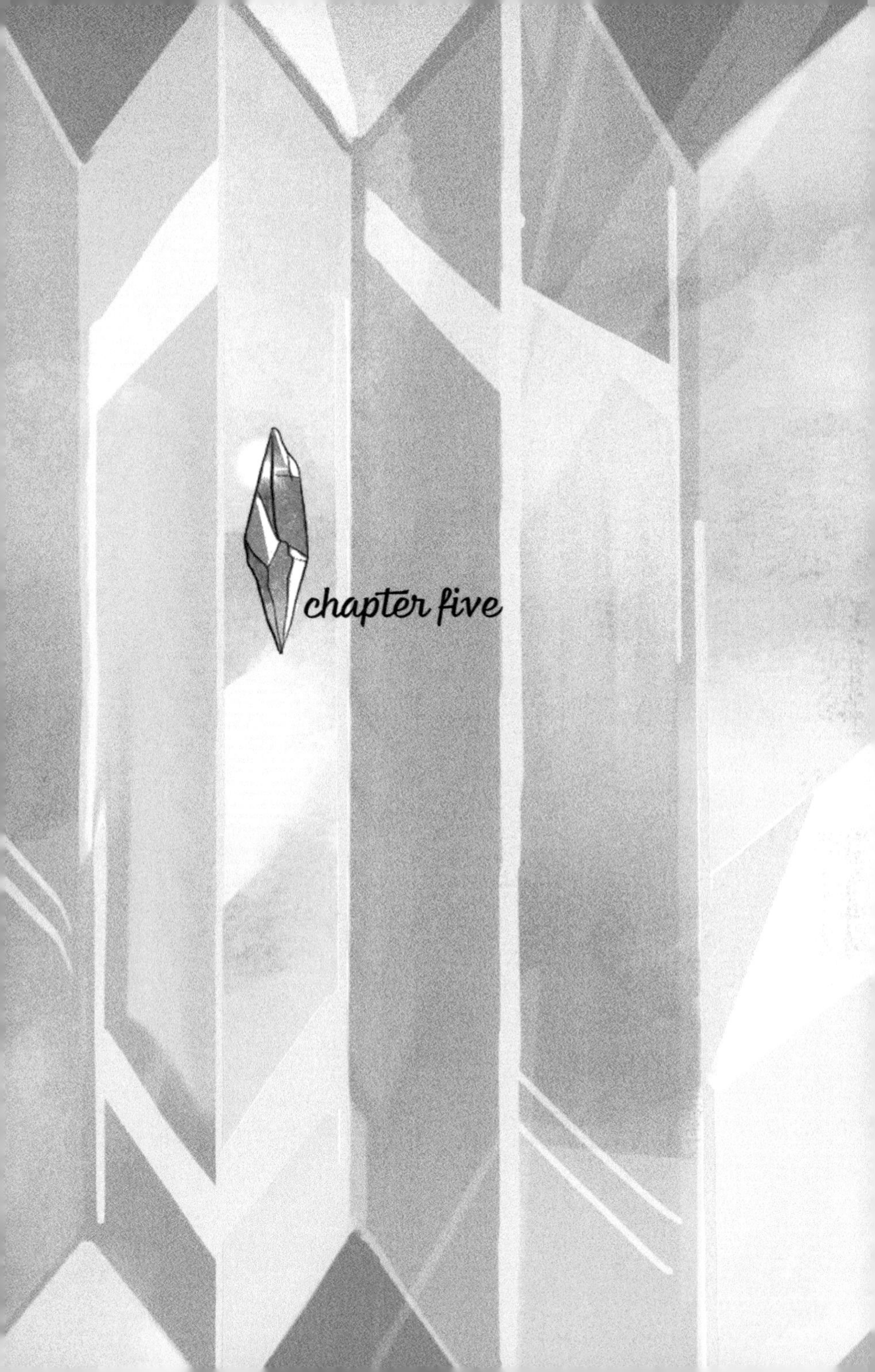

chapter five

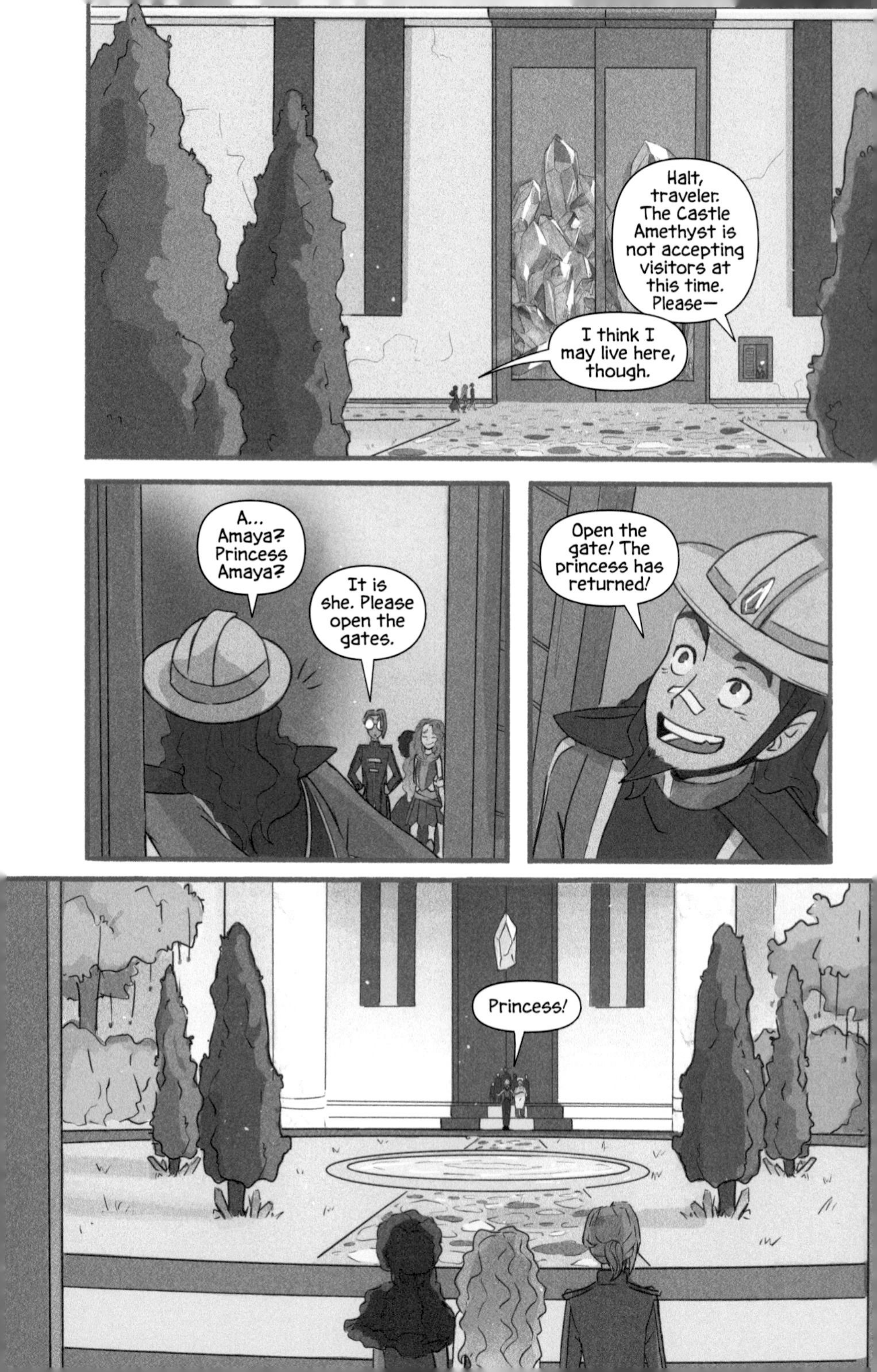
Halt, traveler. The Castle Amethyst is not accepting visitors at this time. Please—
I think I may live here, though.
A... Amaya? Princess Amaya?
It is she. Please open the gates.
Open the gate! The princess has returned!
Princess!

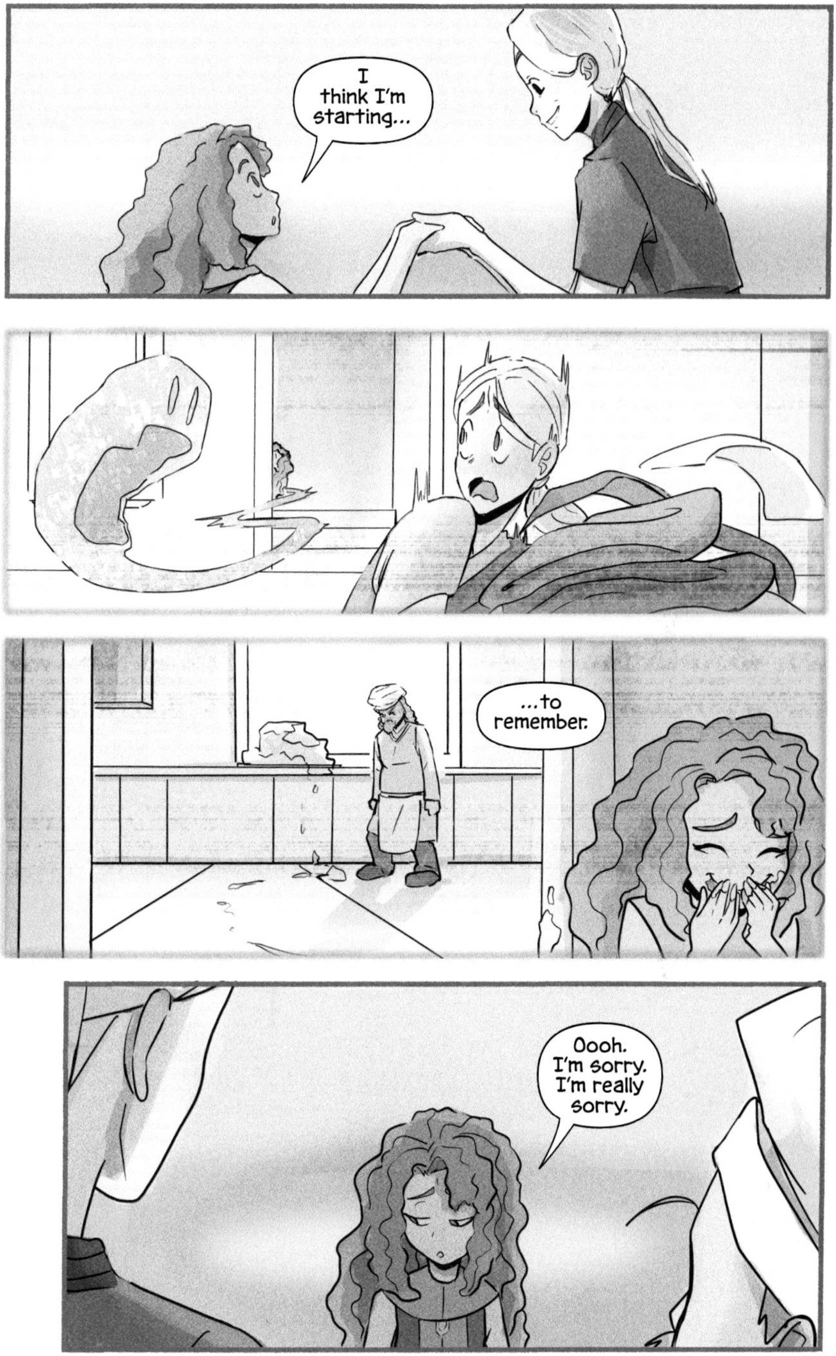
I think I'm starting...
...to remember.
Oooh. I'm sorry. I'm really sorry.

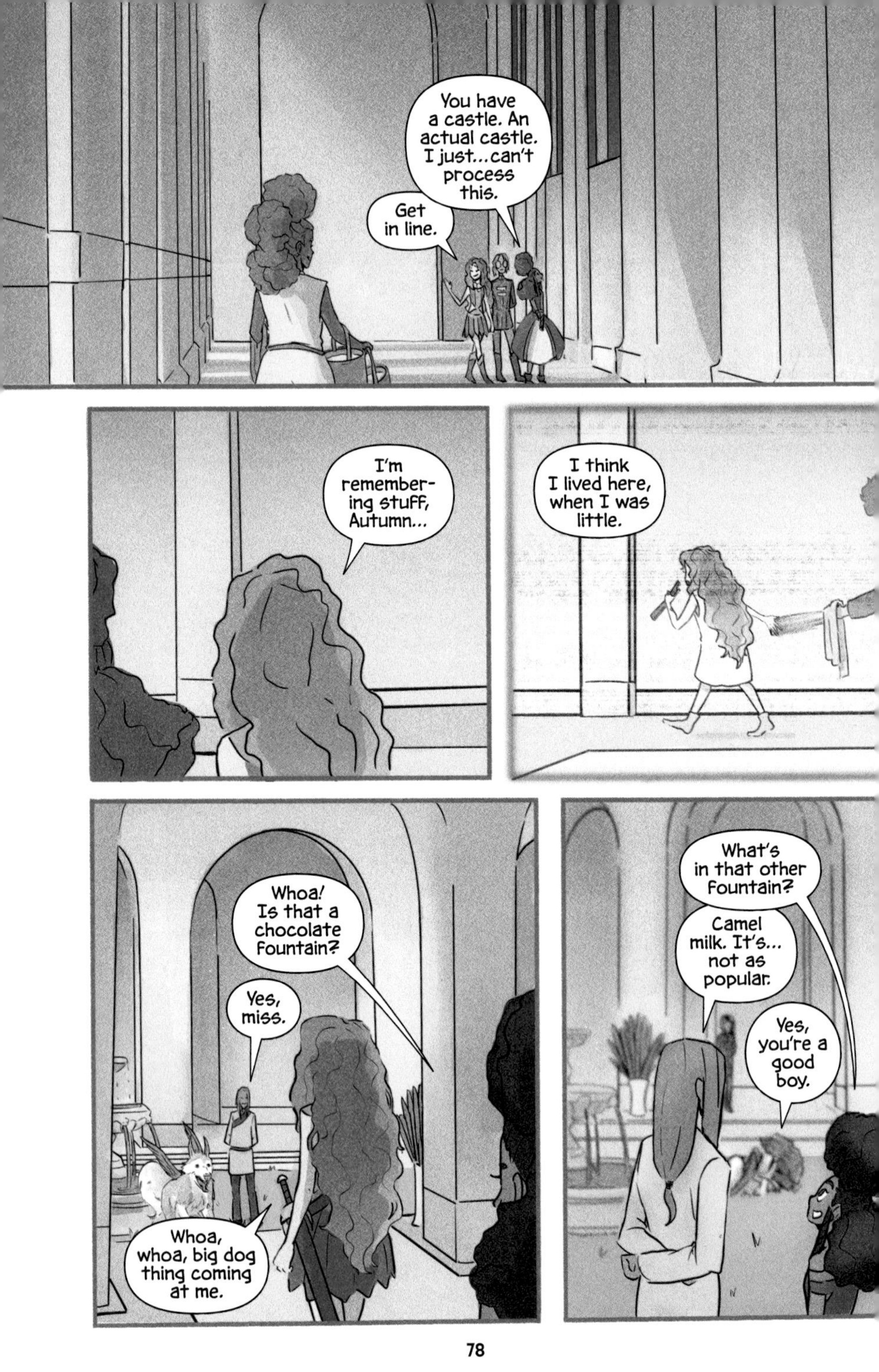

You have a castle. An actual castle. I just...can't process this.
Get in line.
I'm remember-ing stuff, Autumn...
I think I lived here, when I was little.
Whoa! Is that a chocolate fountain?
Yes, miss.
Whoa, whoa, big dog thing coming at me.
What's in that other fountain?
Camel milk. It's... not as popular.
Yes, you're a good boy.

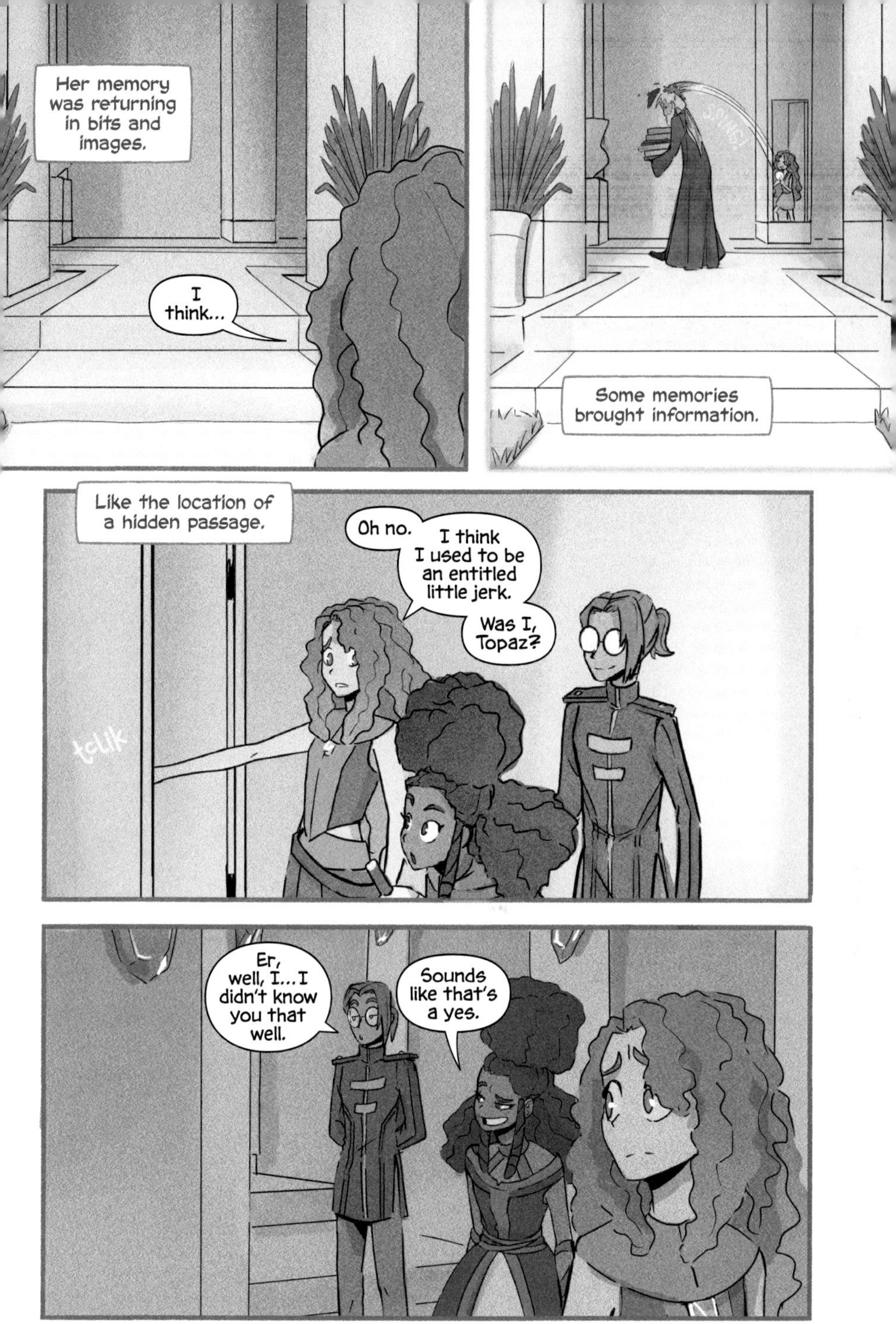
Her memory was returning in bits and images.
I think...
Some memories brought information.
Like the location of a hidden passage.
tclik
Oh no.
I think I used to be an entitled little jerk.
Was I, Topaz?
Er, well, I... I didn't know you that well.
Sounds like that's a yes.

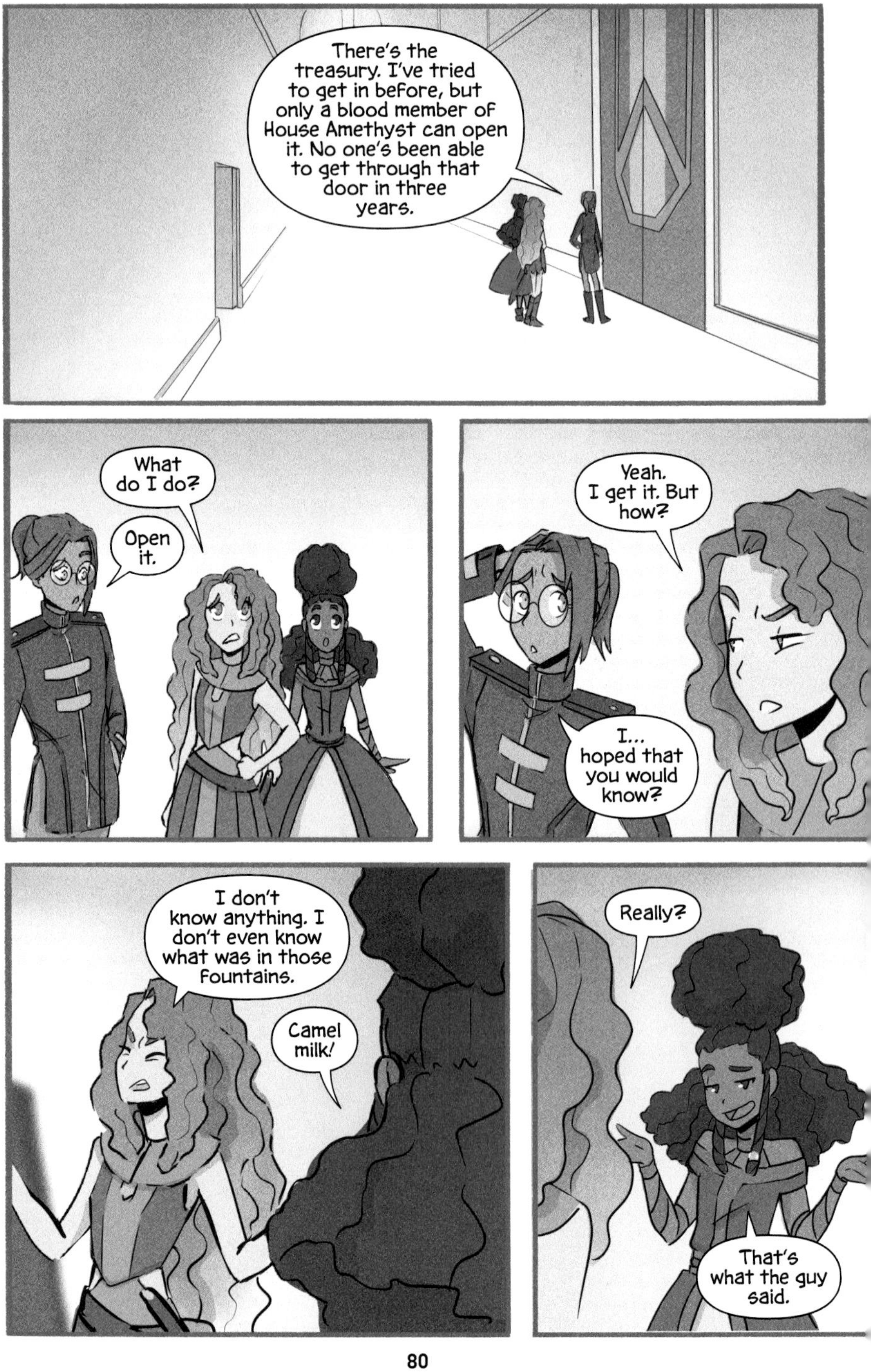
There's the treasury. I've tried to get in before, but only a blood member of House Amethyst can open it. No one's been able to get through that door in three years.
What do I do?
Open it.
Yeah. I get it. But how?
I... hoped that you would know?
I don't know anything. I don't even know what was in those fountains.
Camel milk!
Really?
That's what the guy said.

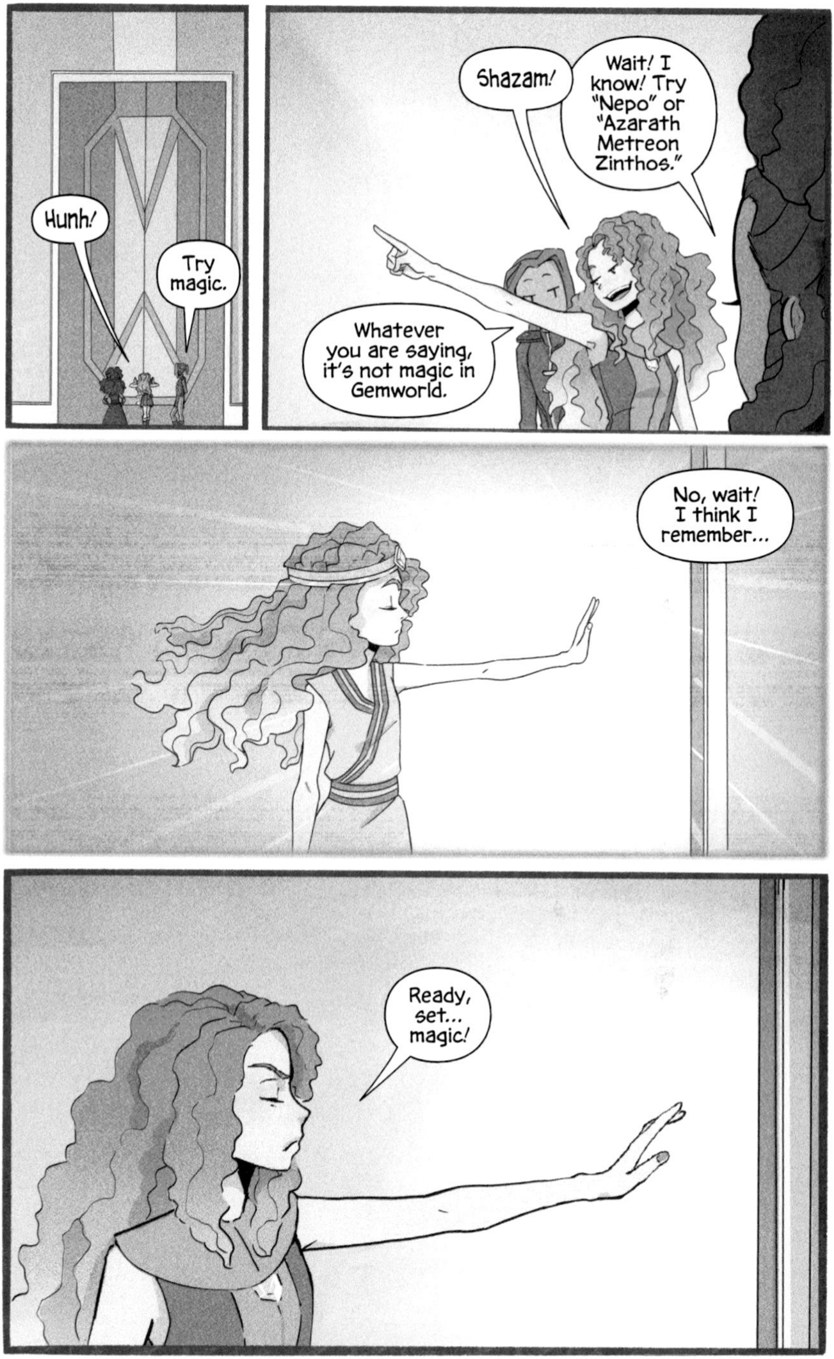
Hunh!
Try magic.
Shazam!
Wait! I know! Try "Nepo" or "Azarath Metreon Zinthos."
Whatever you are saying, it's not magic in Gemworld.
No, wait! I think I remember...
Ready, set... magic!

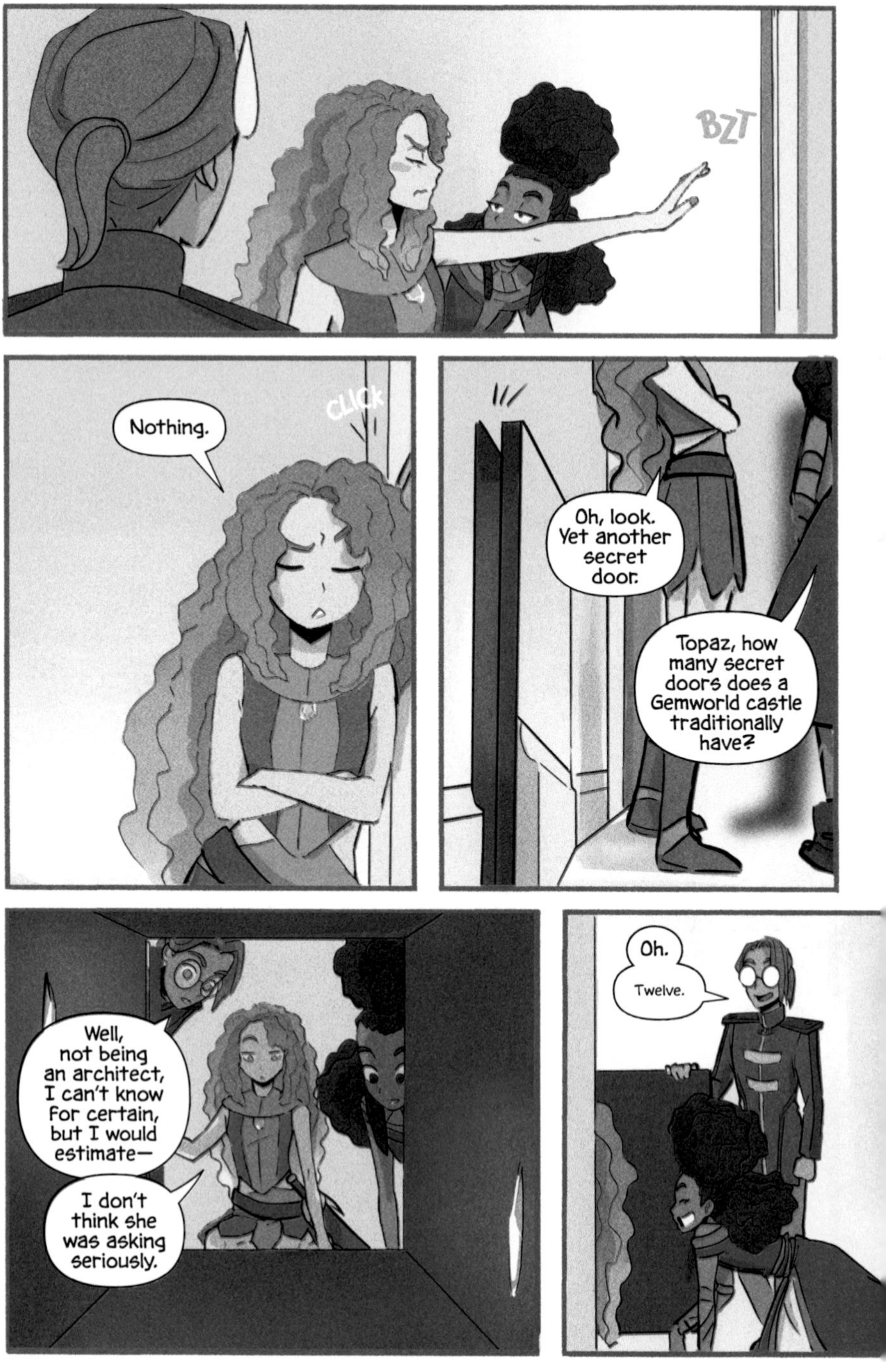
BZT
Nothing.
CLICK
Oh, look. Yet another secret door.
Topaz, how many secret doors does a Gemworld castle traditionally have?
Well, not being an architect, I can't know for certain, but I would estimate—
I don't think she was asking seriously.
Oh.
Twelve.

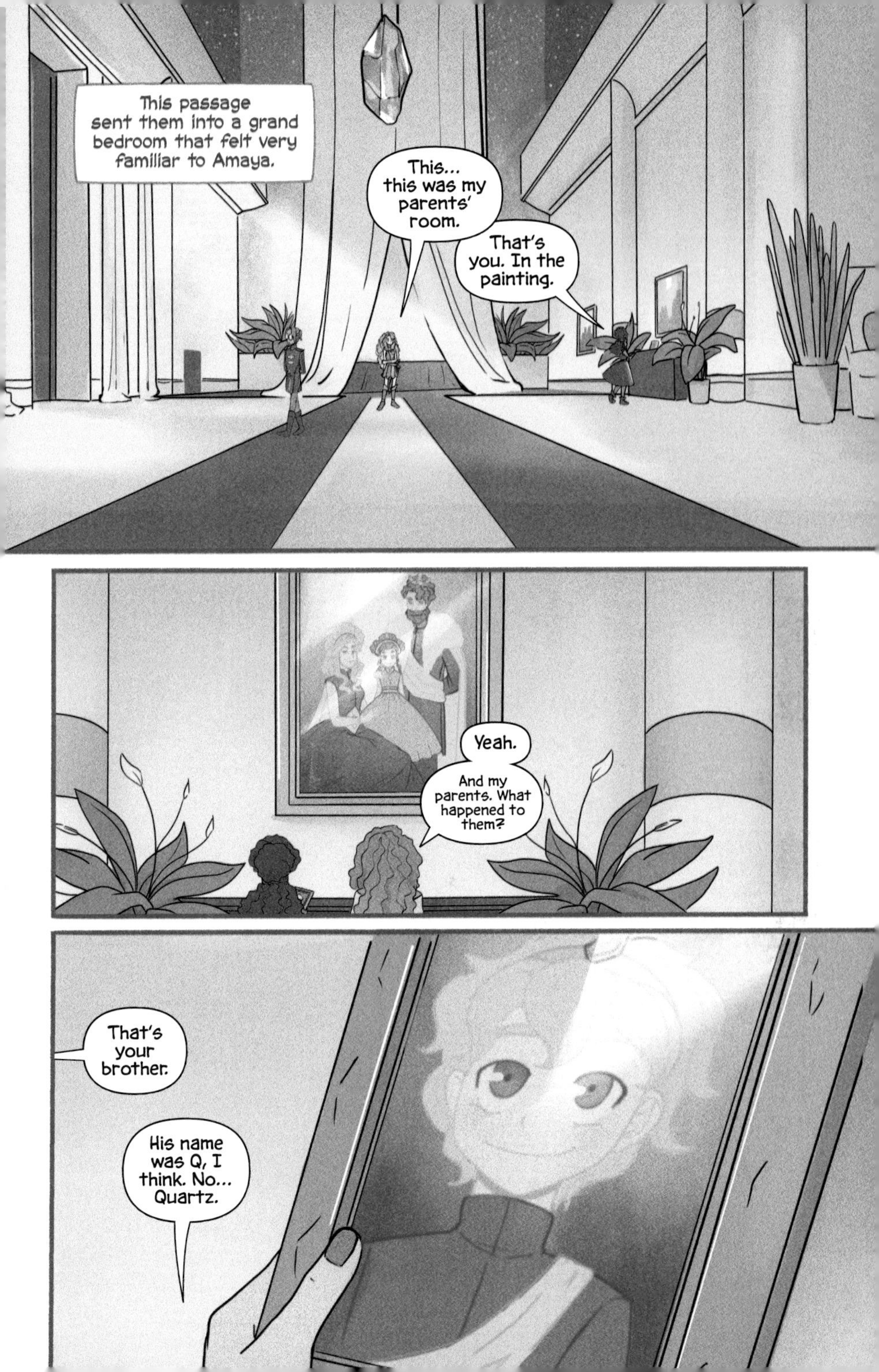
This passage sent them into a grand bedroom that felt very familiar to Amaya.
This... this was my parents' room.
That's you. In the painting.
Yeah.
And my parents. What happened to them?
That's your brother.
His name was Q, I think. No... Quartz.

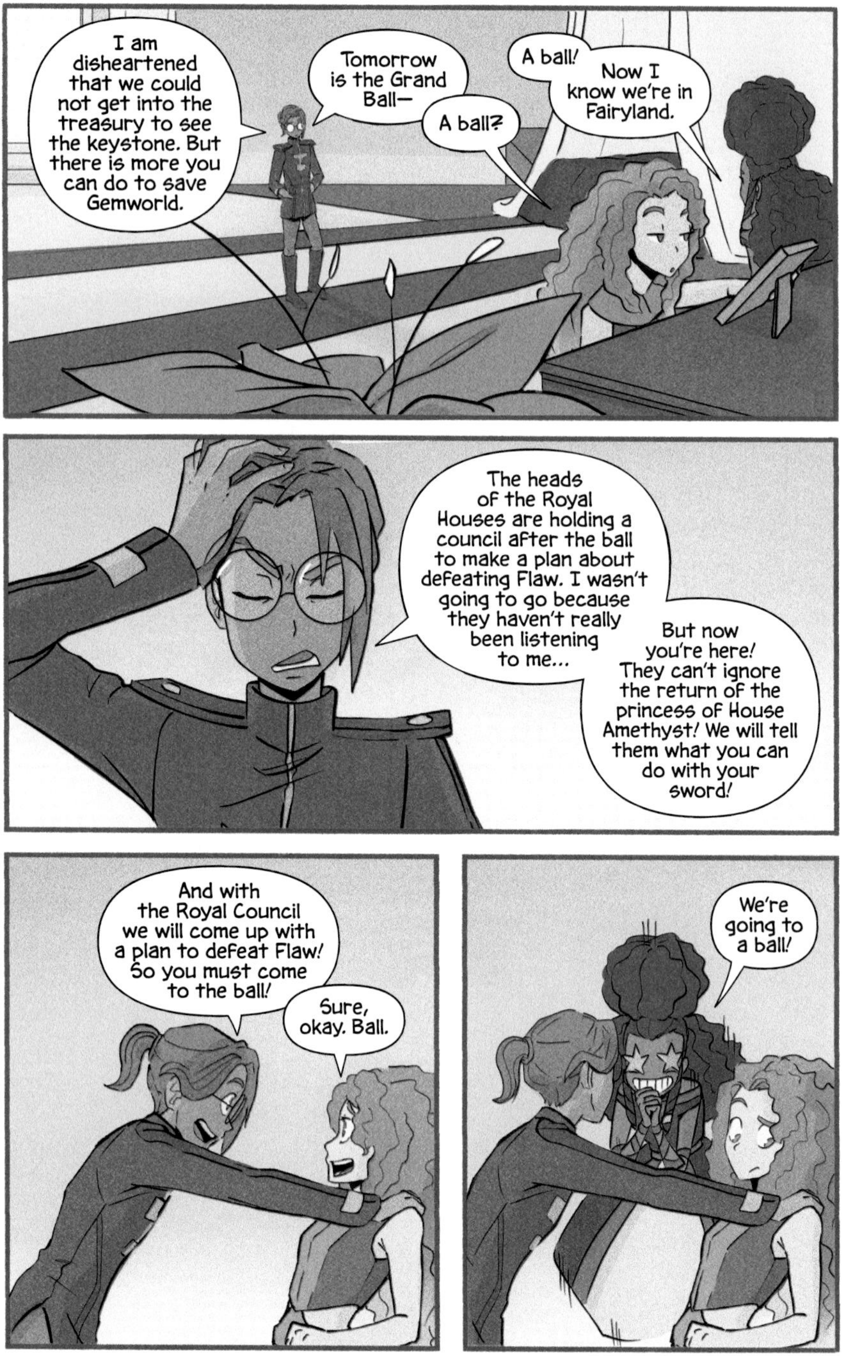
I am disheartened that we could not get into the treasury to see the keystone. But there is more you can do to save Gemworld.
Tomorrow is the Grand Ball—
A ball?
A ball!
Now I know we're in Fairyland.
The heads of the Royal Houses are holding a council after the ball to make a plan about defeating Flaw. I wasn't going to go because they haven't really been listening to me...
But now you're here! They can't ignore the return of the princess of House Amethyst! We will tell them what you can do with your sword!
And with the Royal Council we will come up with a plan to defeat Flaw! So you must come to the ball!
Sure, okay. Ball.
We're going to a ball!

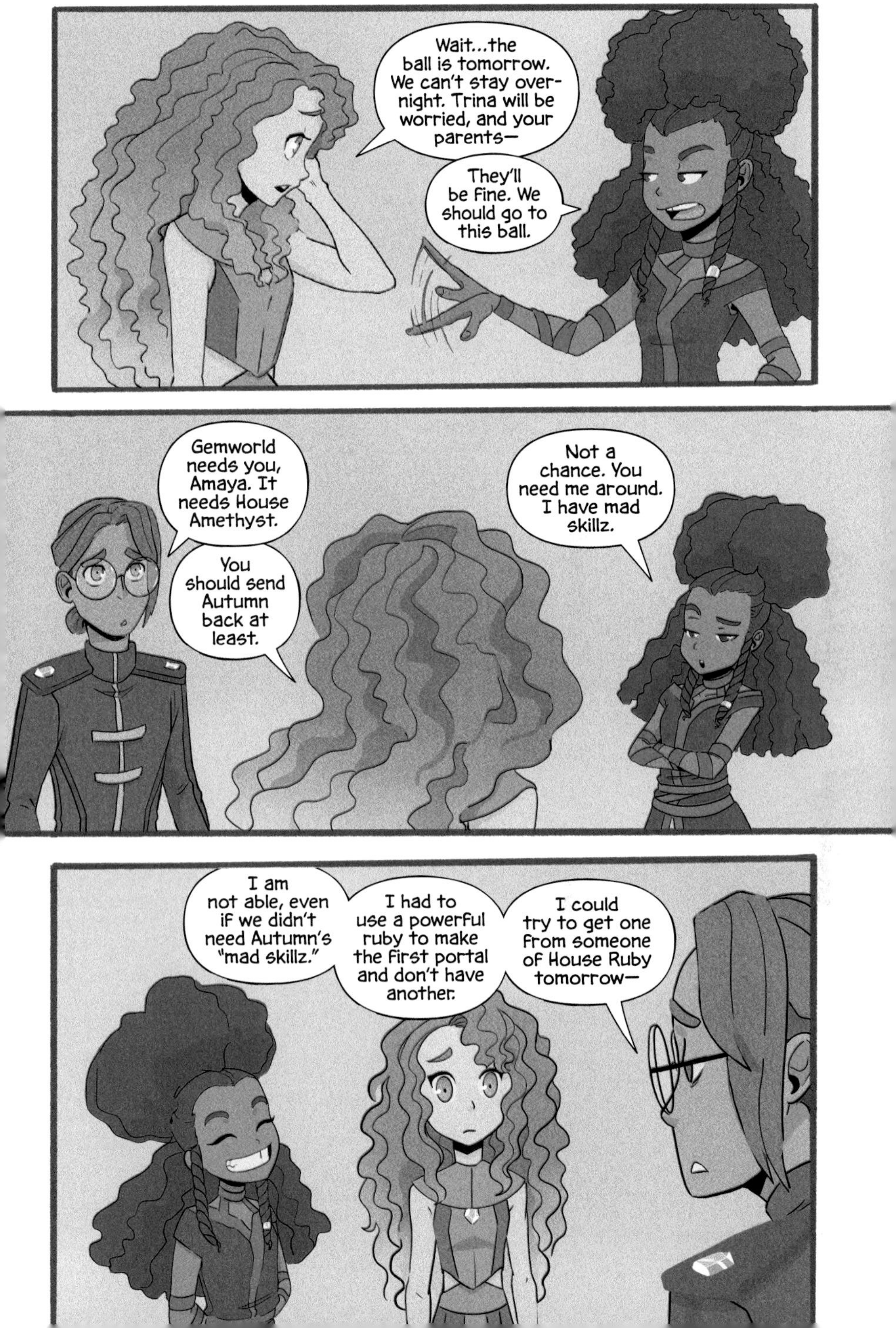
Wait...the ball is tomorrow. We can't stay over-night. Trina will be worried, and your parents—
They'll be fine. We should go to this ball.
Gemworld needs you, Amaya. It needs House Amethyst.
You should send Autumn back at least.
Not a chance. You need me around. I have mad skillz.
I am not able, even if we didn't need Autumn's "mad skillz."
I had to use a powerful ruby to make the first portal and don't have another.
I could try to get one from someone of House Ruby tomorrow—

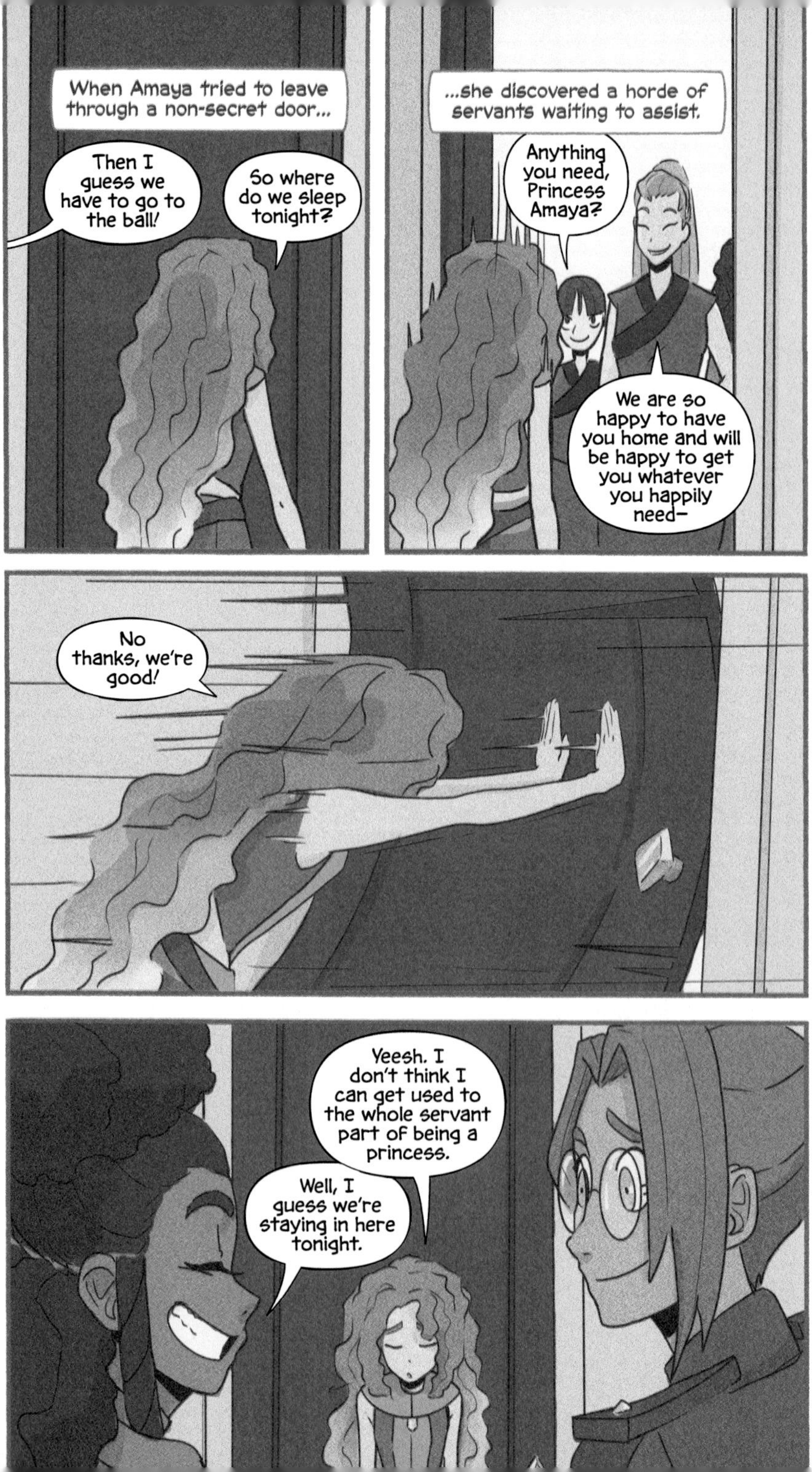
When Amaya tried to leave through a non-secret door...
Then I guess we have to go to the ball!
So where do we sleep tonight?
...she discovered a horde of servants waiting to assist.
Anything you need, Princess Amaya?
We are so happy to have you home and will be happy to get you whatever you happily need—
No thanks, we're good!
Yeesh. I don't think I can get used to the whole servant part of being a princess.
Well, I guess we're staying in here tonight.

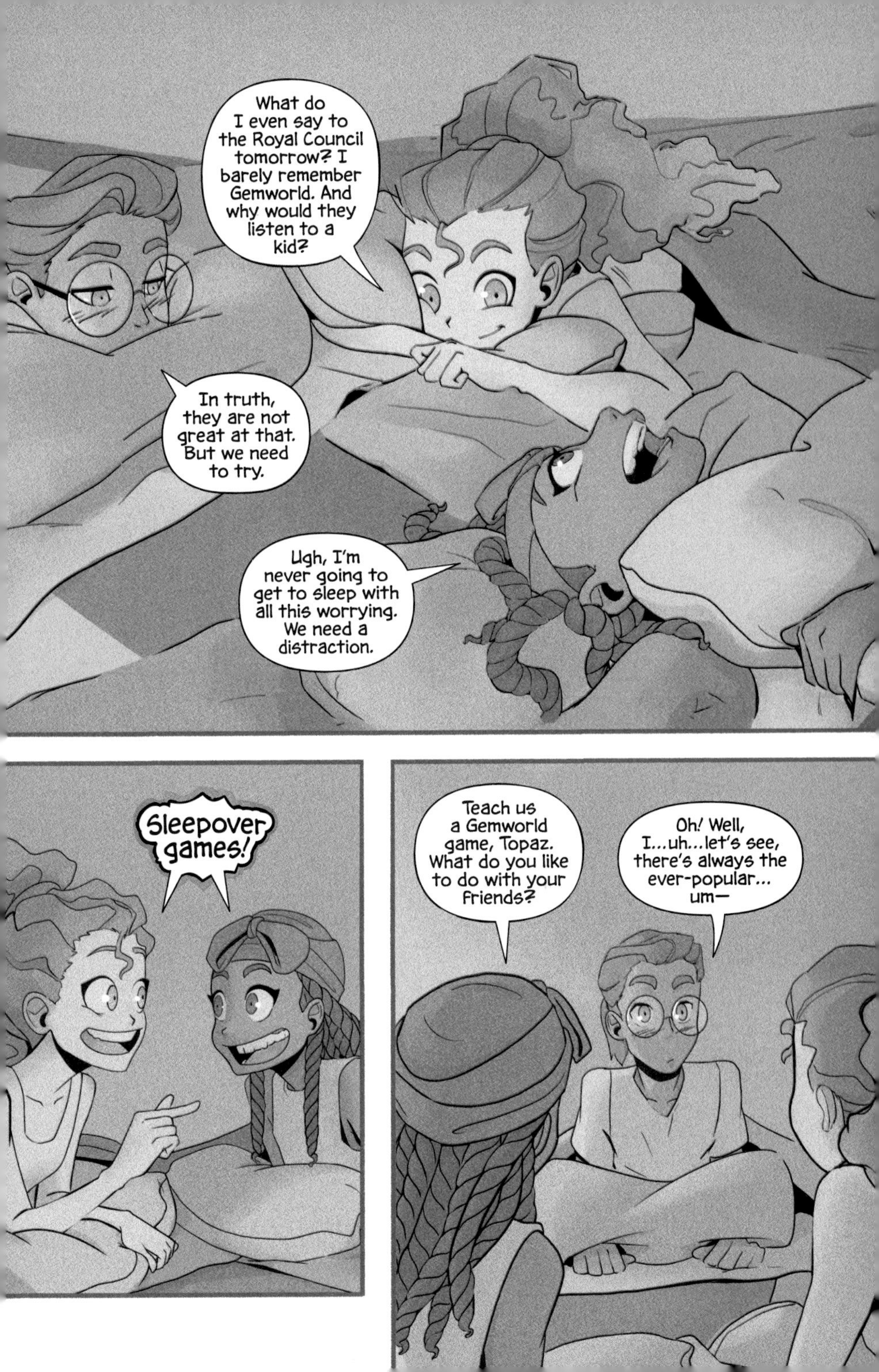
What do I even say to the Royal Council tomorrow? I barely remember Gemworld. And why would they listen to a kid?
In truth, they are not great at that. But we need to try.
Ugh, I'm never going to get to sleep with all this worrying. We need a distraction.
Sleepover games!
Teach us a Gemworld game, Topaz. What do you like to do with your friends?
Oh! Well, I...uh...let's see, there's always the ever-popular... um—

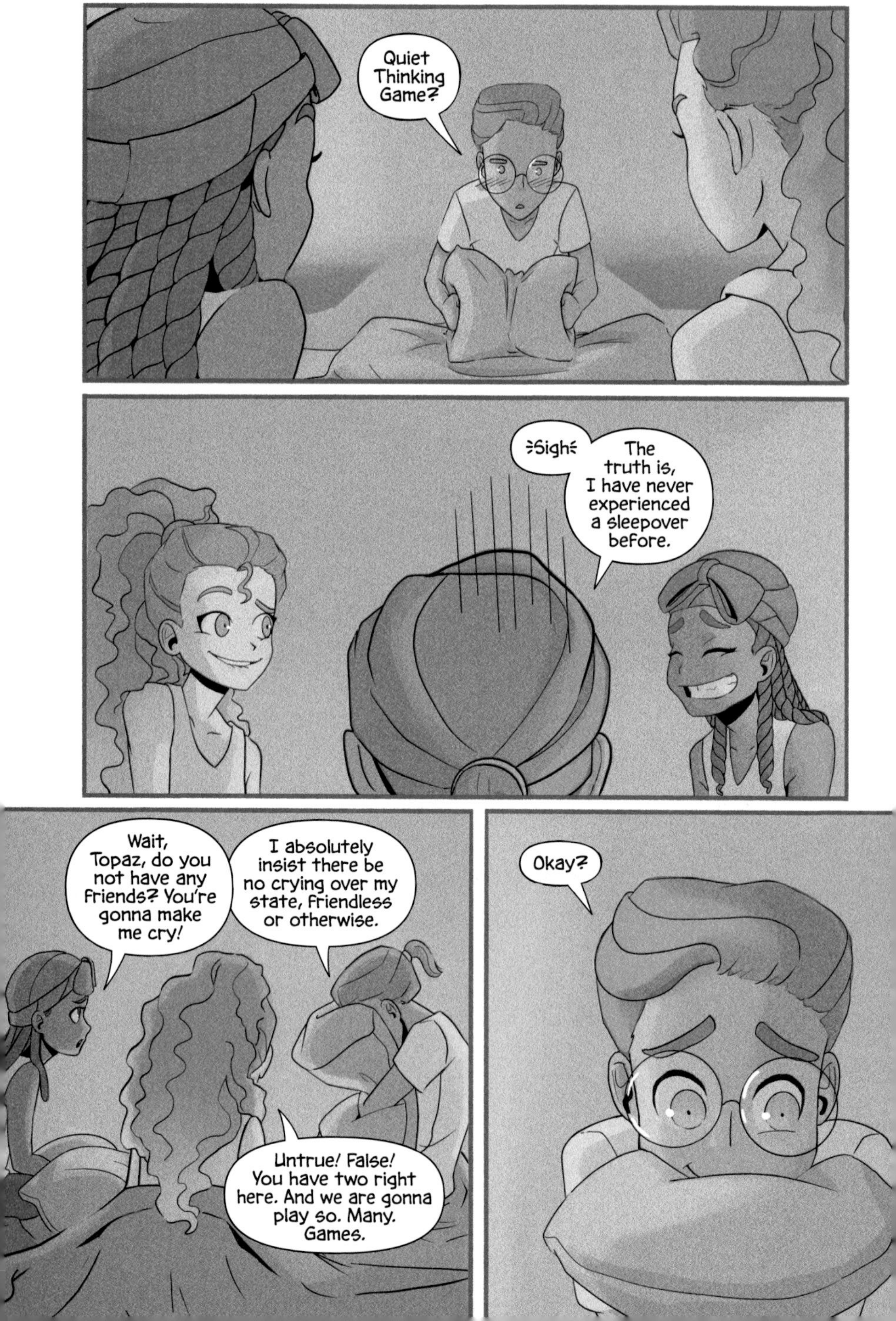
Quiet Thinking Game?
Sigh
The truth is, I have never experienced a sleepover before.
Wait, Topaz, do you not have any friends? You're gonna make me cry!
I absolutely insist there be no crying over my state, friendless or otherwise.
Untrue! False! You have two right here. And we are gonna play so. Many. Games.
Okay?

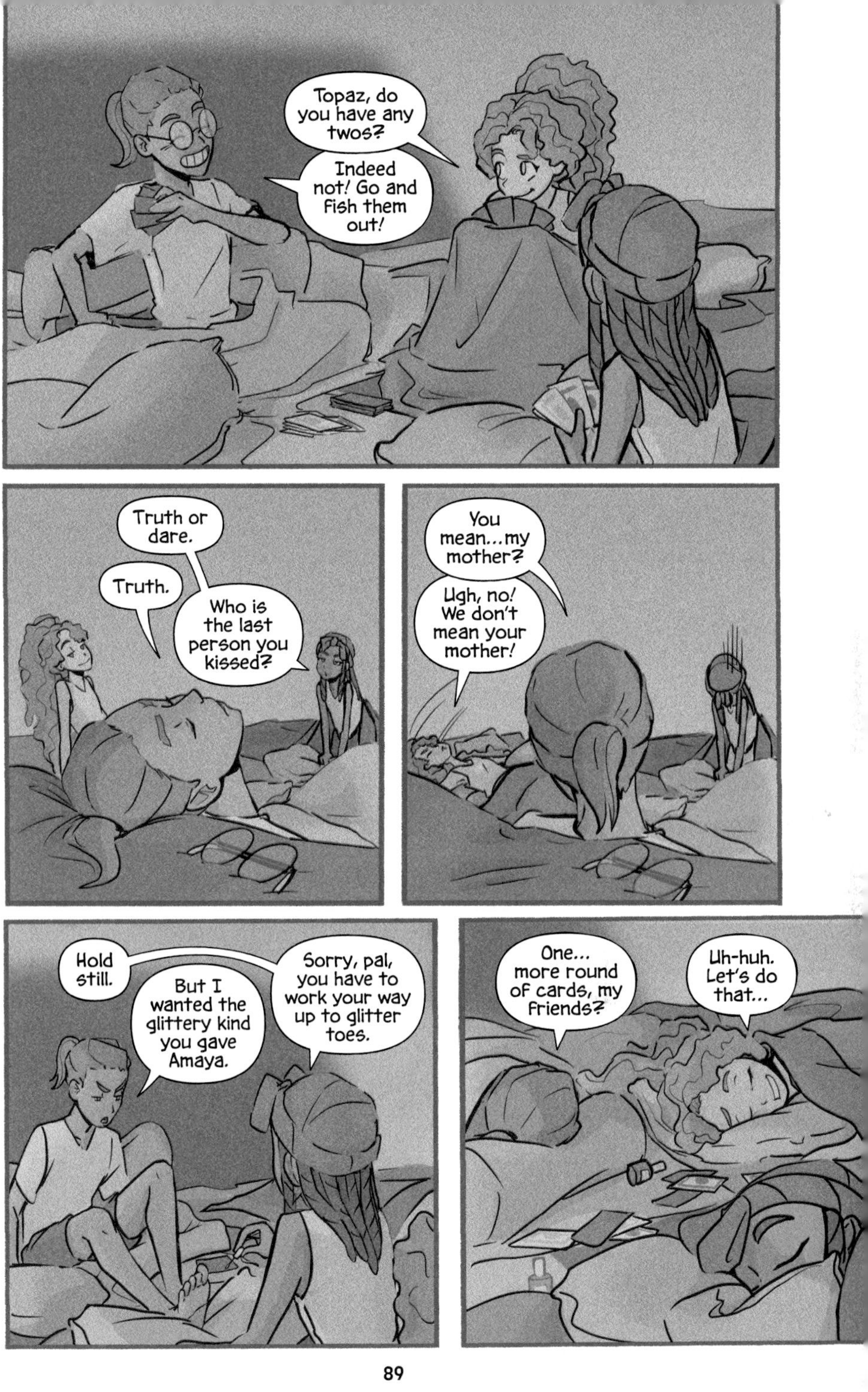
Topaz, do you have any twos?
Indeed not! Go and fish them out!
Truth or dare.
Truth.
Who is the last person you kissed?
You mean...my mother?
Ugh, no! We don't mean your mother!
Hold still.
But I wanted the glittery kind you gave Amaya.
Sorry, pal, you have to work your way up to glitter toes.
One... more round of cards, my friends?
Uh-huh. Let's do that...

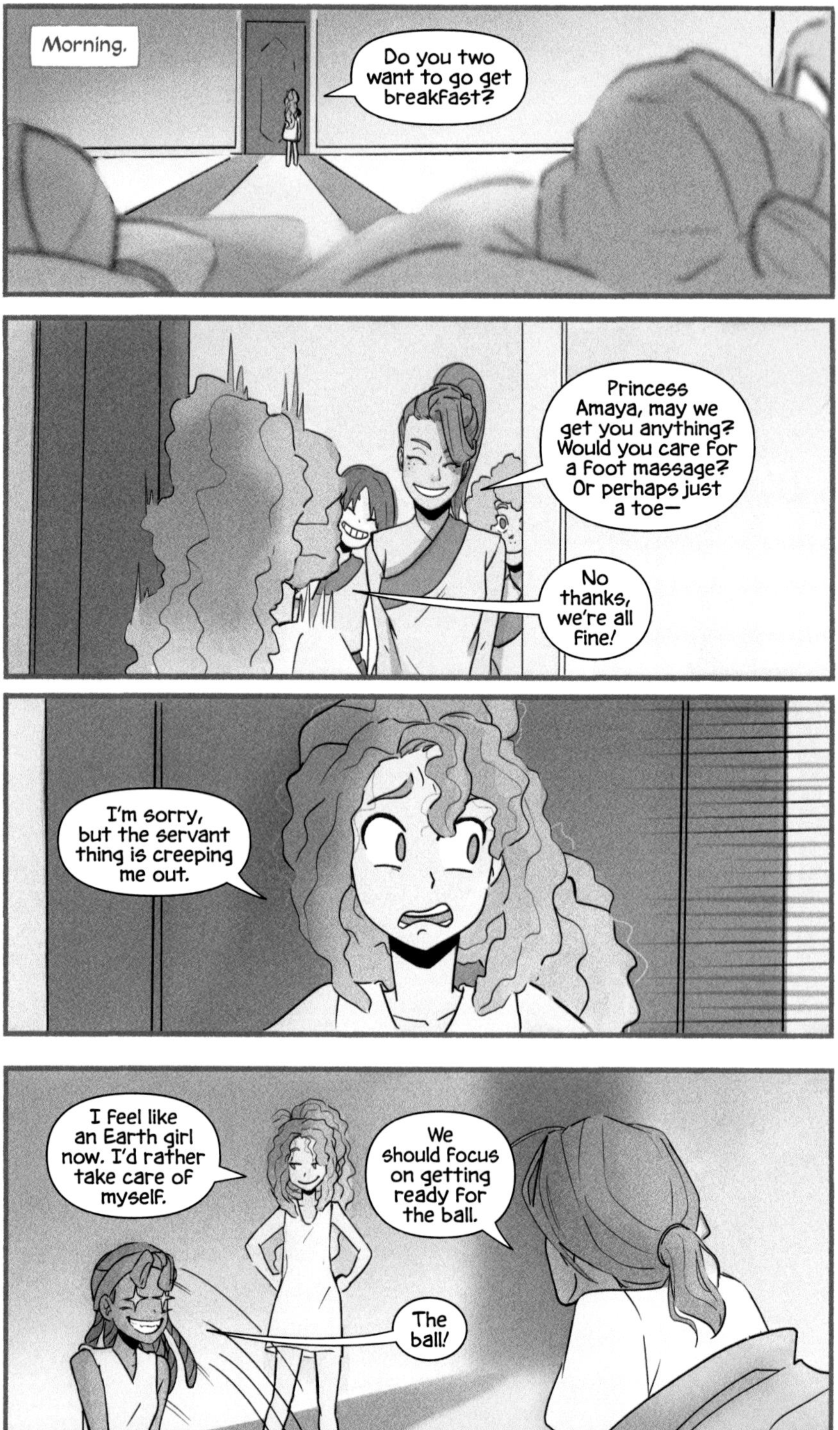
Morning.
Do you two want to go get breakfast?
Princess Amaya, may we get you anything? Would you care for a foot massage? Or perhaps just a toe—
No thanks, we're all fine!
I'm sorry, but the servant thing is creeping me out.
I feel like an Earth girl now. I'd rather take care of myself.
We should focus on getting ready for the ball.
The ball!

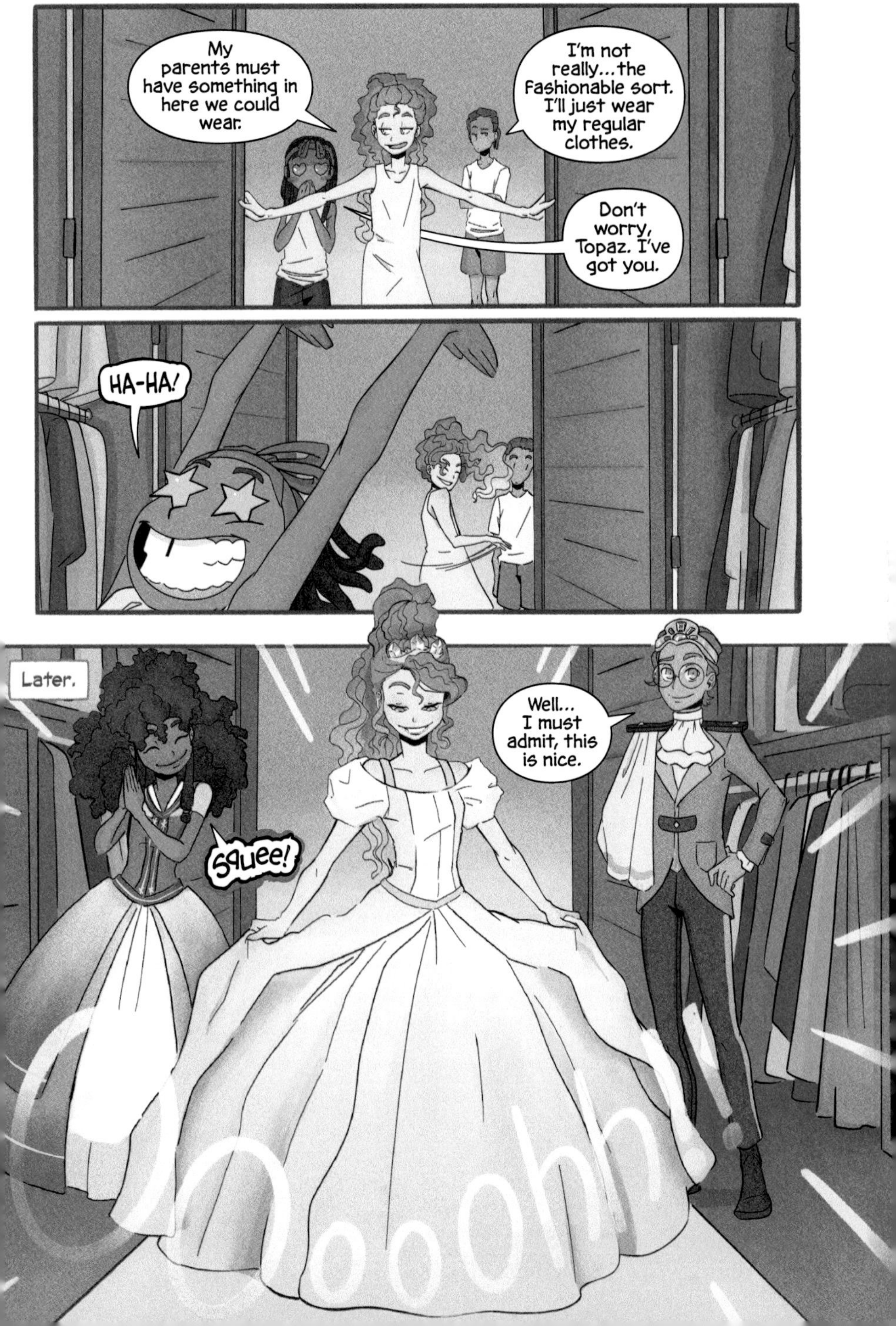
My parents must have something in here we could wear.
I'm not really...the fashionable sort. I'll just wear my regular clothes.
Don't worry, Topaz. I've got you.
HA-HA!
Later.
Squee!
Well... I must admit, this is nice.
OoooOhh!

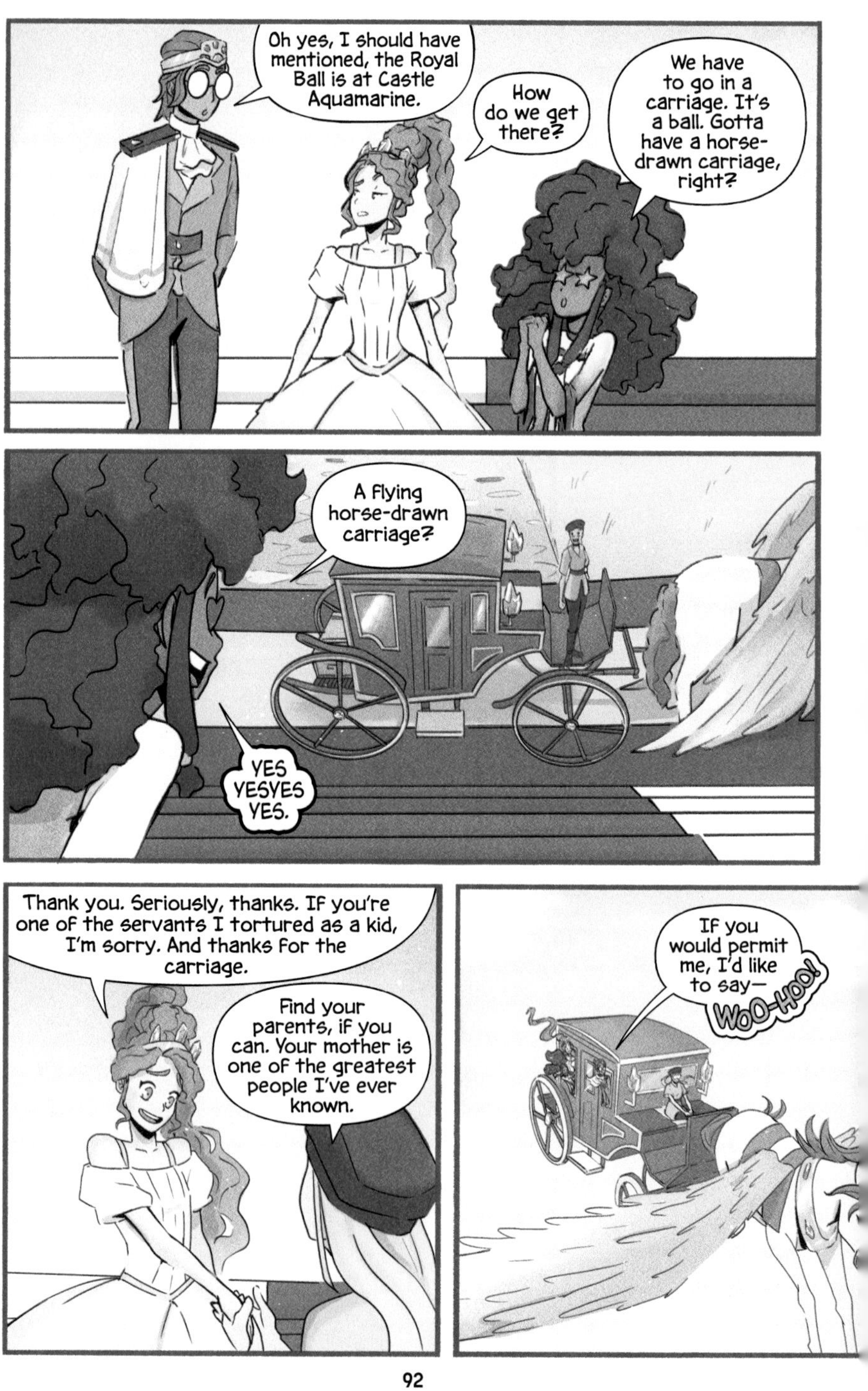

Oh yes, I should have mentioned, the Royal Ball is at Castle Aquamarine.
How do we get there?
We have to go in a carriage. It's a ball. Gotta have a horse-drawn carriage, right?
A flying horse-drawn carriage?
YES YESYES YES.
Thank you. Seriously, thanks. If you're one of the servants I tortured as a kid, I'm sorry. And thanks for the carriage.
Find your parents, if you can. Your mother is one of the greatest people I've ever known.
If you would permit me, I'd like to say—
WOO-HOO!

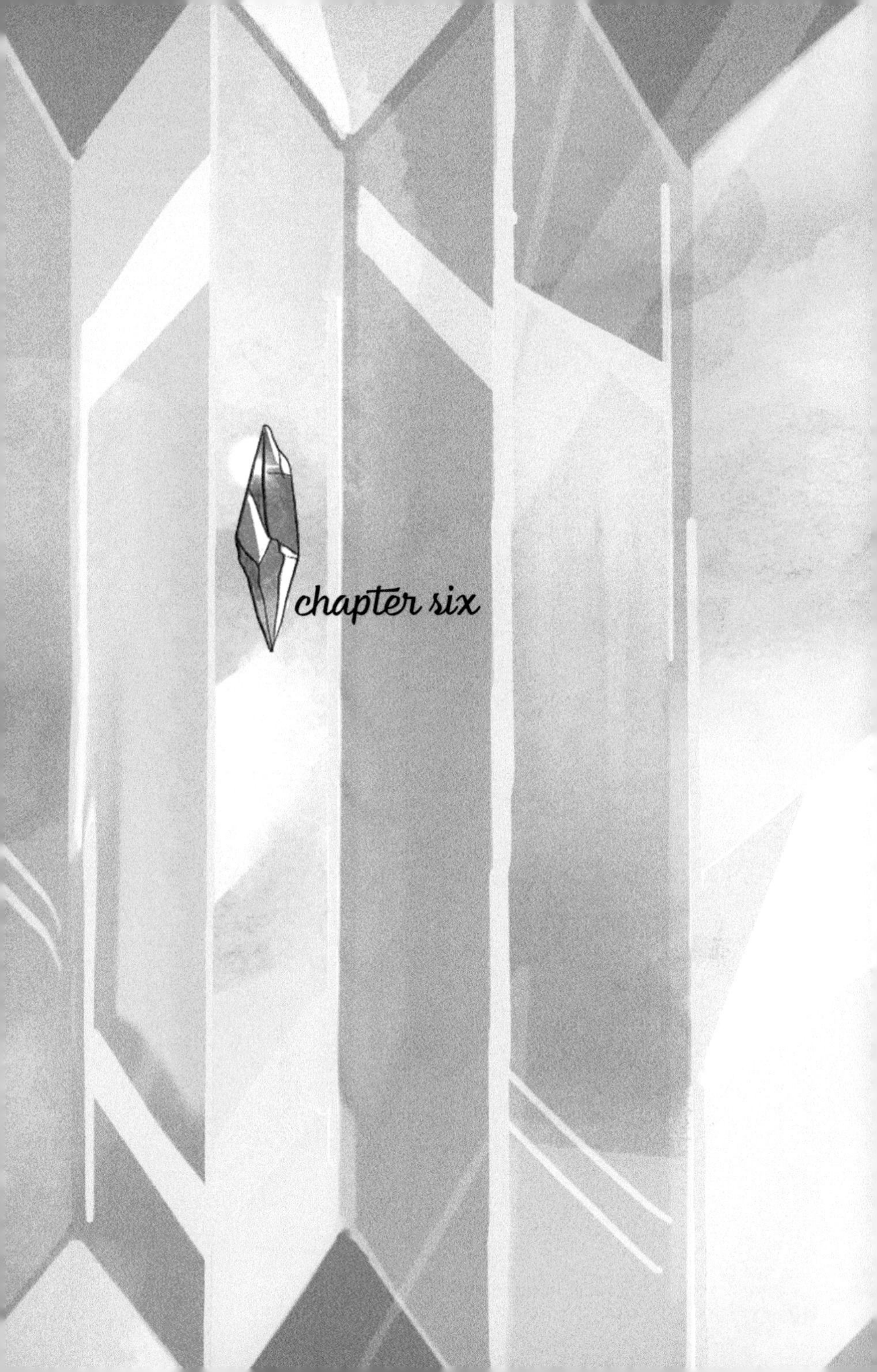

chapter six

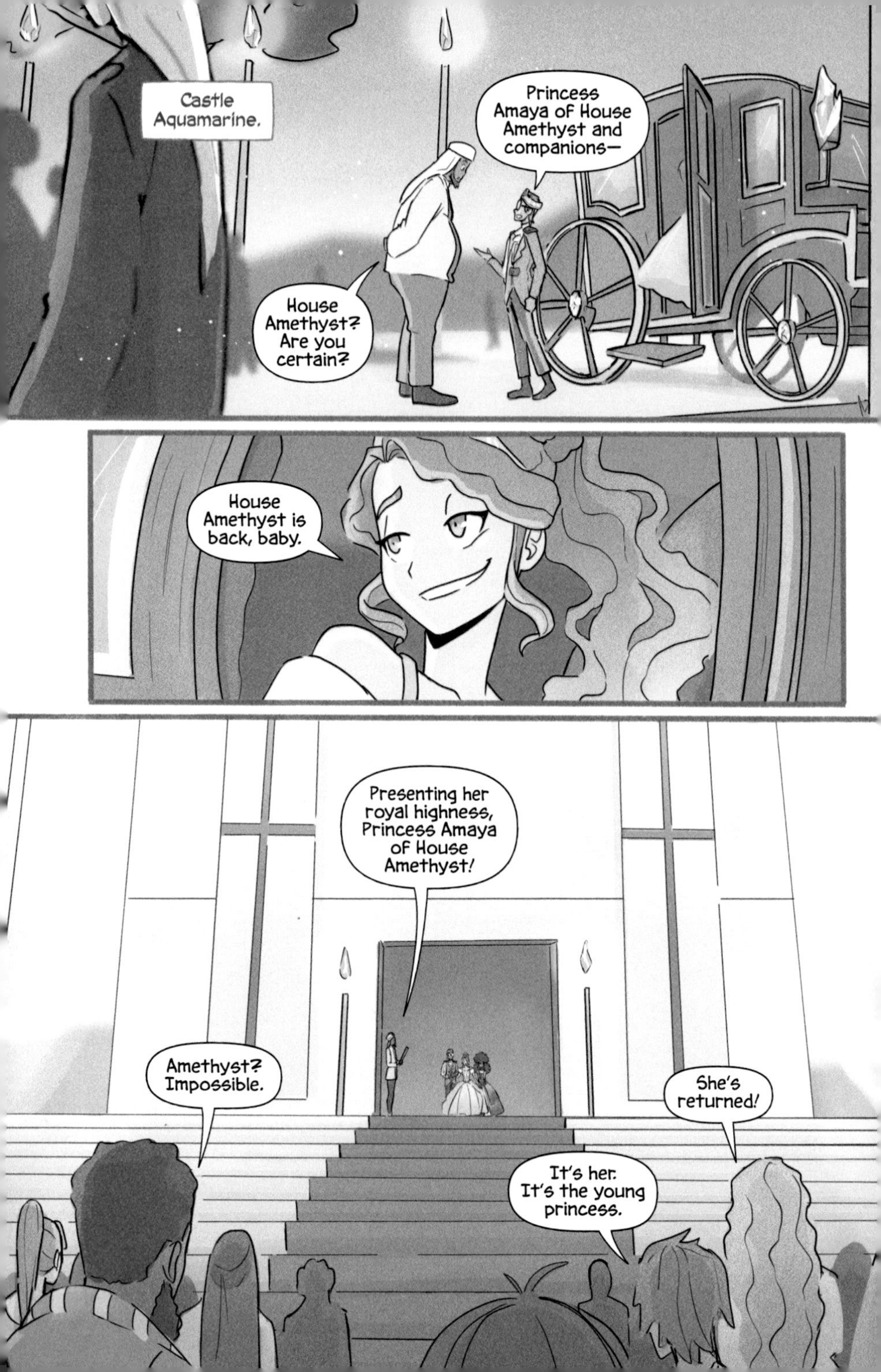
Castle Aquamarine.
Princess Amaya of House Amethyst and companions—
House Amethyst? Are you certain?
House Amethyst is back, baby.
Presenting her royal highness, Princess Amaya of House Amethyst!
Amethyst? Impossible.
She's returned!
It's her. It's the young princess.

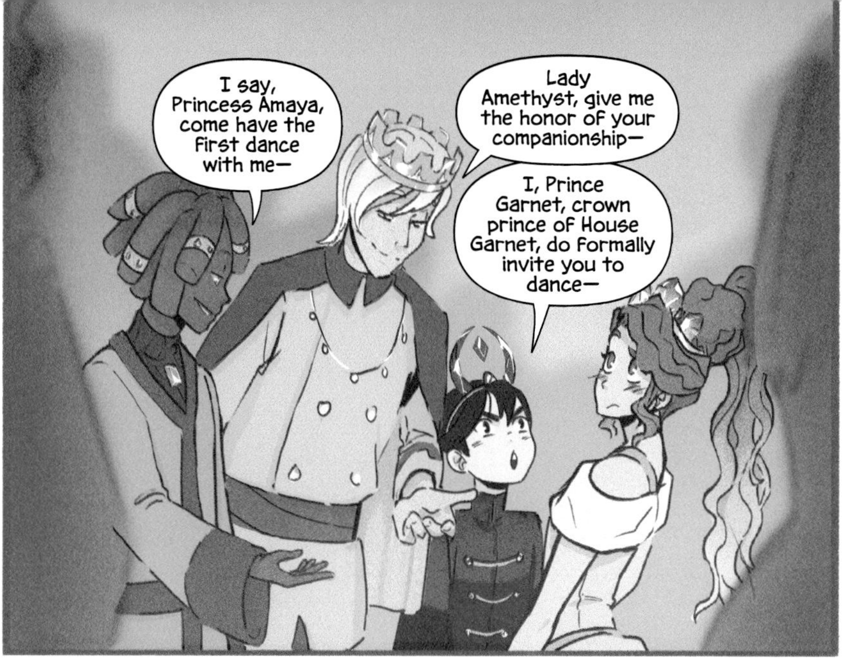
I say, Princess Amaya, come have the first dance with me—
Lady Amethyst, give me the honor of your companionship—
I, Prince Garnet, crown prince of House Garnet, do formally invite you to dance—

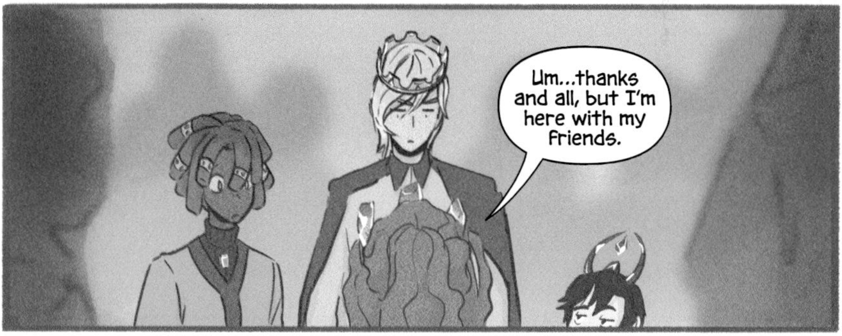
Um...thanks and all, but I'm here with my friends.

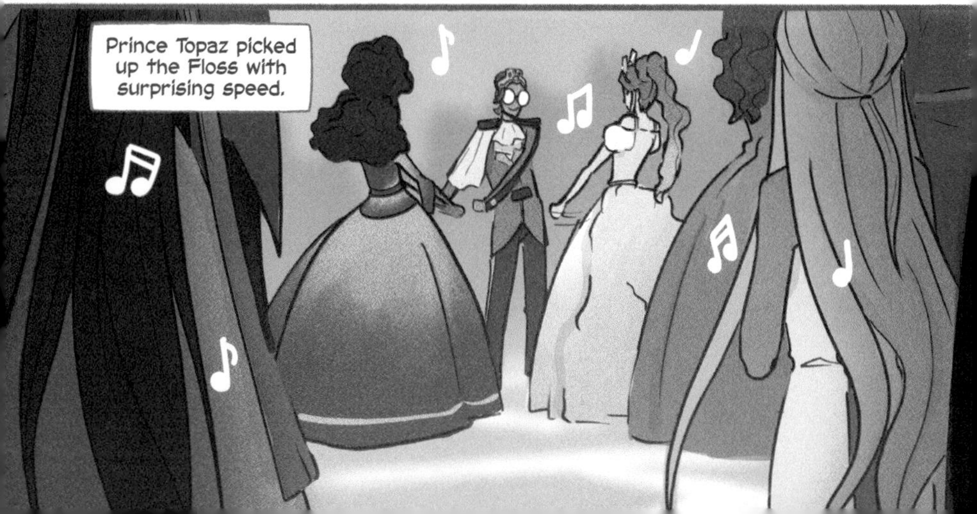
Prince Topaz picked up the Floss with surprising speed.

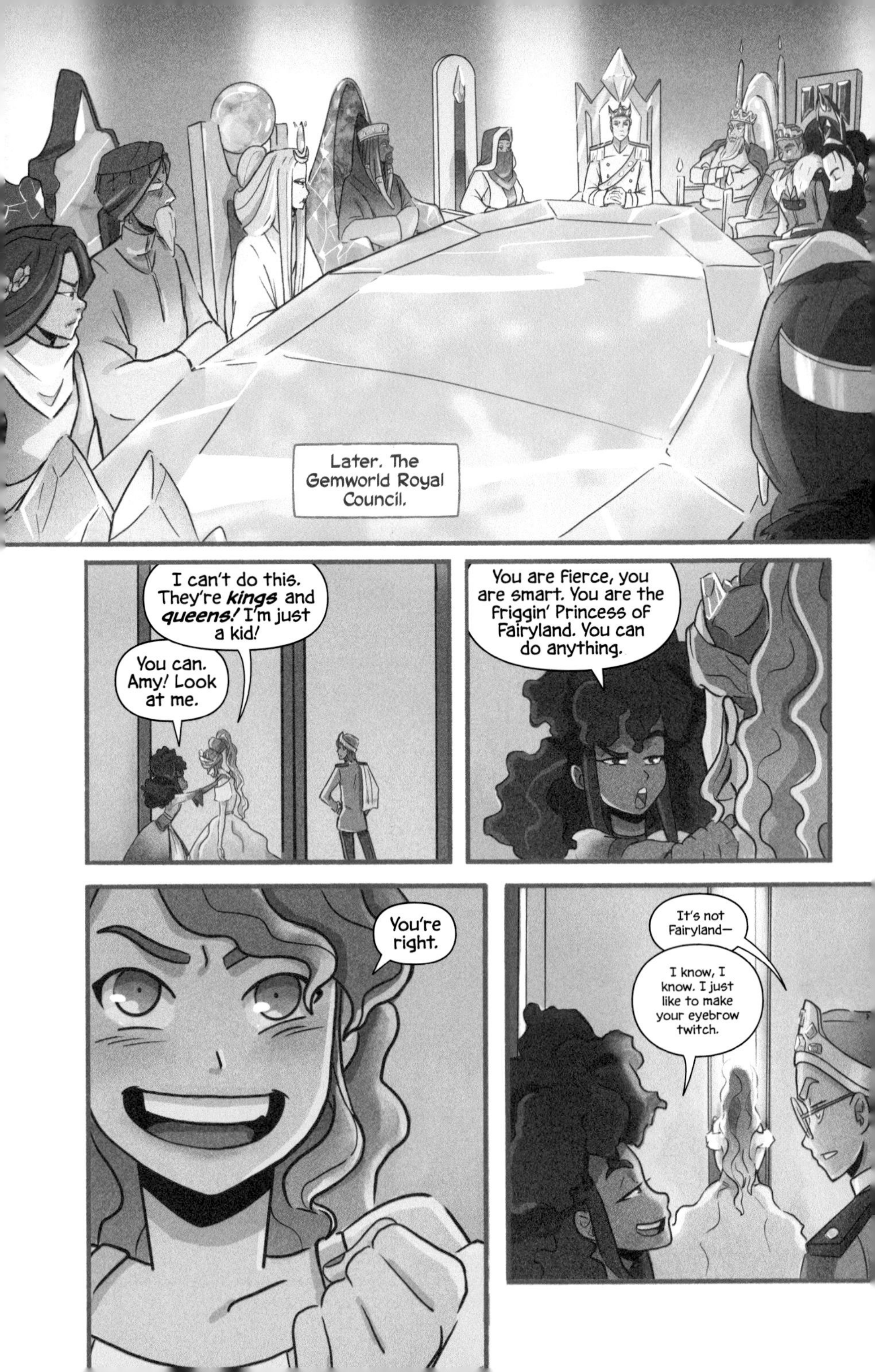

Later. The Gemworld Royal Council.
I can't do this. They're **kings** and **queens!** I'm just a kid!
You can. Amy! Look at me.
You are fierce, you are smart. You are the friggin' Princess of Fairyland. You can do anything.
You're right.
It's not Fairyland—
I know, I know. I just like to make your eyebrow twitch.

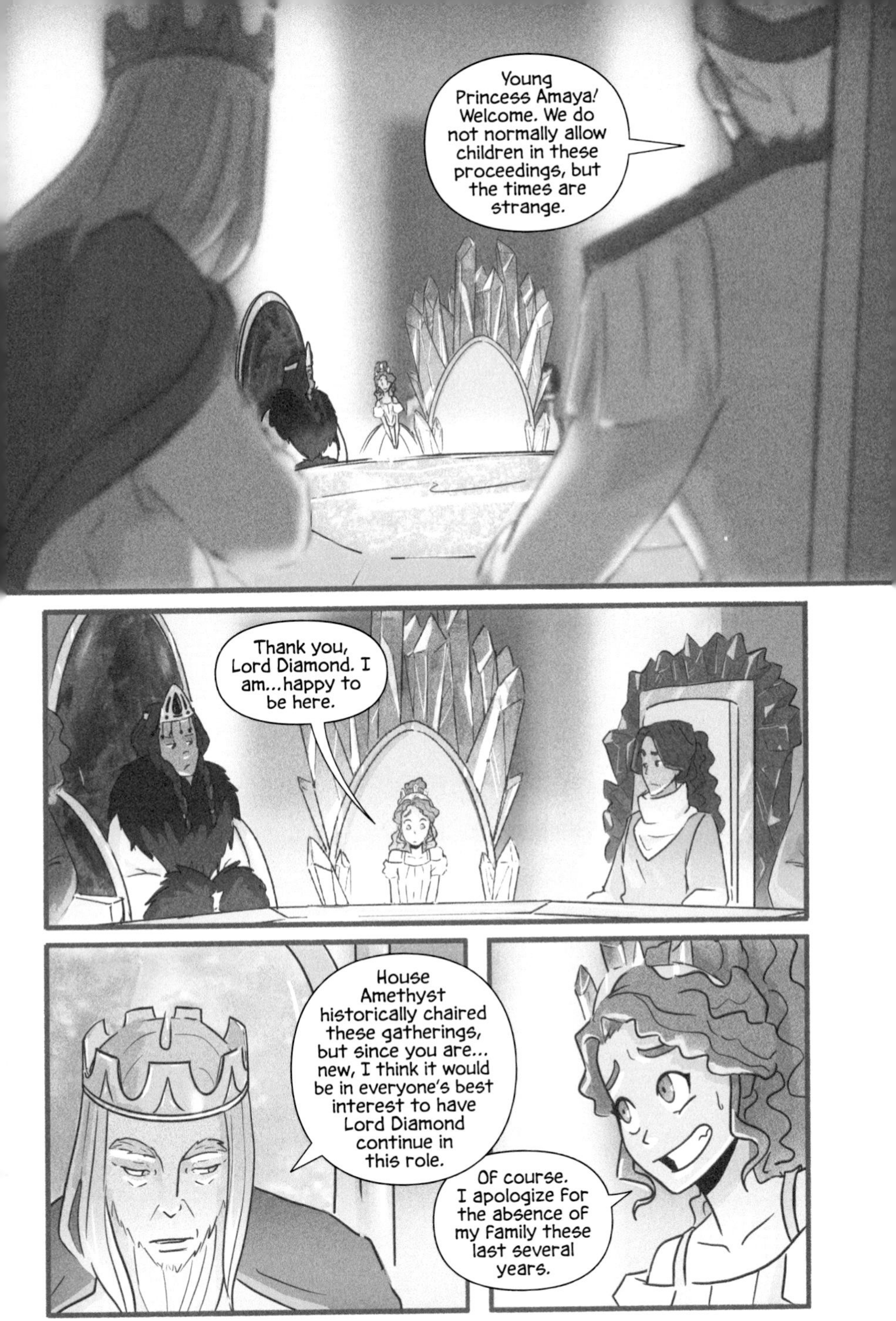
Young Princess Amaya! Welcome. We do not normally allow children in these proceedings, but the times are strange.
Thank you, Lord Diamond. I am...happy to be here.
House Amethyst historically chaired these gatherings, but since you are... new, I think it would be in everyone's best interest to have Lord Diamond continue in this role.
Of course. I apologize for the absence of my family these last several years.

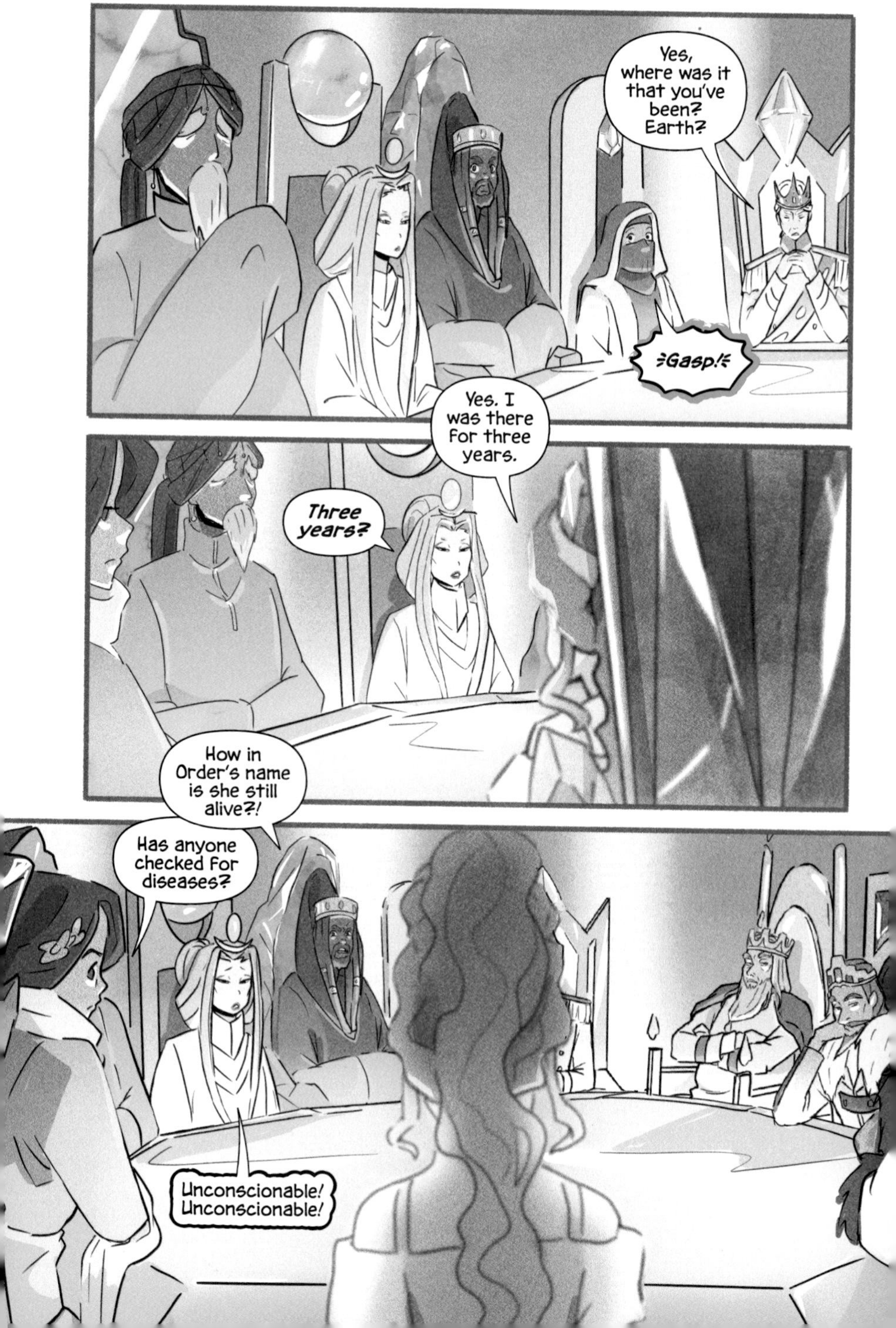

Yes, where was it that you've been? Earth?
Gasp!
Yes. I was there for three years.
Three years?
How in Order's name is she still alive?!
Has anyone checked for diseases?
Unconscionable! Unconscionable!

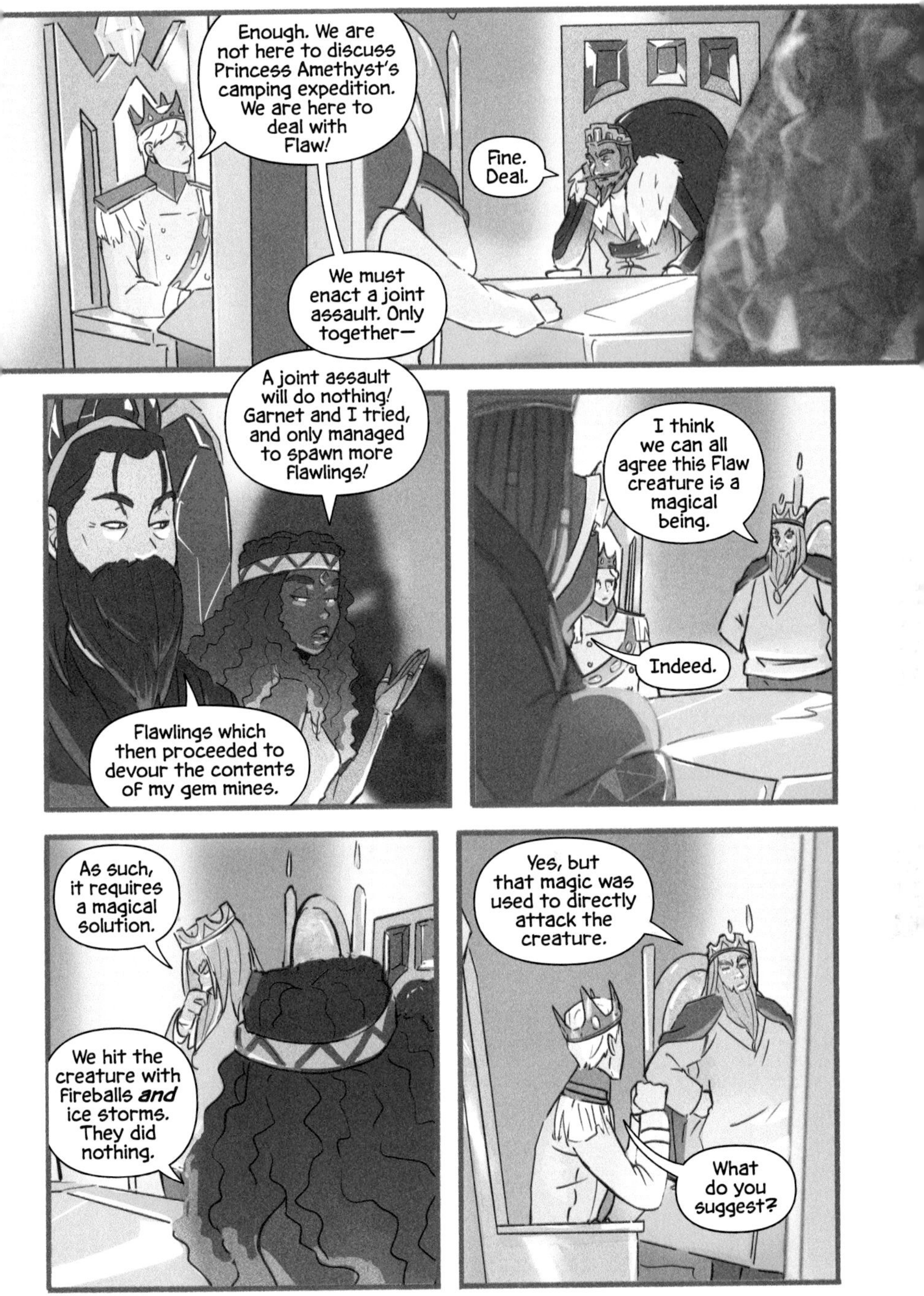
Enough. We are not here to discuss Princess Amethyst's camping expedition. We are here to deal with Flaw!
Fine. Deal.
We must enact a joint assault. Only together—
A joint assault will do nothing! Garnet and I tried, and only managed to spawn more Flawlings!
Flawlings which then proceeded to devour the contents of my gem mines.
I think we can all agree this Flaw creature is a magical being.
Indeed.
As such, it requires a magical solution.
We hit the creature with fireballs ***and*** ice storms. They did nothing.
Yes, but that magic was used to directly attack the creature.
What do you suggest?

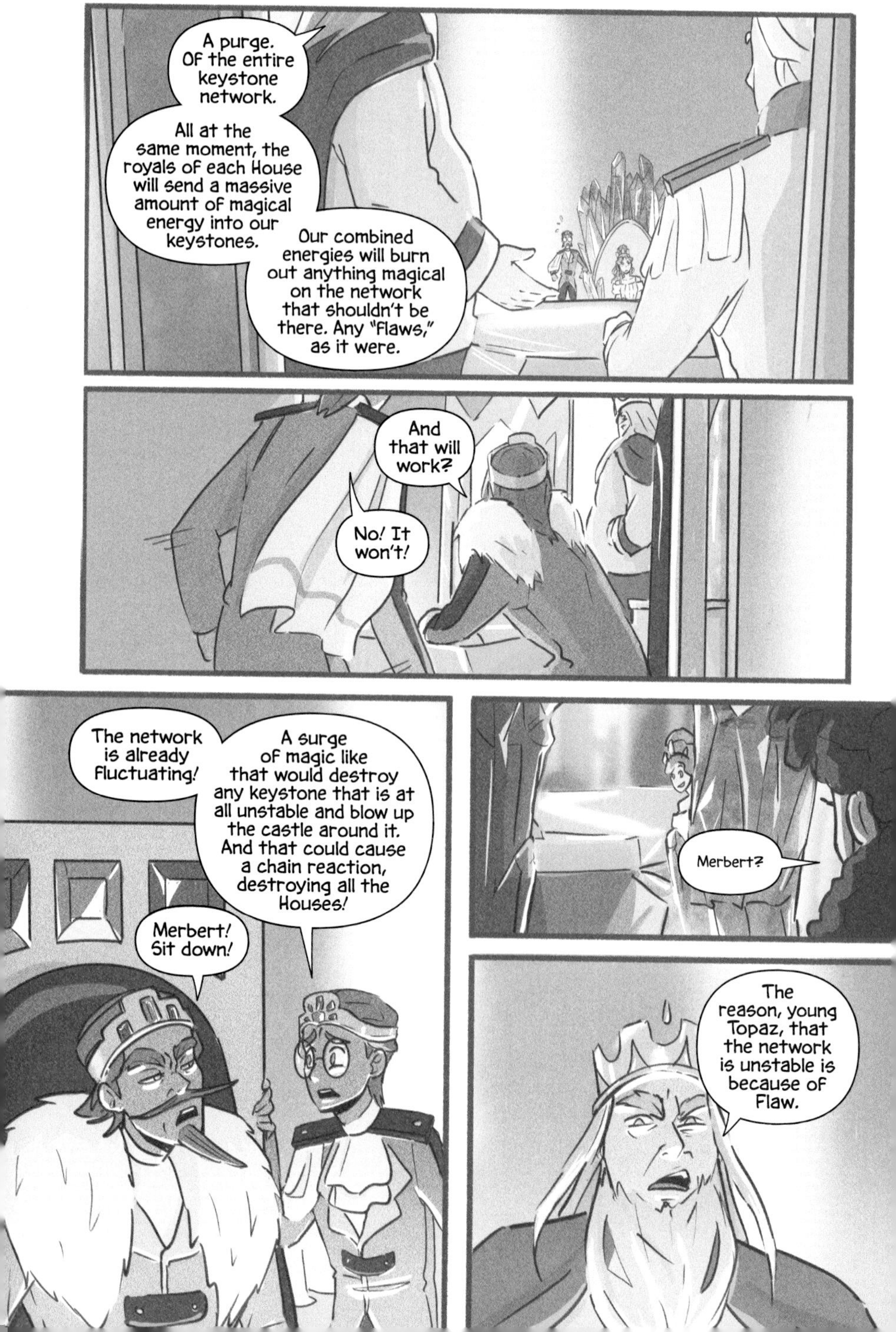
A purge. Of the entire keystone network.
All at the same moment, the royals of each House will send a massive amount of magical energy into our keystones.
Our combined energies will burn out anything magical on the network that shouldn't be there. Any "Flaws," as it were.
And that will work?
No! It won't!
The network is already fluctuating!
A surge of magic like that would destroy any keystone that is at all unstable and blow up the castle around it. And that could cause a chain reaction, destroying all the Houses!
Merbert! Sit down!
Merbert?
The reason, young Topaz, that the network is unstable is because of Flaw.

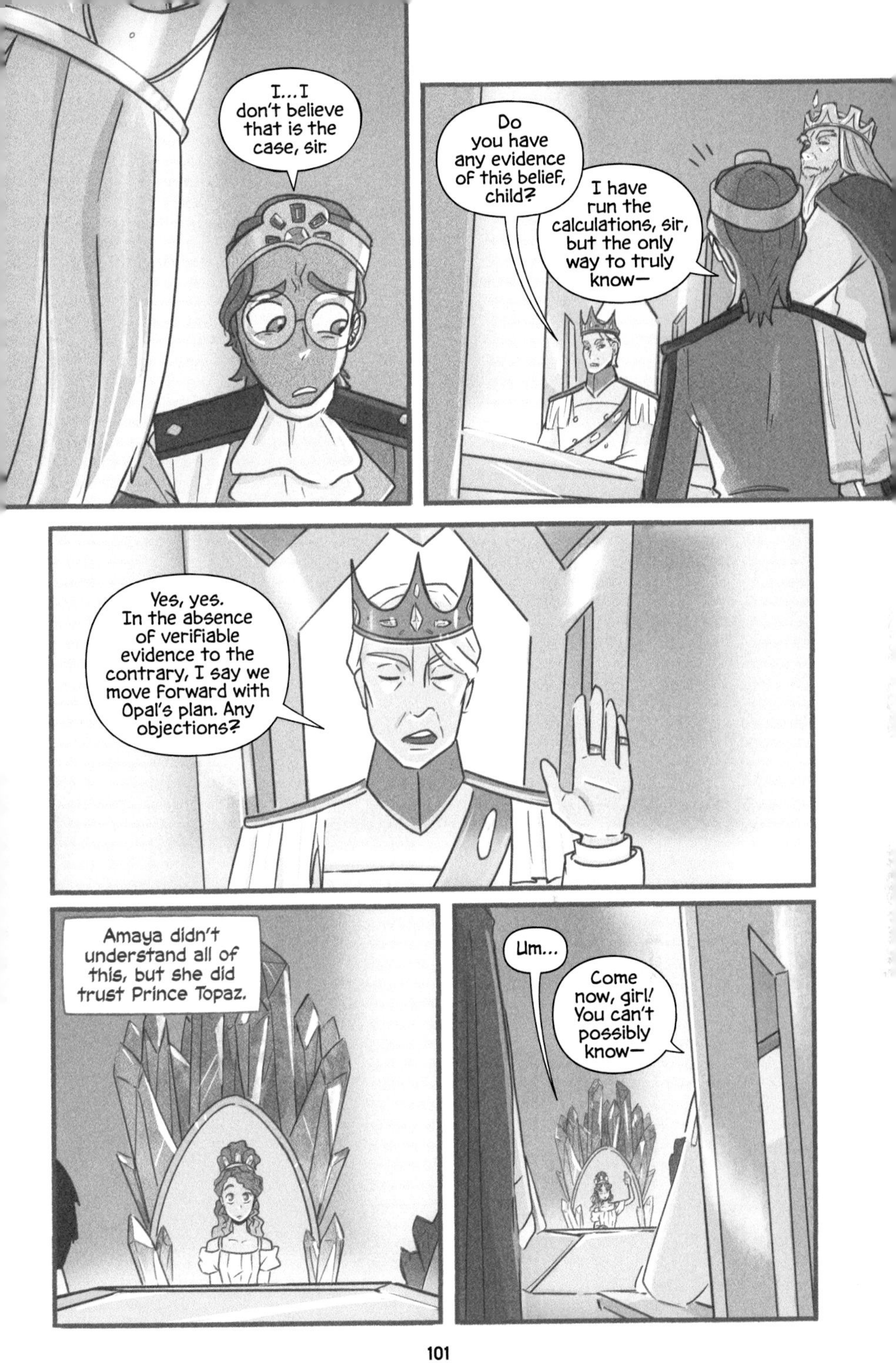
I...I don't believe that is the case, sir.
Do you have any evidence of this belief, child?
I have run the calculations, sir, but the only way to truly know—
Yes, yes. In the absence of verifiable evidence to the contrary, I say we move forward with Opal's plan. Any objections?
Amaya didn't understand all of this, but she did trust Prince Topaz.
Um...
Come now, girl! You can't possibly know—

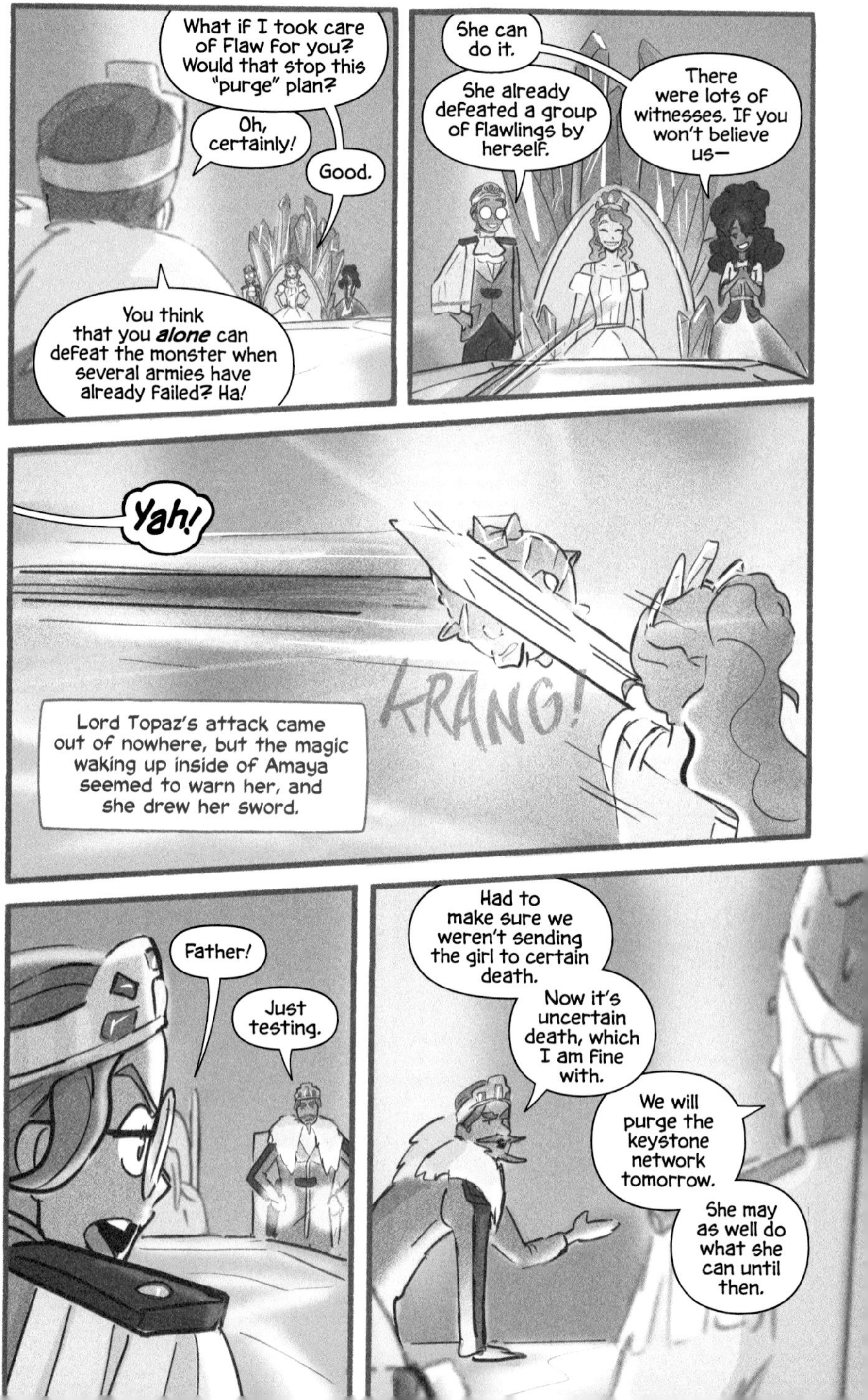
What if I took care of Flaw for you? Would that stop this "purge" plan?
Oh, certainly!
Good.
You think that you *alone* can defeat the monster when several armies have already failed? Ha!
She can do it.
She already defeated a group of flawlings by herself.
There were lots of witnesses. If you won't believe us—
Yah!
KRANG!
Lord Topaz's attack came out of nowhere, but the magic waking up inside of Amaya seemed to warn her, and she drew her sword.
Father!
Just testing.
Had to make sure we weren't sending the girl to certain death.
Now it's uncertain death, which I am fine with.
We will purge the keystone network tomorrow.
She may as well do what she can until then.

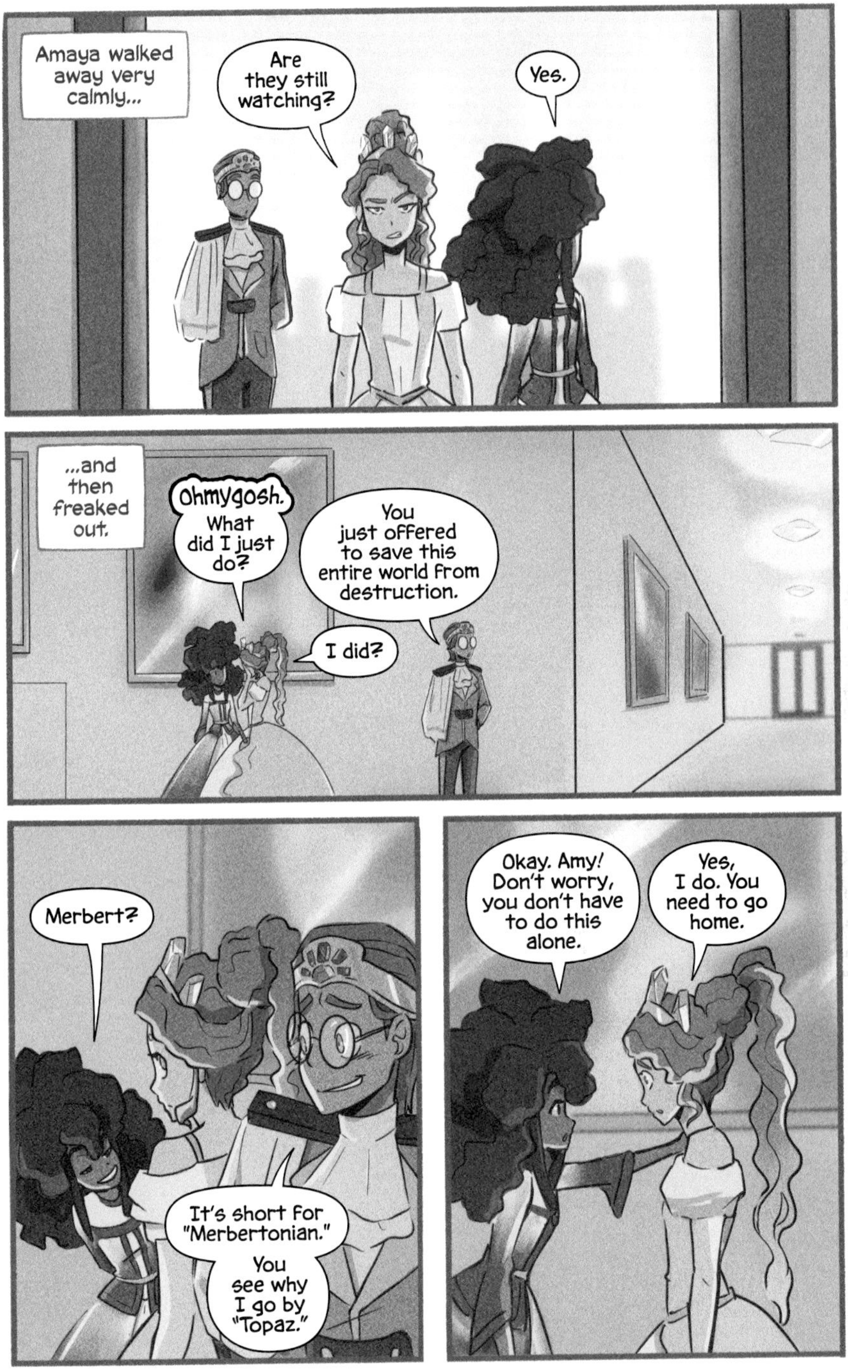
Amaya walked away very calmly...
Are they still watching?
Yes.
...and then freaked out.
Ohmygosh. What did I just do?
You just offered to save this entire world from destruction.
I did?
Merbert?
It's short for "Merbertonian."
You see why I go by "Topaz."
Okay. Amy! Don't worry, you don't have to do this alone.
Yes, I do. You need to go home.

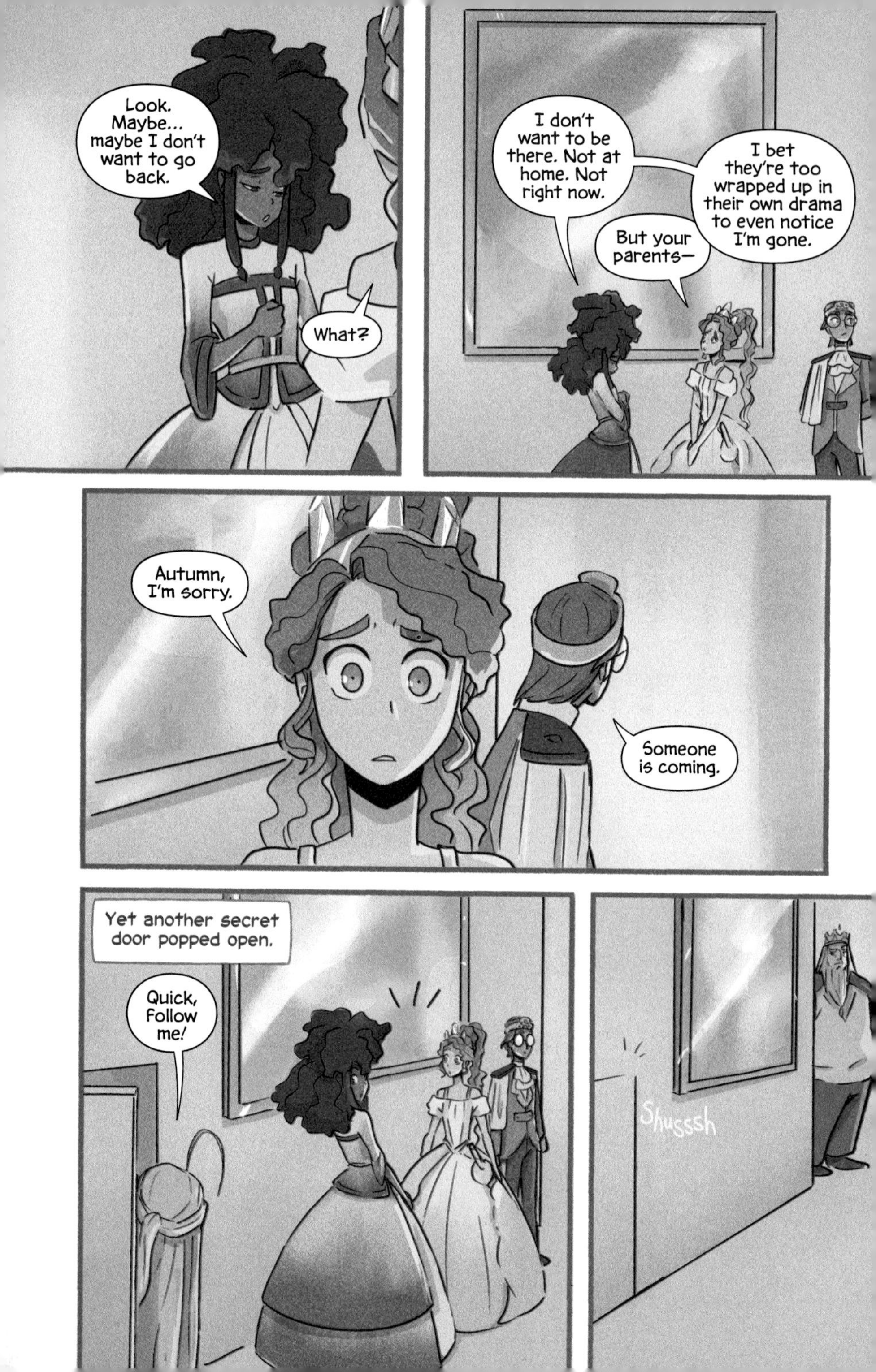
Look. Maybe... maybe I don't want to go back.
What?
I don't want to be there. Not at home. Not right now.
I bet they're too wrapped up in their own drama to even notice I'm gone.
But your parents—
Autumn, I'm sorry.
Someone is coming.
Yet another secret door popped open.
Quick, follow me!
Shusssh

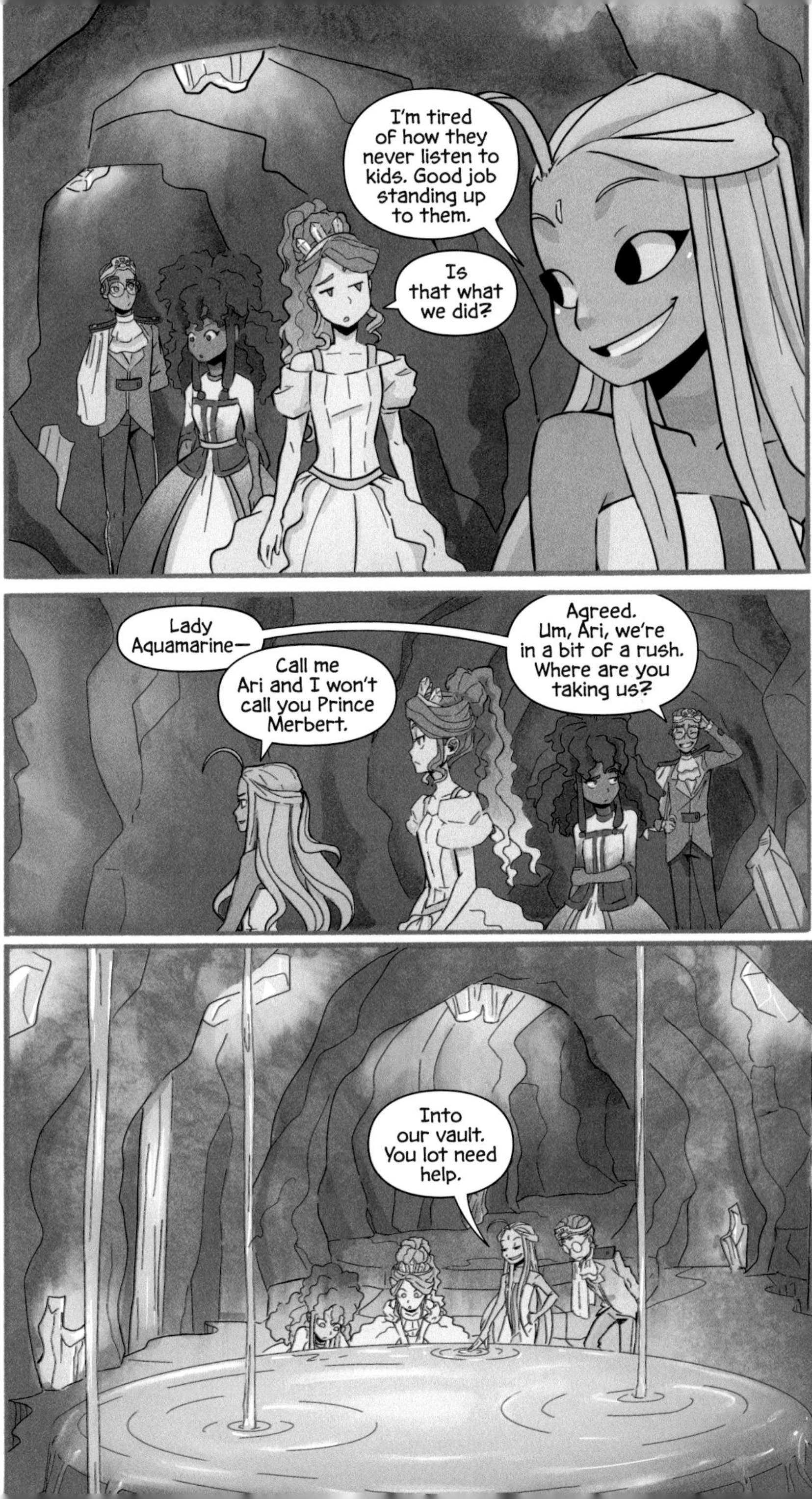
I'm tired of how they never listen to kids. Good job standing up to them.
Is that what we did?
Lady Aquamarine—
Agreed. Um, Ari, we're in a bit of a rush. Where are you taking us?
Call me Ari and I won't call you Prince Merbert.
Into our vault. You lot need help.

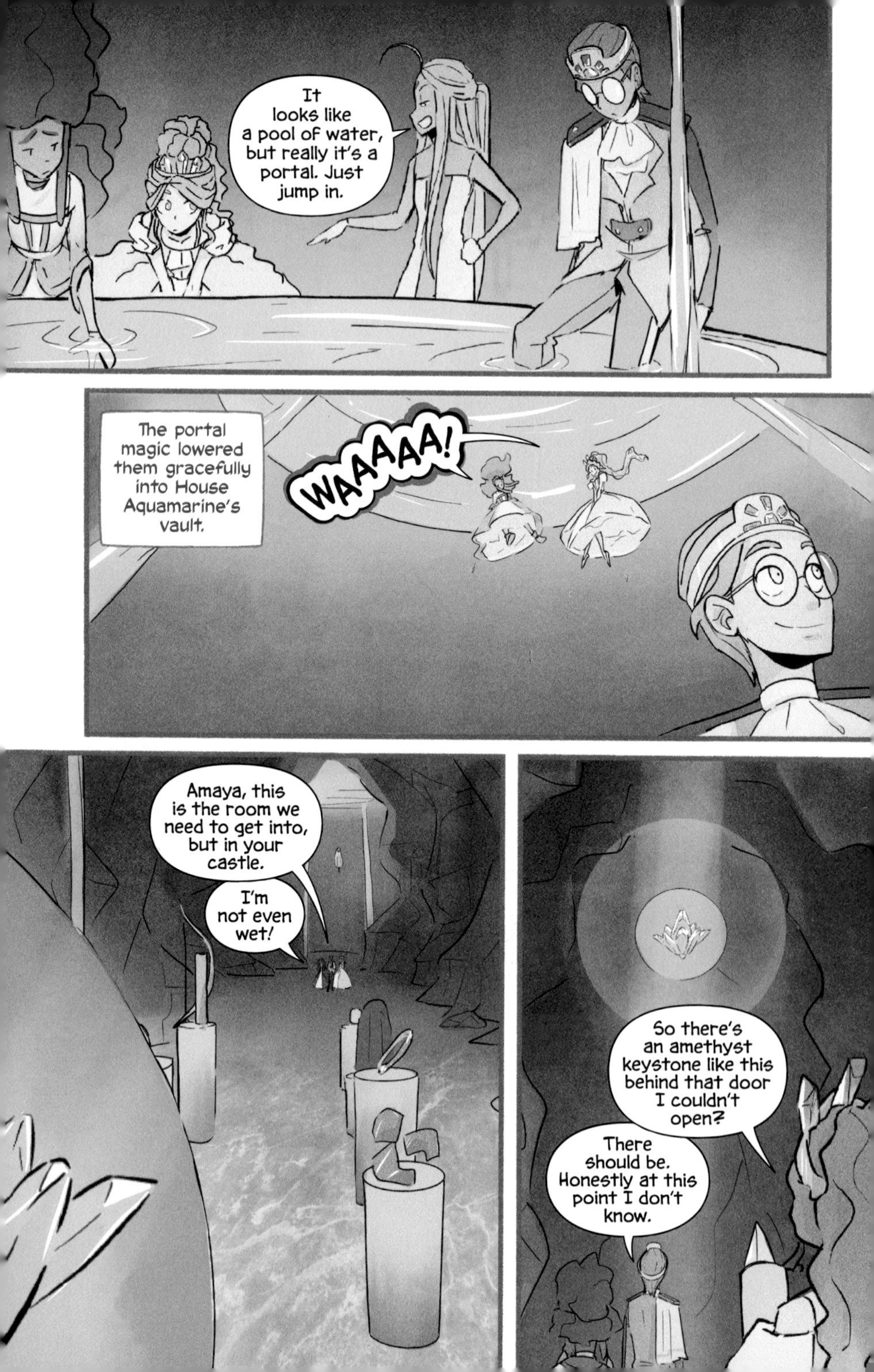
It looks like a pool of water, but really it's a portal. Just jump in.
The portal magic lowered them gracefully into House Aquamarine's vault.
WAAAAA!
Amaya, this is the room we need to get into, but in your castle.
I'm not even wet!
So there's an amethyst keystone like this behind that door I couldn't open?
There should be. Honestly at this point I don't know.

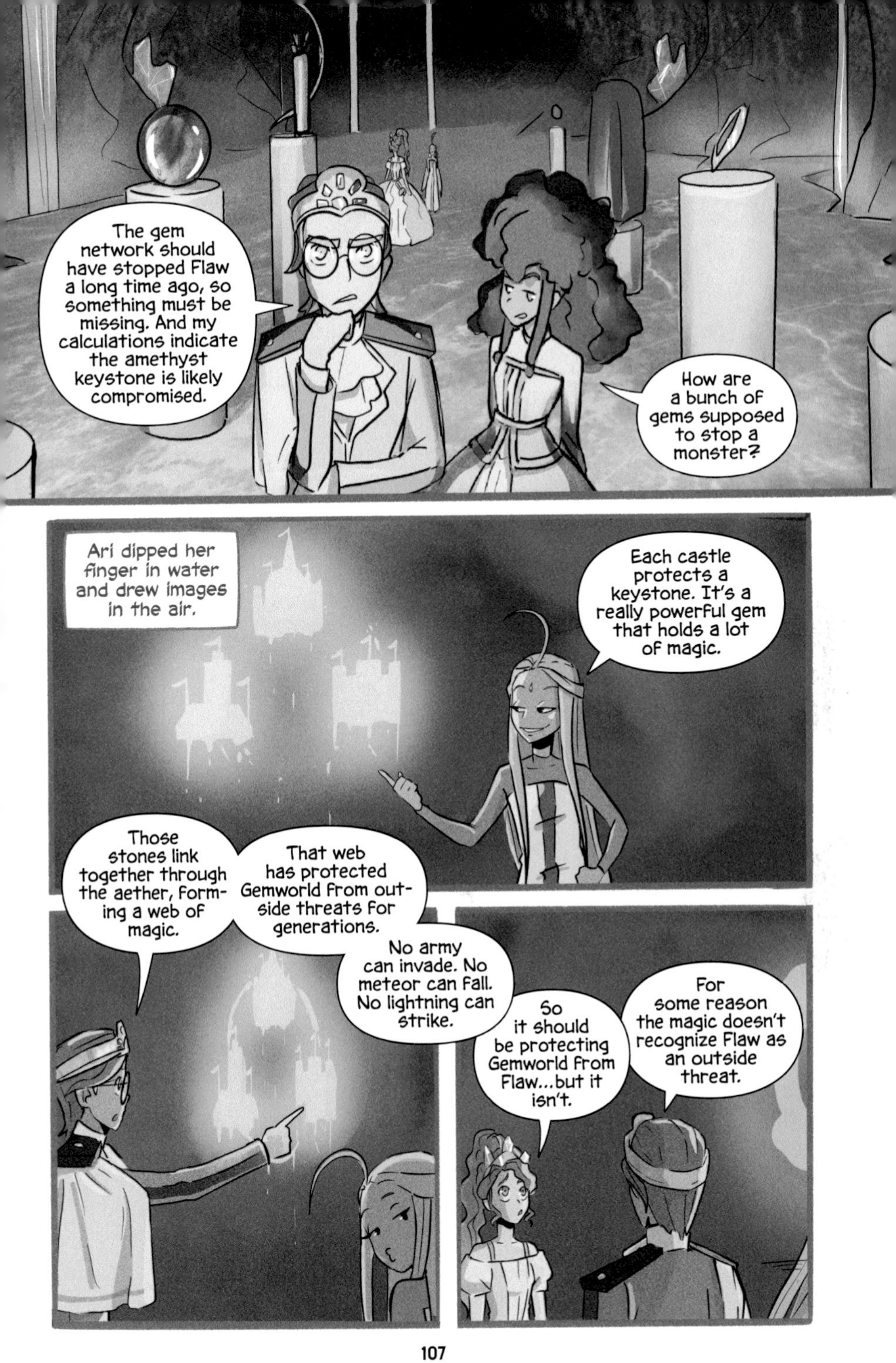

The gem network should have stopped Flaw a long time ago, so something must be missing. And my calculations indicate the amethyst keystone is likely compromised.
How are a bunch of gems supposed to stop a monster?
Ari dipped her finger in water and drew images in the air.
Each castle protects a keystone. It's a really powerful gem that holds a lot of magic.
Those stones link together through the aether, forming a web of magic.
That web has protected Gemworld from outside threats for generations.
No army can invade. No meteor can fall. No lightning can strike.
So it should be protecting Gemworld from Flaw...but it isn't.
For some reason the magic doesn't recognize Flaw as an outside threat.

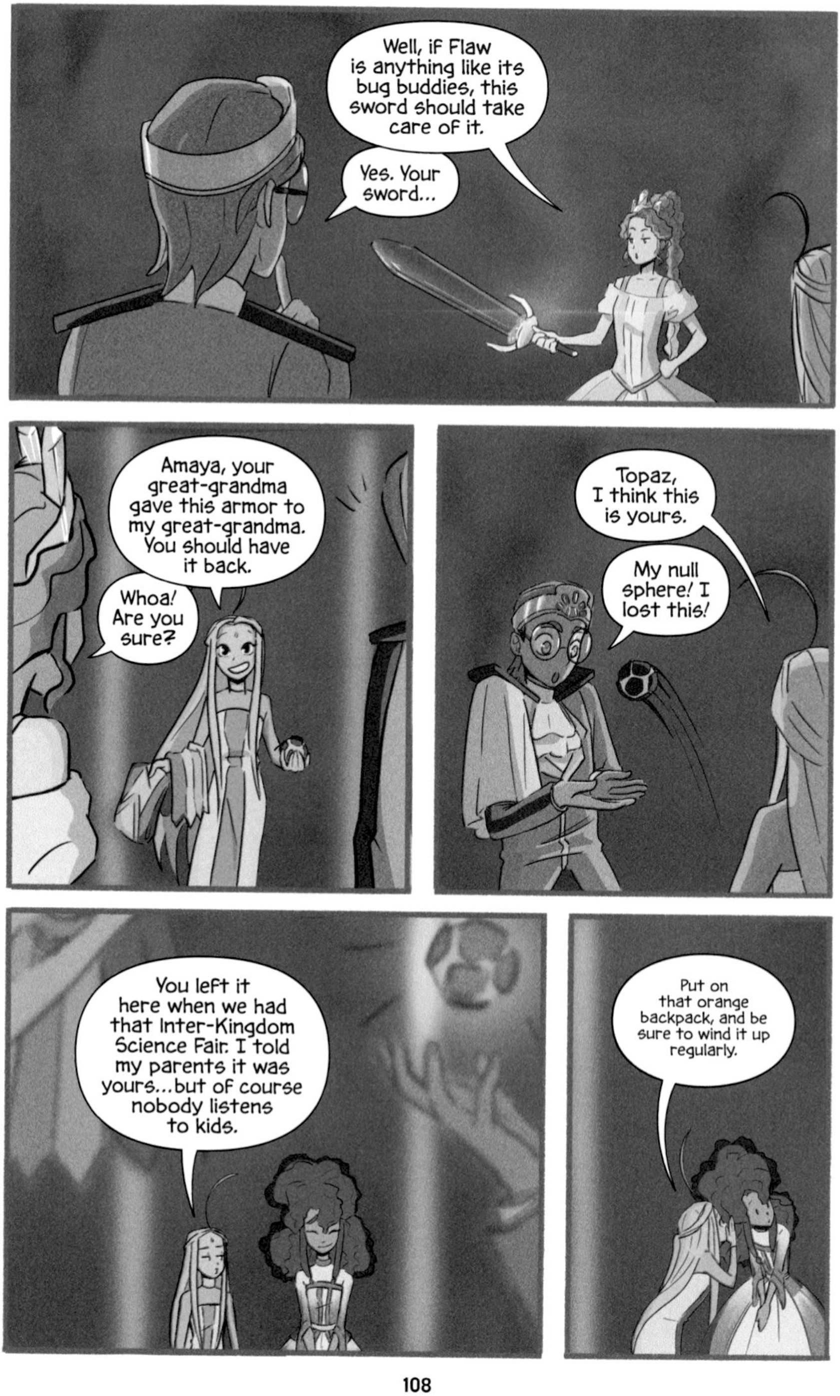

Well, if Flaw is anything like its bug buddies, this sword should take care of it.
Yes. Your sword...
Amaya, your great-grandma gave this armor to my great-grandma. You should have it back.
Whoa! Are you sure?
Topaz, I think this is yours.
My null sphere! I lost this!
You left it here when we had that Inter-Kingdom Science Fair. I told my parents it was yours...but of course nobody listens to kids.
Put on that orange backpack, and be sure to wind it up regularly.

chapter seven

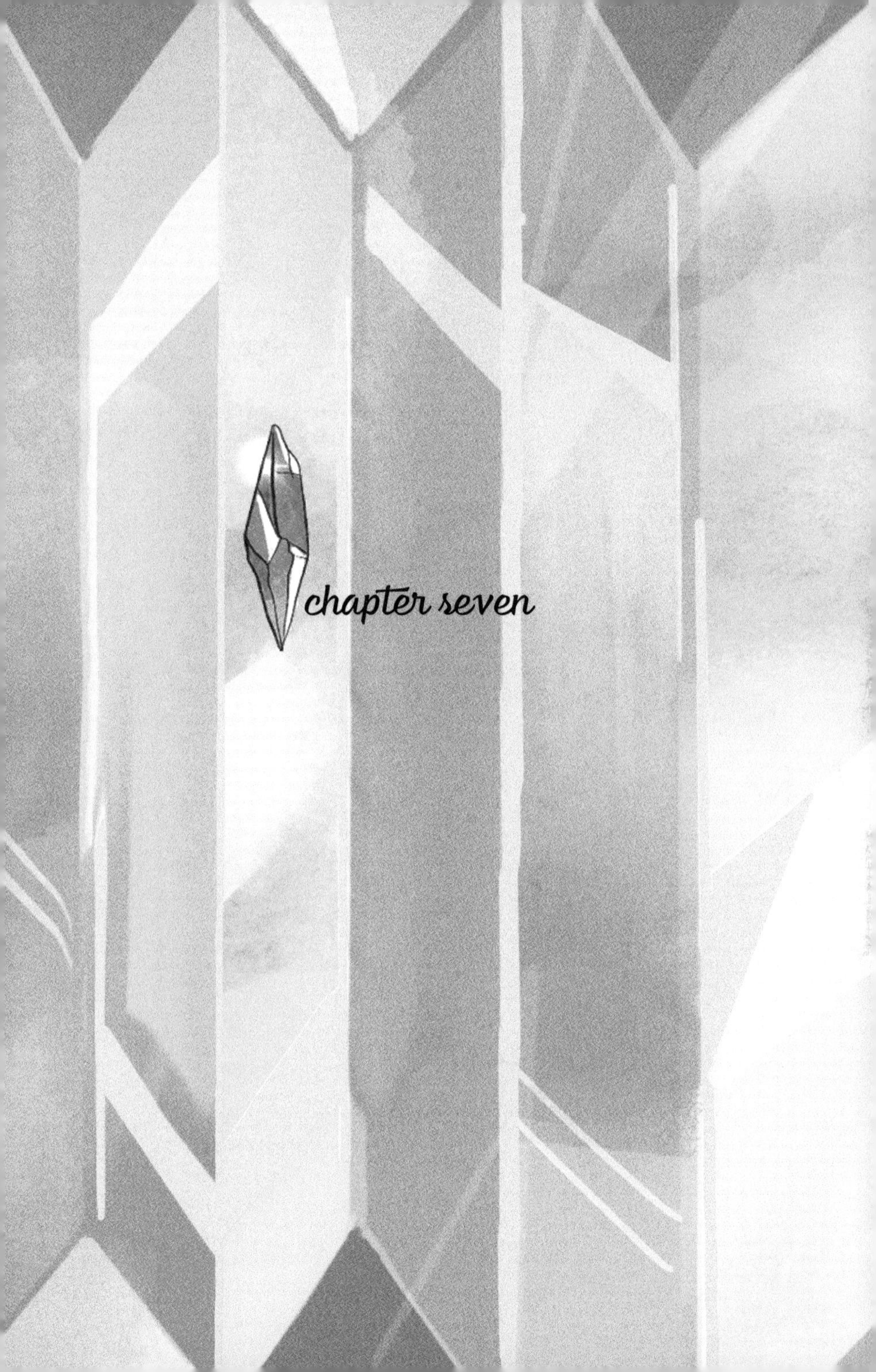

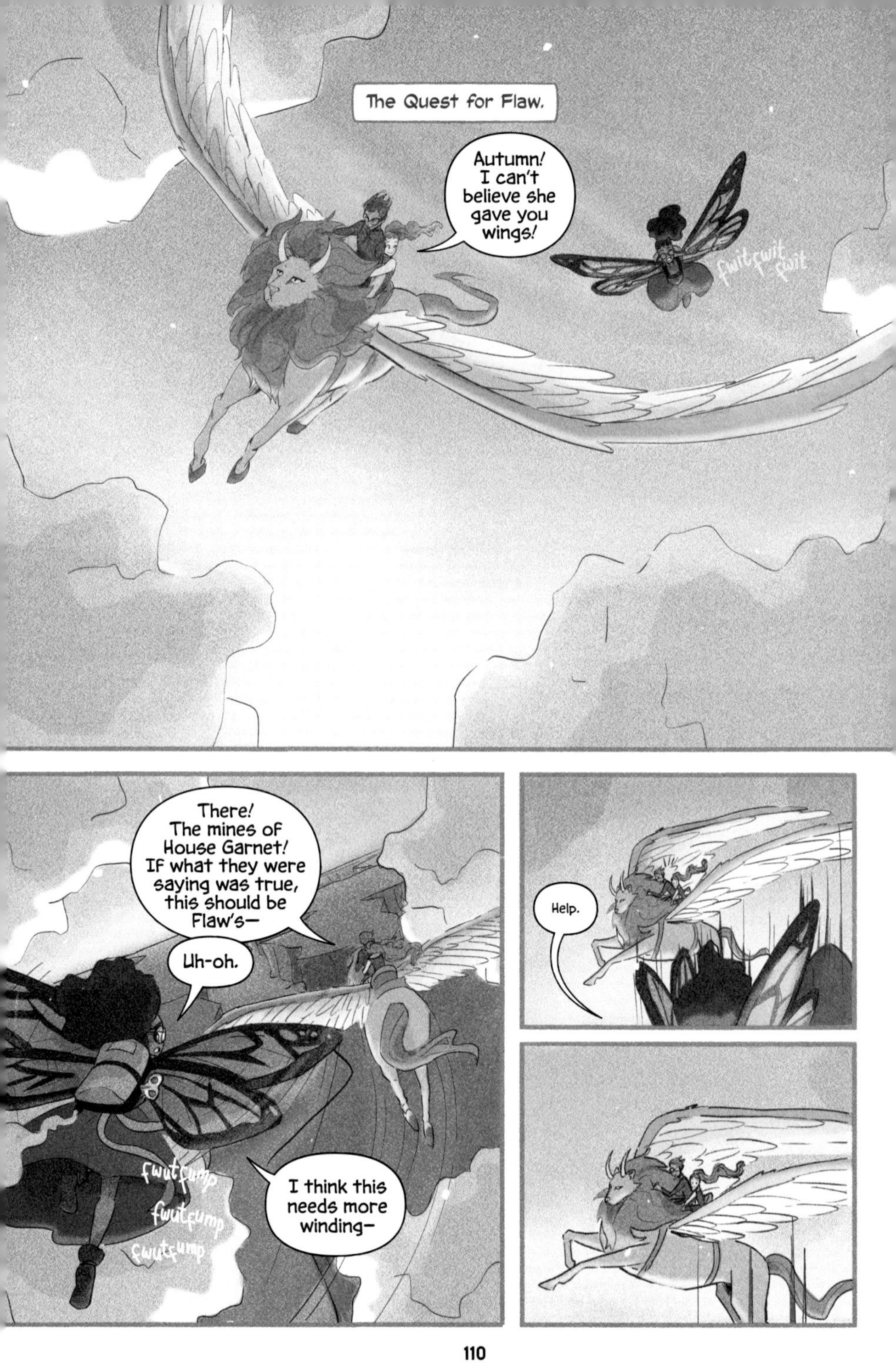
The Quest for Flaw.
Autumn! I can't believe she gave you wings!
fwit fwit fwit
There! The mines of House Garnet! If what they were saying was true, this should be Flaw's—
Uh-oh.
I think this needs more winding–
fwutfump fwutfump fwutfump
Help.

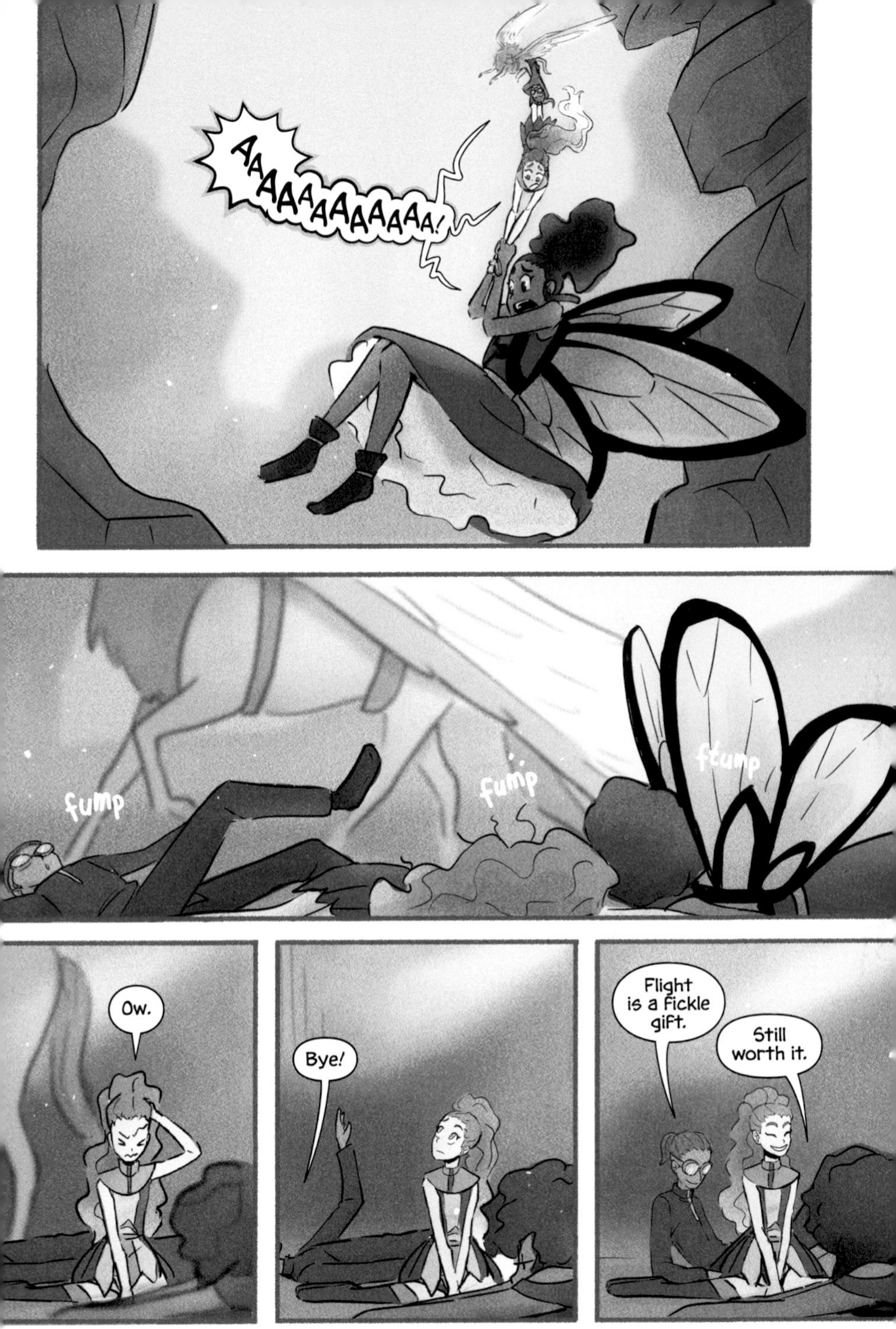
AAAAAAAAAAAA!
fump
fump
ftump
Ow.
Bye!
Flight is a fickle gift.
Still worth it.

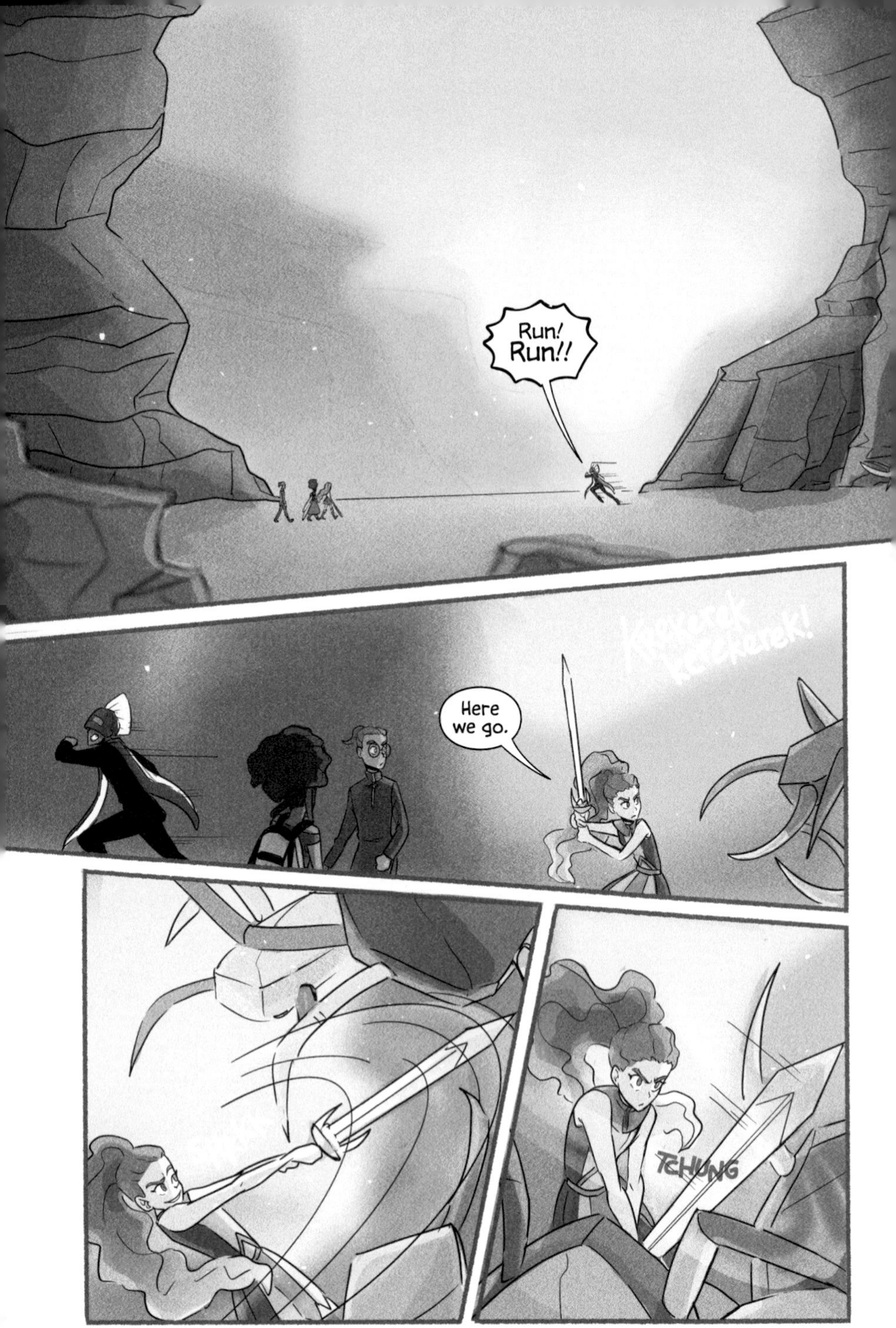
Run! Run!!
Here we go.
TCHUNG

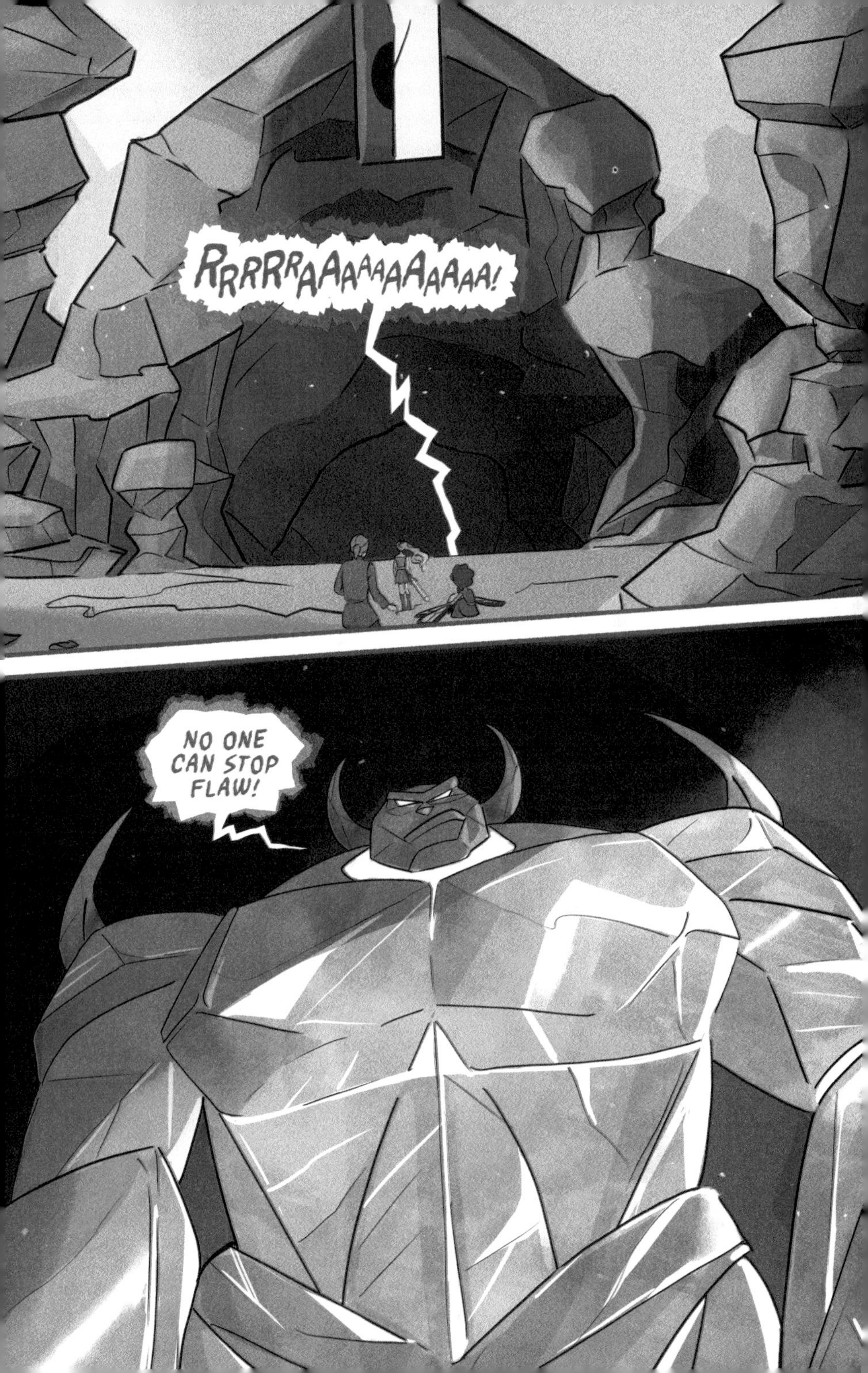
RRRRRAAAAAAAAAA!
NO ONE CAN STOP FLAW!

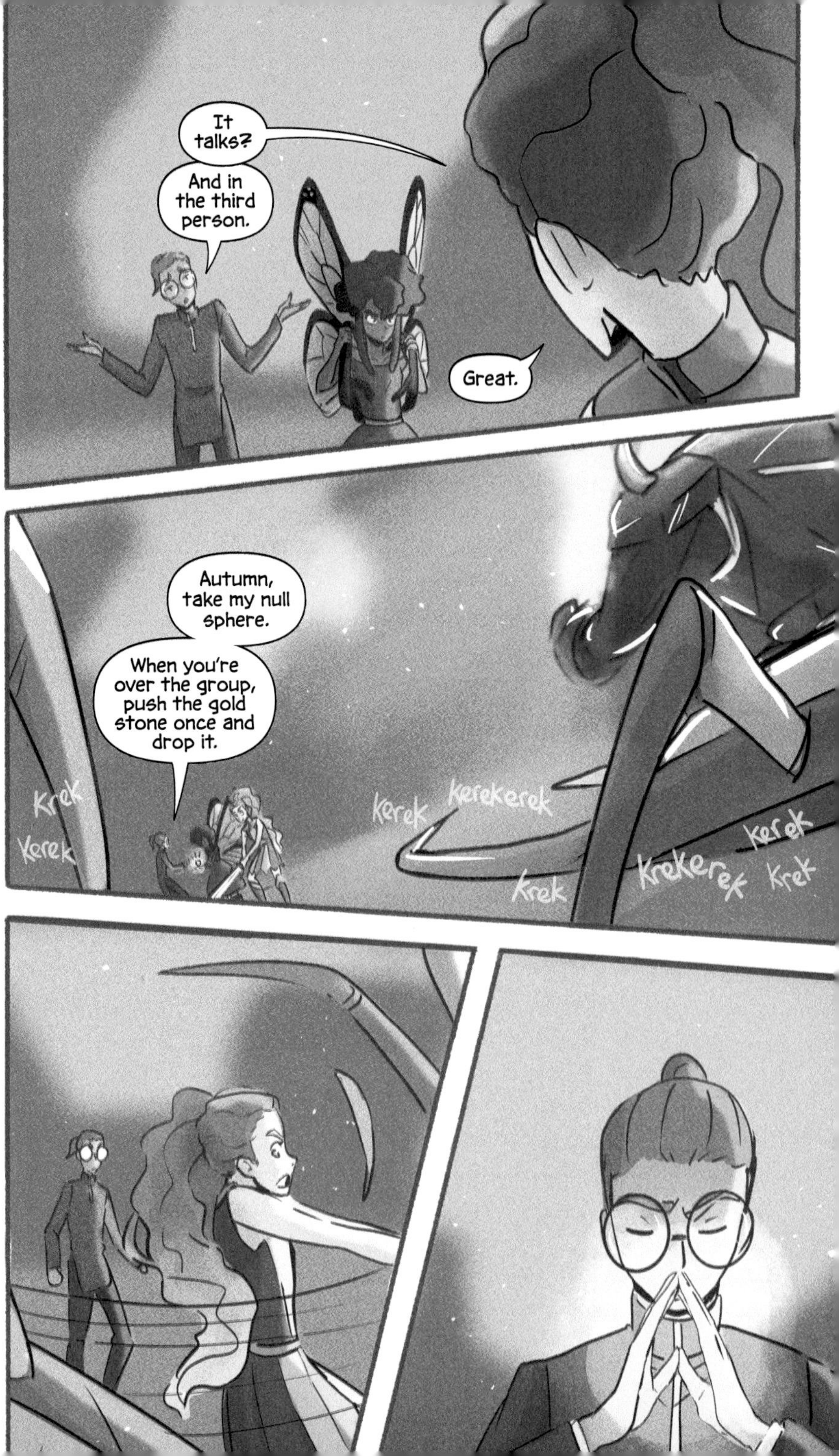
It talks?
And in the third person.
Great.
Autumn, take my null sphere.
When you're over the group, push the gold stone once and drop it.
Krek
Kerek
Kerek
Kerekerek
Kerek
Krekerek
Krek
Krek

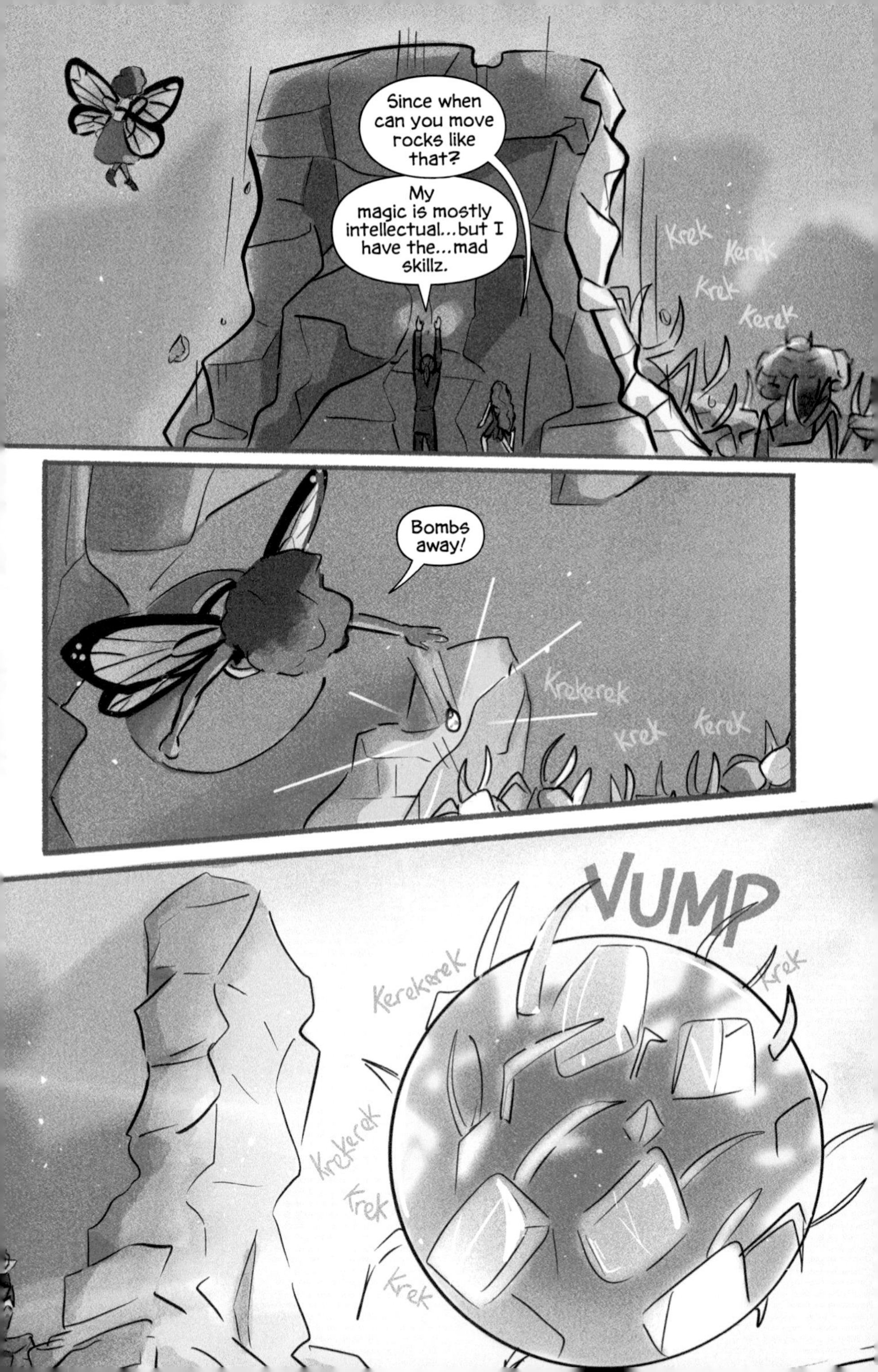
Since when can you move rocks like that?
My magic is mostly intellectual...but I have the...mad skillz.
Krek
Kerek
Krek
Kerek
Bombs away!
Krekerek
Krek
Kerek
VUMP
Kerekerek
Krek
Krekerek
Krek
Krek

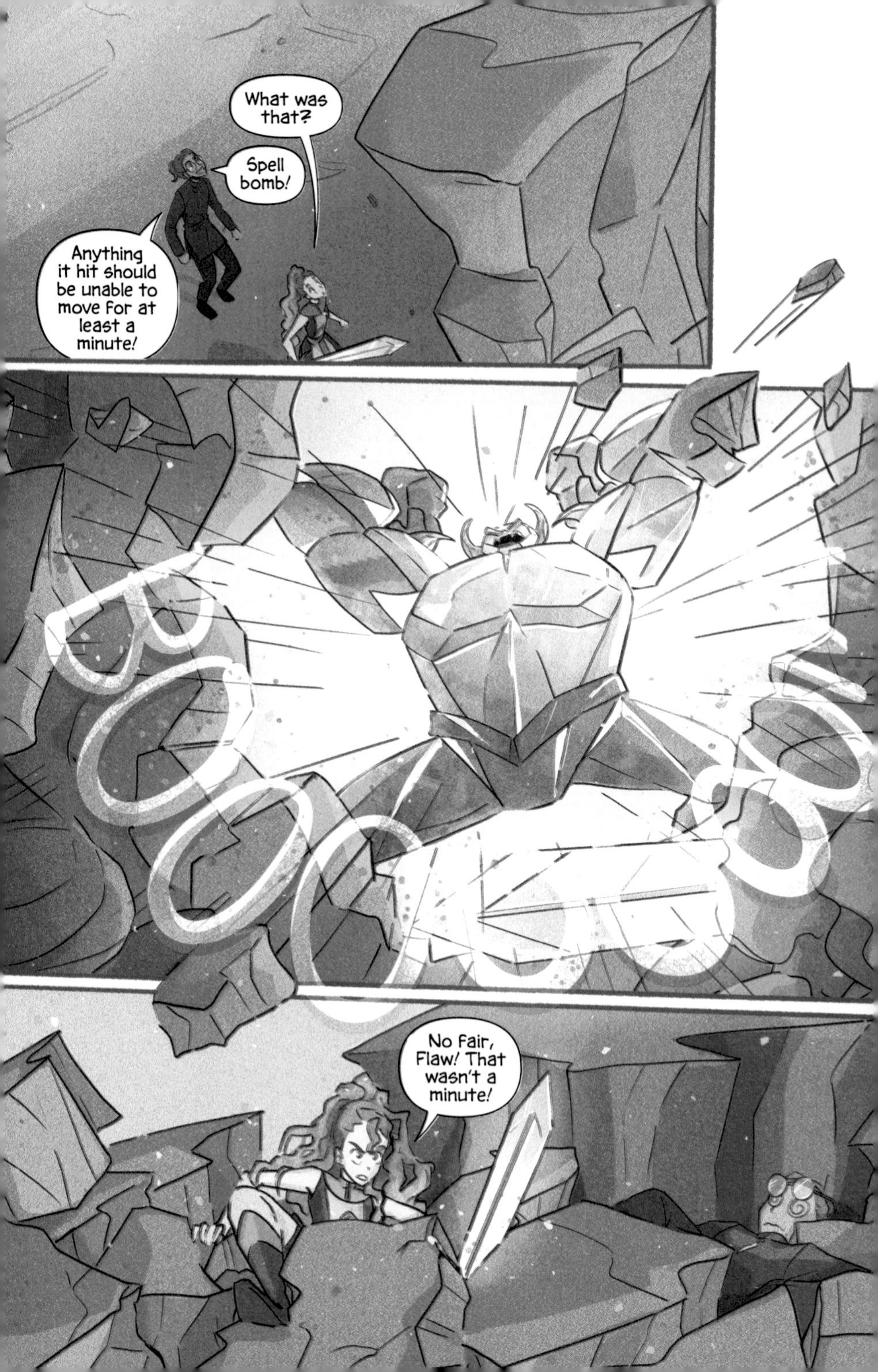
What was that?
Spell bomb!
Anything it hit should be unable to move for at least a minute!
BOOOOOM
No fair, Flaw! That wasn't a minute!

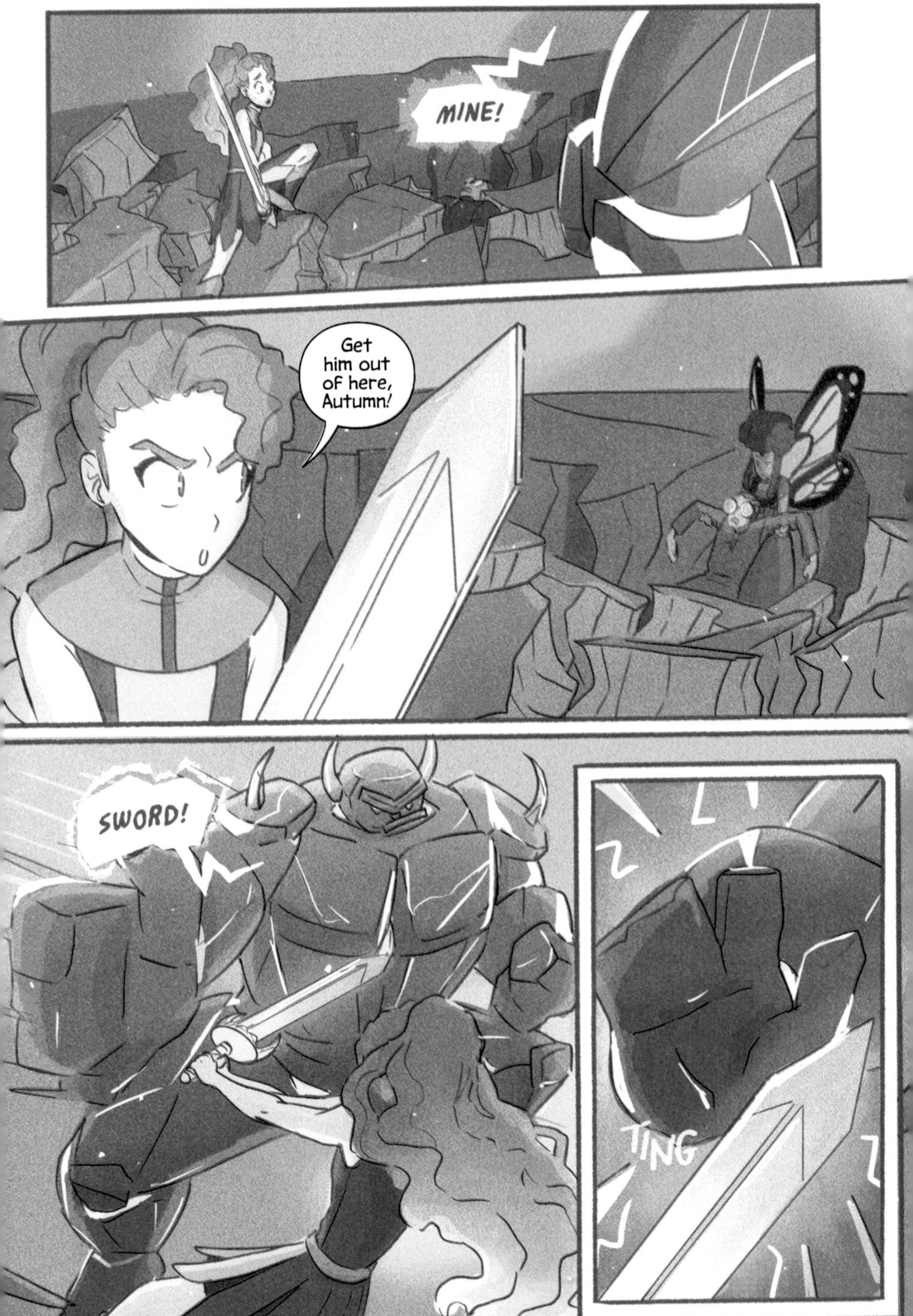
MINE!
Get him out of here, Autumn!
SWORD!
TING

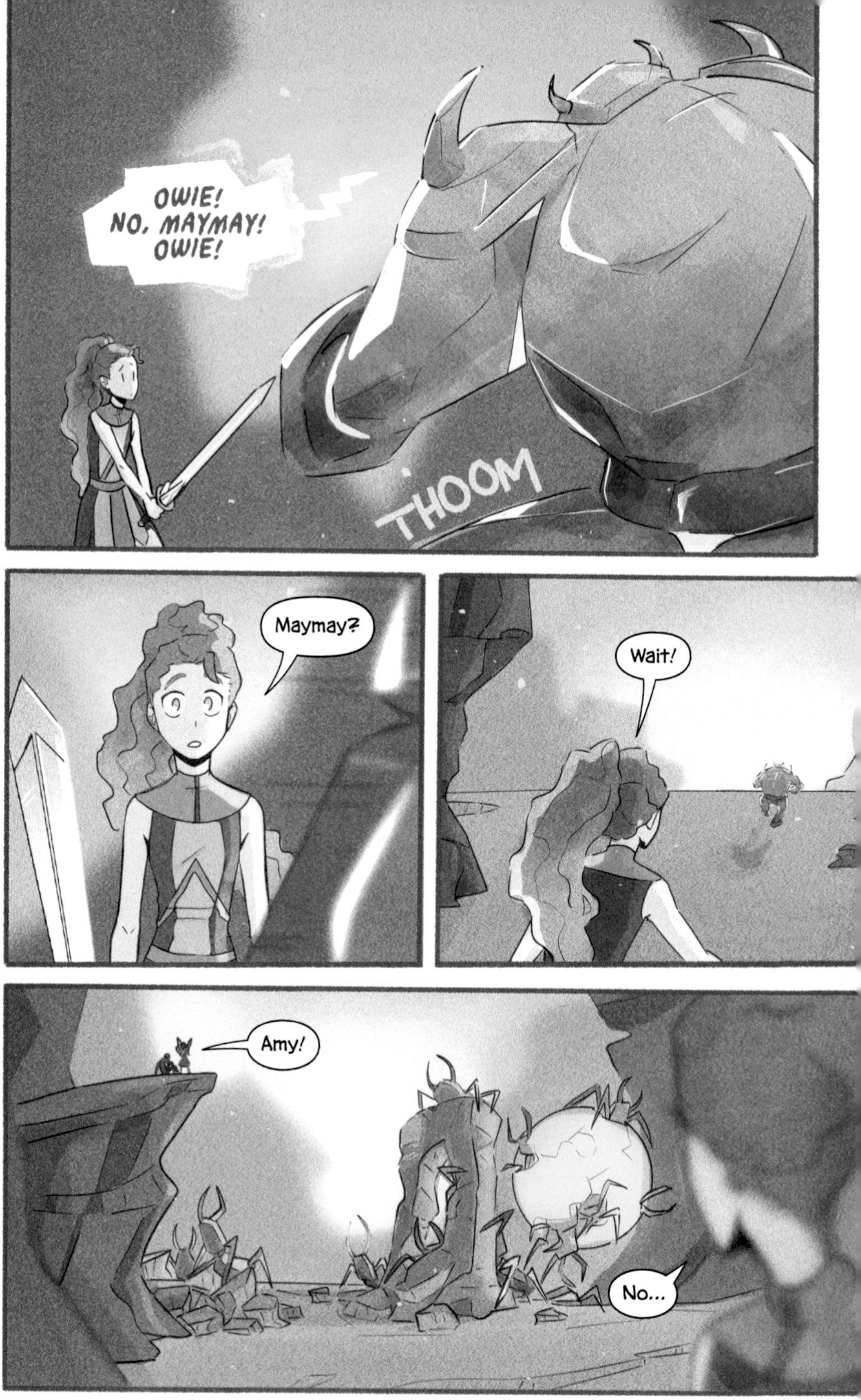
OWIE!
NO, MAYMAY!
OWIE!
THOOM
Maymay?
Wait!
Amy!
No...

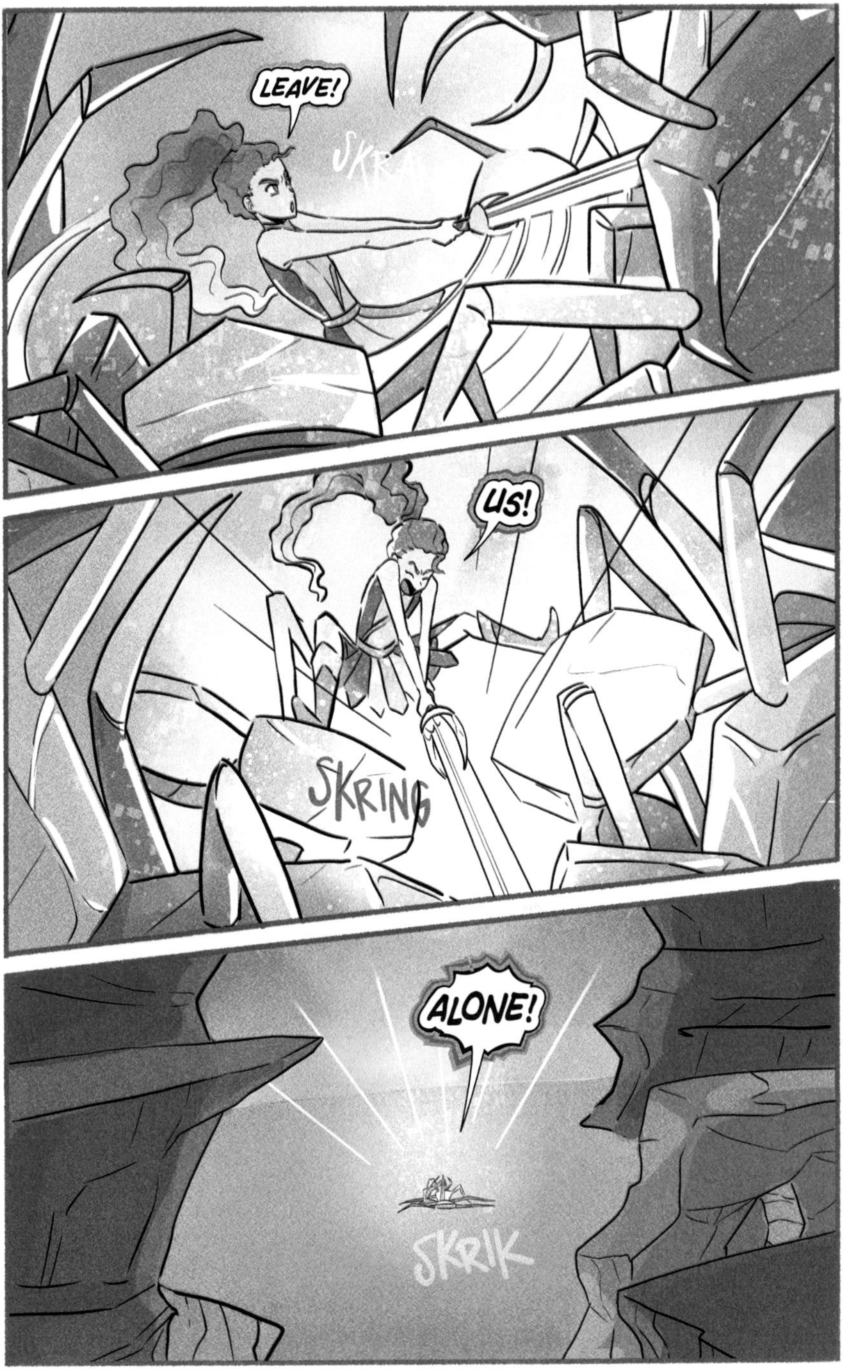
LEAVE!
SKRA
US!
SKRING
ALONE!
SKRIK

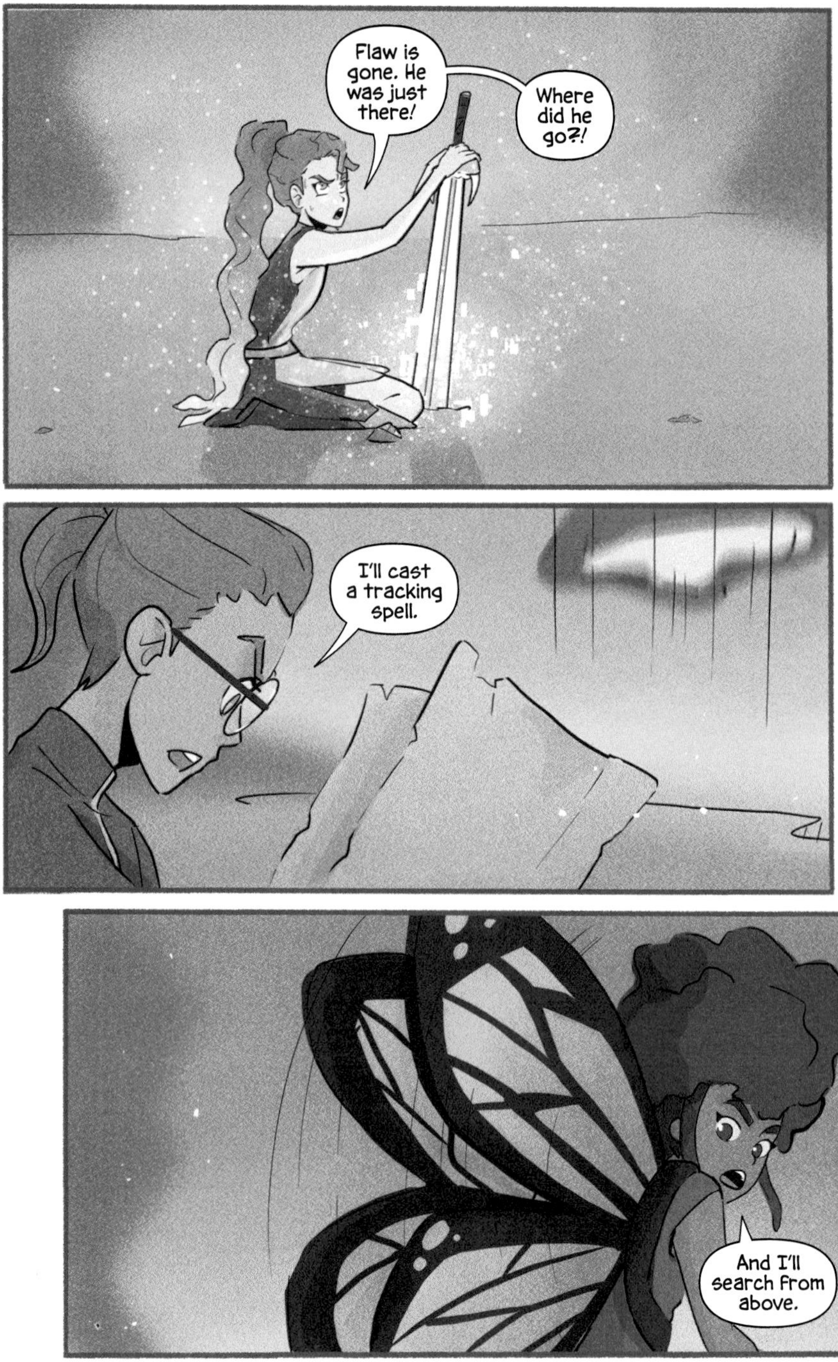
Flaw is gone. He was just there!
Where did he go?!
I'll cast a tracking spell.
And I'll search from above.

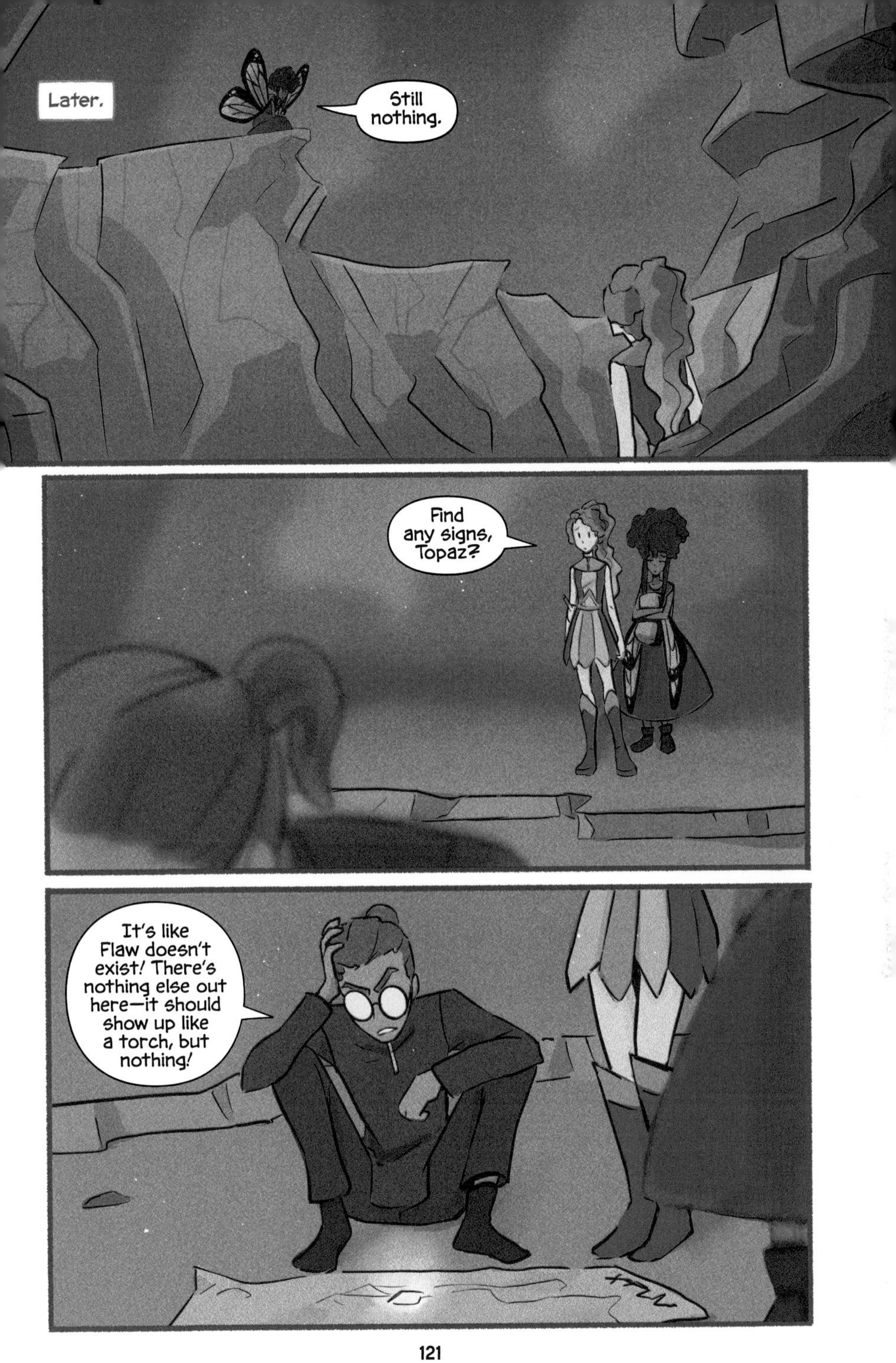
Later.
Still nothing.
Find any signs, Topaz?
It's like Flaw doesn't exist! There's nothing else out here—it should show up like a torch, but nothing!

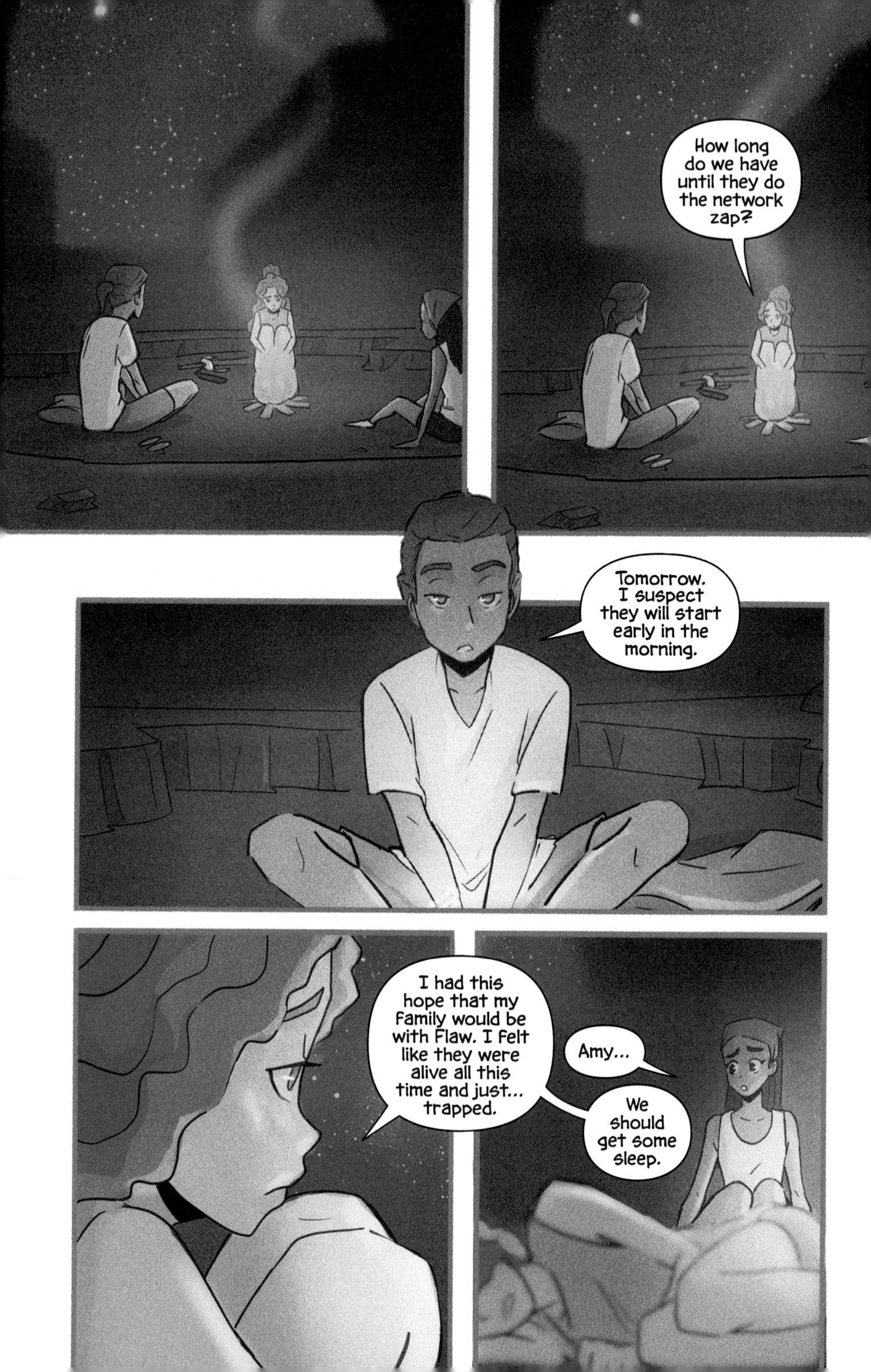
How long do we have until they do the network zap?
Tomorrow. I suspect they will start early in the morning.
I had this hope that my family would be with Flaw. I felt like they were alive all this time and just... trapped.
Amy...
We should get some sleep.

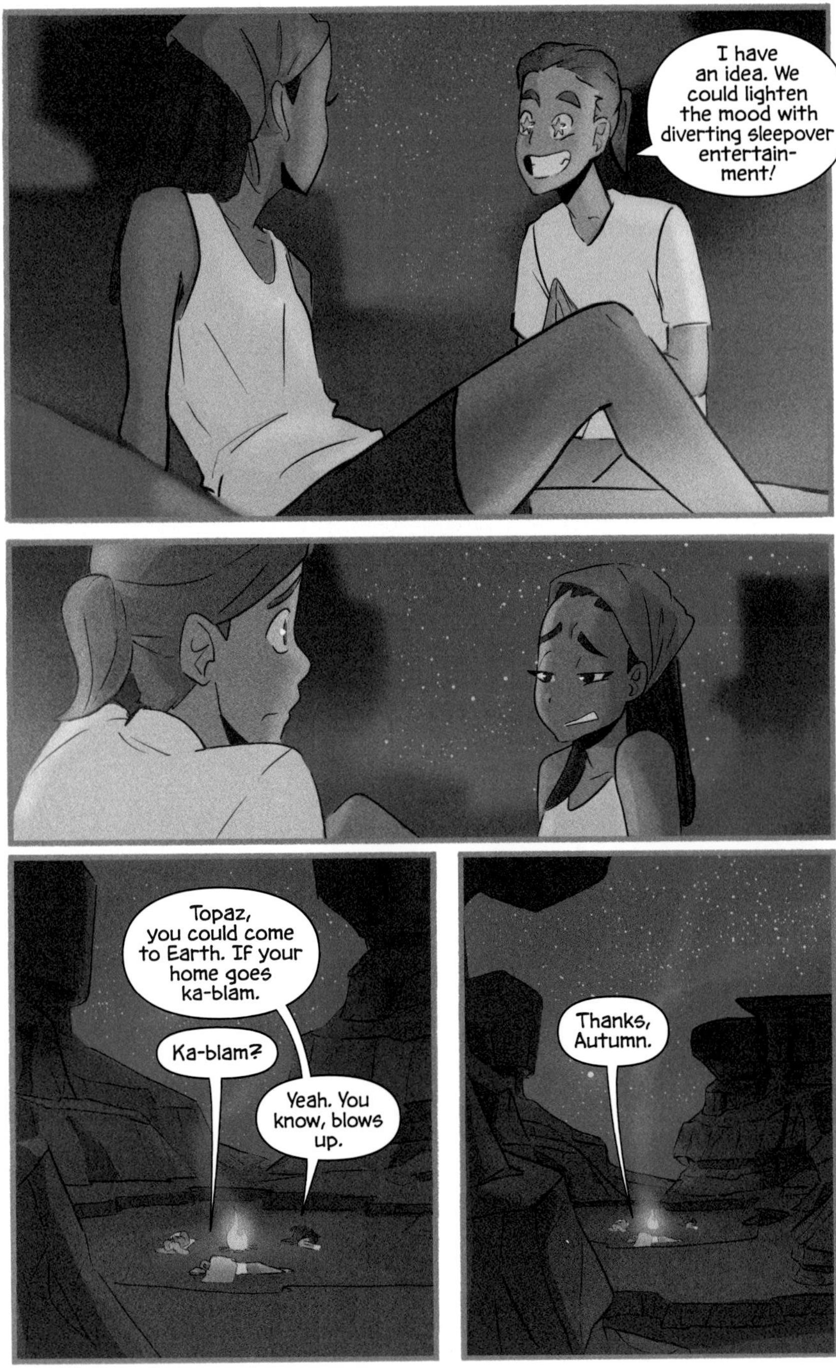
I have an idea. We could lighten the mood with diverting sleepover entertain-ment!
Topaz, you could come to Earth. If your home goes ka-blam.
Ka-blam?
Yeah. You know, blows up.
Thanks, Autumn.

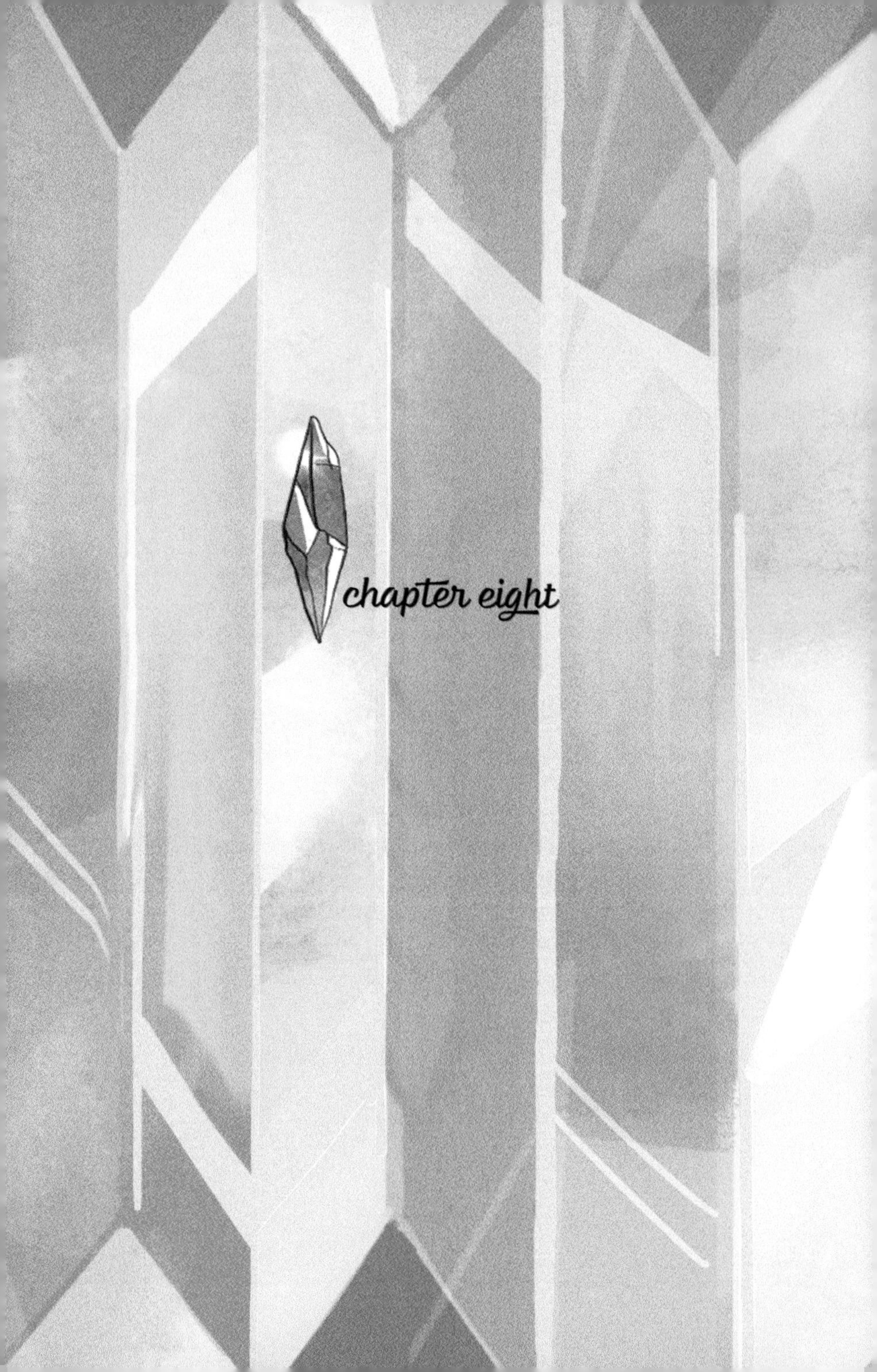

chapter eight

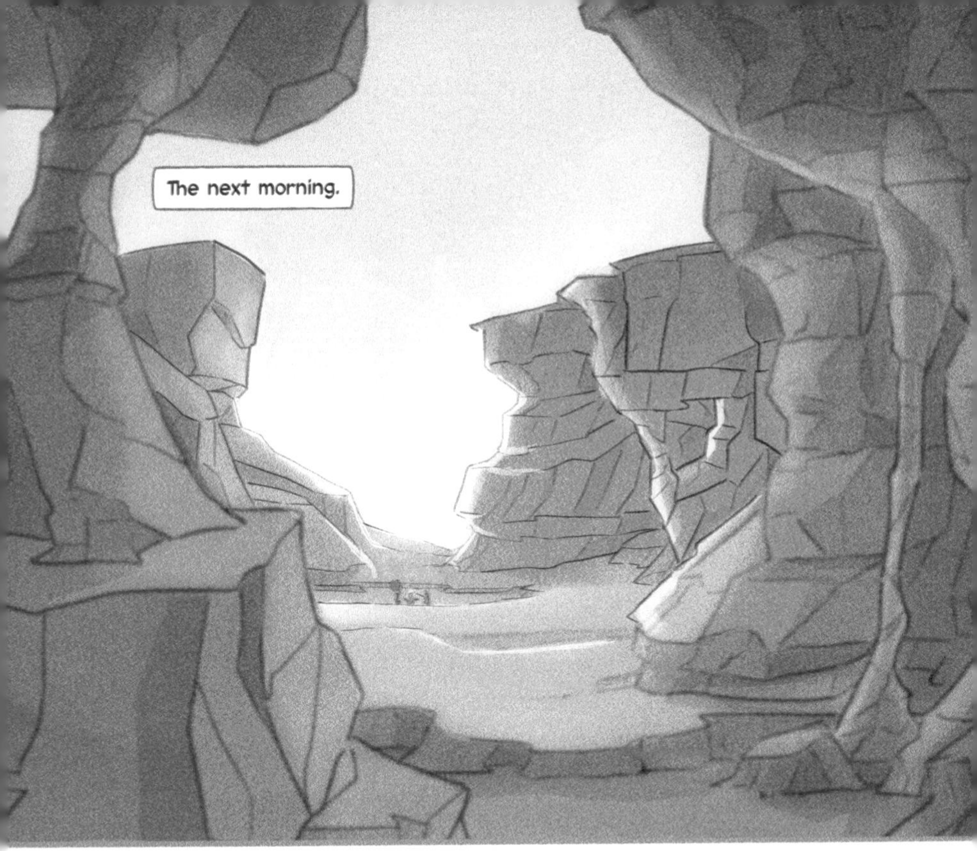
The next morning.

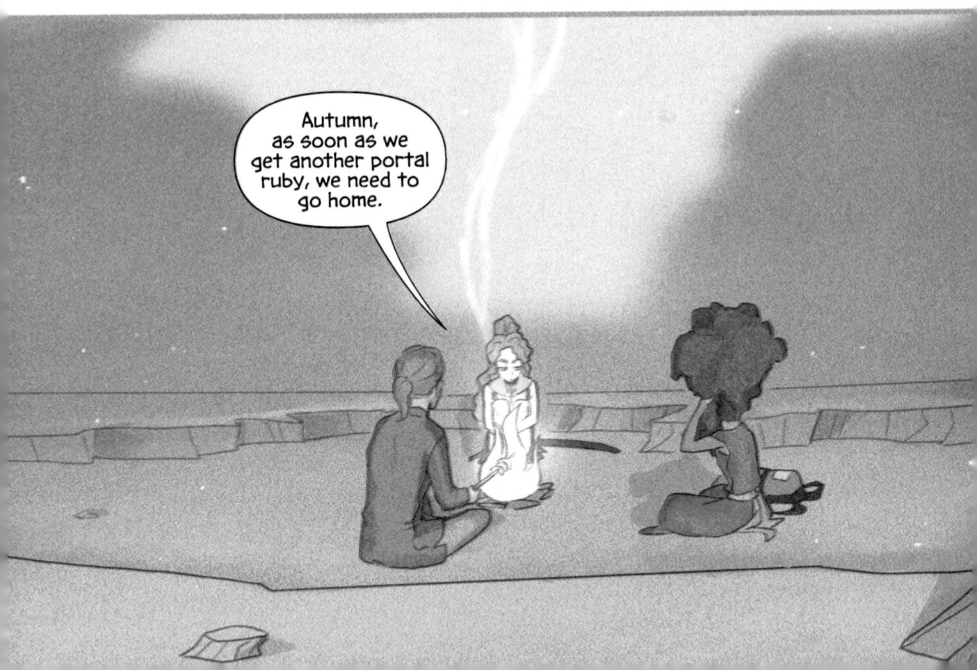
Autumn, as soon as we get another portal ruby, we need to go home.

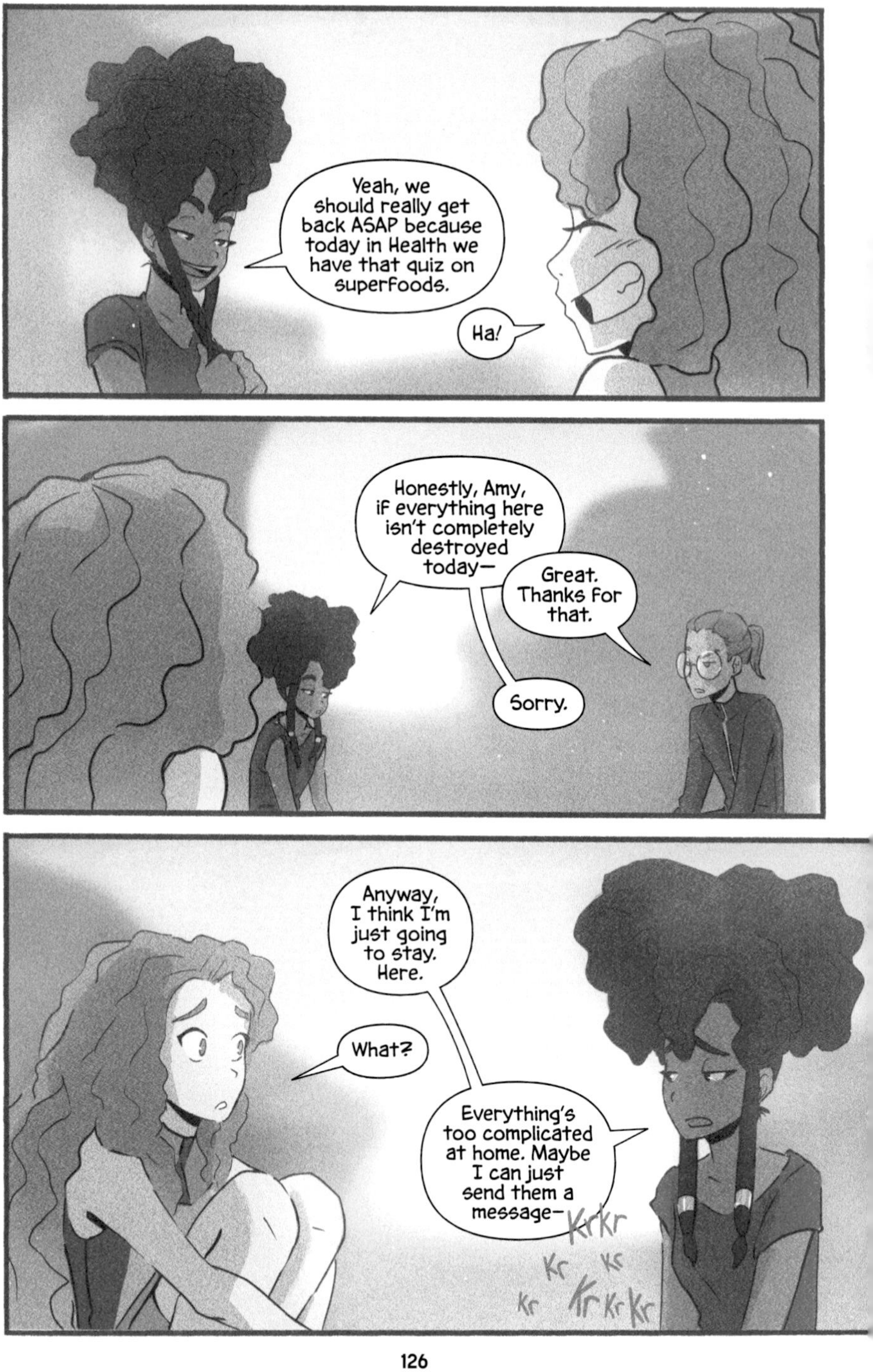
Yeah, we should really get back ASAP because today in Health we have that quiz on superfoods.
Ha!
Honestly, Amy, if everything here isn't completely destroyed today—
Great. Thanks for that.
Sorry.
Anyway, I think I'm just going to stay. Here.
What?
Everything's too complicated at home. Maybe I can just send them a message—
Krkr
Kr
Kr
Kr
Kr Kr Kr

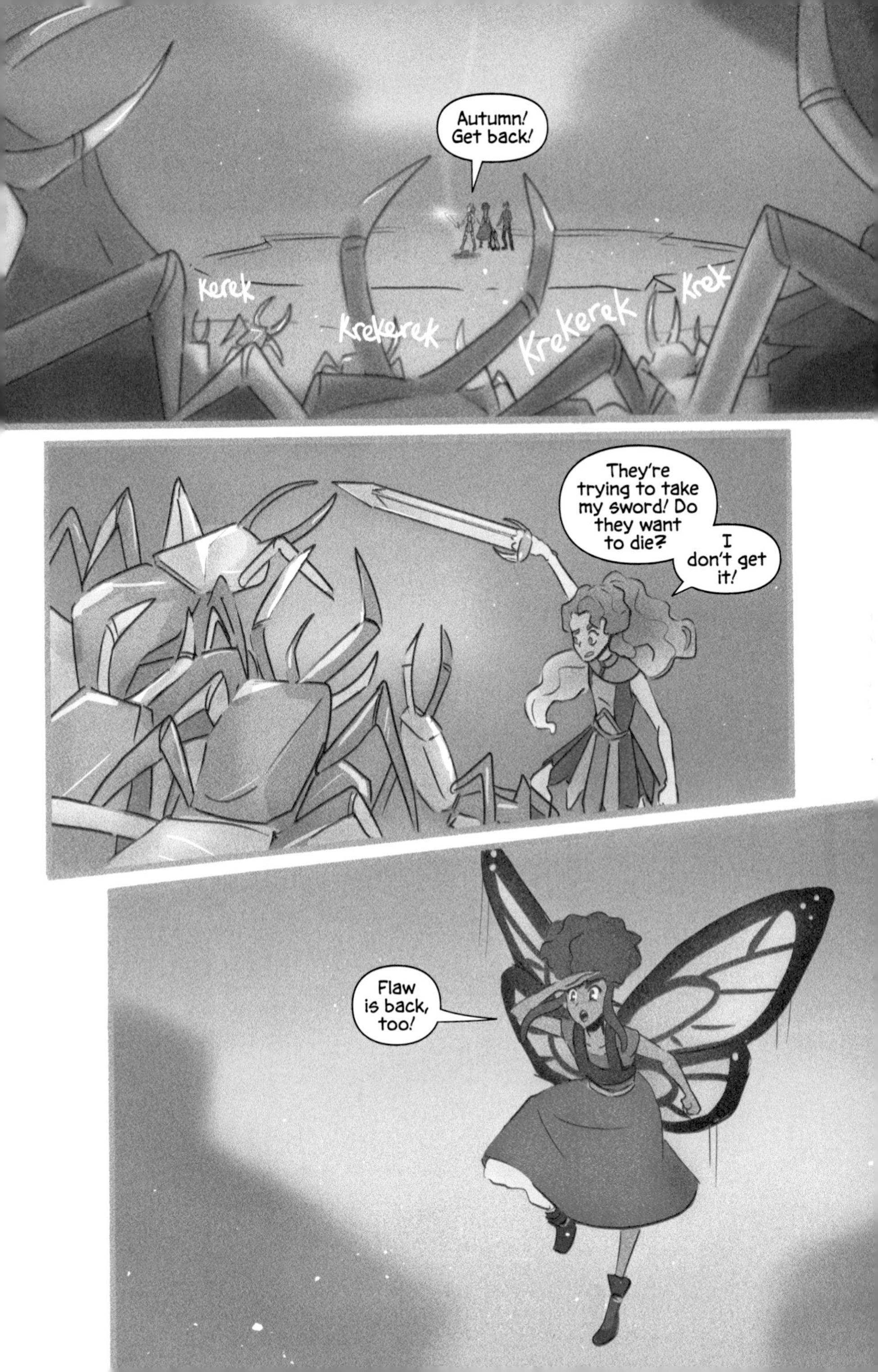
Autumn! Get back!
Kerek
Krekerek
Krekerek
Krek
They're trying to take my sword! Do they want to die?
I don't get it!
Flaw is back, too!

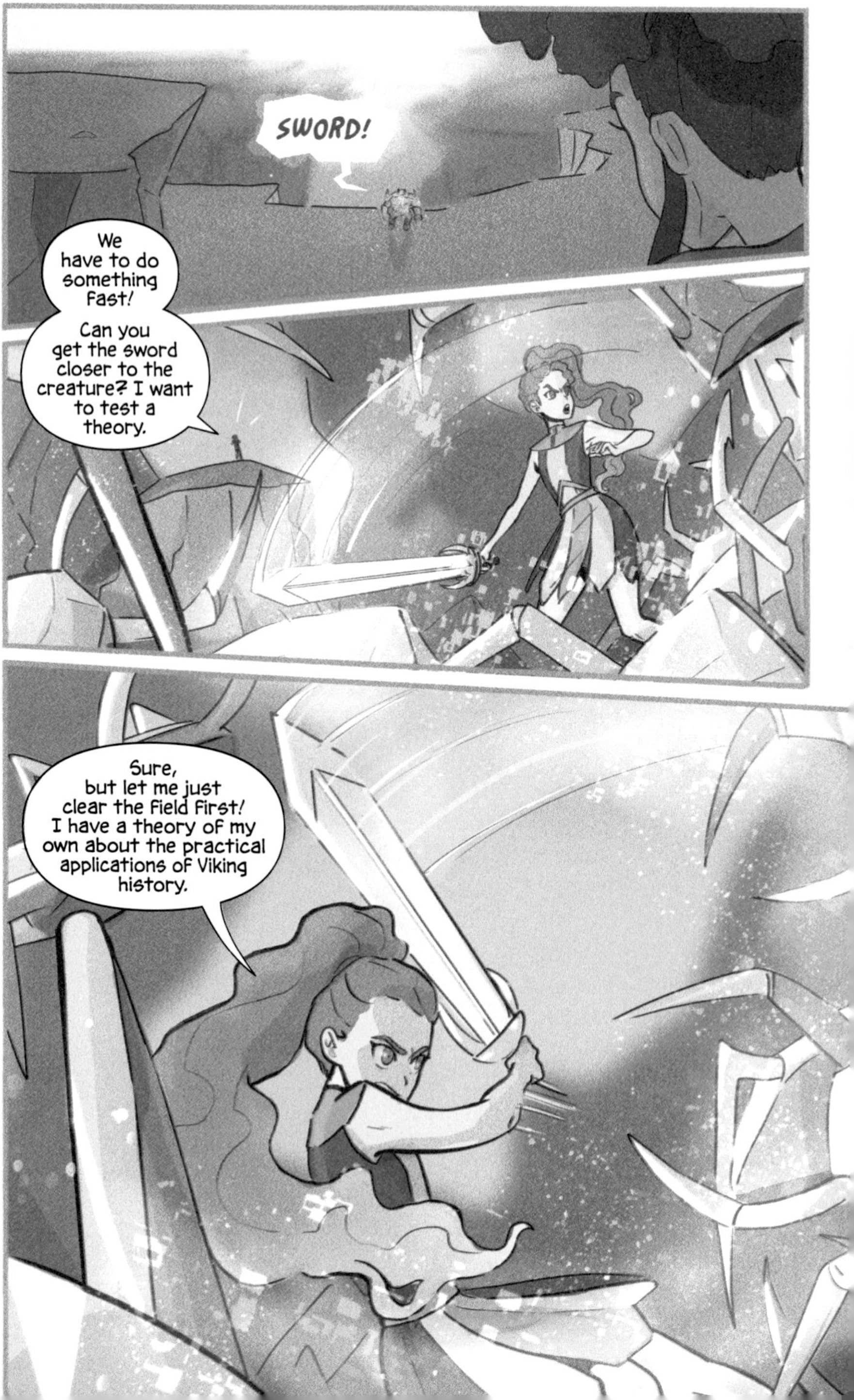
SWORD!
We have to do something fast!
Can you get the sword closer to the creature? I want to test a theory.
Sure, but let me just clear the field first! I have a theory of my own about the practical applications of Viking history.

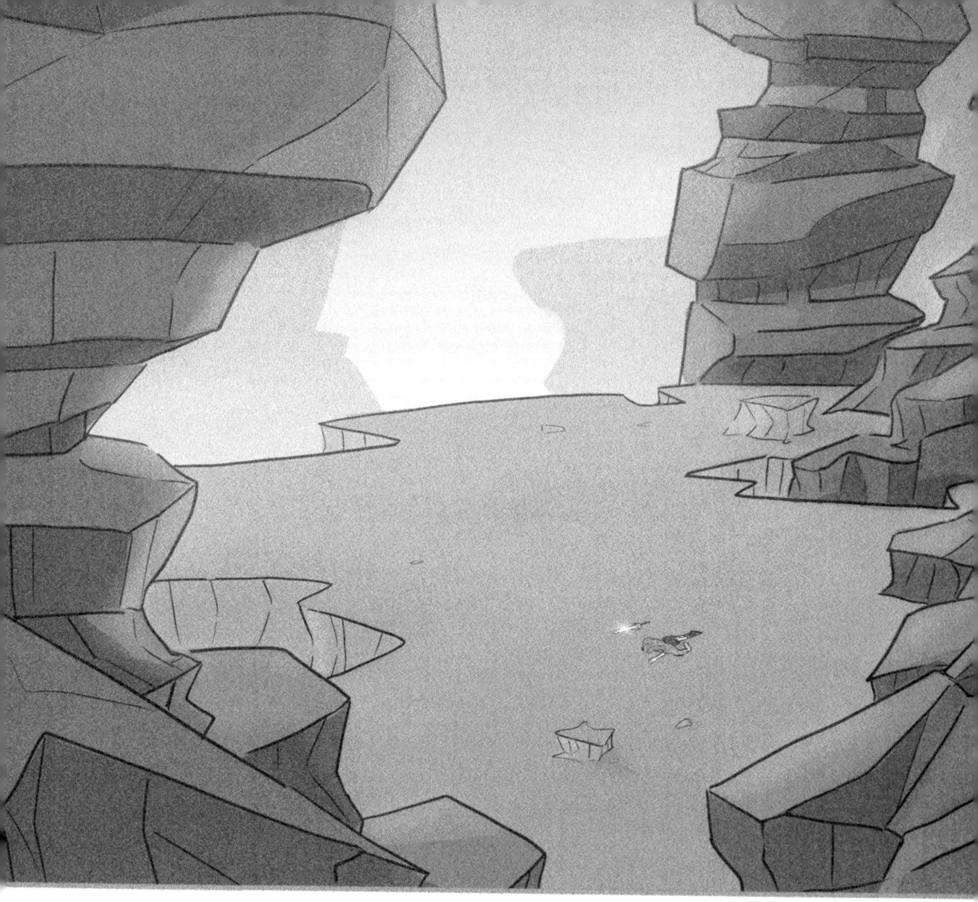

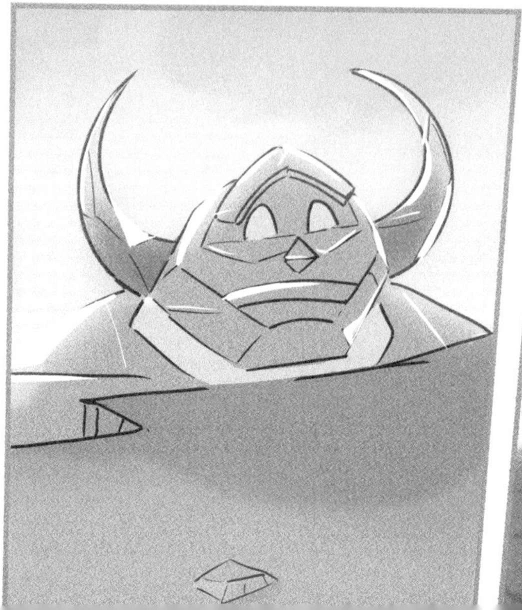

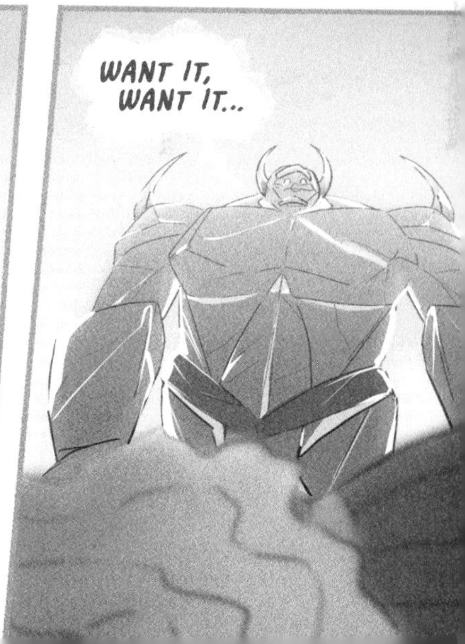
WANT IT,
WANT IT...

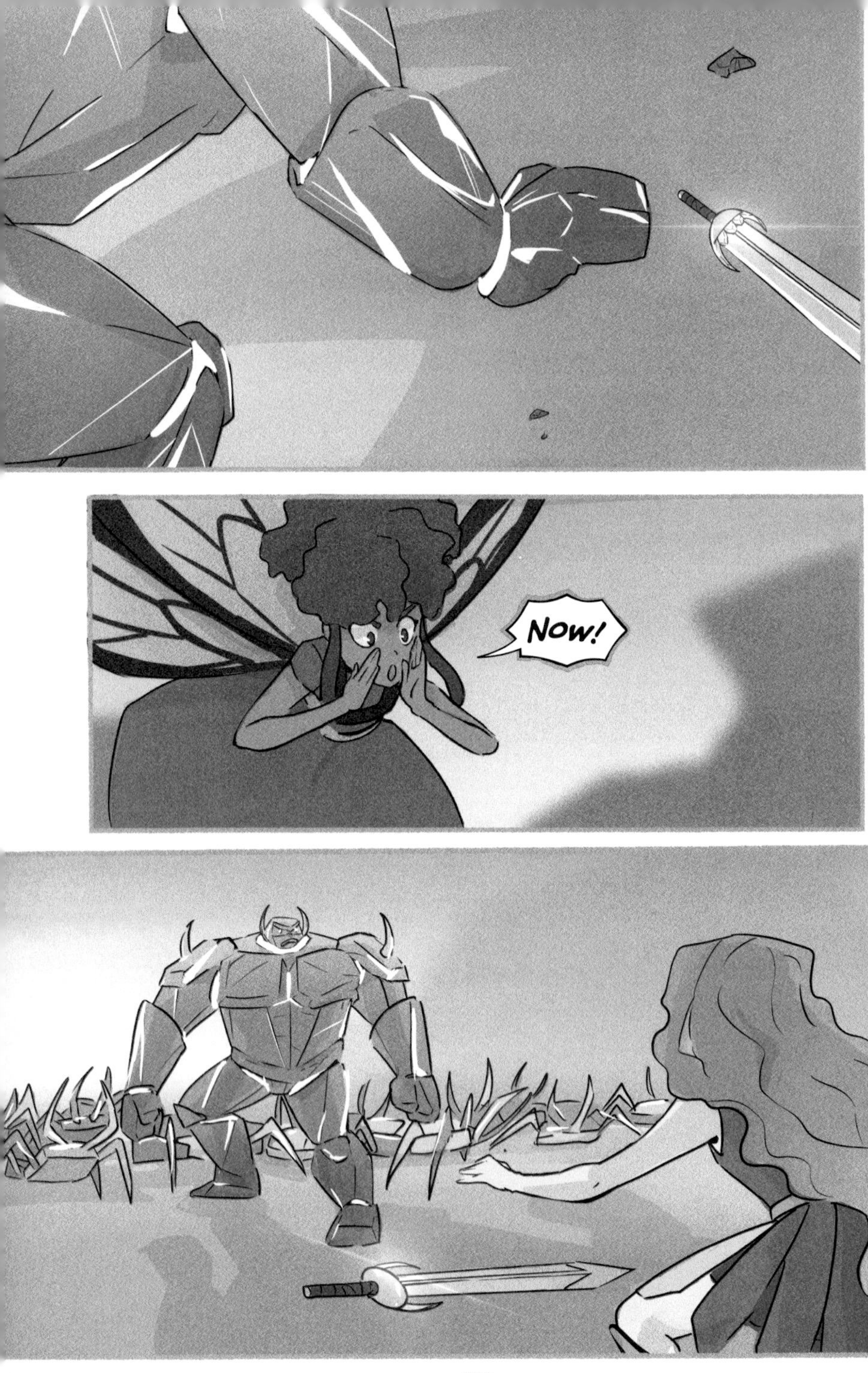
NOW!

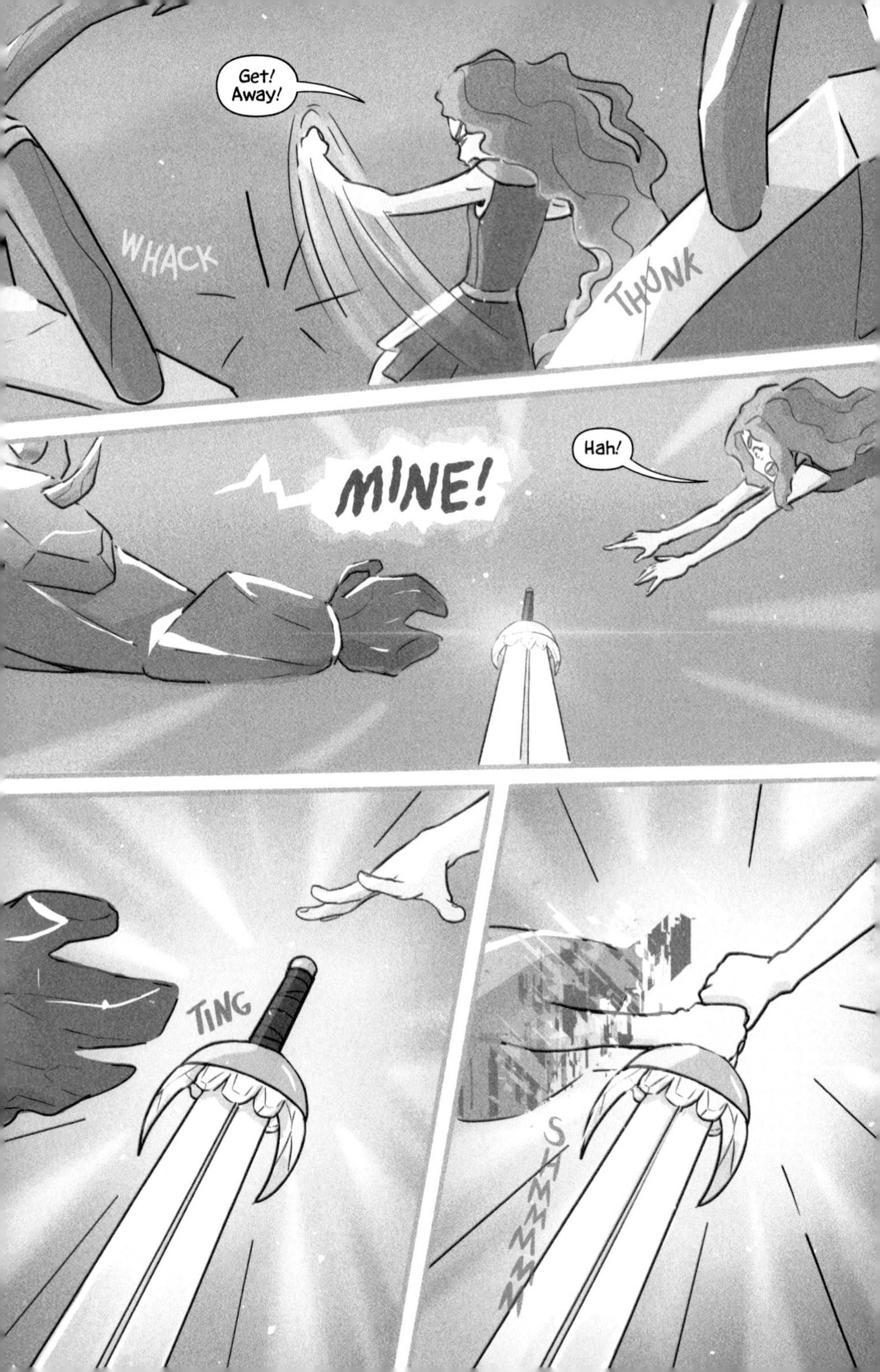
Get! Away!
WHACK
THUNK
Hah!
MINE!
TING
SHMMMMM

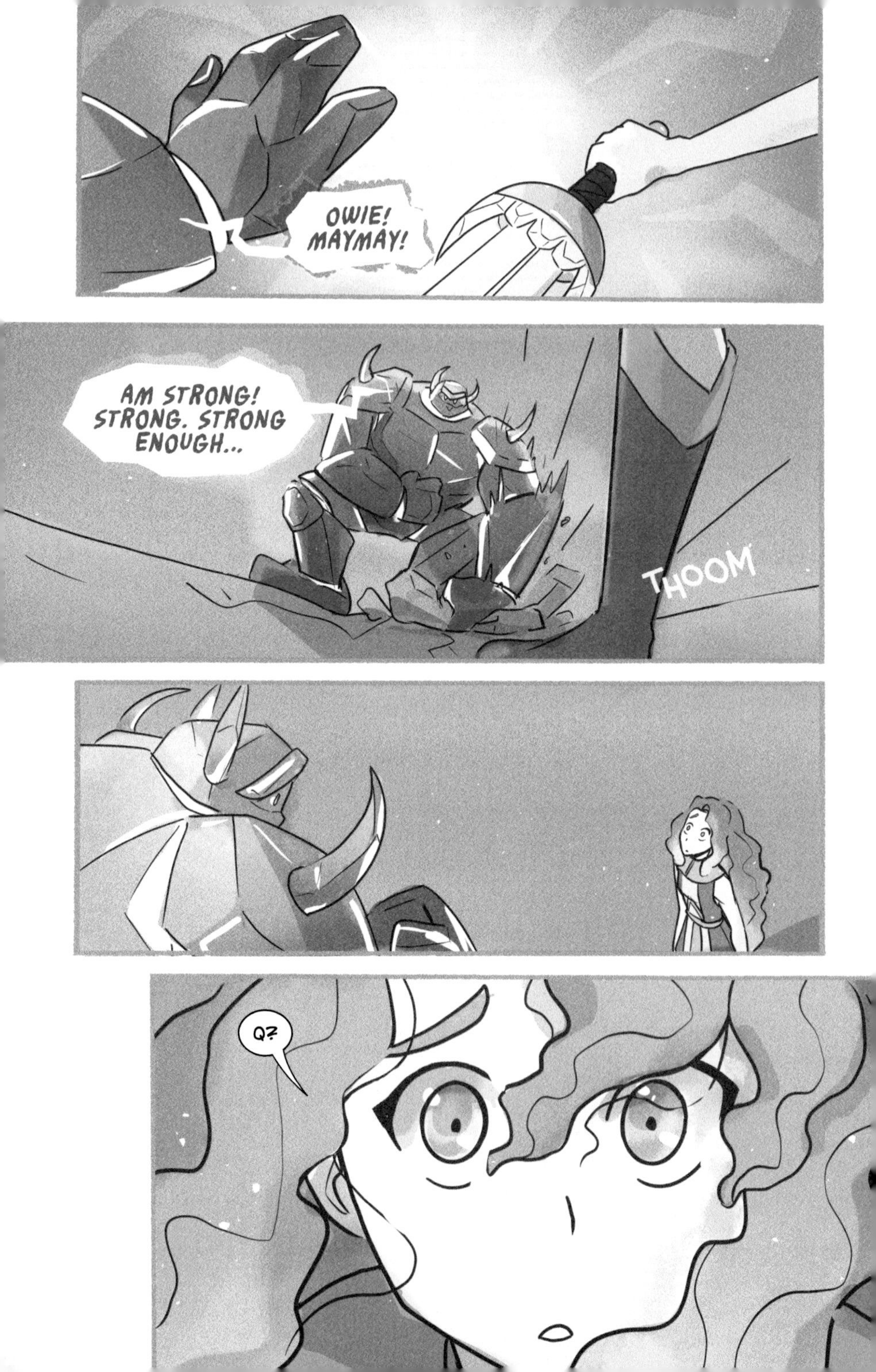
OWIE! MAYMAY!
AM STRONG! STRONG. STRONG ENOUGH...
THOOM
Q?

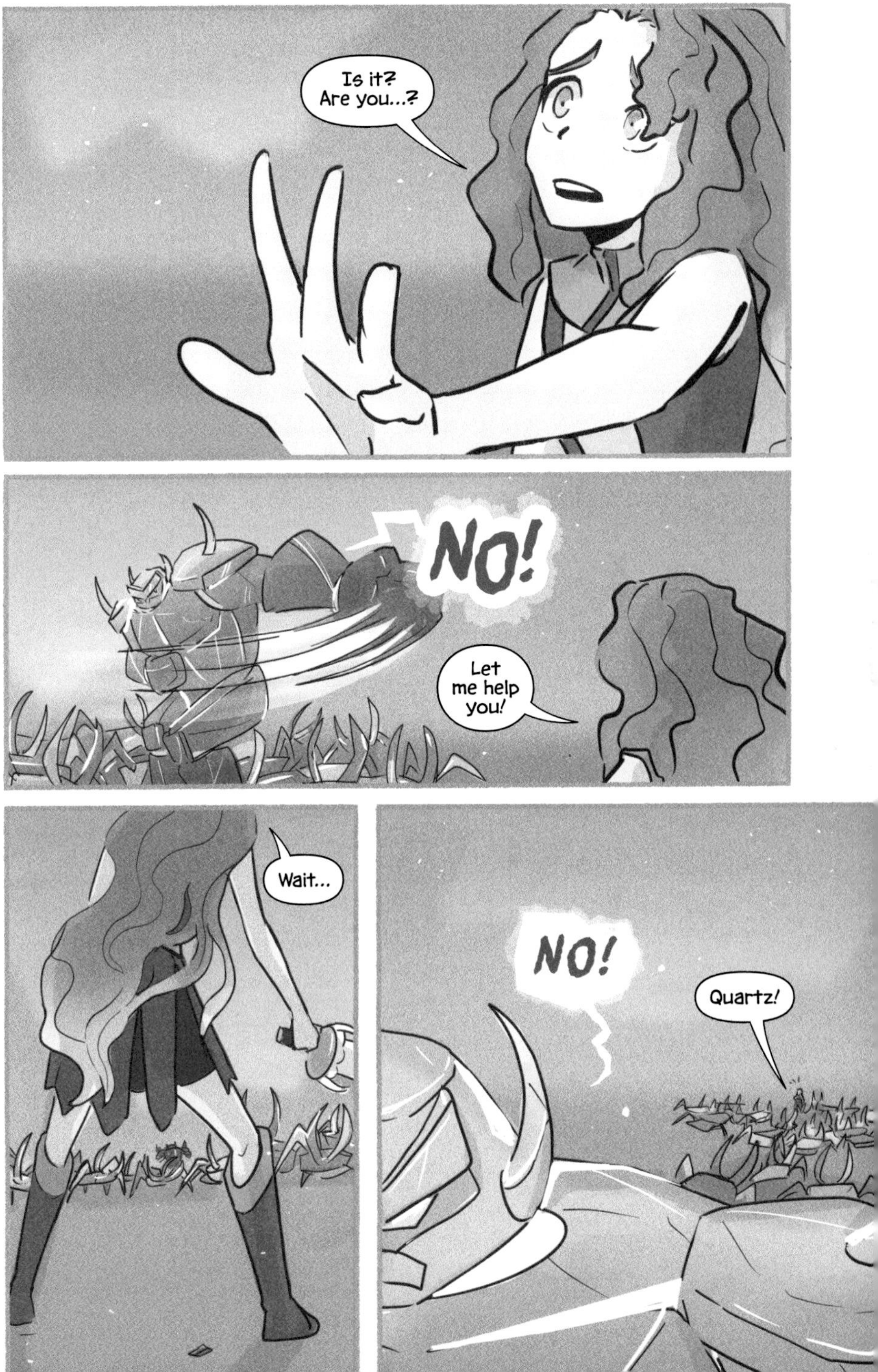
Is it?
Are you...?
NO!
Let me help you!
Wait...
NO!
Quartz!

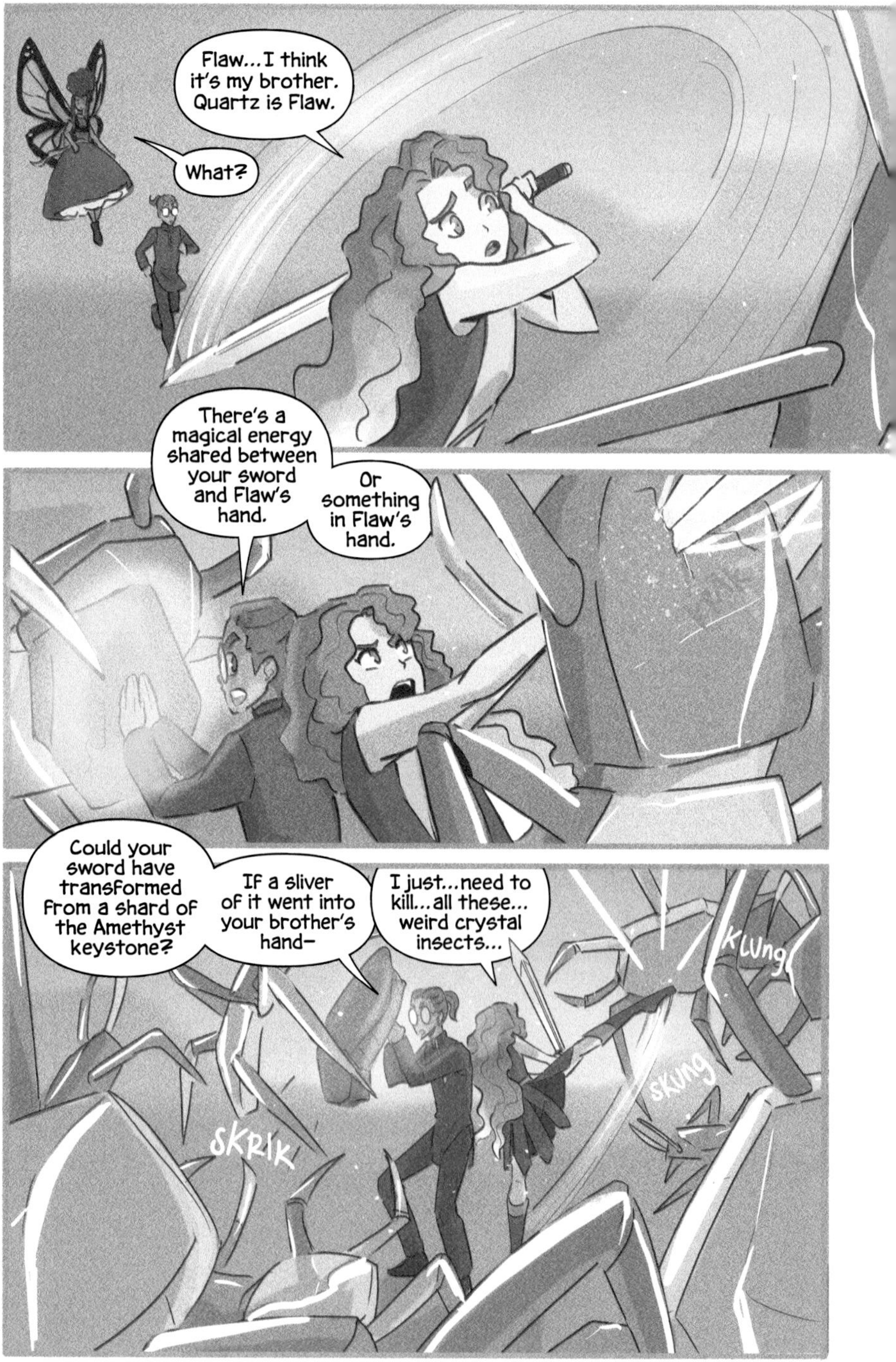

Flaw...I think it's my brother. Quartz is Flaw.
What?
There's a magical energy shared between your sword and Flaw's hand.
Or something in Flaw's hand.
Could your sword have transformed from a shard of the Amethyst keystone?
If a sliver of it went into your brother's hand—
I just...need to kill...all these... weird crystal insects...
KLUNG
SKUNG
SKRIK

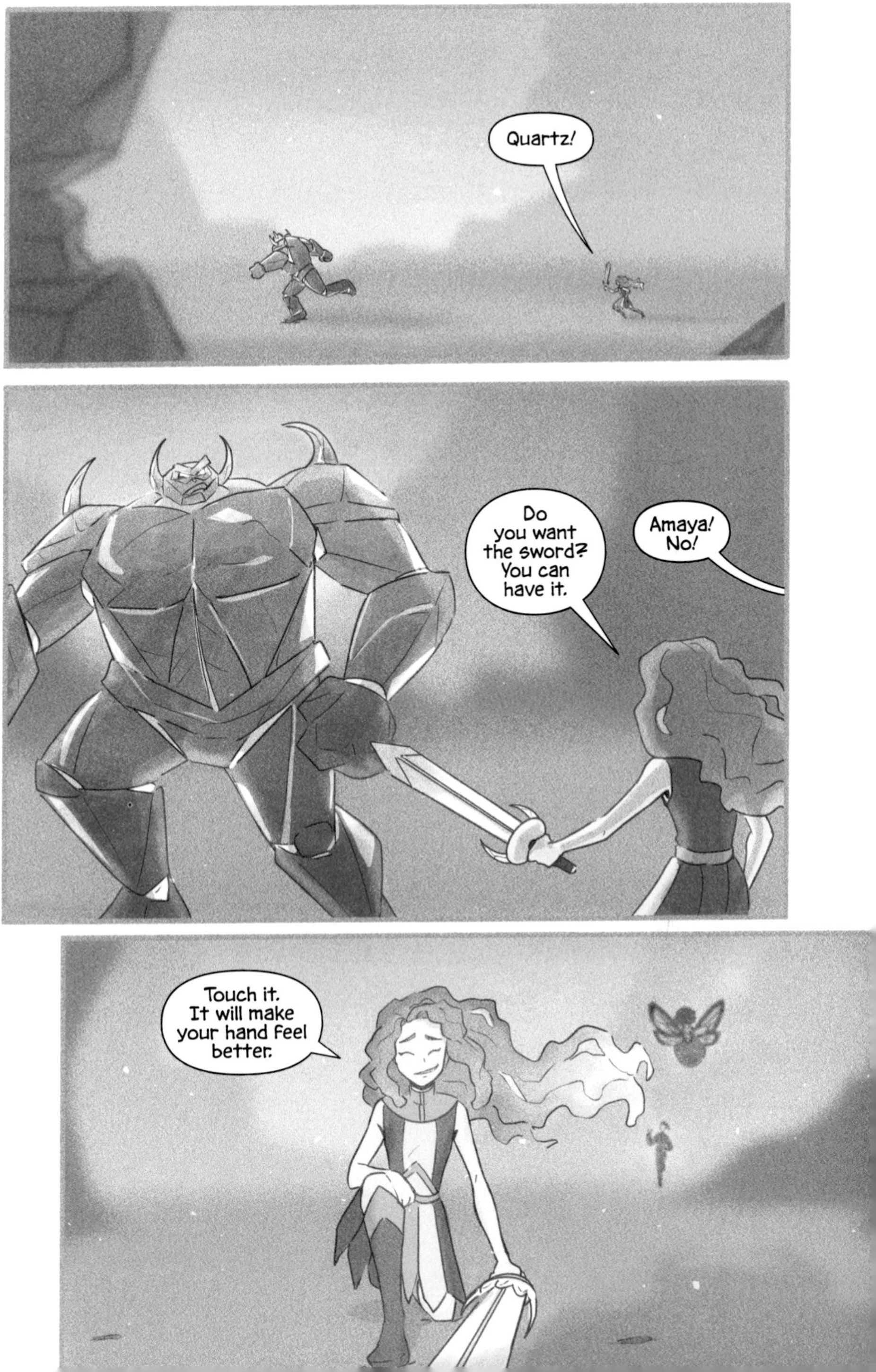
Quartz!
Do you want the sword? You can have it.
Amaya! No!
Touch it. It will make your hand feel better.

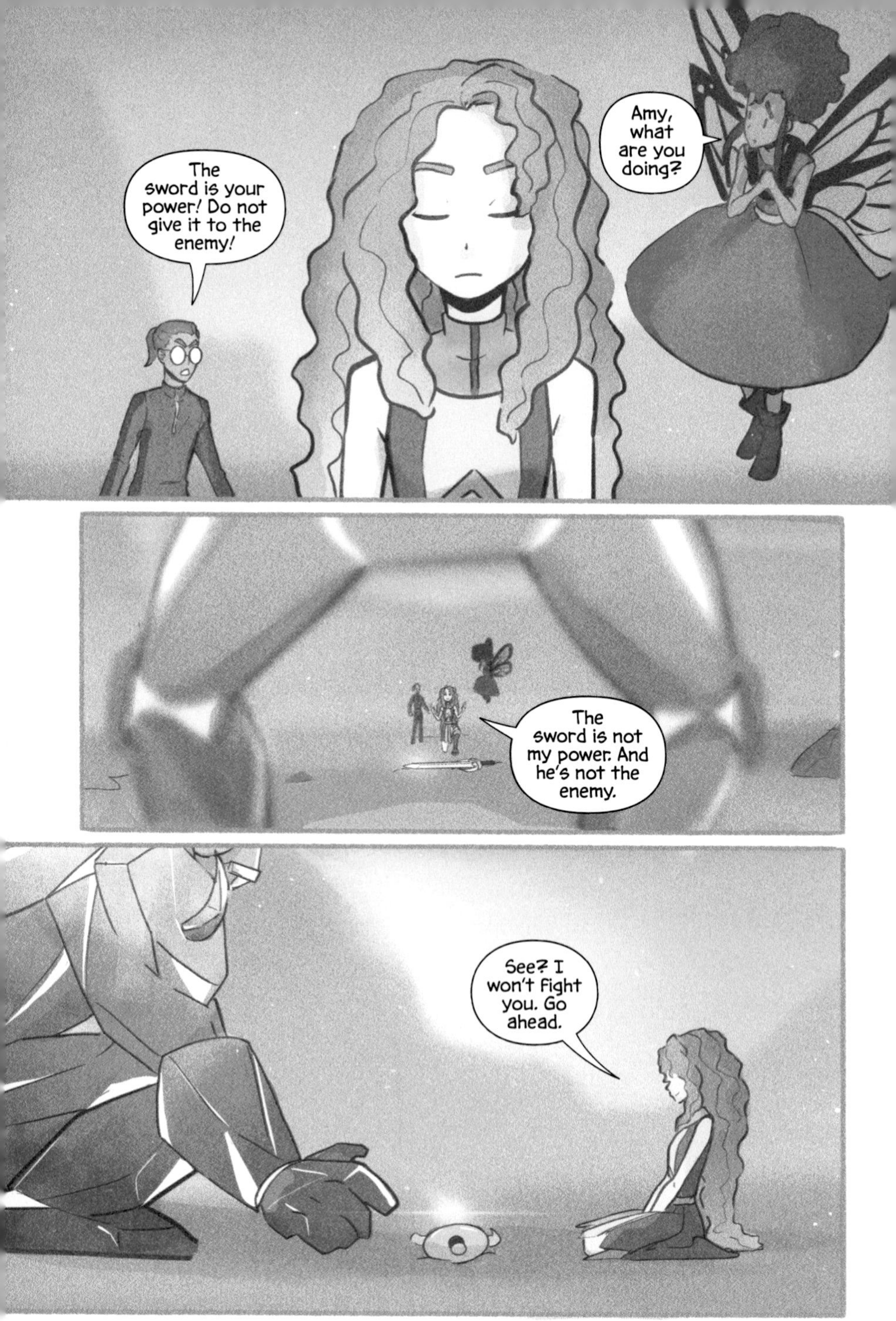
The sword is your power! Do not give it to the enemy!
Amy, what are you doing?
The sword is not my power. And he's not the enemy.
See? I won't fight you. Go ahead.

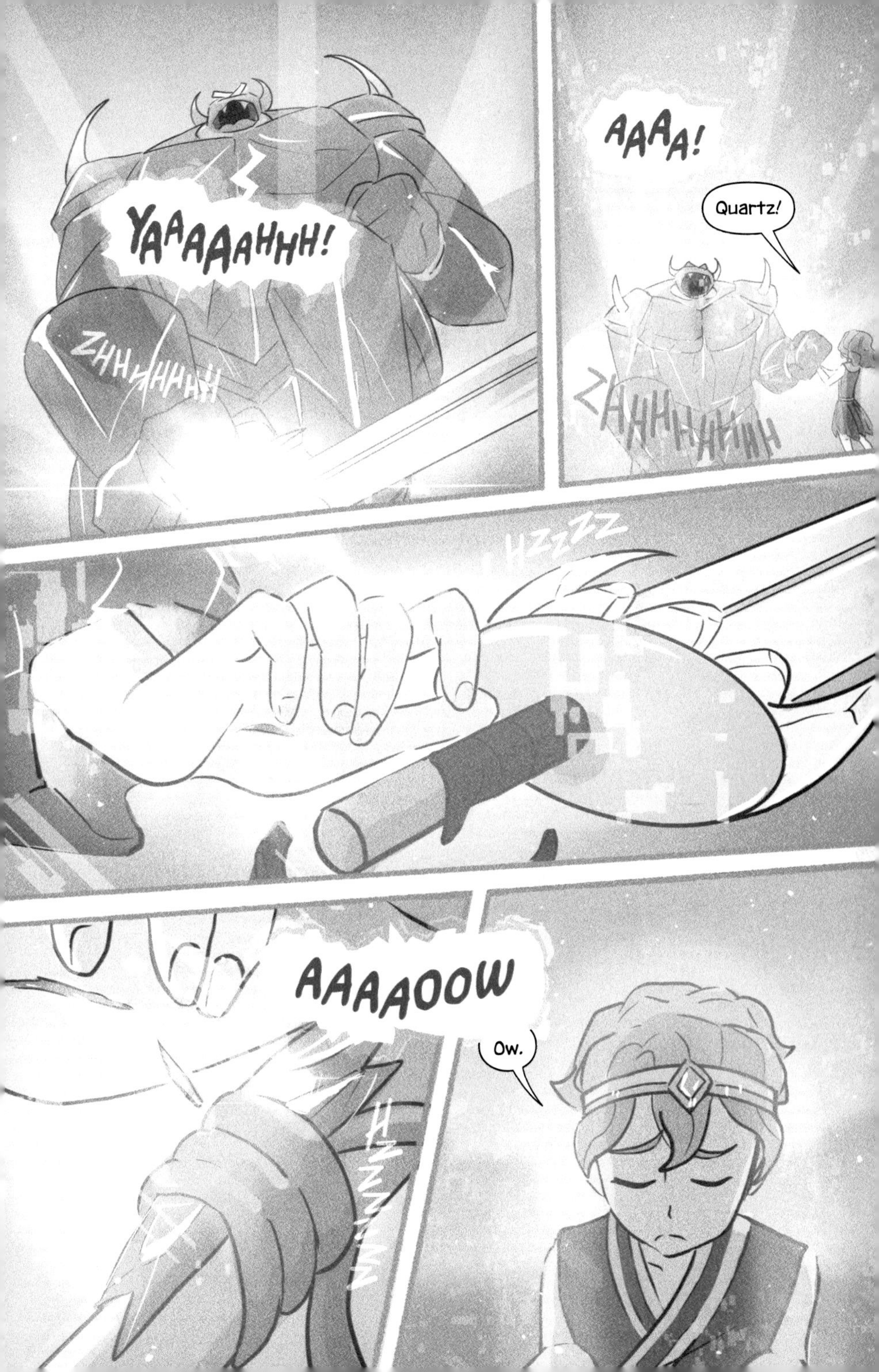
YAAAAAHHH!
ZHHHHHHHH
AAAA!
Quartz!
ZAHHHHHHHHH
HZZZZ
AAAAOOW
Ow.

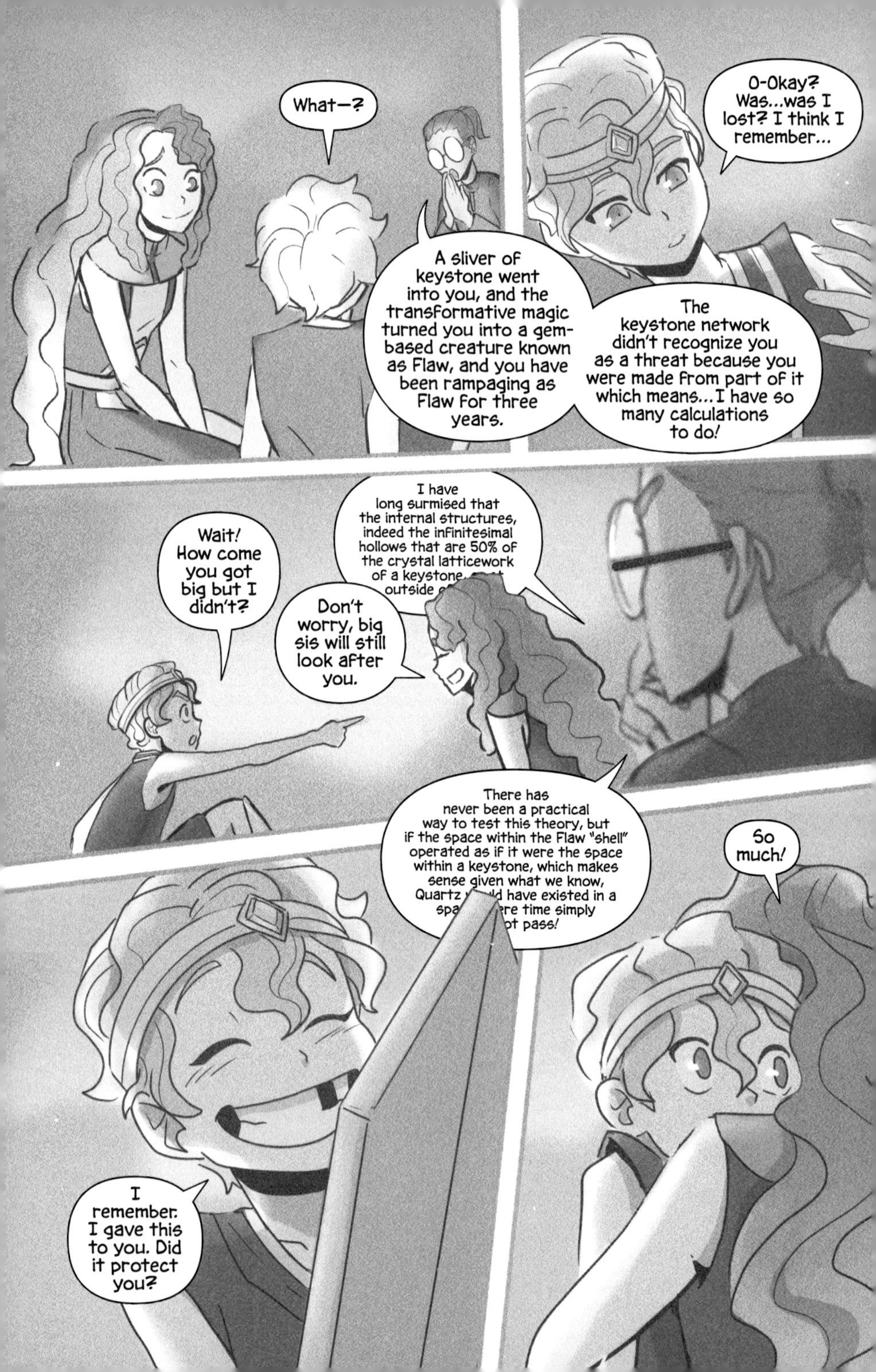
What—?
A sliver of keystone went into you, and the transformative magic turned you into a gem-based creature known as Flaw, and you have been rampaging as Flaw for three years.
O-Okay? Was...was I lost? I think I remember...
The keystone network didn't recognize you as a threat because you were made from part of it which means...I have so many calculations to do!
Wait! How come you got big but I didn't?
Don't worry, big sis will still look after you.
I have long surmised that the internal structures, indeed the infinitesimal hollows that are 50% of the crystal latticework of a keystone,
There has never been a practical way to test this theory, but if the space within the Flaw "shell" operated as if it were the space within a keystone, which makes sense given what we know,
So much!
I remember. I gave this to you. Did it protect you?

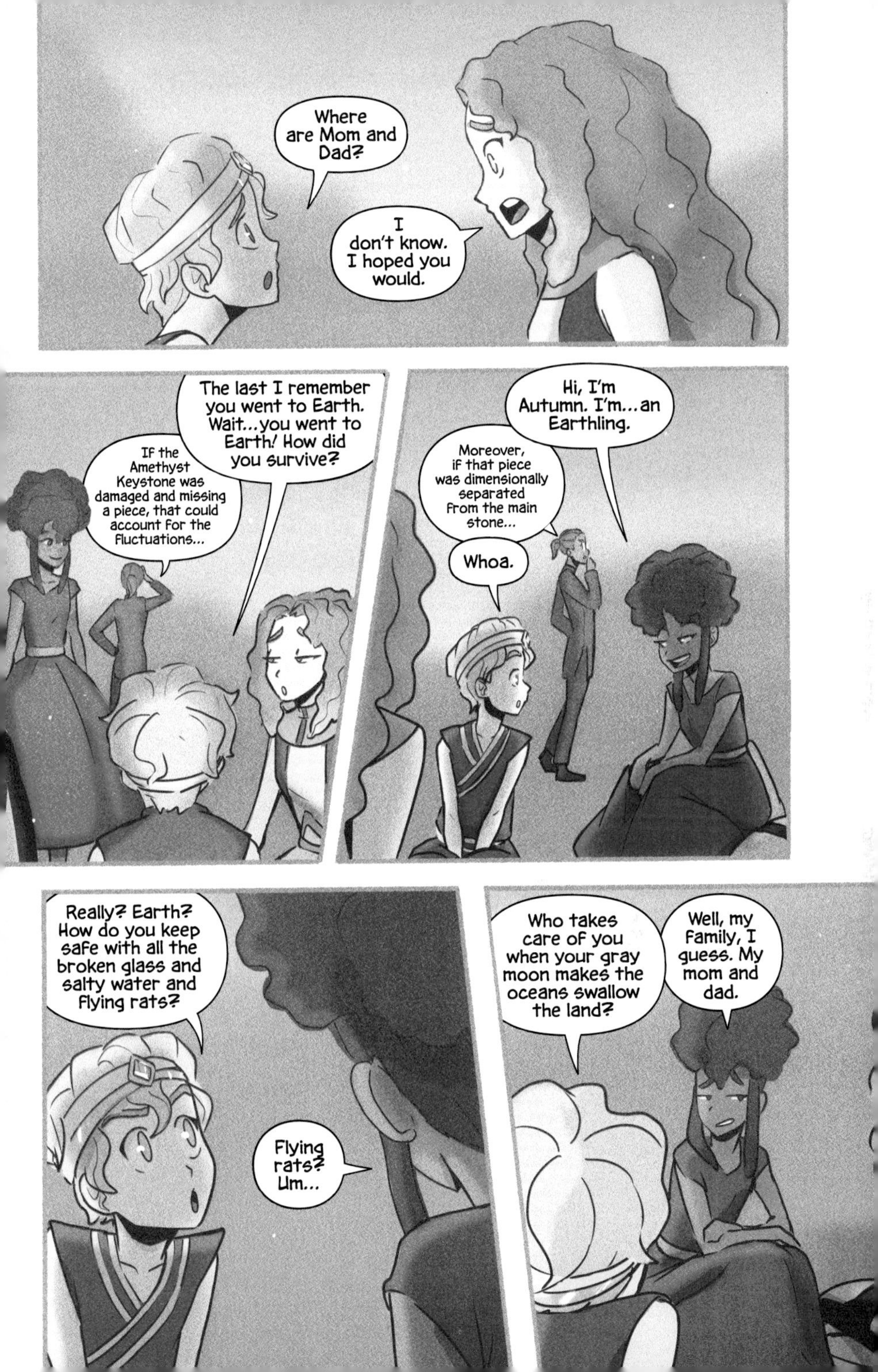
Where are Mom and Dad?
I don't know. I hoped you would.
The last I remember you went to Earth. Wait...you went to Earth! How did you survive?
If the Amethyst Keystone was damaged and missing a piece, that could account for the fluctuations...
Hi, I'm Autumn. I'm...an Earthling.
Moreover, if that piece was dimensionally separated from the main stone...
Whoa.
Really? Earth? How do you keep safe with all the broken glass and salty water and flying rats?
Flying rats? Um...
Who takes care of you when your gray moon makes the oceans swallow the land?
Well, my family, I guess. My mom and dad.

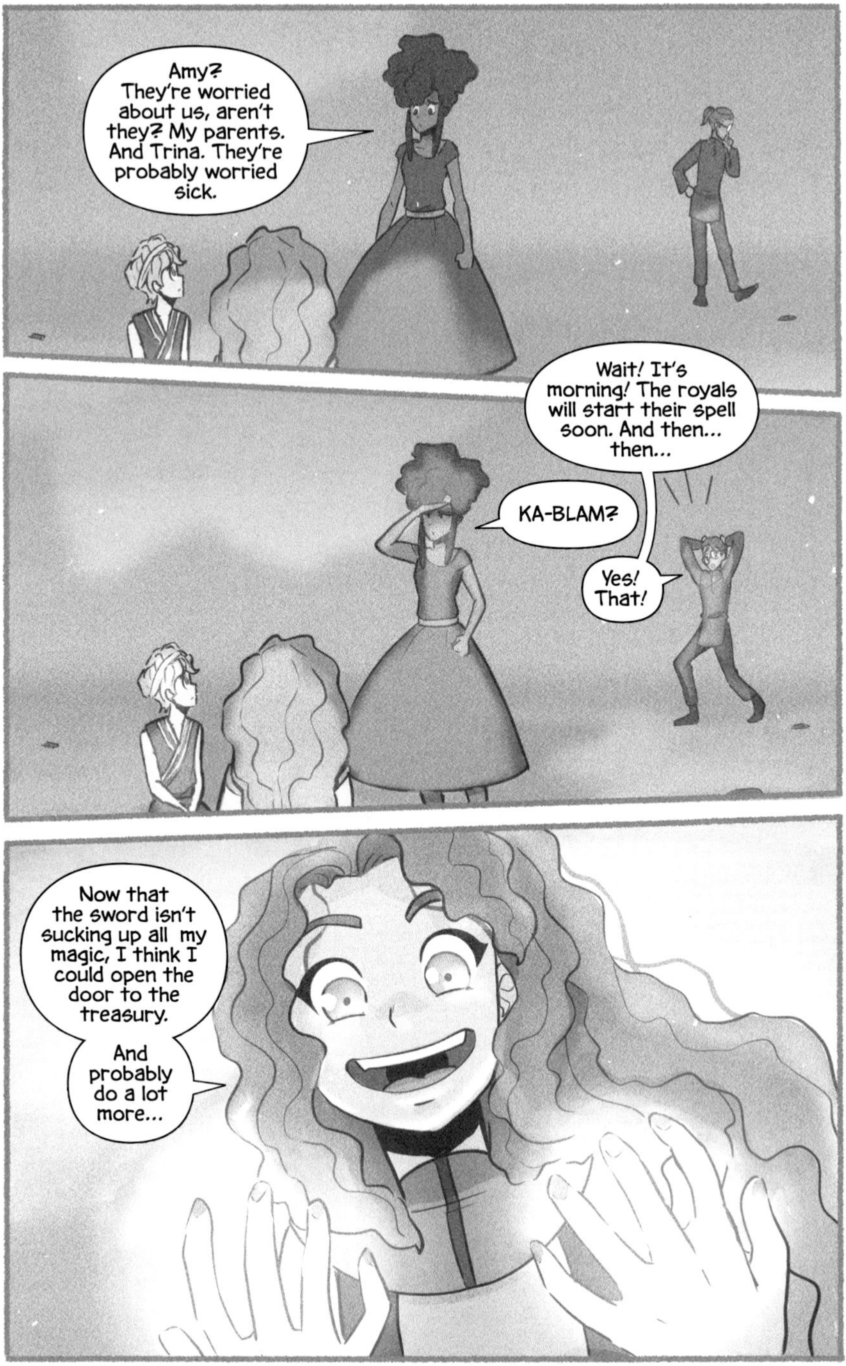
Amy? They're worried about us, aren't they? My parents. And Trina. They're probably worried sick.
Wait! It's morning! The royals will start their spell soon. And then... then...
KA-BLAM?
Yes! That!
Now that the sword isn't sucking up all my magic, I think I could open the door to the treasury.
And probably do a lot more...

chapter nine

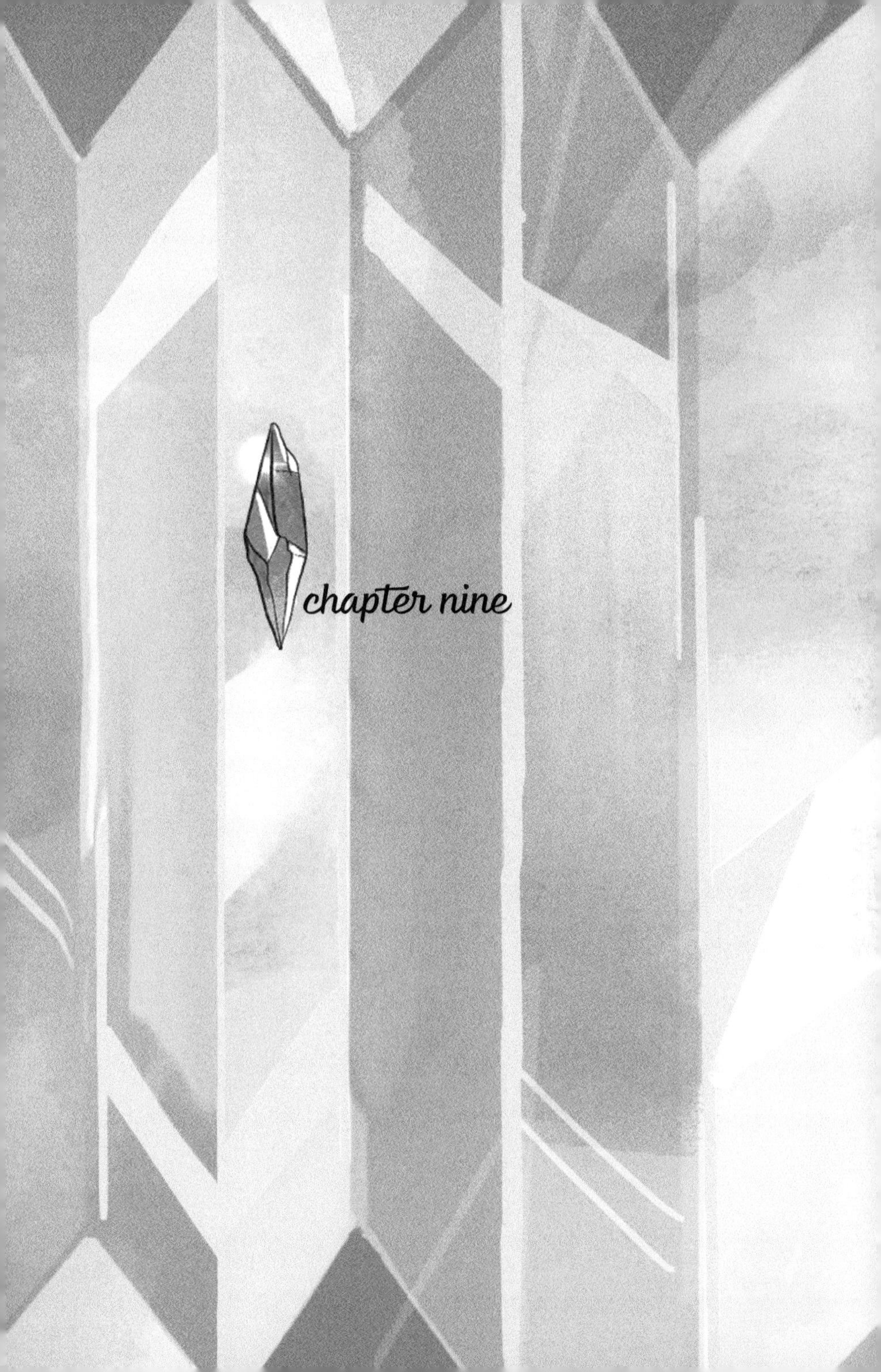

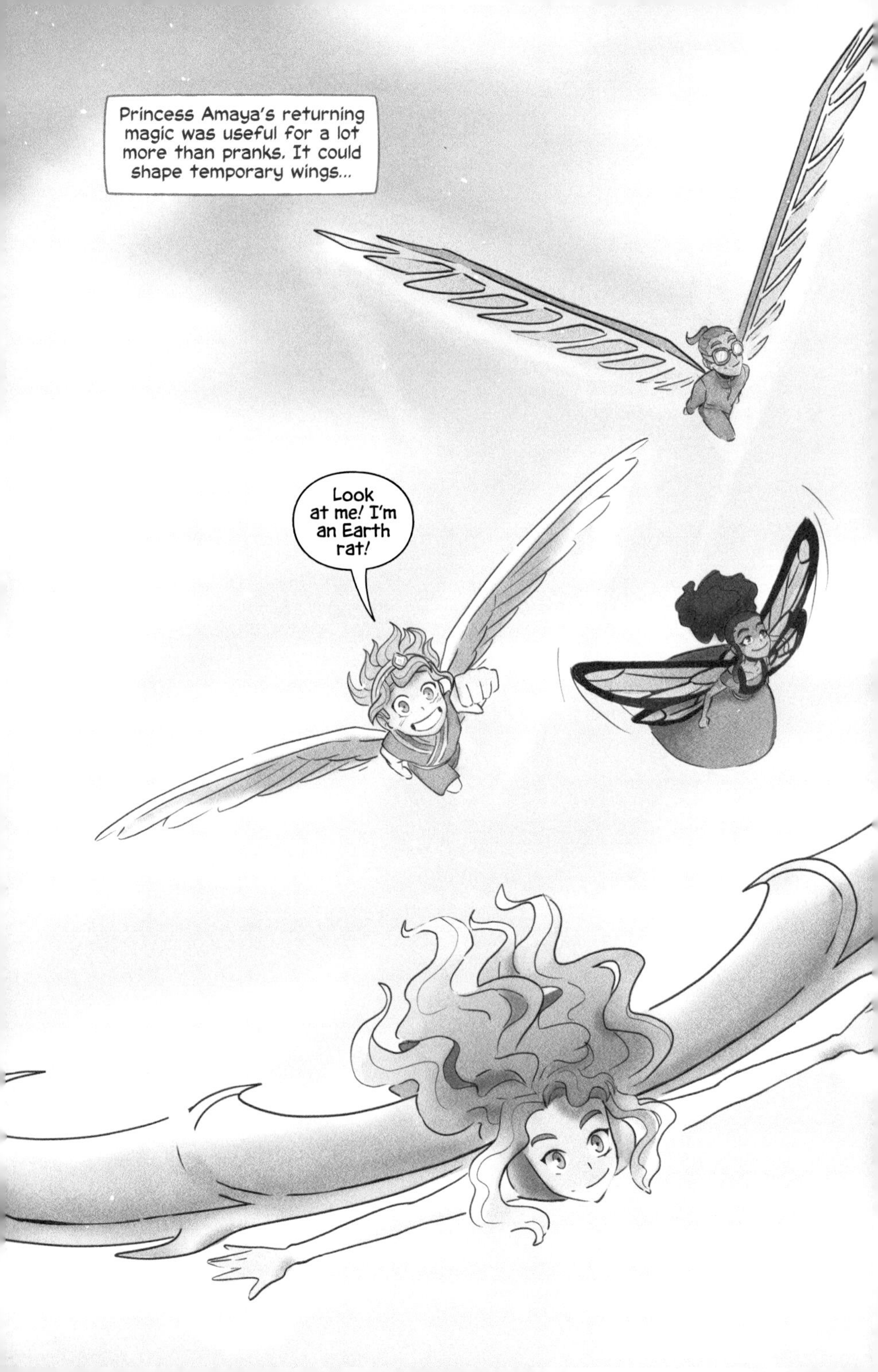
Princess Amaya's returning magic was useful for a lot more than pranks. It could shape temporary wings...
Look at me! I'm an Earth rat!

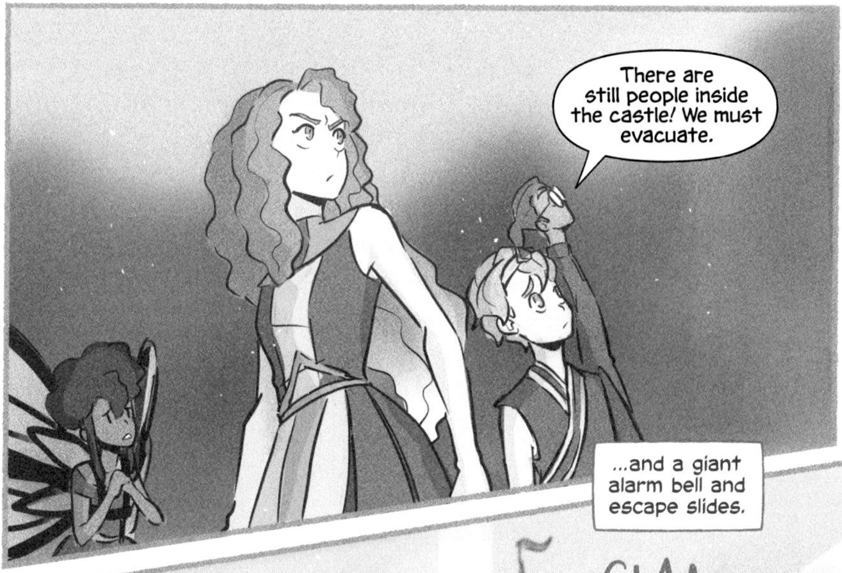
There are still people inside the castle! We must evacuate.

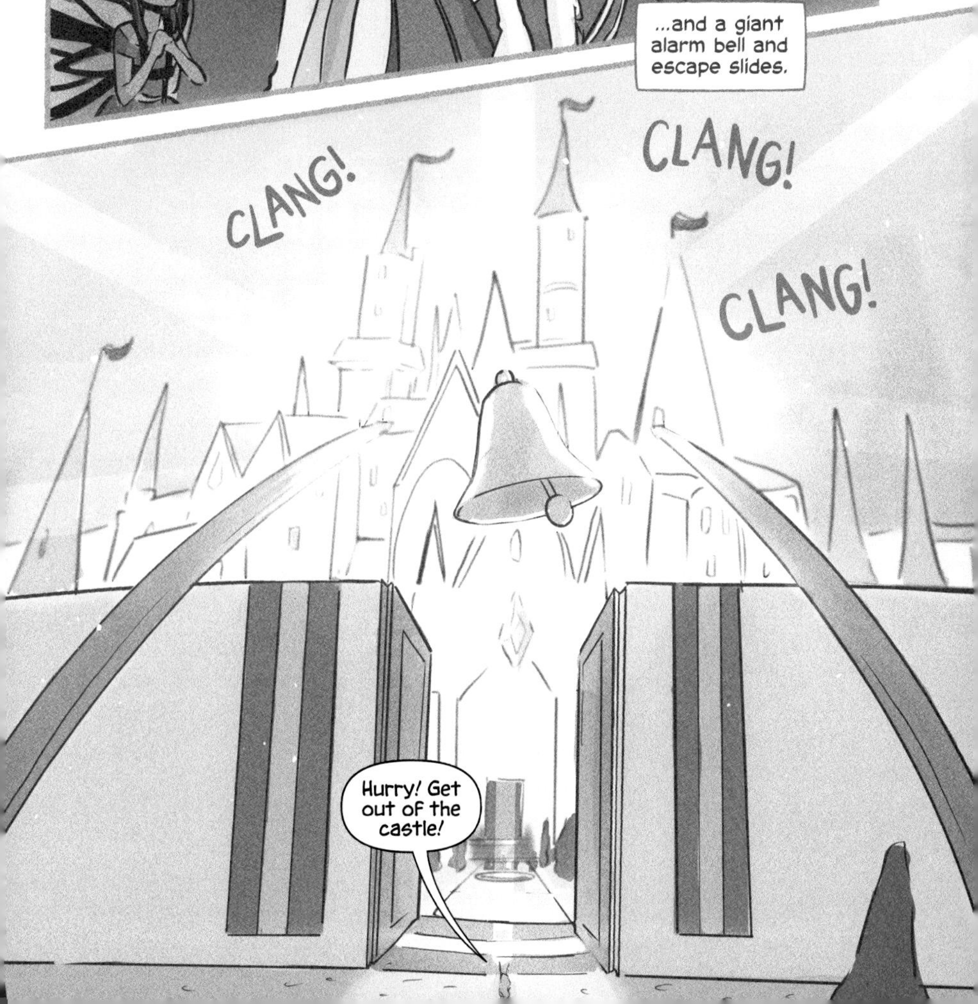
...and a giant alarm bell and escape slides.
CLANG!
CLANG!
CLANG!
Hurry! Get out of the castle!

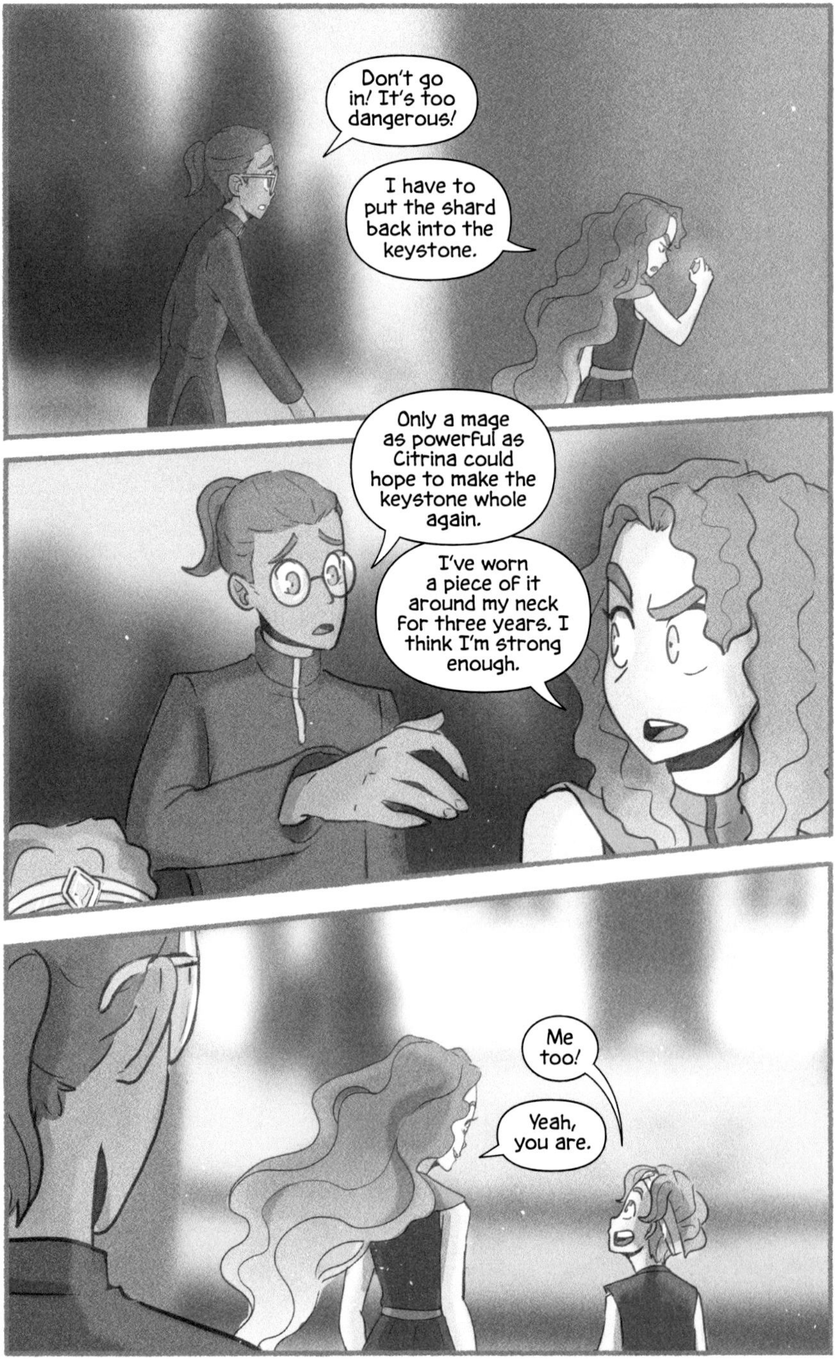
Don't go in! It's too dangerous!
I have to put the shard back into the keystone.
Only a mage as powerful as Citrina could hope to make the keystone whole again.
I've worn a piece of it around my neck for three years. I think I'm strong enough.
Me too!
Yeah, you are.

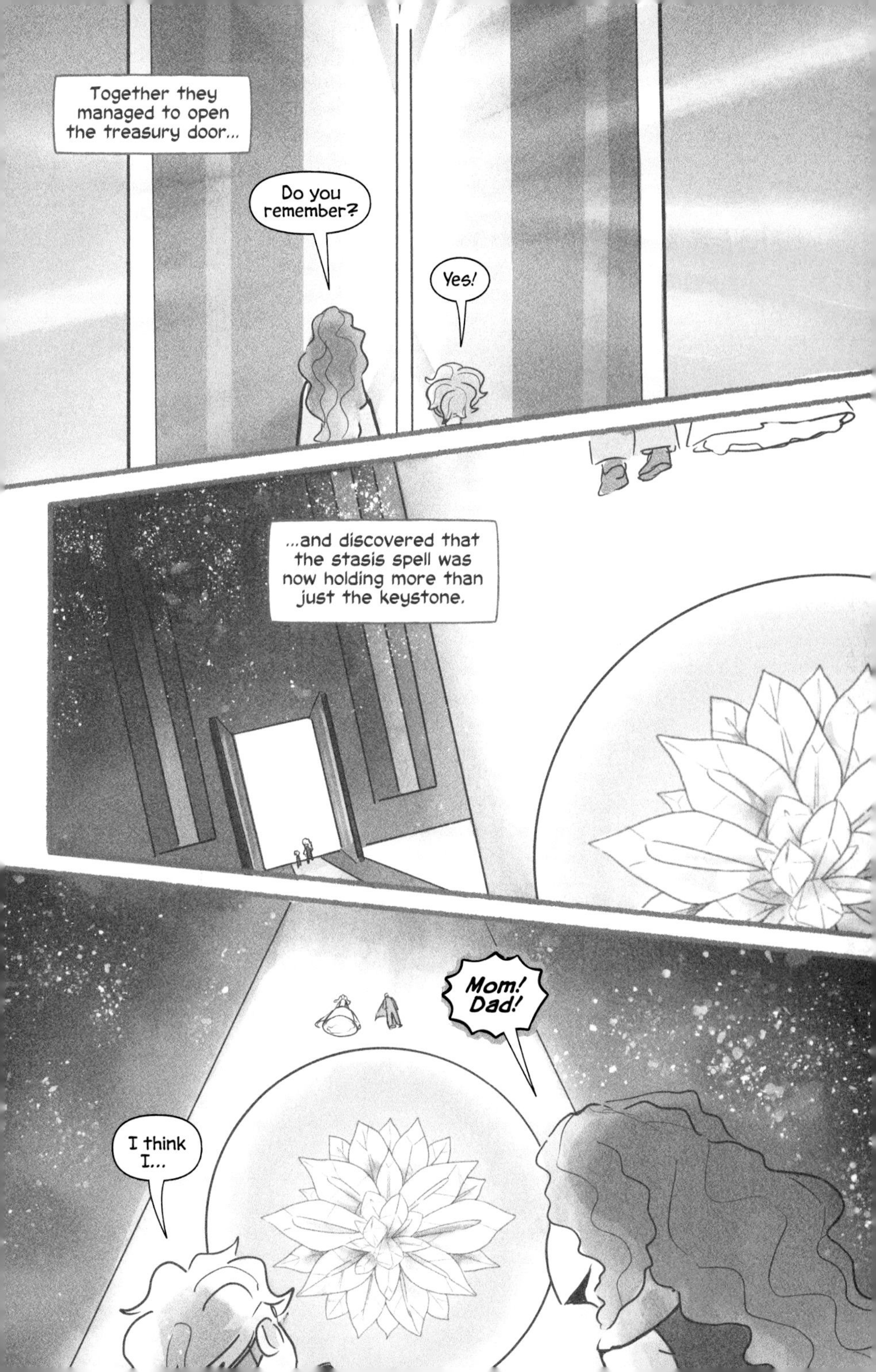

Together they managed to open the treasury door...
Do you remember?
Yes!
...and discovered that the stasis spell was now holding more than just the keystone.
Mom! Dad!
I think I...

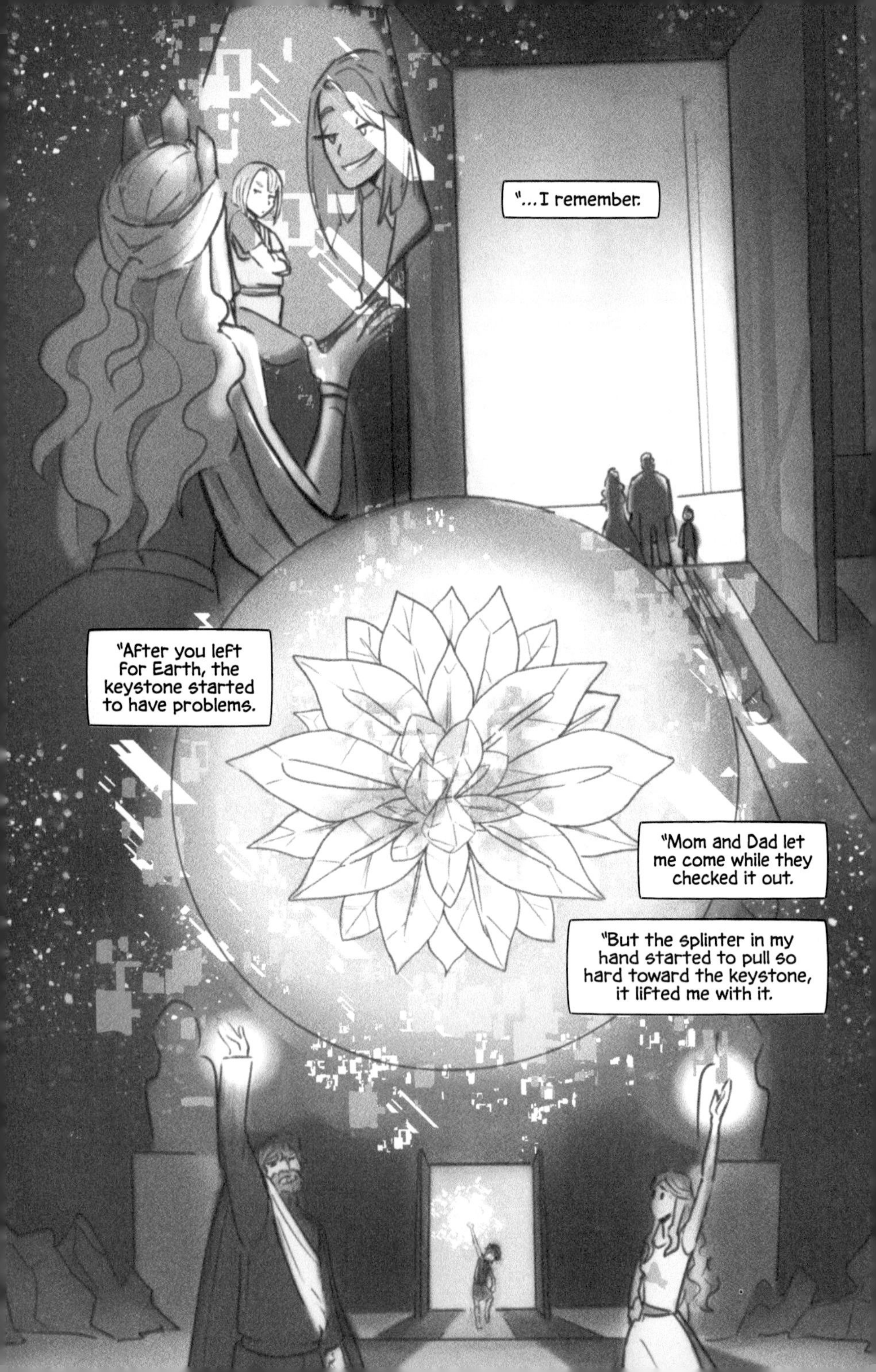
"...I remember.
"After you left for Earth, the keystone started to have problems.
"Mom and Dad let me come while they checked it out.
"But the splinter in my hand started to pull so hard toward the keystone, it lifted me with it.

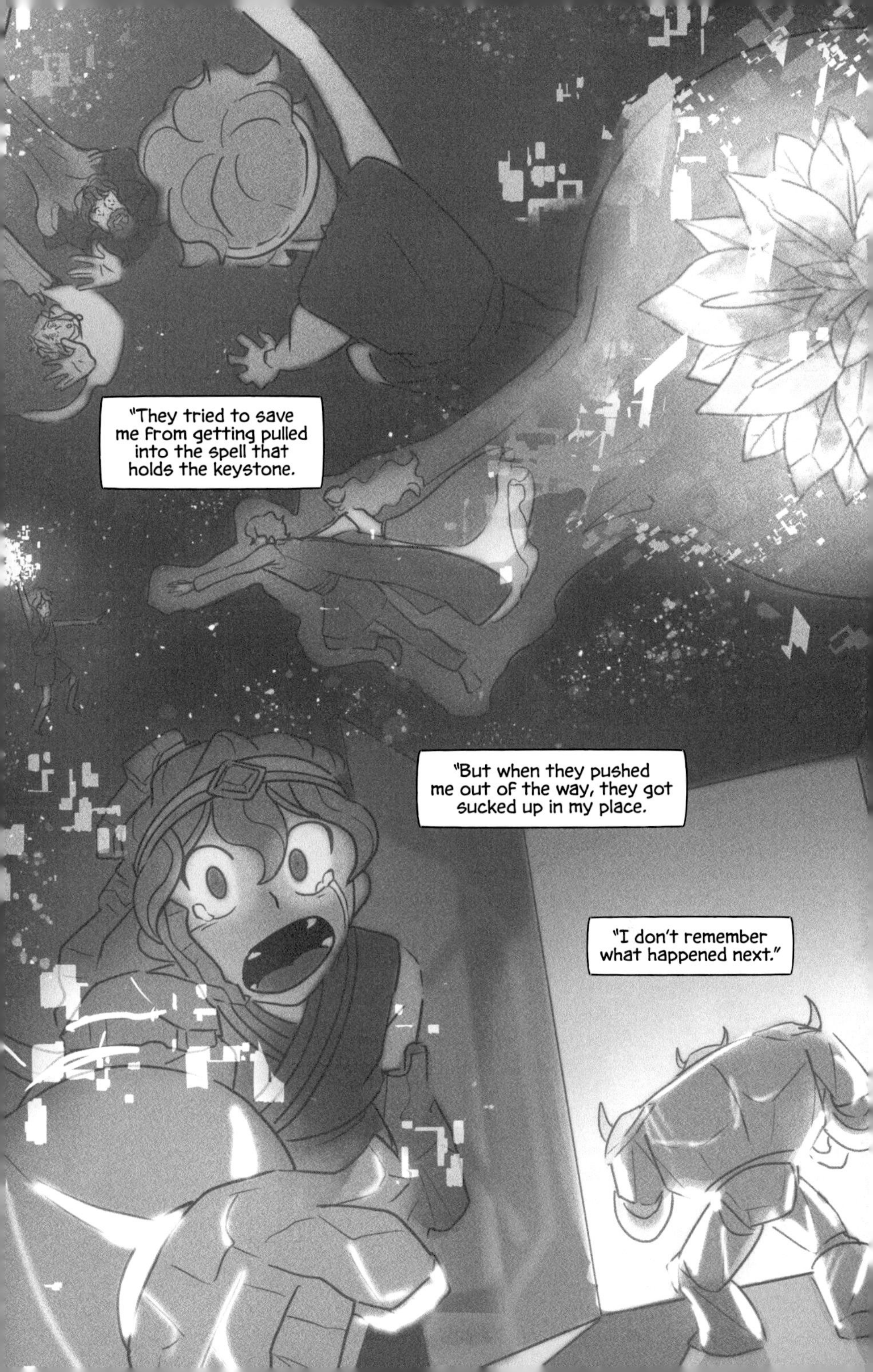
"They tried to save me from getting pulled into the spell that holds the keystone.
"But when they pushed me out of the way, they got sucked up in my place.
"I don't remember what happened next."

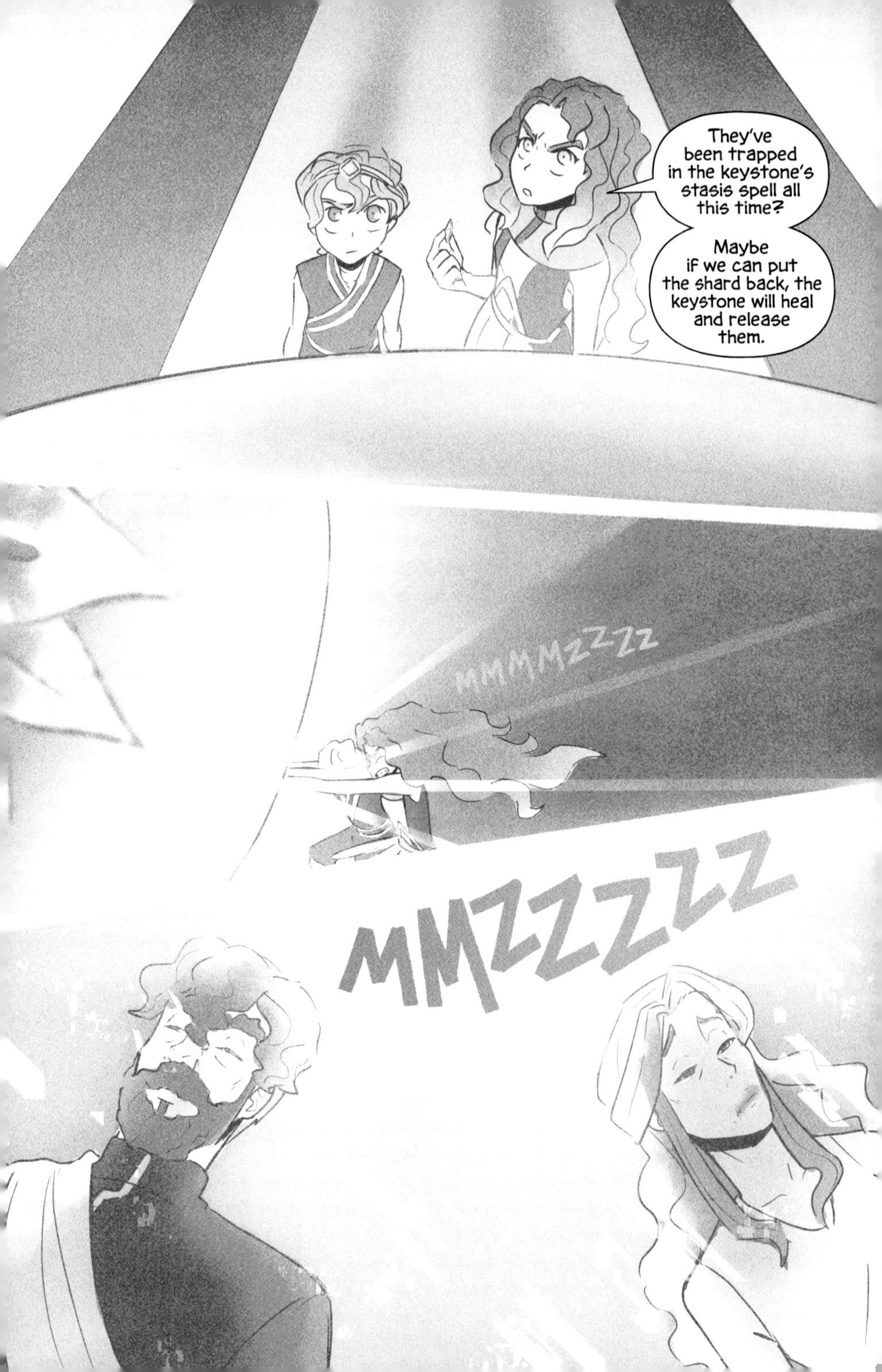
They've been trapped in the keystone's stasis spell all this time?
Maybe if we can put the shard back, the keystone will heal and release them.
MMMMzz-zz
MMZZZZZZ

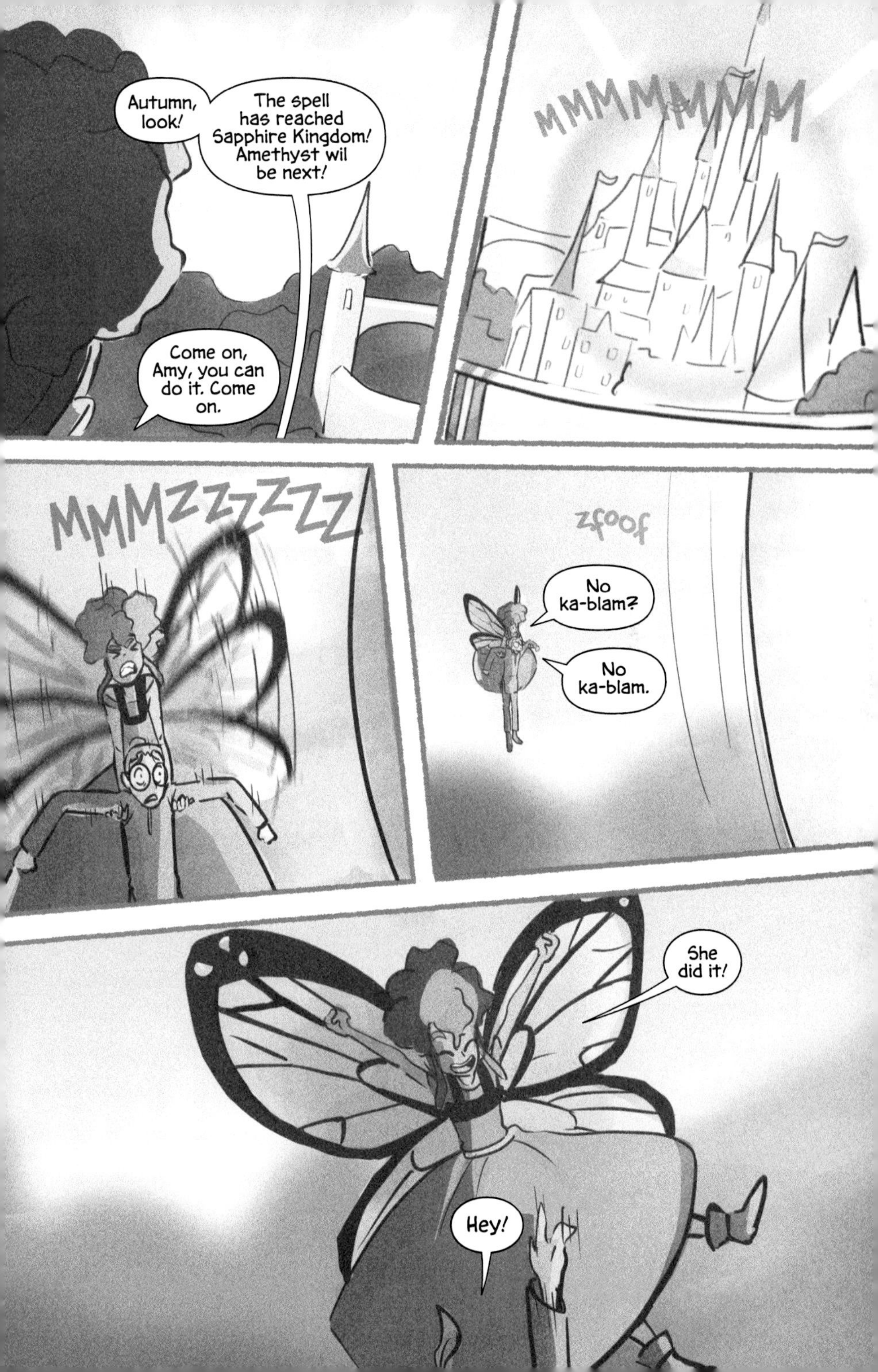
Autumn, look!
The spell has reached Sapphire Kingdom! Amethyst wil be next!
Come on, Amy, you can do it. Come on.
MMMMMMMM
MMMZZZZZZ
zfoof
No ka-blam?
No ka-blam.
She did it!
Hey!

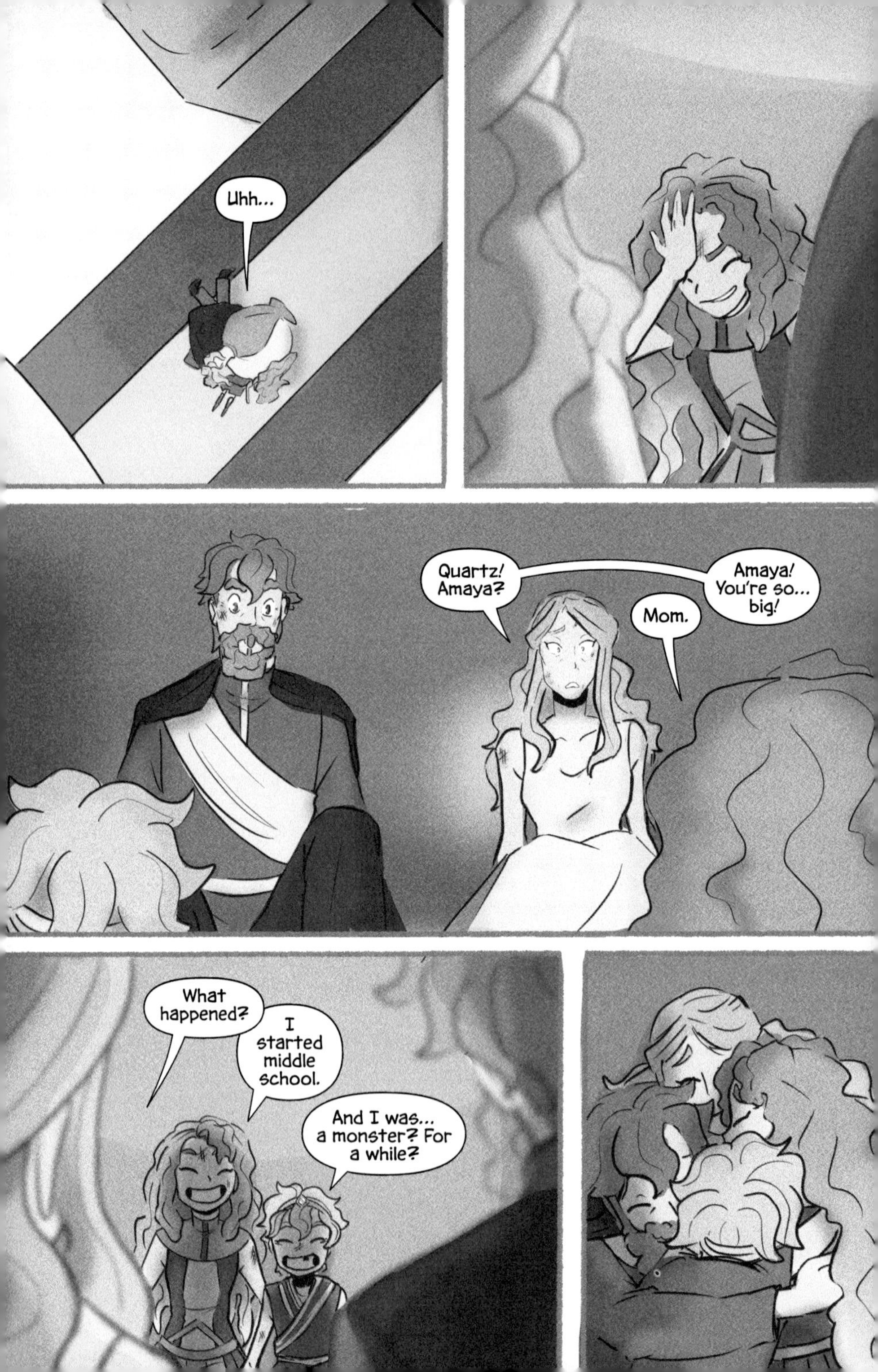
Uhh...
Quartz! Amaya?
Amaya! You're so... big!
Mom.
What happened?
I started middle school.
And I was... a monster? For a while?

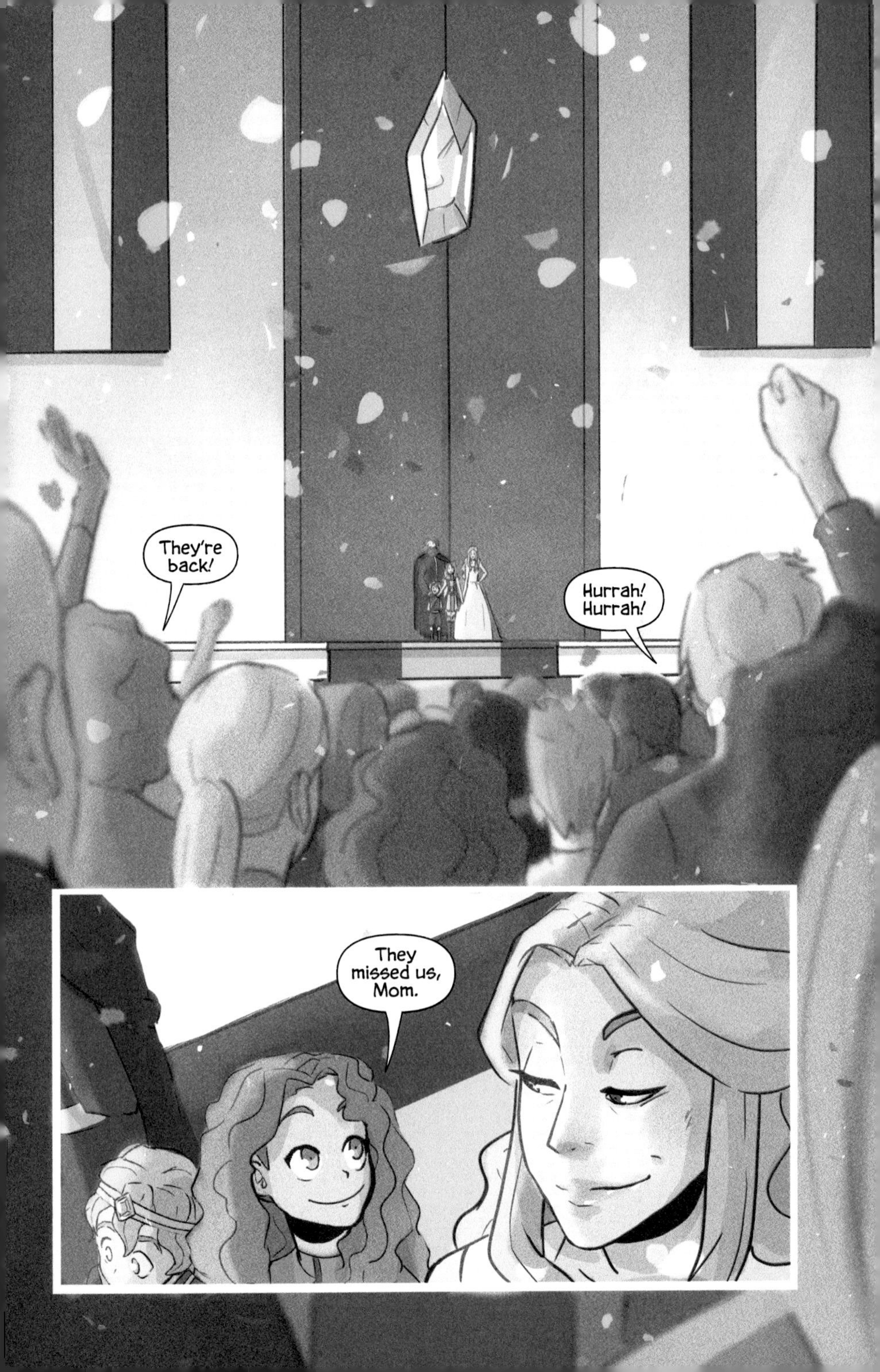
They're back!
Hurrah! Hurrah!
They missed us, Mom.

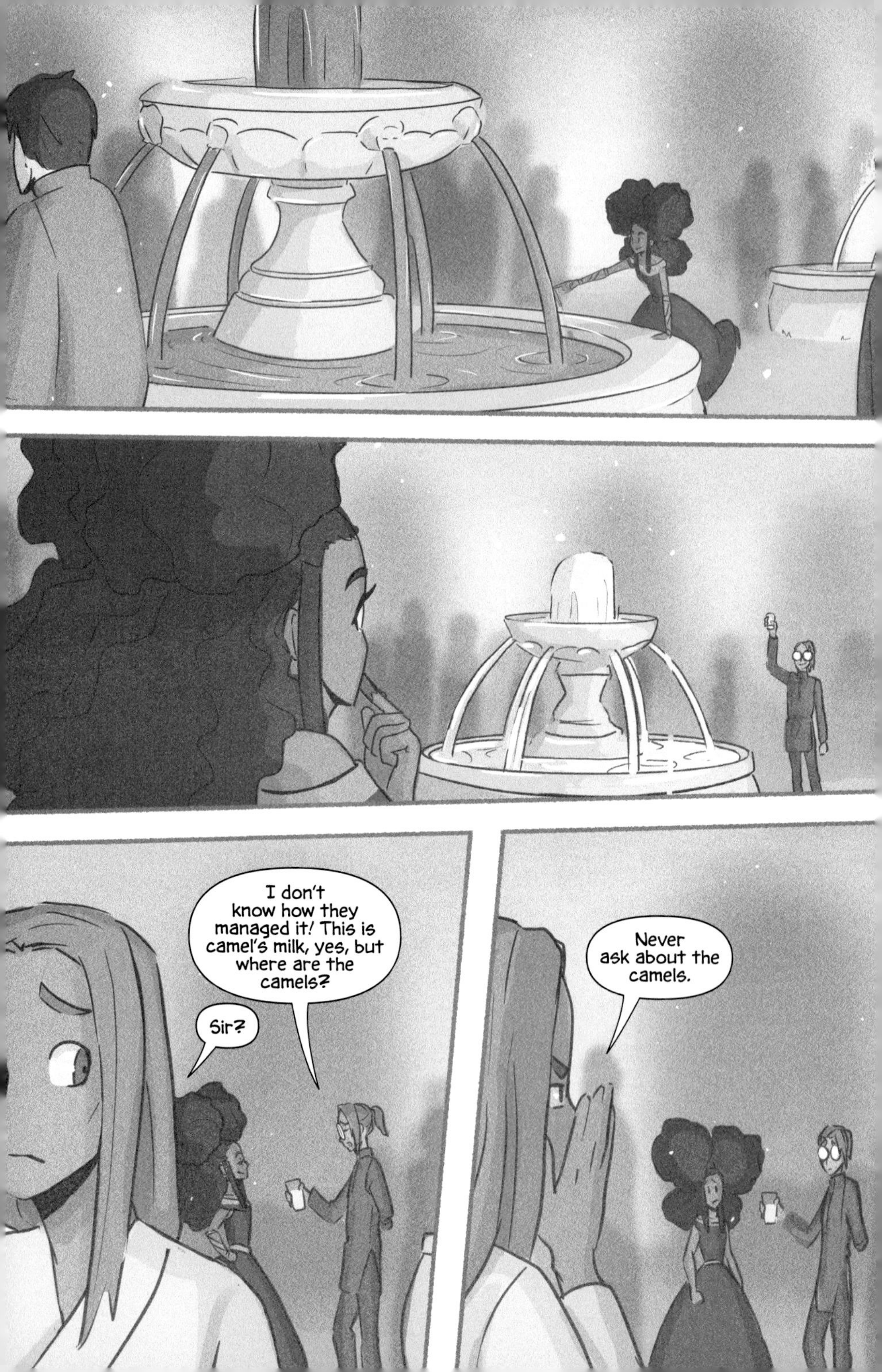
Sir?
I don't know how they managed it! This is camel's milk, yes, but where are the camels?
Never ask about the camels.

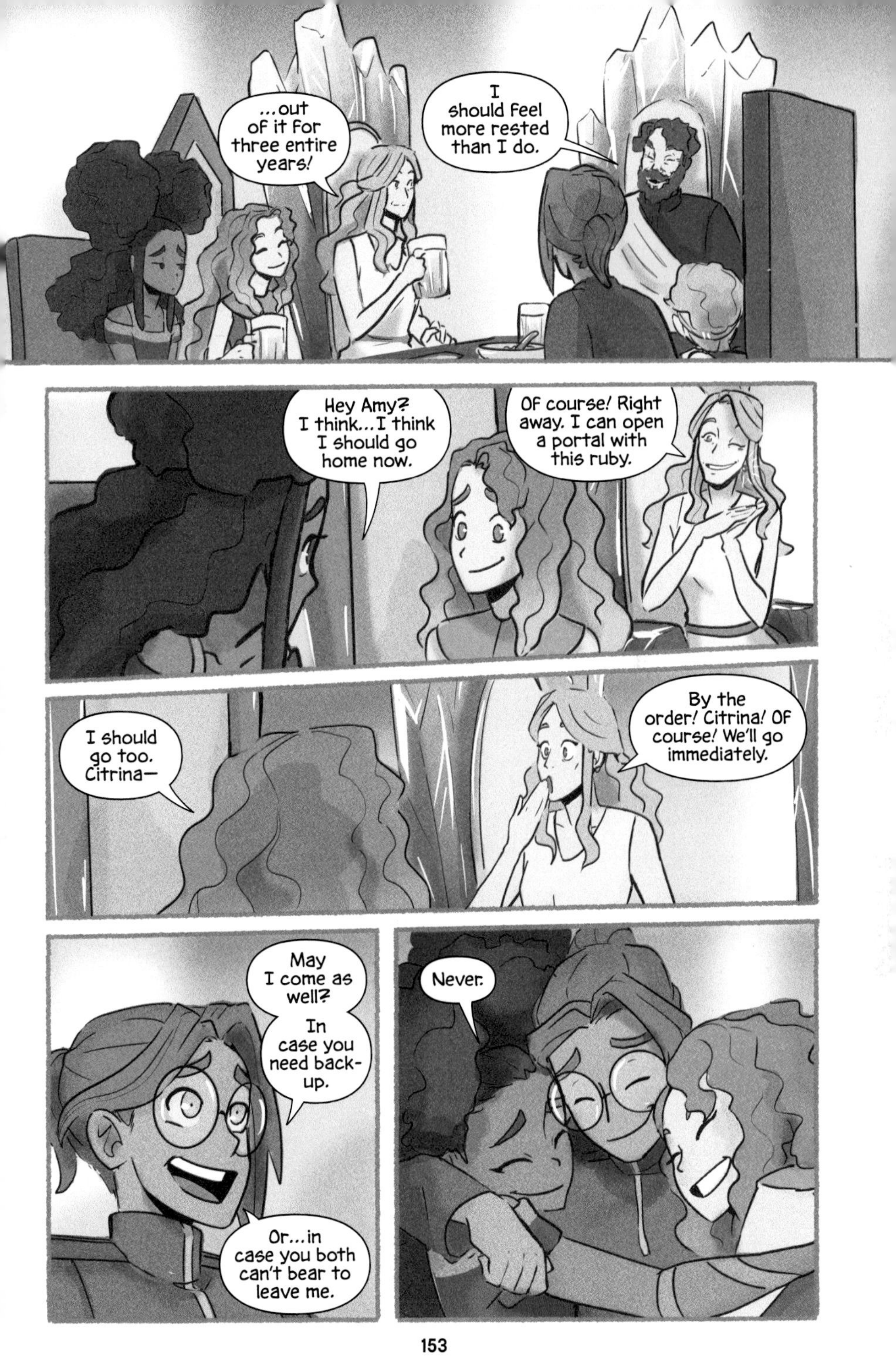
...out of it for three entire years!
I should feel more rested than I do.
Hey Amy? I think...I think I should go home now.
Of course! Right away. I can open a portal with this ruby.
I should go too. Citrina—
By the order! Citrina! Of course! We'll go immediately.
May I come as well?
In case you need back-up.
Or...in case you both can't bear to leave me.
Never.

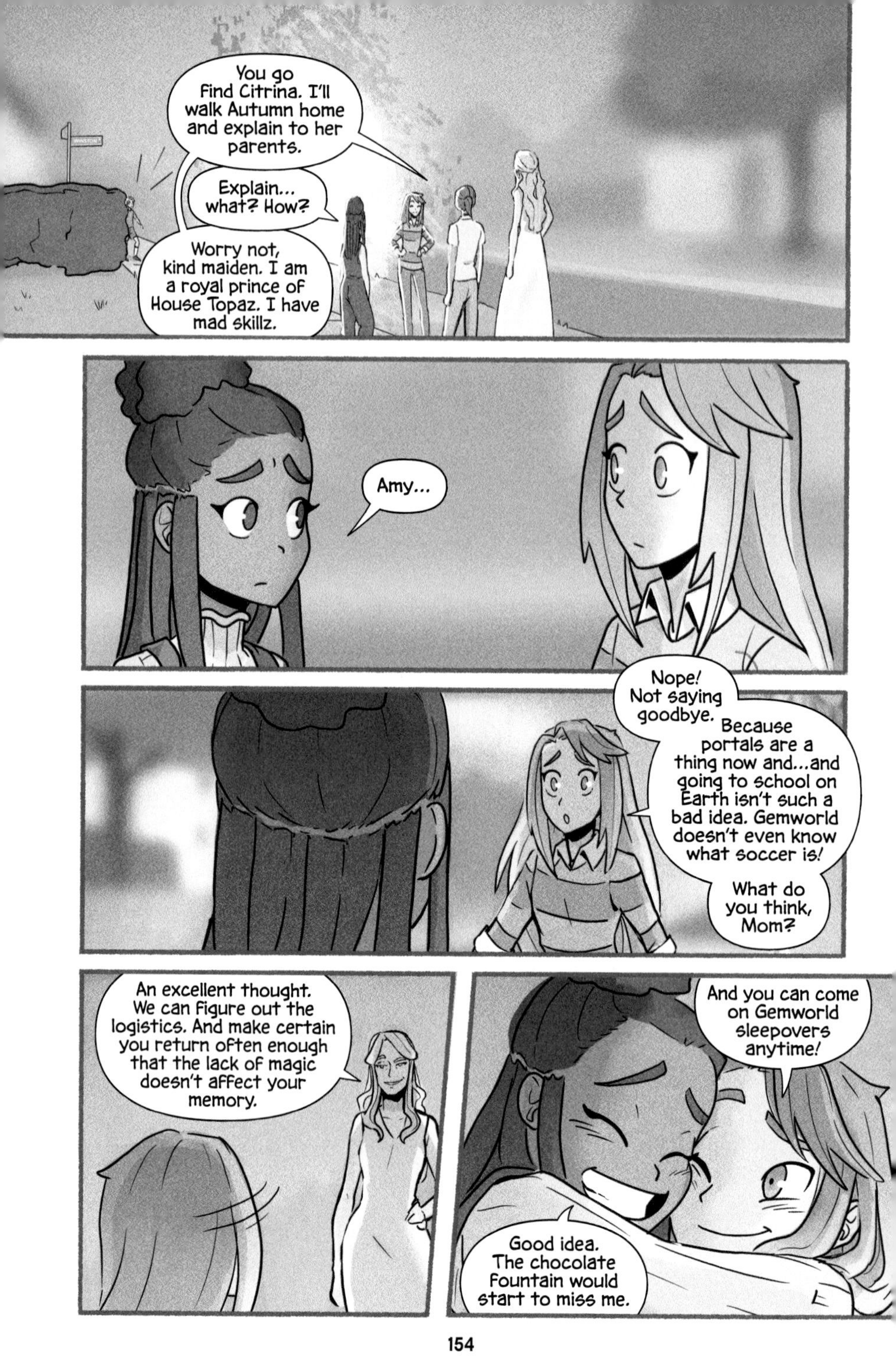
You go Find Citrina. I'll walk Autumn home and explain to her parents.
Explain... what? How?
Worry not, kind maiden. I am a royal prince of House Topaz. I have mad skillz.
Amy...
Nope! Not saying goodbye.
Because portals are a thing now and...and going to school on Earth isn't such a bad idea. Gemworld doesn't even know what soccer is!
What do you think, Mom?
An excellent thought. We can figure out the logistics. And make certain you return often enough that the lack of magic doesn't affect your memory.
And you can come on Gemworld sleepovers anytime!
Good idea. The chocolate fountain would start to miss me.

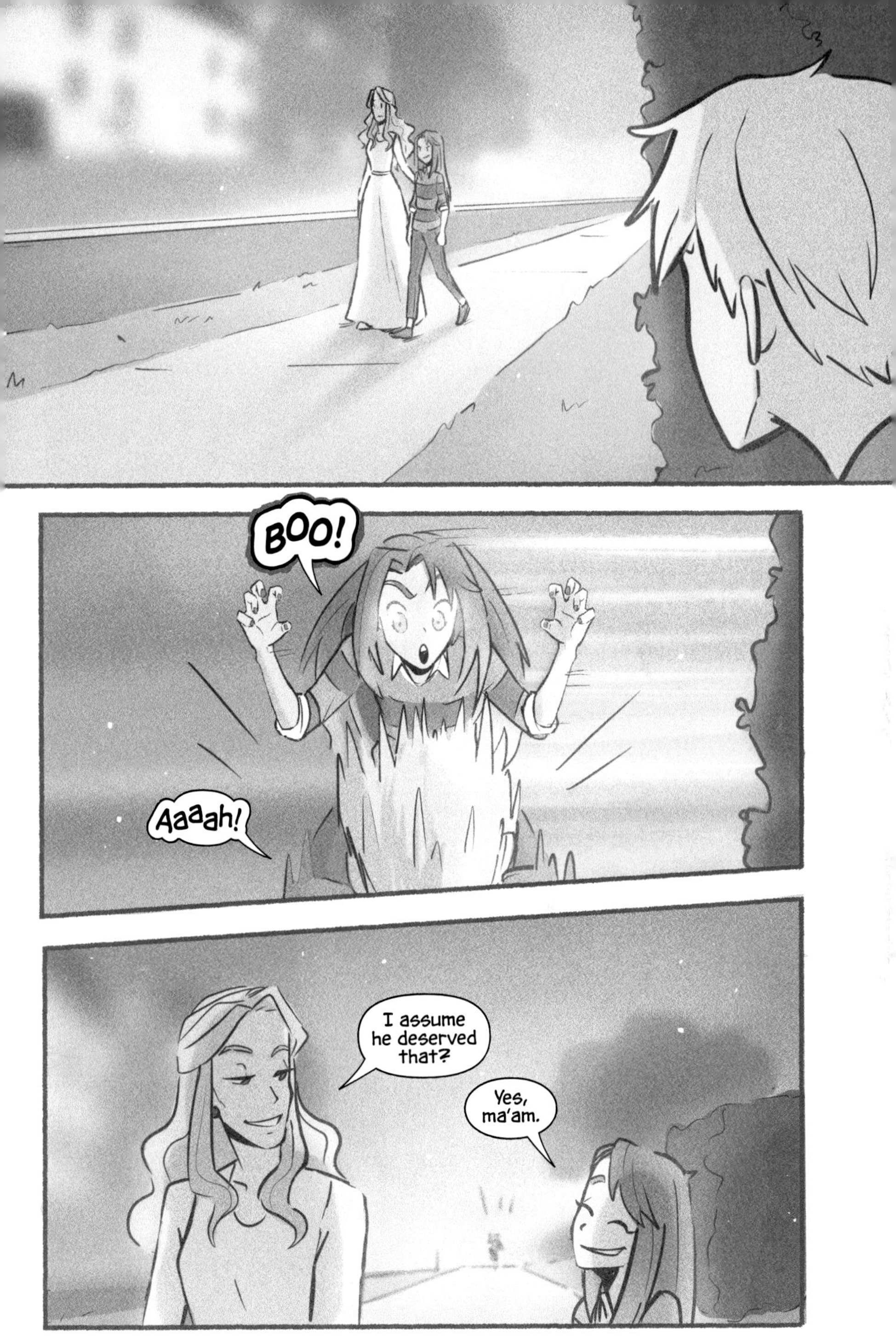
BOO!
Aaaah!
I assume he deserved that?
Yes, ma'am.

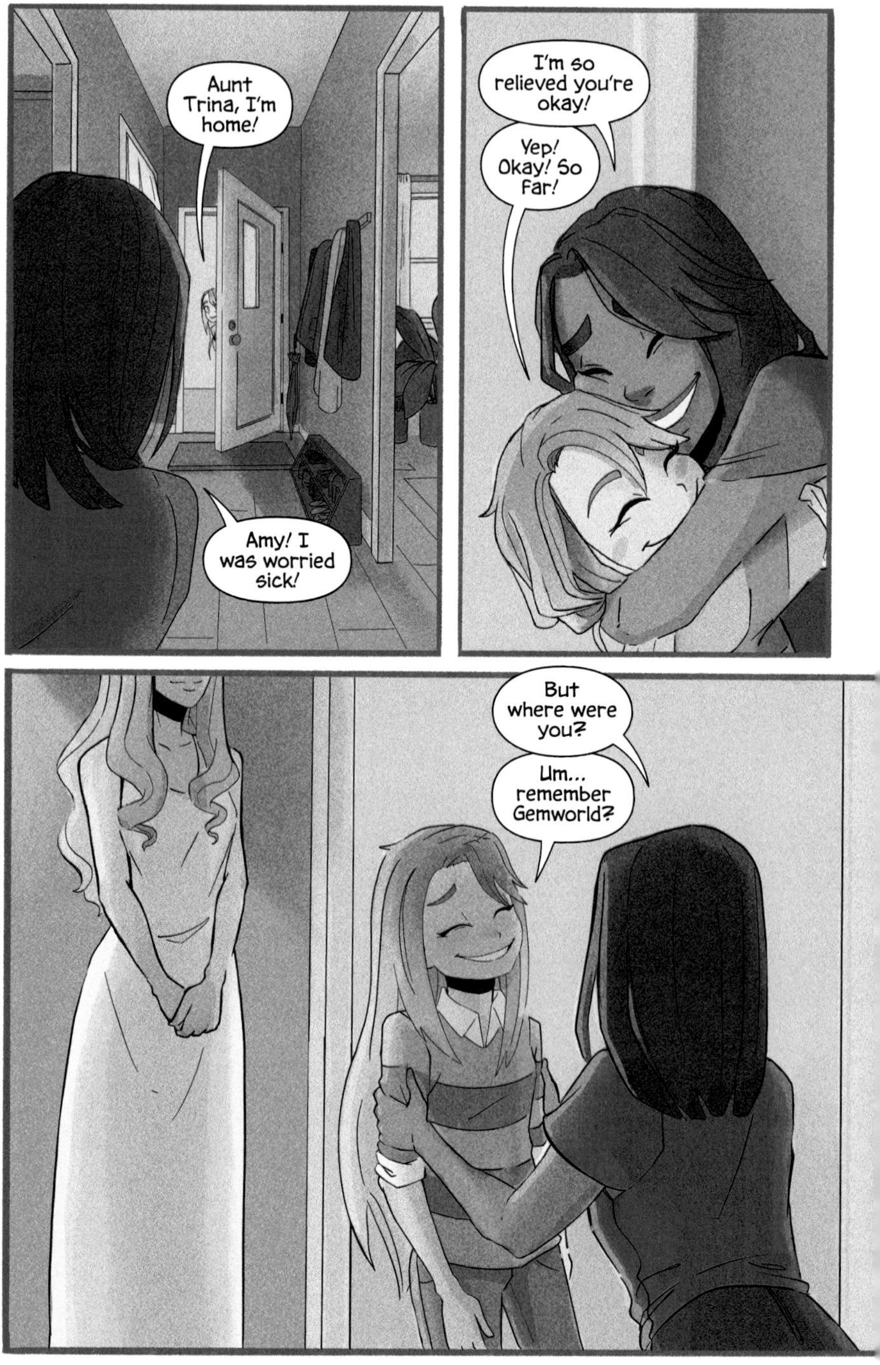
Aunt Trina, I'm home!
Amy! I was worried sick!
I'm so relieved you're okay!
Yep! Okay! So far!
But where were you?
Um... remember Gemworld?

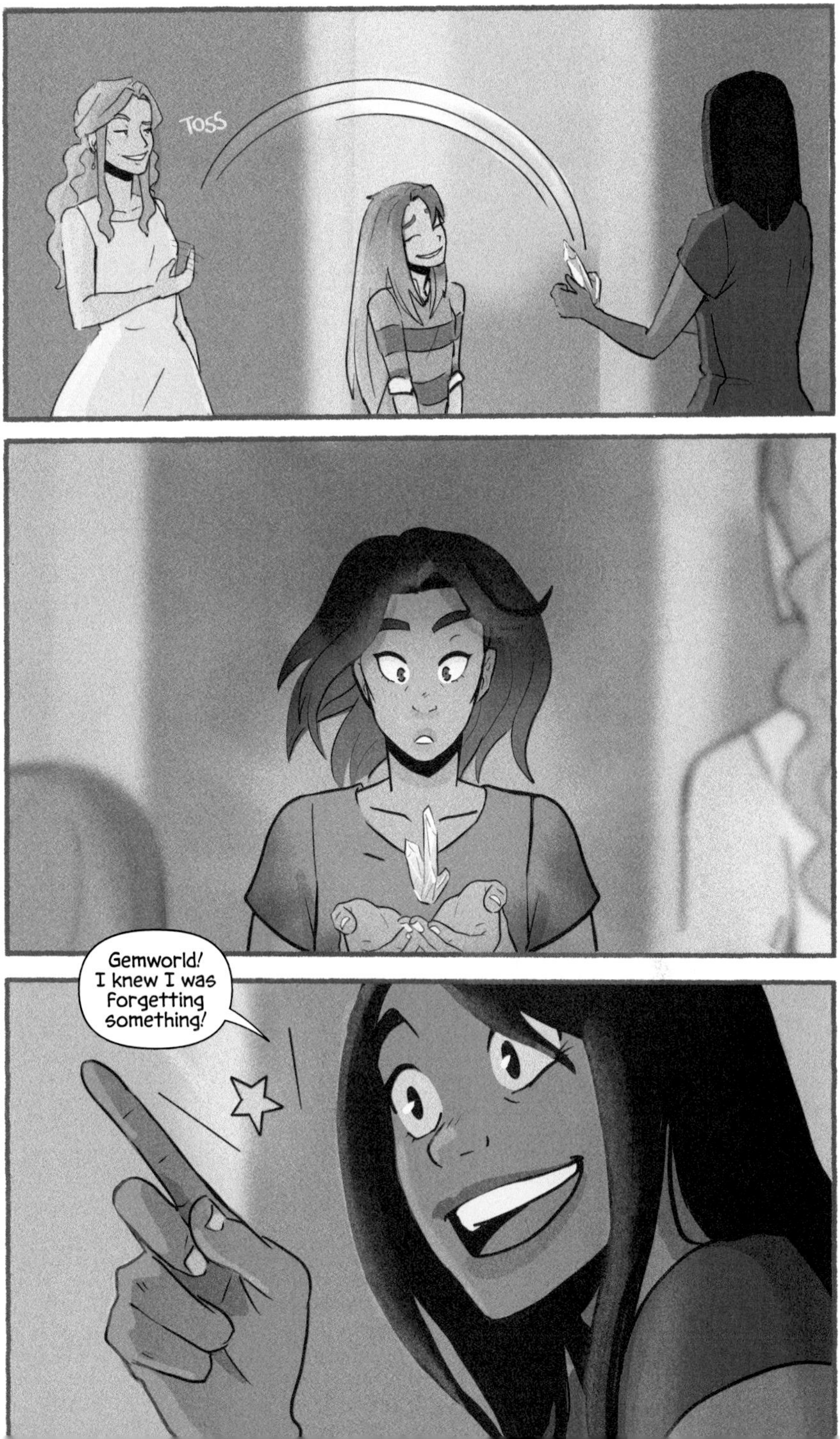
TOSS
Gemworld! I knew I was forgetting something!

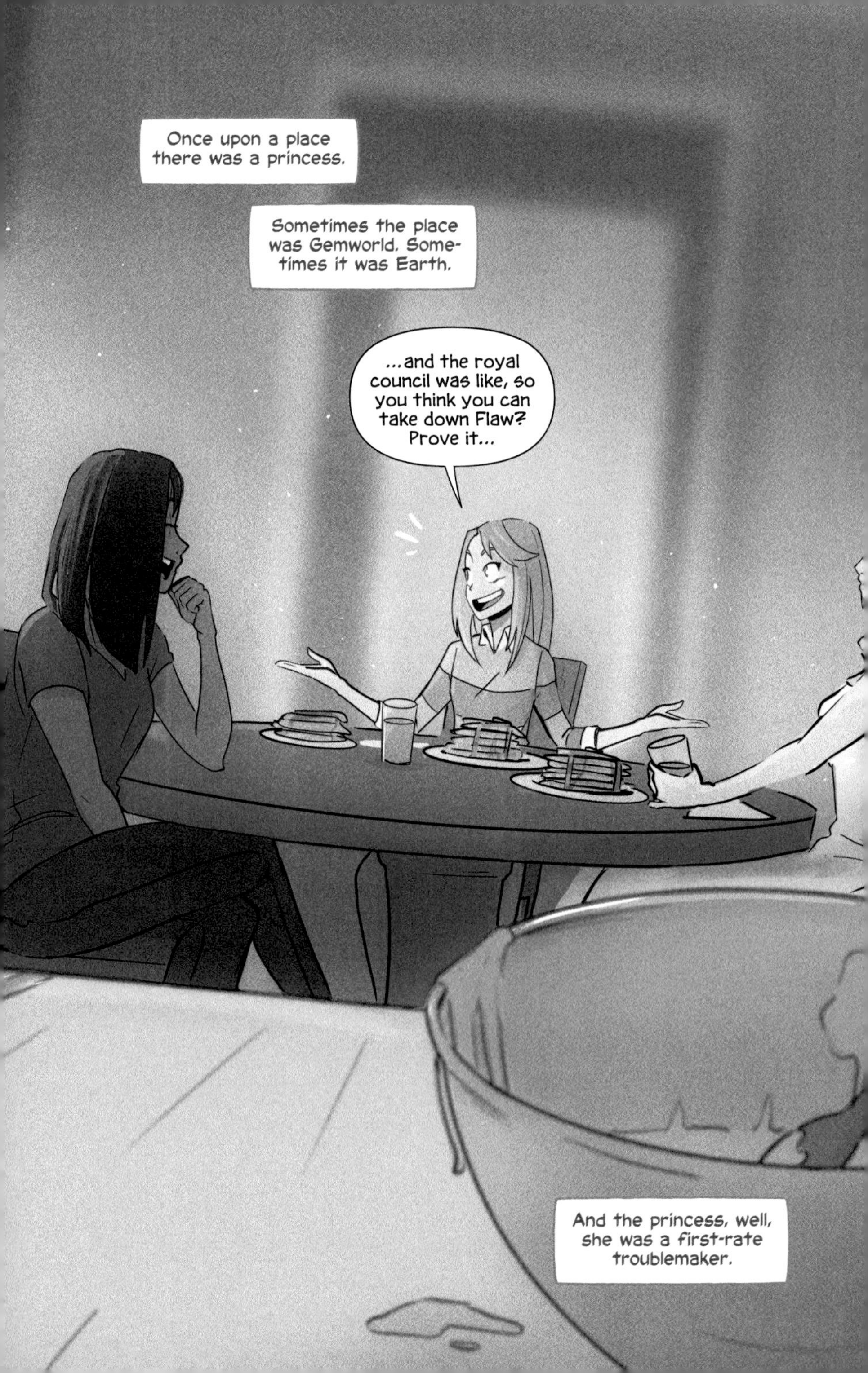
Once upon a place there was a princess.
Sometimes the place was Gemworld. Sometimes it was Earth.
...and the royal council was like, so you think you can take down Flaw? Prove it...
And the princess, well, she was a first-rate troublemaker.

Shannon and Dean Hale are the wife-and-husband writing team behind *Diana, Princess of the Amazons* (illustrated by Victoria Ying), Eisner nominee *Rapunzel's Revenge* (illustrated by Nathan Hale), *New York Times* bestselling series The Princess in Black (illustrated by LeUyen Pham), and two novels about Marvel's *Squirrel Girl*. Shannon Hale is also the author of the Newbery Honor-winning novel *Princess Academy*, the *USA Today* bestselling Ever After High series, the graphic novel memoir *Best Friends*, and others. Shannon and Dean live in Utah with their four children, who are all pretty certain they're secretly magical royalty from another realm and just forgot.

Asiah Fulmore is a freelance illustrator who currently lives in Columbia, South Carolina, with her two dogs, Ali and Ash. She spends her free time reading and loves to travel. If she got the chance to visit Gemworld, she'd hang with House Ruby, because they have the best food, obviously!

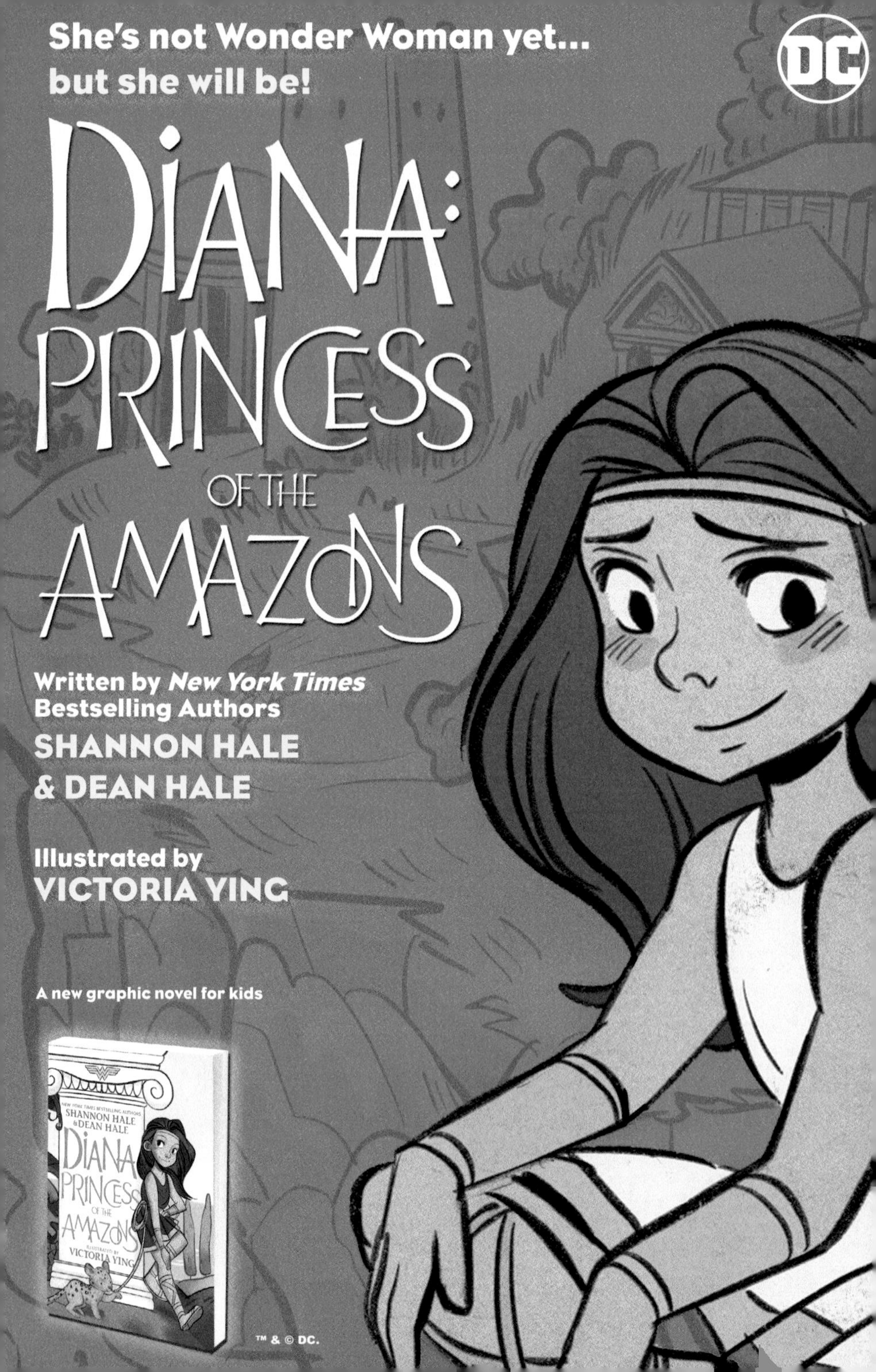
She's not Wonder Woman yet...
but she will be!
DIANA: PRINCESS OF THE AMAZONS
Written by New York Times Bestselling Authors
SHANNON HALE
& DEAN HALE
Illustrated by
VICTORIA YING
A new graphic novel for kids
SHANNON HALE & DEAN HALE
DIANA PRINCESS OF THE AMAZONS
VICTORIA YING
™ & © DC.